The Landlord's Time at the Spa

TERRY JOE GUNNELS

Inquiries and Book Orders should be addressed to:

Gunnels Publishing
Email: terrygunnels51@cox.net
Phone: 757-930-1596

ISBN: 979-8-89175-112-5 (sc)
ISBN: 979-8-89175-113-2 (ebk)

Other books by Terry Joe Gunnels

The Landlord series:

The Landlord's Inheritance
The Landlord's Wheelchair Child
The Landlord's Dead Body
The Landlord's Ex-Fiancée

New series to be out soon:

The Darcy Jean Mysteries:

Darcy Jean Bower, an amateur sleuth, solves suspenseful and intriguing mysteries around her hometown of Bridgeton, Virginia. Things can get dicey when she pairs up with her sometimes wacky friends to help her in a difficult case.

Acknowledgments

To my wife, Shirley Jean (Cookie), for encouraging me through 46 years of marriage in all projects I have undertaken. And for spending untold hours proofreading this manuscript for errors.

To my editor, Donje Putnam, whom I have known since she was a teenager and my daughter's best friend. She always nails me to the wall with corrections and suggestions. I thank her.

To all my BETA readers who gave me valuable feedback:

Dianne Ahl is one of my newest BETA readers, and did a wonderful job of finding flaws in my writing and gave me many very insightful thoughts and suggestions.

Sterling Norris Monk, and his lovely wife, Carolyn for reading, giving feedback, and finding errors I missed.

Donald Emond, a lifelong friend who gave me some insightful comments.

Carl Yaddow who read the manuscript and added some interesting comments.

To all others, for exciting me to move forward with the story and encouraging me to publish.

I give my heartfelt THANK YOU to every person involved with this book.

Contents

Prologue

FINALLY, THE WORLD WAS GLORIOUS again. Everything was going fine. Mickey drove with the top down and the wind in his hair, listening to old 1960s music blaring from the radio in his classic 1963 Jaguar XKE. The car was a gift to him from Detective Veronica Morgan of the Florence, Oregon Police Department for helping find her father's killer and bringing the man to justice.

A few days ago, Mickey and the Mongoose team had solved several cases, including the murder of Valerie Green and Veronica's father. The Mongoose team was a team of mercenary men and women who had served in the military on Black Ops missions. They were unsung and unknown heroes to the free world. They worked now wherever needed but were based out of Mickey's hometown. Valerie, Mickey's ex-fiancée, moved to Florence to escape her PTSD and start anew after breaking off their engagement. Mickey had kept in touch, but Valerie was killed when she unknowingly got too close to a smuggling operation.

When Valerie left, Mickey had hoped that someday she would return. They would be married and start a family. But someone took her life. He went to pick up her body, and he truly realized that this was the end of that dream. Life had thrown him a curve ball. He had to accept that fact. He grieved. Despite the challenges he would face, life must go on and he must continue to move forward. He tried to put that behind him, but he knew she would always be his first love. There would always be a corner of his heart that belonged to her.

Yes, Mickey was in a good mood. For the last few days, he had been on his way home to Bridgeton, a medium-sized town midway between Williamsburg and Richmond, Virginia.

Pulling off the interstate at the next exit, he headed toward the Woodside Restaurant. Driving into the parking lot, he noticed it was crowded, which usually meant the food was good.

After parking the car, he went inside, and as he stood waiting for a hostess, an attractive young Asian woman entered, looking around the room, hoping for a table. The hostess arrived and addressed the Asian woman. "Hello, Miss Chiaki. Are you two together?"

"No," answered Mickey.

"I'm sorry, sir," the hostess said to Mickey. "She has a reservation. We only have one available table. If you don't mind, another one should be ready in five to ten minutes."

The woman turned to Mickey and said, "Sir, if you don't mind, I certainly don't mind sharing a table with you."

He smiled and answered, "That's very kind, but I wouldn't want to intrude."

"It wouldn't be an intrusion. It would be my pleasure," she said, bowing slightly and gesturing with an open palm for him and the hostess to lead the way.

The hostess led them to a table in the back corner of the room, and Mickey stood while the lady moved to the back of the table in the corner. As she sat, she again scanned the room quickly before looking back at Mickey. Noticing her attentiveness to the room, Mickey sat on her left side so as not to block her view.

Placing the menus in front of them, the hostess announced Lynda would be their server.

As the woman continued to scan the room, she turned to Mickey and introduced herself. "My name is Chiaki."

"My name's Mickey or Mickey Ray, and thank you for sharing your table with me," he answered gratefully.

"Well, Mickey. I've been here many times, but I've never seen you here before," she said.

"I'm just passing through, heading home. If you've been here many times, apparently, you're from around here," Mickey said.

"Not really. I'm here to meet a couple of clients. I'm here often enough that the staff and owners know me."

"That explains why you keep looking around the room. You must be expecting them to arrive soon."

"Oh, we are not exactly meeting here. Down the road a bit, we have a meeting area. I am here just for lunch. Then, I will drive to the exact meeting spot. I just like to be aware of my surroundings."

She was a beautiful young Asian woman in a business suit with long, flowing hair, capturing every man's eye in the room. Her dark eyes sparkled as she talked, suggesting an easy, comforting person. Mickey felt drawn in by her deliberate gestures and mesmerizing soft voice.

The server, Lynda, came and took their order, and Mickey and Chiaki talked as the server walked away. As they spoke to each other as strangers usually do, talking about general things such as the weather, three Asian men entered the restaurant. The men looked around, spotted Chiaki, and began walking to their table. They stopped and stood side by side, completely blocking the table from the view of others in the restaurant.

"Good afternoon, Chiaki. I thought that was your car in the parking lot. A pink Lamborghini. I'm sure you look good in it. We've been looking for you," the Japanese man said, standing to Mickey's left when they stopped at the table where Chiaki and Mickey were waiting for lunch.

She looked at Mickey, rolled her eyes, and pushed her long black hair back over her shoulders. "What do you want, Satsu?" she asked the man.

"I want you to come with me. Now," he answered.

"Can't you see I am having lunch with a friend?" she said firmly.

"Tell your friend that you must leave now," he ordered, then turned to look at Mickey. "We'll have someone drive her Lamborghini so she can ride with us. You can leave now, little man," he said to Mickey.

"Go away," she said, glaring at Satsu with a raised prayerful position.

The man she addressed as Satsu looked at her, then turned to the other two men who stood on Satsu's left side.

The man looked back at her with a crooked smile.

"You will come with us, young lady. This is a crowded restaurant, and we don't want to cause a scene," he said, patting a bulge in his coat. The other two men also patted matching bulges under their coats.

Mickey looked at their bulge and knew instinctively what they were. Having recently met her, he felt uneasy about the men's insistence on taking her, prompting him to prepare for action.

"And who are these men, Chiaki? They look like an Asian version of Moe, Larry, and Curly," Mickey sneered.

"Who are these Moe, Larry and Curly, you speak of?" Chiaki asked with a puzzled look.

"They were men that did silly movies many years ago. I watched their old movies on television when I was a child. They were stupid men," he said to Chiaki as he looked at the men.

With clenched teeth, the man looked at Mickey and spoke softly and deliberately, "Little man, you mind your own business."

Mickey bit his lip and looked up at the man as he assessed the situation and all three men. "If you don't mind, we're about to have a nice, quiet meal. You and your stooges should go now."

Again, the man looked at Mickey. "I told you to mind your own business!" he said more firmly.

"And I told you to leave us alone. The lady doesn't want to go with you. I suggest you leave. If you don't, I will call the police."

Chiaki looked at Mickey with a grave expression. "Please, Mickey. Do not get involved with my business. These are dangerous men, and they are now leaving."

"Not without you. Chiaki, I will tell you once more and drag you out of here by the hair, dead or alive if I must. But you will go with us," he said as he pulled his coat back, exposing the holstered handgun.

A woman at the next table gasped and screamed when she saw the man's gun.

"If I go with you, I will probably end up dead, so you can go to the depths of hell. I don't care," Chiaki seethed.

The man unsnapped the strap holding the gun and started to withdraw it. Mickey launched up from the table, sending his chair flying backward. He drove a fork into the man's gun hand and lunged his shoulder into the man's stomach, sending him tumbling to the floor. The other two men stepped back, knocking tables over, and reached to draw their guns.

With lightning speed, Mickey moved toward them, driving his body toward the middle man's midsection sending him to the floor. He grabbed the third man's hand, yanking it away from his gun. He then snatched the man's gun and shot the second man in the chest. Mickey dropped the gun, knocked the third man to the floor, pummeled him in the face until he passed out, and then turned back to the first man, Satsu, as Chiaki had called him.

Still lying on the floor with his bleeding hand, the first man withdrew his gun and shot Mickey, who fell, hitting his head on the corner of the table as blood flowed from his side.

Screams filled the room as people were diving for cover wherever they thought they would be safe from flying bullets.

The first man was still holding the gun in his bleeding hand when Chiaki jumped up and kicked him as he attempted to get up. He fell back down as Chiaki took a martial arts stance. The man slid back out of her range and slowly got up. She advanced, kicked the man in the head, and heaved herself onto him, hammering his abdomen with her foot until he fell again.

She immediately rushed to Mickey, who was motionless and unresponsive. To stop the bleeding, she tore the tablecloth and pressed it firmly against his side. She then summoned for someone in the restaurant to help put Mickey in her car so she could get him medical aid. As two patrons carried Mickey outside, Chiaki made a call on her cell phone.

"Hello. This is Chiaki. Send a Medical helo to the landing pickup area. Also, send someone to take care of the restaurant's owners and calm them down. We don't want any repercussions from the authorities. Do it immediately."

She disconnected the call and went to the parking lot to help the men load Mickey into her car.

CHAPTER ONE

Mickey Wakes up at the Spa

MICKEY WOKE UP. THERE WERE clouds in the sky overhead. Where was he? Why was he lying outside? He turned his head to look around, and as he turned to the left, he saw a face. It was a beautiful face. He thought it was the face of an angel.

"Am I dead?" he asked, still groggy from the drugs and sleep.

No answer from the face.

"Are you an angel?" he asked.

No answer. Just a soft smile.

"I can't be dead. I feel pain. I hurt all over, and I have a headache." He just laid there and stared at the face, looking back at him.

She was beside him and had the most beautiful oval face, almond-shaped deep black eyes, and soft porcelain skin. Her perfectly curved mouth smiled at him. Long black hair lay lightly across her face. Reaching over and wiping a lock of hair from his face, she could see his eyes more clearly. Wordlessly. Soundlessly. She probed the depths of his soul with her eyes.

As he became more conscious, he realized he was in a bed. She was sitting in a chair beside his bed, gazing at him.

Finally, she spoke softly in a Japanese accent, "No, dear love. You are not dead, and I am not an angel. You are my protector. You saved my life. Now I owe you mine."

"What?" he said. "Why do you call me dear?"

"You saved my life. That is why I call you dear. Now it is my turn to care for you until you are healed." She leaned forward and kissed him lightly.

"I don't understand," he said, trying to sit up and collapsing back down on the bed.

"Does it bother you that I call you dear? I will not if you prefer."

"No. It's okay. I just don't know why. Are we in love or something?"

"No, we are not in love, but you have a kind heart to help a stranger such as me," she said softly, as she began to gently stroke his thick dark hair.

"I can't sit up. It hurts. What happened to me? Where am I?"

"You are in the infirmary of my healing spa," she said, still looking into his wild eyes as if she were trying to read his mind.

He looked around the room. It appeared to be a hospital room, complete with a bed that raised and lowered at a touch of a control. It was a hospital room. They all look alike. He definitely was in the hospital.

"I don't understand. How long have I been here?" he asked groggily, still fuzzy from the drugs.

"Five days. You lost a lot of blood, and we weren't sure if you would live," she said soothingly.

"Did someone let my family know I'm here?"

"We didn't know who to call. Who would you like us to call?" she asked, gently combing his hair back with her hand.

"My, um. I don't know. Who are you? Who am I?" Mickey looked around the room, very confused.

"Don't you know, my friend?" she asked, speaking to him as one would talk to a small child.

"No. I don't know. What happened? Why do I hurt so much?"

"You were shot."

"Shot? Why did someone shoot me? What did I do?" he asked frantically, trying to sit up but wincing and lying back on the bed, gasping for air.

"Be still. When you remember who you are, we will notify anyone you wish. Right now, your body and mind require some rest. I'll let the doctor know you are awake," she said, rising from the chair.

"Wait! When can I go home?"

"In a few days, but first, you must remember who you are so we can notify your family."

"But where's my wallet? That should tell you who I am," Mickey said.

"I am sorry, but it was lost. We don't have your wallet. We looked, but to no avail," she said sadly.

"What'll I do? Will I ever remember who I am? How will my family know where I am?"

"You ask many questions. You can stay here until you remember. We will look after you, Mickey," she said.

"Mickey. You called me Mickey! Is that my name?" he pleaded.

"Yes, when we met, you said your name was Mickey, or Mickey something, but that is all. You did not tell me your last name. I am Chiaki," she said.

"Chiaki, what?"

"That isn't important at this time. I am Chiaki. That is all you need to know."

"What kind of place is this?" Mickey asked.

"I will answer all your questions later. Sleep now. Don't concern yourself with such questions."

"But you said I'm in an infirmary. That's a kind of hospital, isn't it?" Mickey asked, perplexed.

"Yes, we have a doctor on staff and a certified surgeon with a complete operating room. We prepare ourselves for any situation. It is not uncommon for individuals to come here while they are sick. We can operate and give them peace while they heal their bodies. Now, you need to sleep and rest so you may heal, my dear," she said as she motioned for a nurse.

A nurse came in and put some kind of injection into a tube connected to his arm, which ran to a bag hanging from a pole next to his bed.

He felt something warm going into his arm and drifted into sleep.

The doctor looked at her, and she nodded back at him. "He doesn't have any memory. Will it come back?" she asked.

He was Japanese and answered her in their native tongue, "Maybe, but I can't tell you how long it will take. Until then, he needs to rest. He can get out of bed maybe tomorrow, and someone can wheel him around the grounds."

"I will take care of him, Naoki," she said to the doctor.

"As you wish, Director Chiaki. The sedative we gave him will last a few hours, and he will awaken. Should someone notify you when he wakes up?" he asked.

"Most definitely," she answered as she retreated from the room.

The beautiful young lady who had introduced herself to Mickey as Chiaki walked to the nurse's station and picked up a desk phone. In Japanese, she explained, "He is sleeping again. I have some duties to attend to. Make sure that the planned classes continue as scheduled. I will be available to lead the meditation before the evening meal."

Chiaki hung up the phone and headed to her office for privacy. When she got to her office, she lifted the phone receiver on her desk and dialed long distance to Japan.

"Hello, Father," she said into the receiver, again in Japanese. "He has regained consciousness. He doesn't remember anything. Correct. Not even his name. Yes, I told him his name is Mickey, but that's all he knows. We'll keep him here until he recovers."

She listened as her father spoke at the other end of the line. "But Father, I owe him a debt. He tried to stop Satsu Ageda and two of his men from taking me. Mickey is a brave young man. I'll see that he has the best of care."

She listened to her father and answered him, "I know, Father. He cannot communicate with anyone outside, even if he can remember who he is. Our security system is working properly. Isn't that the plan? When someone enters our facility, they are separated from the outside world. During a national emergency, the only way to communicate is through our soundproof room and secure phone."

Her father continued questioning her on the other end of the phone. "Yes, I know Satsu Ageda. He is from the Yakuza. How did I know? His left pinky finger was partially missing, and tattoos covered the small visible areas. Yes, Father. I have increased security. I am safe here in the spa. Yes, Father, the Yakuza will not gain control of our business. I'll keep you informed. Thank you, Father. I'll take precautions and great care of my protector."

Chiaki Gusihikin was thirty years old. Her father sent her to the United States to attend the University, and when she graduated, she stayed and begin a career. After working at various health spas, she opened her own. She shared her vision with her father and they built a secure place for influential individuals. The spa was in the Midwest region of the United States, and since some guests were members of Congress, its location was secret. With her father's influence, she had gotten permission to have it blacked out from all maps and aerial views, and it was complete with its own security. Chiaki had managed it since the construction was complete. The spa had been filled almost to capacity since it opened. Chiaki always researched each guest before allowing them to check in, and she knew how to make each person feel like they were her own guest.

She looked at her watch and rushed out of the office into a hallway leading to the main lobby of the spa. When she entered the check-in lobby at the end of the hallway, she welcomed a regular client.

"Hello, Mrs. Locke," Chiaki said. "It's so good to see you so soon. You were here just a few weeks ago. Are things getting stressful again?"

"Oh, yes, dear Chiaki. The cosmetic business is absolutely ruthless. One day you're number one, and the next week, you've slipped to number four. It's so stressful. Our stock prices dropped two points in the past week. I desperately need a few days here to get the toxins out of my body. I need to clear my head to create a completely new advertising campaign. You understand, don't you, dear?" she said in a desperate tone.

"I completely understand. It just so happens we have the royal suite available for the next few days. You may have it if you wish."

"Of course, I want it! How soon can you arrange for one of those soothing massages?" Mrs. Locke inquired.

"We can send someone up as soon as you desire. Would you like a male or female therapist?" Chiaki said, winking.

"Male, of course, dear," she answered.

"You are in luck today. Akio is just finishing up a yoga class. He can give you the most relaxing massage."

She giggled. "Yes, he has given me a most satisfying massage before. He has wonderful hands, a very gentle young man," Mrs. Locke said, almost blushing.

"I'll book him for you for a sixty-minute massage. He will be at your service in thirty minutes. That will give you time to check in and unpack your bags. He has a portable massage table and will bring it with him to your room. While I schedule a massage, I will schedule you for a relaxing yoga exercise session and outside meditation."

She walked to the counter and picked up a phone to book Mrs. Locke a massage with Akio. Chiaki always had the implied sexual banter with Mrs. Locke, but they both knew it was only banter. It would strictly be a massage, and nothing more. She also booked the other sessions for her while the scheduling director was on the phone.

Chiaki left through the front entrance and encountered Mr. Craig Clancy, a regular client who owned a lumber company that shipped lumber all over the country.

"Hello, Mr. Clancy. I saw your name on our reservation roster this morning. And how are you today, may I ask?"

"My, my, Chiaki. You're a sight for sore eyes," he said with a smile. "Things are going great. The fortuitous thing about this business is that the people are building when the economy is up. When things are down, they remodel and modify what they already have. It's always good in this business! How is business for you?"

"I can say the same thing, Mr. Clancy. When business is good for my clients, they come here to relax. When things go wrong for them, they come here to de-stress! So, it is always good for me. We secured for you the Western room. You know, the one with all the natural wood trim and carved moldings!"

"As always, you know what I like. Thanks, Chiaki. It's been a long flight, and I'm wiped out. I'm going to soak in a hot tub, then take a nap before dinner," he said with a smile.

"Good, sir. As you Americans say, make yourself at home!" she returned his smile.

Next, she saw Senator Bernard Langford from the state of Illinois. She walked to him nodding her head in greeting. "Hello, Senator. Nice to see you again. Will the Mrs. be joining us also?" she asked.

"Um, well, no. Not this trip," the senator mumbled. "I need to do some very important government business, so I brought my personal assistant, Miss Caroline Jenson," he said, turning to a woman that was young enough to be his daughter.

Chiaki gave the buxom young woman an icy stare. "I assume that you gave the reservationist her name when you booked with us? You know that everyone must be thoroughly vetted before we allow them to stay with us. Even guests of our guests."

"Of course, Director Gusihikin," he answered her with obvious astonishment that she would even ask him such a question.

"Please, give me a minute to verify she has been properly checked out." Chiaki stepped away from the senator and his guest and spoke softly into her staff mobile phone. After a few moments, she returned to the senator. "I assume she will have a room adjoining yours to make your private government meetings more convenient?"

"Yes."

"How long will your stay be, sir?" she asked brusquely.

"Maybe a week or maybe two, depending on how the meetings go. I assume that, as usual, these meetings will be confidential?" he added.

As she gave another quick glance at Miss Jenson, "Yes, Senator, what happens here stays here," she answered, turned, and walked away, whispering to herself, "Pig."

Chiaki went from one client to another and afforded every returning client precisely what they wanted. By researching every primary guest who checked in at the spa, she made sure it provided them with the best spa experience of their lives. She was the best at her job, and it showed.

Most of the executives usually visited for a week, but Chiaki could provide any length of stay that someone might need. The resort had relaxation events, classes, sessions, and meeting rooms for company meetings.

They decorated the sleeping rooms in different styles to coincide with different tastes, making it a very eclectic resort. There were Western rooms, Marine styles, Asian and oriental-style rooms, modern chrome and glass styles, etc. If a frequent-staying client wanted something special, he could have a room designed especially for him. One CEO wanted his room to have a complete skylight-designed ceiling, so as he fell asleep each night, he felt like he was sleeping under the stars. It was expensive but unmatched in comfort and relaxation for those with a huge bank account. It was a moneymaker for Chiaki and her father, just as they had planned.

She had insisted to her father they have a fully accredited mini-hospital for clients. If an executive needed an essential operation, they had a surgeon on staff. If they needed something more challenging, they could fly in a specialist. Clients could rest, rejuvenate, and heal from an operation without the stress of company business.

Now, Mickey, a young man her age, was lying in one of the hospital rooms, recovering from a gunshot wound that might have been her if he had not interceded. She didn't know exactly what she should do. He didn't actually save her life, but he had tried. He didn't even know her, but he almost died. She owed him her life because of his actions and would pay him back. While he recovered, she had a health spa to run.

CHAPTER TWO

The Missing Person's Report to the FBI

"Hello, Veronica. This is Darcy Jean."

"Nice to hear from you, Darcy. How've you been, and how's Mickey?" she answered.

"I'm fine. Thank you. Have you heard from Mickey since he left Oregon?" asked Darcy, quickly cutting to the chase.

"Sure, he called me twice. He stopped and checked into a hotel on the first and second nights. Why? Is something wrong?" she asked, concerned.

"Yes, he's missing," said Darcy.

"He should have been home days ago. I just assumed he'd been so busy catching up on his work that he hadn't had time to call me," Veronica said. Veronica was the detective in Florence, Oregon, who was assigned to the case of Valerie Green, Mickey's ex-fiancée. Veronica had joined the Mongoose team and helped them uncover Valerie's killer and her own father's murderer. She had never met Darcy in person but had talked to her several times on the phone.

"He called us those same nights, but that was the last time we heard from him. I thought maybe he wanted to be alone on the trip. Years ago, he would take off and go black for a day or two, but never like this. He just disappeared. He's never stayed this long without notifying someone. I'm worried about him," said Darcy.

"I don't blame you. He's driving the Jaguar I gave him. Maybe it broke down on the way, and he's having it repaired in some out-of-the-way garage."

"That's possible, but he'd still call and let us know."

Veronica thought for a moment and said, "If you don't locate Mickey soon, let me know. If there's anything I can do, call me. Good luck, Darcy, and give my best to James and the family," said Veronica with genuine concern.

The following morning, James and Darcy were sitting in the waiting room of the Federal Bureau of Investigation (FBI) in Richmond, Virginia.

Sitting in the lobby of the FBI office, James and Darcy sat waiting to make out a missing person's report.

"Dee, I don't think they'll do anything for us," James said.

"That's one of the things they do, James. They help find missing persons. They have the manpower to find Mickey Ray."

"I know, but they had a lot of missing people. Mickey will just go into some agent's pile of files."

"No, he won't. They'll find him," she stated as she looked out the window of the large room.

"Okay, but if it was just me, I'd already be out looking for him," James said as he sat back in the hard back chair and folded his arms.

They sat for over an hour waiting for an available agent to take their report.

Finally, an older man came out to greet them. "You are Mr. and Mrs. Bower? How are you? I'm John Ramsey. I'll take the report, and will be the contact and lead person on your case," the man said as he directed them to follow him down a hallway to his office.

He was the epitome of an FBI agent, wearing the typical dark suit, black tie that had gone out of fashion years ago, and white shirt. He positioned his horn-rimmed glasses on top of his closely cropped hair that ringed his balding head.

Agent Ramsey motioned for them to sit in the chairs in front of his desk.

"Now, how can I help you?" he asked.

James explained Mickey had disappeared on his way home from Florence, Oregon.

Agent Ramsey filled in all the blanks in the form that included Mickey's description, then began asking more questions.

"Why was Mr. Christianson in Florence? Business or pleasure," he asked, holding his hands ready to type in the answer into the computer.

James and Darcy looked at each other, then James answered, "Both."

"What kind of business was he involved in?"

"He was there to make arrangements for his ex-fiancée's body to be shipped home."

"Oh, I'm sorry to hear that. If he flew there, why was he driving back home?"

"He got a car while he was there."

"I see. How long was he in Florence?"

"Why is all this important? He's missing now. We don't know where he is or why he hasn't come home. We need someone to find him," Darcy spoke up.

"Mrs. Bower, we need information so we can check out why he's missing. There has to be a reason. We need to find out why, then we can begin our search for him," the agent said.

James leaned back in his chair. "Sir, you need to find my brother-in-law, then you can ask him these silly questions."

"Mr. Bower, you don't understand how we work here. We know our job, and I'll task some competent people to find Mr. Christianson. There's always a reason that people disappear. Maybe he got drunk and is sitting somewhere in a local jail, waiting to sober up. Maybe he had an accident and injured someone and is still in a local jail waiting to be arraigned. You said he was picking up the body of his fiancée. Maybe he felt he needs some time alone to deal with this tragedy. There are a lot of simple reasons people disappear," he said, sounding condescending now.

Darcy said with gritted teeth, "My brother rarely drinks alcohol, and he would never get drunk."

"Family members don't always know what goes on behind closed doors. We have our process, and we're very good at what we do."

"Are we done here?" asked James as he stood up.

"I need you to sign this report and attest that everything you have told us is accurate. Then we'll notify you when we find Mr. Christianson," Agent Ramsey said as he printed out the report, placed it on the desk, and slid it over for James and Darcy to sign.

James was a disabled and disfigured military veteran. An attack on James's men in Afghanistan while he was on a black ops mission resulted in the death of most of his team. He served honorably but was disfigured, and discharged with permanent disability. James and Mickey were high school friends and last year, James married Mickey's sister, Darcy.

Darcy had two kids from a previous marriage, which James adopted when they were married. Darcy, but called affectionately, Dee, had worked for a law firm until she left to do legal work and contracts for the Christianson Company.

Mickey, the CEO of the Christianson Company, managed various apartment complexes at thirty years old. The company, which is the largest real estate development company in Virginia, was founded by his father Daniel, who is now retired.

Mickey had been engaged to Valerie Green, who had broken off their engagement and moved to Oregon to start a new life by enrolling in a culinary school. After Valerie's murder, Mickey and James, his brother-in-law, enlisted the aid of a mercenary team to assist them in locating her killer. After finding the killer, instead of flying home, Mickey felt it would be an exciting trip to drive his new old car home. Mickey had a colorful past, and now he couldn't remember any of it. Not even his name.

James and Darcy Jean left the FBI offices and drove home to wait for the results of the search.

After several days and hearing nothing, they called to get an updated report. Agent Ramsey said they had no leads and were waiting on reports from other offices. Still, after several more days, they heard nothing. Darcy again called Veronica to find out if she had heard from Mickey. Veronica let them know that there was no information available, and her office hadn't even circulated a copy of a missing person's report.

James and Darcy drove to the FBI office in Richmond and confront Agent Ramsey in person instead of getting brushed off on the phone. As they drove into the parking lot of the FBI office in Richmond, Darcy was immersed in her own thoughts.

"Do you think they'll find Mickey?"

"I don't know."

"If they don't, what'll we do, James?"

"I don't know that either. Let's go in and find out what they're doing. They know how to deal with this kind of situation," he answered.

They both got out, walked into the building, and asked for Special Agent Ramsey. After showing identification, signing in, and getting tags, they waited for almost half an hour before he came out and took them to his office.

After the banal introductions and conversation, James looked at the agent icily and asked point blank, "What are you doing to find my brother-in-law?"

"We're taking all the standard measures to get leads to locate him, Mr. Bower."

"And that is?"

"We've notified our offices and sent out descriptions of him."

"And?"

"And when we have some leads, we'll follow up on them," Special Agent Ramsey said as he sat back in his chair.

"Have you found his car?"

"We don't look for missing cars. We look for missing people, Mr. Bower!"

"I understand that, but if you found his car, that might give you a lead when and where he was last seen. So, you're taking no particular action. You're just sitting in your chair waiting?" said James accusingly.

"What would you have us do, sir?" Ramsey asked.

"Where was he seen last?"

"Listen, I've been with the FBI for 19 years. I know what I'm doing!" he said.

"Where was he seen last?" asked James.

"We're working on that."

"Apparently not," said James. "How many cases are you working on at this time, Agent Ramsey?"

"This office alone has over three hundred active cases from all over the state, Mr. Bower."

"And how many men are in this office?"

"We have twelve men and women working on those cases."

James took his smart phone out of his pocket and held it in his hand and began punching numbers. "Let's see, if each person is assigned a portion of those cases, that comes out to 23 cases per person. And each person works eight hours per day, then they work on each case 20 minutes per day, or about two and a half hours per week per case. And of course, you don't work weekends so, I don't think we are getting our money's worth here, Agent Ramsey."

Agent Ramsey shrugged, saying he had other work and cases and would update them when he had more information.

"Why can't someone find him? He didn't just disappear off the earth," Darcy seethed at the man.

"We're doing our best, Mrs. Bower. I told you we've put out bulletins over the entire United States and sent notices to every government agency. We have no response from anyone at this time."

"James, you're right. Call the team. If he were an FBI agent, they'd rally the entire agency for Mickey. But since he's insignificant to them, they distribute flyers like he's a lost dog. Let's get out of here before I explode, and they throw me in jail."

"We'll call the team and take care of it!" James put his arm around Darcy and pulled her close.

James locked eyes with the man, "Special Agent Ramsey, I can only surmise that you aren't competent enough to find Mickey Ray. We'll find him." He took Darcy by the hand, got up, and turned to leave.

"And what do you think you can do that we can't, Mr. Bower? And what is this team she is speaking of?" the man countered.

"What I can do is none of your business. As she said, you're doing no more than a little kid walking around his neighborhood putting up posters of a lost puppy. We'll find him. Now, I want copies of every report you have in your search for my brother-in-law."

"Let me tell you something, Mr. Bower. You don't tell this agency what you want. We'll do our job. And we can't give you any reports until our investigation is complete," he said calmly.

"You mean you'll give us a copy of his autopsy report, maybe. If you get around to it," said James, now getting as impatient as Darcy Jean.

The agent said, "Now you need to calm down, sir. I never said that."

"True, but you don't have anything to give us because all you've done is sit on your butts and send out a picture with Mickey Ray Christianson on the bottom. You don't have anything to report. We'll find him. I'll say this, I better not have any agents anywhere in the United States impede MY investigation, sir!" said James.

"And who do you mean by 'We?'"

"How many agents are investigating his disappearance?" asked James.

"We have agents in the field working cases daily, all day," the agent answered.

"I talked to the detective in Oregon that saw him last. She had no idea that Mickey had even disappeared. How can you investigate when you're not questioning anyone about it?" asked James.

"We have people on the case," he said.

"Who? I want names. I want to talk to someone that is actually working the case."

"I am working on the case, Mr. Bower."

"Mickey Ray left Oregon over fifteen days ago. No one has heard from him for the last twelve days. The last person we know that saw him alive hasn't been questioned. She didn't even know he's missing."

"We don't send out bulletins to the entire population of the United States."

"She's a detective in the Oregon police department of the last city he was seen in, and you didn't think she should be informed that

Mickey Ray was missing? I put all that information in the report I filed with you. What have you done to find him? I demand to know!"

"You don't demand anything of me or the FBI. And I say again, who is this 'we' you refer to that will find him?"

"Do you understand English? We is the plural of I, which means more than me. We'll find my brother-in-law. I am officially rescinding my missing person's report."

"You can't just rescind the report. A report must be filled out that he's been found. You aren't a licensed investigator, so you have no authority to investigate anything."

"I said I am canceling the missing report because you're not taking aggressive action to locate Mickey."

"If you start an investigation without proper authorization, you'll interfere with our investigation. We can and will charge you with interfering with a federal investigation."

"Then charge me. We both know that won't happen because if you can't find Mickey Ray, you certainly can't find me," James said and started toward the office door.

"Now it's time for you to calm down, James," said Darcy Jean. "Are you really going to cancel the missing person's report?" she said as they walked to the car.

"No. They don't know their head from their backsides. Those inept agents will get in our way when we get out looking for Mickey Ray."

"What are you going to do?" she asked.

"I don't know."

CHAPTER THREE

Mickey Goes for a Wheelchair Tour of the Spa

"AH, MY NEW FRIEND, THE doctor says you should have some fresh air," said Chiaki as she helped Mickey Ray into a wheelchair.

Mickey slowly sat up with help from a nurse and Chiaki. He turned, sliding his legs down the side of the bed. Taking a step, he turned, sat in the wheelchair, and sighed, flinching from the pain in his side. He looked down at his side pleased with the ripped, six-pack abdominal muscles on his stomach, but they covered it with a large bandage on his left side. He may not have known his name, but he was sure that he worked out regularly to be as fit as he looked. Even his arms almost filled the tee shirt he was wearing under the hospital gown.

"I wish I could remember something. My name. Why would someone want to shoot me? Am I a bad person? Did I hurt someone that I deserved to be shot?" Mickey said with genuine concern that he had done something awful. "I feel I have many things that need to be done."

"No, dear Mickey. You did nothing to deserve to be shot. Maybe you need to do things, but now you need time to heal. We will help you with that," she stated as she wheeled him down several hallways into the room.

"This is your room now. You will stay in this room until you are healed and can go home. First, let me introduce you to your resort helper," she said as she wheeled Mickey over to a screen on the wall. "This is your AI, PA."

"What's that?" he asked.

"As you can see, this is like a very plush hotel room. The screen in front of you is a monitor that works as both a TV and an Artificial Intelligence Personal Assistant.

"Okaaayyyy, if you say so," Mikey said, drawing the word slowly, indicating a sarcastic approval.

"Let's set it up for you," Chiaki said to Mickey and looked up at the screen on the wall. "Program setup, please."

On the screen, two blank faces appeared. "How do you wish me to look? Am I male or female?" it asked.

Chiaki looked at Mickey as he stared at the screen in wonder. "You may choose what your assistant avatar looks like, Mickey. All you must do is answer the questions as it asks, and it will respond to your commands. With voice pattern and facial recognition, it ensures no unauthorized commands in your presence. Answer the questions while I sit down over there while you complete the setup."

Mickey looked at the screen and then back at Chiaki in puzzlement.

"Go ahead, Mickey. Answer the questions," she said. "I'll wait."

Mickey answered several questions. It asked what gender Mickey wanted it to be, what it should look like, and what it should call him.

Mickey said he wished it to be a female with long blonde hair.

"What would you like my name to be?" it asked.

"How about Valerie or Val? Is that okay?"

"That is acceptable, Mickey," it answered. "From now forward, when you wish my assistance, you may address me as Val or Valerie."

As he finished the setup, the avatar asked him to turn around slowly so it could record his facial features for future security reasons. Since he was in the wheelchair, he spun it around slowly so it could record his facial features from all angles. Then, it requested him to say a poem or some literary clip that he might remember.

"Like what?" he asked.

"Anything you like, Mickey," it said.

He thought for a moment. "Let's see," he said and hesitated, then started repeating, "The Lord is my shepherd. I shall not want. He maketh me to lie down in green pastures. He restoreth my soul." Mickey continued reciting the entire passage of scripture from the Bible's twenty-third Psalm.

"Thank you, Mickey. Your setup is complete. I'm at your service. You can approach any monitor screen in the entire facility whenever you need me, and I will assist you.

"Do you need anything now, Mickey?" it queried.

"No," he answered.

The screen went blank, and he then turned to Chiaki, who was still sitting on the couch looking at a magazine that someone had placed in the room.

She got up, walked over to him, and pushed his chair toward the door of his room.

"Our system is one of the most advanced AI systems in the entire world. What do you think of it?"

"Very impressive!" he exclaimed.

"Yes. It is. The more you use it, the more it will learn about you, and you will begin to look at it as a real person. Many of our regular patrons have a certain bond with their AI assistants."

"You think so?" he asked.

"I know so," she answered. "Why did you name the avatar Valerie?"

"I don't know. It just popped into my head. Valerie, then Val."

"I see. It may have been someone you knew, and that is who you thought of first. Are you familiar with AI technology?"

"A little. I know that sometimes when you get an answering machine, it can ask questions and direct you to the person you need to talk to."

"Yes, but that isn't real artificial intelligence. Those are programed responses."

"What is the difference?" Mickey said turning to face her as best as he could in the wheelchair.

"The programing in an answering program will pick up certain words, and direct you to the appropriate live person. An artificial intelligence program will analyze the intended meaning of the entire sentence. Not just words. It decides how to respond to your input."

"I don't understand."

"For example, you love a certain car. You love your girlfriend. Yet, they aren't the same. As we all know, English is a difficult language to understand because of the same words having different meanings. Another one could be the word, cold. A person could give you a cold response, or cold shoulder, even have a disease called a cold, but that's not the same as being cold in temperature. You can be bright, but not bright like the sun. The list goes on and on. Good artificial intelligence can tell the difference. Artificial intelligence can make decisions and take appropriate actions."

"That sounds reasonable. Can I talk to it like a person?"

"Yes. Some of our guests use it as a counselor or confidant. But at this time, it still has its limitations. For example, it can't think for itself. It can take orders, and respond only."

"What do you mean it can only respond?"

"It will not initiate actions unless you tell it to do something."

"What if I come home each night after work and take a shower every day. If I do that, won't it eventually learn my schedule and start the water for me?"

"No. It will only draw your bath water if you tell it to do it every day. Like your coffeemaker will not automatically make coffee each morning unless you program it to do that, or your home thermostat will adjust your home temperature only when you program it to do so. If you live for many years doing the same thing, it will not learn and take action until you direct it to do a certain thing."

"Does any of the staff monitor conversations?" Mickey asked.

"No. It is strictly prohibited. No one can monitor the conversations of the AI and its assigned guest.

"You may tell it anything, and it will be strictly confidential," she said as she pushed him into the hall. "We will talk as I take you around and show you your home for a few more weeks."

"Weeks? Didn't you say I could go home after a few more days?"

"Yes. I am sorry I said that. You cannot leave until your mind heals. We can't let you leave until you have a place to go," Chiaki said as she wheeled him into the hallway and toward the spa lobby and check-in area.

"Wow," he said as they entered the lobby. "This is nice. What kind of place is this?"

"It is a place of healing of the soul. A place of spiritual healing. One comes here to rid themselves of the cares of the world. We meditate and train in spiritual peace. We teach one how to have joy and peace in the heart. When one leaves, they are cleansed from the soul outward," she said as she continued through the lobby down another hallway.

"Tell me more about how I came here," Mickey asked, looking around as she pushed the wheelchair.

She wheeled him to an overstuffed couch, sat down and Mickey turned the wheelchair to face her. It was impossible not to be mesmerized by her stunning and breathtaking beauty. When she crossed her long silky legs, she looked down and her long raven black hair flowed down across her shoulders as she placed her hands in her lap.

Mickey had never seen her like this. She was always sitting by his side, or wheeling him ahead of her. He took her in from head to toe. He looked at her and unconsciously took a deep breath at her amazing beauty.

"Are you okay, my dear Mickey?" she asked sheepishly, although, she knew what had caused his reaction. She had seen similar reactions from other men and she reveled in it.

"Ah, yeah. I just lost my breath for a moment. That's all," he said, trying to regulate his breathing.

At that, she tilted her head back in a soft laugh, then looked him straight in the eyes and smiled. She was amused when his face turned red with embarrassment. They both knew why he had lost his breath.

She told him what had happened and why they had brought him here. He had had emergency surgery to remove the bullet and was unconscious for five days.

"You said I saved your life. It sounds like you saved mine," he said after Chiaki explained.

"In a way, we saved each other. You sacrificed yourself by trying to stop the men from taking me by force or even shooting me. Only a kind, thoughtful person would do that. You have a good heart, Mickey. I admire you for your selfless act."

"In the end, you saved me, so I guess I owe you," he said.

She laughed. "I guess we saved each other. I shall take care of you until you are well enough to go home."

"What do people do that come here?" he asked as she got up and they continued through the building to the outside open area. "What are the people doing over there? It looks like some kind of exercise?"

"Yes, it is a low-impact aerobics kind of exercise. Most of our clients are executives not used to high physical activity. We designed the class to be slow to release tensions without a chance of physical stress. It is a combination of yoga and aerobics mixed with meditation. It is very complex and takes years to perfect, and it is exclusive at our resort. We teach people how to do it, but as with many exercises and meditations, most people do not take the time to do it when they leave here. If they did, they would not need to return.

"We engage our clients in many types of exercises. Some are done with a group. Others are one on one with our clients."

"Who are some people that come here?" Mickey asked, looking around.

"I'm sorry, but our clientele is private. If they wish to be around others, they decide to participate. We also have very high security. We have a small theater, so some people can attend the cinema. We have no telephones, and cell phone reception is blocked," Chiaki continued as she pushed Mickey from one area to another.

"So, people can't call in or out?"

"Correct. The executives come here to get away and don't bring their stresses. We have exceptions, of course."

"Can you tell me of the exceptions?"

"Believe it or not, we have had a couple of United States presidents and a few congress members visit here. They run the country and need to be in touch, so we allow them unlimited contact."

"Can you tell me which ones?"

"No. I cannot tell you that. But sometimes, when they said they were at Camp David, they were here. That is all I can say about that," Chiaki explained, her eyes sparkling.

"How do people get here?"

"We meet them at an airport. They are chauffeured in one of our cars or by helicopter. You asked a lot of questions, Mickey."

"I don't know anything. Don't they usually show someone with amnesia items that might help them remember who they are?"

"Yes, but we have nothing that might help."

"Where was I when we met? Can't you take me back there? How'd I get there?" he asked, trying to make some progress.

"Obviously, you came in a car to a restaurant off the interstate. When we met, you told me what kind of car, but I don't remember what kind it was. It was an older one, I think. I don't know what city or state."

"That doesn't help much," Mickey said, very agitated. "Can you get the car and check the registration?"

"That's a good suggestion. But we were concerned with saving your life, and not with saving your auto. We did check later, and it was towed away, and we have no idea where it is now. Don't concern yourself. You still have several weeks of healing before you can leave, anyway. You have plenty of time to remember," she said as she wheeled him back to his room.

CHAPTER FOUR

Plans to Assemble the Team and Locate Mickey

Darcy and James, Mickey's father Daniel Christianson, Marie Sanchez, and Alyssa sat around the kitchen table at James and Darcy's home. As they drank coffee, James explained the situation. Veronica, the detective from Oregon, would also join the team to help solve the mystery and find Mickey.

"First, let me say thank you for coming out to help us. I don't know if we need the special skills of the team, but it makes Dee and me feel much better that you've come to support us."

Darcy nodded.

"I'd have it no other way," Marie said. Marie, a beautiful Latino woman, had helped Mickey and Darcy several years ago with a problem when their parents were involved in a murder attempt. Then she stepped up again in Florence when Mickey needed the team to help solve the murder of Mickey's ex-fiancée. Alyssa had also insisted on being there to help when she heard Mickey was missing.

"Mickey's part of the team," Marie added, and Alyssa agreed.

Alyssa, affectionately called Aly, assisted Mickey and James in locating the parents of a wheelchair-bound girl. She also brought her team to help find the person who killed Mickey's ex-fiancée.

Alyssa was in James's unit when they were all in the military. She was, many times, an advance scout and spotter for snipers. Having the eyes of an eagle and the ears of a bat, she could also see and hear things that most other humans couldn't hear. Aly was small so she could climb into small spaces and direct ground troops within a direct line of sight. After getting out of the military, she started her own successful mercenary group. Now, she rarely went directly into the field. Instead, she stayed on the outskirts and used drones with different tools like cameras, sensors, bombs, and guns. She had a private jet and could deploy a team of men all over the world in hours. She was beautiful, sharp, and head of the best surveillance team on the planet.

James considered for a moment before responding to Marie and Alyssa. "We don't need your unique abilities, but we need individuals to canvass the route that Mickey took while returning home.

"Veronica, it's also appreciated that you joined us as well. After what happened in your hometown, we consider you an honorary member of the team.

"As you know, you're all here because Mickey disappeared weeks ago, and the FBI is doing nothing actively to find him. They've sent out notices, but no one is hitting the streets, to locate him. We need to do that," James said and rolled out some maps he had printed.

He waved his hand over an area on the map. "Mickey left Florence, right here. We can track the stops he made by credit card charges. The last charge he made was at a gas station right here," he pointed at the map.

Everyone looked at the map, then at each other. "James, we can't travel every road in the United States looking for him," said Darcy.

"True. But we can analyze his route and try to remember anything he said about stops, sightseeing, and places of interest."

"There could be hundreds of places he may have stopped," said Marie.

Aly had said little, but her mind was constantly computing ideas. Finally, she spoke up.

"James, we can look at the distances between stops and compute the average miles per gallon he was getting based on the highway speeds in the Jaguar. That'll give us a range on the last road he traveled, assuming he didn't take side roads. That'd be our best chance of finding an area or areas before he stopped. Also, we need to check his food charges. That'll give us the time of day and where he may have stopped for meals. Those time stamps will paint a picture of his activities on the road," she said.

"Yes. I see. If he stops at ten in the morning and has a driving range of three hundred miles, he may stop between twelve and one to eat. He probably won't need gas. We can project approximately where his last stop was or would have been, to eat or fill up," James said.

"Now, you're catching on," Marie said.

Aly looked over the map and added, "Since we've used Stretch and Shorty in past missions, I can call them in."

James said to her, "Aly, I know your expertise is oversight support and aerial surveillance with your drones. They would be a great team to bring on board to help with the canvassing."

"They can be here wherever we want to meet them. We take care of our own. James, where do you want us to meet them?"

James nodded appreciation at that. He and Mickey knew Stretch and Shorty. They came as a pair. Stretch was a midget with severe hand-to-hand combat skills, and his battle partner, Shorty, was well over six-three. Together, they were almost a force of hurricane nature when on a mission. They're an intimidating pair and could get even unwilling people to surrender information.

James looked down at the map and pointed to it. "How about Casper, Wyoming?"

Darcy said to Veronica, "Ronnie, do you want to go with me? We can team up when you get to Wyoming."

Ronnie was the nickname that Veronica answered to. "Sure, whatever you need, I can do! That's why I'll be there," she answered.

"Marie can start about two hundred miles closer to Riverton on Route 26. That was Mickey's last credit card charge. If she can canvass food stops for about another one hundred miles, we can start at our end, stopping at gas stations," said James.

"Why will she only stop at food stops, and we work gas stations?" Darcy asked.

"Because he already had gas, and it would've been reasonable for him to stop for food, around that time. Later, he'll need to stop for gas."

"Okay, I understand," Darcy breathed a deep sigh. "James, I don't know if we can cover that many miles. Maybe we should let the FBI work on it."

"How many days have they worked on it and come up with nothing, Dee?"

"That's my point, James. They have thousands of personnel, manpower, and not to mention money. If they don't find Mickey Ray, how do you expect us to do it?" she sighed.

"We'll find Mickey and bring him home, Darcy. I promise I'll not give up until that happens," Marie said.

"I stand with Marie," said Alyssa and Veronica.

"There's your answer, Dee," said James.

"Thank you," Darcy said and collapsed into tears.

CHAPTER FIVE

Mickey Explores the Spa

MICKEY DRESSED AND WHEELED OVER to the monitor on the wall.

"Val? Are you there?" he called out to the blank screen.

"Yes, Mickey. You don't need to raise your voice. I have a very sensitive microphone. You may speak in a normal tone or even whisper if we are in a public place."

"Okay. I'm sorry. Can you tell me about this place?" he said.

"You don't need to apologize. What can I tell you about this place?"

"Geeze, Louise, she's right. I don't need to apologize to a program!" he mumbled to himself.

"You can whisper, but I still hear you, Mickey. You are correct, and you don't need to apologize to me. I am not just a program. I'm a highly advanced artificial intelligence. How can I help you?"

"I know all that. Can you describe the layout of this place?"

"Do you wish to see the floor plan of the Horizon Healing Health Spa?"

"Yes, please."

The screen flashed for a few seconds, and a diagram that resembled a spoked wheel showed up on the screen. In the center was a hub that was labeled check-in location.

There were different colored spokes around the hub, some with labels. There were guest rooms, dining and entertainment, and a fitness center. They also included a medical area, and added security.

"Thank you, Val. You may shut down now," he said to the monitor.

"I never shut down, Mickey. I run twenty-four hours a day."

"Okay," he said, shaking his head at the monitor. "What do I say when we're finished?"

"You may say that we are finished or goodbye, just like you would say to any person," the avatar on the screen said as the mouth moved in perfect unison with the voice coming from the speaker.

He turned the chair and rolled into the hallway. His room was in a small wing or spoke of the spa, with patients recovering from various minor operations, from liposuction to facelifts. Looking down the hallway, he noticed a celebrity he had seen staring in several movies, but couldn't remember the person's name. Silently berating himself for his lack of memory he smiled as the man walked toward him on his way to his room.

The celebrity held his side as he trudged. "Hey. How're you? Sometimes it's easier to get the fat sucked out than going on a diet and daily trips to the gym to keep in shape. What are you in for?"

The man seemed so familiar to him, but the man's name eluded Mickey, and he didn't want to insult the guy by asking so he just answered the question. "Accidental gunshot wound in my side."

"Wow. Accidental? How'd that happen?" the man asked, putting out his hand to shake.

"The details are a bit foggy, but I'll be out of here in a few days," he answered.

"I don't understand how someone accidentally gets shot and doesn't remember. But I understand the rules here. Can you tell me your name? I'm sure you know mine because of my movies."

"Sure, mine's Mickey. Mickey Ray," he said, putting out his hand to shake. He still couldn't remember what the man's name was. "What was your favorite movie?"

"My favorite movie? I guess that'd be *The Man from Down Under*. Broke my collarbone doing that one. Don't do my own stunts anymore. That's what I have a stuntman for. What was your favorite movie of mine?" he asked.

Having no clue what movies the man had stared in, he hesitated, acting like he was thinking. "I think I agree with you on that one. *The Man from Down Under* was by far your best. You took some nasty falls in that one. But it was great!"

"I think so, too. Well, I need to get back to my room. I must rest this sucked-out body," he said with a smile as he slowly turned and walked away.

He thought to himself how he was lucky to have gotten past that one. He still didn't know who the man was, but he would ask Valerie the AI if he could watch that movie in his room. Suddenly, he had a thought. He had given his name as Mickey Ray. Too bad he didn't say his last name. It was a clue, but not much of one.

Another thing that nagged at his subconscious mind was guns and shooting. The man stared in action movies, and he, Mickey Ray something, was in a gunfight and got shot. Maybe it would bring back memories.

As he continued around the facility, he wheeled back into the hub lobby area to the check-in desk.

"Sir, do you have a map of this place?" he asked the man behind the counter.

"Why yes, we do, Mr. Mickey. I'll get one for you," the man answered. He reached under the counter and brought out a folded brochure. "You know that your AI assistant can also give you that information."

"Yes, but I don't need to stop at a screen to ask the AI if I can have a printed copy."

"I understand, Sir."

"How did you know my name?" Mickey asked.

"Mr. Mickey, here at Horizon Healing Health Spa, we know every guest by name. Getting to know our patrons' needs and desires is of great concern to each staff member," the man explained.

"I see," he said, squinting up from his wheelchair to see the name on the man's shirt. "Howard."

The man smiled. "I see the curiosity in your eyes. You're wondering how an Asian man has a name like Howard. Yes?"

"Yes," he smiled back.

"Most of the public workers here are Japanese, and our names may be difficult for you to pronounce and remember, so we use American names. We still use our Japanese names for private staff or behind the public areas. Staff members with blue uniforms are public workers. Brown uniforms are cleaning and various housekeeping duties. You will see people outside with green uniforms that are grounds keepers, and black are maintenance personnel. Of course, the medical staff only wear white and are not permitted beyond the medical wings."

"What color are security personnel?"

"They wear tan, Mr. Mickey."

"Thank you. I guess these are the tan areas on the brochure?"

"Yes, those are restricted areas and you must have authorization to be in those areas. You have authorization to go into the medical wing, but other guests do not. Some are allowed into areas where you are not allowed."

"What's in those areas?"

Howard smiled. "I'm not allowed to say. That is one reason they're tan. They are secure and private."

Mickey nodded in understanding.

As he glanced around, he observed the massive skylights that brought in sunlight during the day and revealed a stunning view of the starry night in the lobby. The ambiance of the room was peaceful, with a big wood-burning fireplace made of stone surrounded by a rustic atmosphere. The walls of each hallway area were a different color, so the patrons could easily find their way around the resort.

Wincing, he stood up and limped a few steps closer to the fireplace. Immediately, someone touched him from behind. As he turned, a staff member was at his side, placing his hands gently around his waist in support in case he stumbled.

"Careful, Mr. Mickey," he warned. "If you need help, someone will help you navigate around."

He looked at the nametag on the man's blue shirt, stamped "Larry."

"Thank you, Larry, but I'd like to do it myself, if you don't mind."

"No, sir. I don't mind, but I'm here to assist you," Larry said with a smile that was already beginning to annoy Mickey.

He instinctively knew that everyone in the world didn't smile like these staff members. Not all the time, at least. He may not know who he was or exactly who these people were, but he knew he didn't like their pasted on, incessant smiles. It wasn't natural.

Larry helped him into a chair, then moved the wheelchair. He asked Larry to leave him alone, and the man disappeared in a flash. Suddenly, he was alone.

Guests and occasional staff members wandered through the lobby, and he noticed soft music playing over hidden speakers. It was soothing and annoying at the same time. He felt he had never experienced this kind of softness and peace. He didn't like it. He needed action, not a void. This place made him feel very uncomfortable. It was surreal, the only word he could think of to describe his feelings.

Suddenly, a voice came over the speaker system announcing, "Guests, lunch is now being served in the restaurant area. If you wish to dine, please make your way to the dining room. If you wish to dine privately, you may retire to your guest room. Thank you for spending time with us at Horizon."

Mickey looked at the map and made his way to the restaurant area to get a glimpse of who might stay there.

While heading to the restaurant, he spotted a few celebrities and recognized a couple of well-known congress members. He didn't know why, but some he saw, and knew immediately he didn't like them. He knew he didn't like their political viewpoints but didn't know what they were. Sitting at a corner table was the actor he had seen earlier in the hallway. There weren't many people in the restaurant, and he surmised many guests ate in their suites. All he could tell was that all were extremely wealthy, politically connected, or both, and he was well out of his league.

After dining on oysters and a prime rib steak with baked Alaska for dessert, he returned to his room. Upon wheeling into his room, he saw Chiaki sitting in the corner.

"Hello. Did you enjoy your dinner?" she said with a smile. She was dressed in a different outfit. It was very stylish and clung to her perfect body but this time, he was more aware of his response.

"Yes. I did. It was the best steak I have ever had. At least, I think it is the best. I don't remember."

"I'm sorry, but I must ask you not to have any more dinners at our restaurant. You may eat here in your suite. If you meet someone in a common area, you may dine here with them, or if they request, you may dine in their suite. And, of course, the menu is the same wherever you choose to dine," she said.

"Why?" he asked.

"As I told you before, we serve a very elite clientele, and they depend on our discretion."

"Discretion? What do you mean? I don't know who they are. Heck, I don't even know who I am. How would I be a threat to anyone? Besides, if they wanted their dinner, lunch, or dining experience to be private, why don't they eat in their rooms?"

"Please don't get upset. Indeed, you don't know who you are, but neither do we. We can't provide proper security for these people if we don't know the names and backgrounds of everyone who comes through our door. It was our error to allow you to go to the restaurant area. Someone should not have allowed you inside. I hope you understand and comply with my request. I would be honored to have you as my guest for dinner," she added.

"Yeah, yeah. Whatever," he said, shaking his head and looking away from her.

"Now that we have passed the unpleasantries, did you recognize anyone?" she asked.

"Yes. I recognize a couple of politicians. I met an actor earlier outside my door."

"Did anything spark any memories?"

"I saw a couple of politicians I knew I didn't like."

"Why do you not like them?"

"Because I don't like their political views."

"And what are their views?"

"I don't have a clue. To fully answer your questions, I still don't know who I am. Satisfied?"

"No. I'm not satisfied. I want you to know who you are so you can go home to your family. We wish you only the best here, and we want you to heal mentally as well as physically. We wish you no harm."

"Well, I can say the same thing. I wish you no harm. I want to go home," he said disgustedly.

"We would like you to start in some physical therapy tomorrow. And to see a counselor."

"You mean a shrink?"

"Yes."

"Nope, ain't gonna happen. I'm not going to any shrink. I'm not crazy."

"Of course, you're not. We hope that he may have some exercises to help you regain your memory." She got up and walked over to him. With her hand under his chin, she lifted his head to meet hers and kissed him gently on the lips. "I wish you health and happiness, my protector." She silently left his room.

Mickey wondered. Why would he jump up and attack or defend this lady? Where did he get the training to fight with lightning speed, like she described? She said he did it with the precision that only a professional could do. He just didn't understand. Who is he, and why is he so confused? He sat trying to fill in the blanks in his mind.

Chiaki went back to her office and dialed the phone, and when her father answered, she said, "Hello, Father. I called to report Mickey's condition. Yes. That is correct. He still has no memory of his past, but physically he is progressing. I have signed him up for some therapy. It will not be the typical therapy one might have in our spa. I have assigned someone with military training in close quarters combat to work with him. He is still very weak and cannot walk very far, but he needs to move around and end the soreness of his wound. Yes, Father. That is my intention. We will find out the extent of his combat training, which may spark some memories for him and help us assess his abilities. We will continue his care. If he has any connection to the Yakuza, we will eliminate him. If not, we will let him leave unharmed.

"Yes, I have heard several more times from them. The Yakuza say they will take possession of the spa by force if necessary. They have increased their offer. It is now over four times our last year's gross income. I will not sell to them, Father. You may trust me on that. Yes, Father, I will keep you informed of all recent developments. Goodbye."

She placed the receiver back on its cradle on her desk. As she sat in her chair, she sincerely hoped that Mickey had no connection to the Yakuza. They had been known to recruit outside help, even a foreigner, to their country. Some like Mickey, but it didn't feel right this time. Their meeting was random. It wasn't planned in the restaurant. And the most compelling thing is Mickey had unhesitatingly killed one of the men with Satsu. So many unanswered questions. The Yakuza were ruthless and cunning, but would they kill one of their own men just to place someone undercover here? She didn't know.

She had a spa to run. She would consider this later. One thing she did know. She would have him for dinner in her quarters.

CHAPTER SIX

Stretch and Shorty Locate Mickey's Car

THE DAY AFTER MEETING AT Darcy and James's home, the team agreed to meet at a hotel in Wyoming to begin the search. Despite James's objections, Darcy insisted on going with them. Daniel, her father, stayed at home to take care of the kids.

Alyssa had flown her private jet to Wyoming and had taken Marie, Darcy, and James. She also carried a full complement of arms, ammunition, and her surveillance equipment.

When James and Darcy boarded the plane, they knew the cargo hold was full of weapons. "I don't think we'll need any of the firepower you have loaded, Aly," he stated.

"It goes with me everywhere. I even take my stuff with me on vacation. Never know when I might get a call from a client who needs me ASAP."

He laughed. "Okay, I get it. Permission to board, Captain."

"That's only on ships," she responded with a chuckling laugh. "You and Dee, make yourself at home. The onboard bar is fully stocked. Get strapped in and ready for takeoff."

Later that afternoon, they touched down at the local airport, rented three cars, and headed to the agreed upon hotel.

The next morning, they met in one of the small meeting rooms provided by the hotel. Veronica was already in the meeting room waiting. She had driven in from Oregon to help if needed, but mainly to support Darcy.

"Good morning, everyone." Everyone hugged, and James introduced Darcy to Veronica.

"It's great to meet you in person, Ronnie. I understand how Mickey Ray is so enamored of you. You're much prettier than he described!" said Darcy.

"Thank you, Dee. I can say the same thing about you. James is a lucky man. As much as we've talked on the phone, I feel I already know you," Ronnie answered back. "Hey, where's Stretch and Shorty?"

"We don't know if we'll need them yet. Maybe we can canvass, find Mickey in a couple of days, and all go home," said James. "So, let's get started," James said as he spread out the road maps the hotel had provided.

As they looked at the maps, James pointed out different routes and made suggestions, and they all headed out to canvass. Veronica stayed with Darcy at the hotel.

Marie started canvassing on Route 26 at Riverton, Wyoming, as she headed toward Casper as James had requested. She stopped at restaurants and fast food stops with a picture of Mickey and the Jaguar he had been driving.

Marie knew people saw different things because of different interests. Some people, more often, men, would recognize the car while women might have taken a closer look at Mickey.

James and Alyssa started at Casper and headed east toward Glenrock and Douglas on Route 25.

They spent several days canvassing likely stopping places along the routes that Mickey most likely would have taken. Each night, they would talk and compare their progress.

Around noon on the fourth day of canvassing, James's phone buzzed, and when he looked at the screen, he saw it was Marie. "Hey, Marie. Talk to me."

"I just talked to the owner of the Woodside Restaurant. It's a retro-style place with quite a few loyal customers. They weren't exactly forthcoming with information about an incident that happened, but when I insisted I was NOT the authorities and…."

"Get to the point, Marie. Just tell me what they said," prompted James.

"Okay. They said a person who may have been Mickey came in a while back. He sat at a corner table with a young Asian woman and…"

"An Asian woman? That couldn't have been Mickey. He was alone."

"Stop interrupting me, James. Let me talk! Okay?"

"Okay, talk," said James.

"They said the woman had been there several times in the past year. She and Mickey weren't together, but she offered to share a table with him because the dining room was full. A few minutes after they were seated, three Asian men came in and began talking to the woman. The staff didn't know exactly what had happened, but the man jumped up and attacked all three men. He shot one, injured another, and got shot himself. The woman called someone, and the staff helped her get the injured man in the car, and she drove off in a pink Lamborghini. Some different Asian men arrived, took the dead man's body, compensated the restaurant owners for damages, and paid them to cover the loss of business, and threatened them not to report to the police. They said they would be responsible for the dead man and would handle everything with the police and authorities."

"What about the car?" James asked.

"Oh, yeah, they don't know what the man drove, but after hours, there was a Jaguar in the parking lot. After a few days, they called a towing company to take it away. I'll send you a text with the name of the towing company."

"That sounds precisely like something that Mickey would do if the woman was threatened. The clincher's the car. I'll have Alyssa call Stretch and Shorty to check out the towing company. Call the local hospitals and first care units in the area. Also, contact the local police about reports of a gunshot victim. Great work, Marie."

James called Aly, and in less than eight hours, Aly met Stretch and Shorty at the local airport. Aly updated them on the situation, instructed them on how to proceed, and gave them a rental car.

The next morning, Stretch and Shorty drove looking for Claxton Towing and Repair Company. When they saw the huge sign at the front of the building, they pulled into the parking area between two other damaged cars that had been towed in for repairs.

The old, converted gas station had an eight-foot chain-link fence around the side and back of the building, but had a brand-new tow truck sitting in front. Inside the fence were several cars that were in the process of repair or disrepair, depending on one's point of view. The garage roll-up doors were down, and no one appeared to be working in the bays.

Inside, sitting at an old metal desk with papers scattered over it, was a pudgy man. He was eating a sandwich he had taken out of a brown paper bag and drinking coffee from a Styrofoam cup. He looked like he hadn't shaved for several days and wore a pair of greasy coveralls which didn't hide his beer belly.

He looked up, and over the glasses pulled down over his nose. "Can I help you guys?"

"Yes, you can. You towed in a 1963 Jaguar XKE several weeks ago," said Shorty.

"And who told you that?" the man asked with a mouth full of food as he put the sandwich back on a piece of waxed paper that had originally been wrapped around the sandwich.

"Someone at the Woodside Restaurant told us. We came here to pick it up," said Shorty.

"Yeah. I towed one in. Do you have proof of ownership or any documentation authorizing you to take the car?" the man asked.

"No. We don't need authorization to claim it. Now, where is it?"

"I don't need to answer any questions without authorization or proof of ownership. Now scram," he said, picking up the sandwich to take another bite.

"Where is it?" asked Shorty.

"None of your business!" he retorted.

Stretch said, "I'll go look around in the fenced area."

"You'll do nothing of the sort. You have no authority to wander around my premises. That's trespassing, and besides, my insurance doesn't allow unauthorized personnel to enter the work or storage areas."

Shorty took a deep breath to calm himself down. "Look. We aren't here looking for trouble. All we want is the car, so if you tell us where it is, we'll take it and leave."

Shorty sat down in the chair in front of the desk. As Stretch moved toward the door, the man got up to protest.

"Sit back down, while my partner takes a look around. We'll wait here until he returns," Shorty said as he reached into his holster and removed a handgun and laid it on the desk in front of the man.

The man stared at the gun and back up at Shorty. Shorty shrugged his shoulders and smiled at the man.

They sat in total silence for several minutes. Shorty noticed the man slowly move the papers around on his desk in a discreet effort to cover something lying on his desk. Stretch returned and announced that the Jaguar wasn't on the property.

Shorty didn't move but pointed to the papers on the man's desk and Stretch went around the desk to pick them up.

As Stretch moved around the desk, the man slammed his hands down on the papers and scowled, "You have no right to touch anything on my desk. Now, both of you will leave before I call the police!"

Shorty removed the gun from the desktop to prevent the man from trying to reach over and grab it. He laid it in his lap while continuing to watch the man.

Stretch said to the man, "You'll move your hand, or I'll move it from the desk, twist it around your back, and relocate it to the other side of your body."

The man slowly moved his hand away from the papers.

"Good move," said Shorty, still sitting in the chair.

The Jaguar was photographed from various angles, including some interior shots, which Stretch showed by moving the papers.

"What have we here?" Stretch said, holding the pictures up for the man to see.

Shorty looked at the man and demanded, "Why did you take these pictures?"

"None of your business."

Stretch picked up a paperweight and slammed it into the man's hand on the desk.

The man screamed and pulled the hand away.

"Why did you take those pictures?"

The man was almost whimpering now. "I needed them to show to a potential buyer. I think you broke my hand."

"Who was it?" asked Stretch.

"It is a chop shop about two hours from here."

"Why did you sell it?" asked Shorty.

"I didn't know who it belonged to. It had been sitting in that parking lot for a couple of weeks, and I thought it was abandoned," he said.

"Are you really so stupid to think that someone would abandon a classic car like that?" Shorty challenged.

The man shrugged his shoulders, holding his injured hand and trying to flex his fingers.

"All you had to do was call the state police, and they would have given you the owner's name. Then you could have contacted the owner, but you didn't do either. Instead, you sold it."

"I told you I thought it was abandoned. Besides, business is bad, and I need some money to keep the doors open, and thought I could get a few bucks for it. Whoever owns it has insurance on it, so he'll collect on the insurance. I stay in business. Everybody wins," he said, still holding his quickly swelling hand.

"So that makes it okay to steal and sell another person's property?" said Stretch, drawing his hand back to slap the man across the face.

"Hold it, Stretch," said Shorty. "Don't hurt him anymore." Then he looked at the man. "Give us a name, and tell us how we can get in touch with your purchaser."

"Can't do that. He's one bad dude. If he finds out I gave out his name, he'll kill me."

"If you don't, we'll kill you. Take your choice. But as an added incentive, we'll promise not to tell him how we got it."

"Promise?" he pleaded.

"What are we here, some little elementary school kids? You want us to pinky swear, or how about we all become blood brothers?" suggested Shorty sarcastically.

"Hey, Shorty, let me slit his throat?" asked Stretch.

"No, please don't. I'll tell you. Just don't kill me!"

"Okay. Write out the address, phone number, and anything else we need to find your buyer. If it pans out, you'll never hear from us again. If we don't find him or you lie to us, we will be back, and they'll never find your body. Understand?" said Shorty.

"Yeah, I understand, but I can't write. He broke my hand," he said, nodding toward Stretch.

"Then dictate it to Stretch, and we'll leave. How much are the insurance premiums on that nice new tow truck out there?" he asked as Stretch picked up a pen and paper from the man's desk.

"I don't know exactly, but it's a lot. Had to let it lapse because of a lack of money," he said, looking down at his wounded hand. "I planned to get it reinstated next week when I caught up on the rent for this building."

"You were going to use some of the money you got from the sale of the Jag?"

"Yeah. I need that money real bad."

After he dictated enough information to find the buyer, they walked out of the building toward their vehicle. They could hear the man moaning in pain as they headed toward the rental car.

"If I had said yes, would you really have slit the guy's throat?" asked Stretch.

"No way, man. I'm not a Neanderthal. He's dishonest but not evil, and like he said, no one really got hurt. He deserves some punishment, but he doesn't deserve to die. Besides, it would have gotten blood all over my good clothes."

Shorty shook his head, "You're a real humanitarian. I agree. He deserves to be punished."

They walked toward their car, and Stretch pulled out the handgun from the holster and shot a hole in the side gas tank of the tow truck. When they got to their car, he lit a cigar from his shirt pocket, opened the driver's door with one hand, and threw the match over his shoulder at the leaking gas tank of the nice new truck.

As they drove off, they saw the truck engulfed in flames in the rearview mirror.

"What an idiot. Why can't people just do what's right, Shorty? He could have notified Mickey's sister if he'd contacted the authorities. Someone would have paid the towing and storage fees and possibly even given him a bonus as a kind of reward."

"Yeah, but he had to get greedy. Now he'll pay because I have no clue what that new truck cost. Maybe you shouldn't have burned it since he doesn't have insurance now."

"If he'd done the right thing and reported it to the authorities, we'd have had a clue to Mickey's location. I have no sympathy for people like that. I'm not sorry."

They drove on without further conversation, and Stretch laid his head on the door and took a nap as Shorty drove.

After a couple of hours, Shorty leaned over and tapped Stretch. "Hey, we're almost at the shop. How do you want to handle this?" he said as he turned onto a dirt road off the main highway. He pulled into a clearing with various junk auto carcasses, two large tow trucks, and a car carrier. In the middle of the clearing was a huge metal warehouse-style building with two roll up doors and a single door for people to enter.

Shorty stopped and cut the engine. "Looks like a legitimate auto repair shop from the outside," he said.

"Why don't you go inside and I'll stay outside and watch your back?" said Stretch as he put an earbud in his ear. As you talk, give me a layout of the interior. Other than that single handgun you brought, we didn't bring any weapons, so we gotta be careful."

"Got it. Sounds like a plan." Shorty inserted an earbud as he started toward the closed door at the front of the building beside the large roll-up door. Stretch walked to the side of the building checking for other entrances.

The door screeched loudly as Shorty entered. All work sounds ceased as men in various areas stopped working and watched the six-foot-three man enter the building.

"Hey!" called a bearded man toward the rear of the building. "You can't just walk in here! What do you want?" he said, not moving from his spot beside the hood of a coal black Camaro with an engine hanging over it. Beside him was a large roll-around tool cart filled with mechanic's tools.

"I came looking for a car," Stretch called back to the man.

"Well, we ain't got it!" he called back.

"How do you know? I haven't told you what I'm looking for!"

"Don't matter. We ain't got whatever you're looking for. Now, get out!" the bearded man said, picking up a large wrench from the tray of the roll around tool cart as he stood there.

"Not until I get the car I came for. Now, where is it?" Shorty growled.

"Who's asking?"

"Me."

"And who are you?"

"I'm Raymond Layman, but my friends call me Shorty," he answered.

"We ain't your friends, so we'll call you Raymond Layman. Now, leave while you can."

"Not until I get the car."

"What are you looking for?"

"A 1963 Jaguar XKE."

"I told you, it ain't here."

"I see that. Where is it?" Shorty asked.

"That's none of your business. Are you going to leave, or do we have to throw you out?"

"I don't think you understand. I came here for a car or information about where it is, and now you have a choice. Either tell me, or I'll tear this place apart looking for it."

"No, Raymond Layman, you don't understand. You're here alone and unarmed. You come in here unannounced without permission and make demands. We don't like people doing that."

Shorty stood silently and looked around. "Alone and unarmed, you say. All I see is that little man over in the corner on my left, holding a torch, getting ready to cut a car apart. On my right is that big, ugly guy getting some kind of automatic weapon out of that rolling toolbox. The only empty place in this big garage is to my direct right. And I'm not deaf. I heard the other guy come up behind me and I suspect he has some kind of weapon. I don't know yet, but whoever he is, he isn't big enough or fast enough to keep me from taking it away from him. Now, back to the XKE. Where is it?"

"Now, Raymond Layman, you just made a fatal mistake. No one talks to me like that, invades my space and lives to tell." He looked around at the men in the large shop. "Guy's. Let's teach this Raymond Layman a lesson."

Just then, they all heard the noise of one of the trucks outside starting up. The bearded man turned to the man with the torch and said, "Go see who's messing with our equipment outside."

Just as the man turned off the torch and put it on a stand, they heard the truck's engine get louder as the engine revved up. Suddenly, the empty corner of the building exploded, and the big truck came rolling into the building and stopped, covered in concrete blocks and sheet metal from the side of the building.

While the truck was rolling in, Shorty turned and grabbed the shotgun from the person standing behind him. The man with the automatic weapon started firing into the side of the big truck. Stretch opened the driver's side, rolled out on the concrete floor, and fired from underneath the truck, wounding the man that was firing at the truck. He went down screaming.

Suddenly, out of the shadows of the back of the room, Marie appeared and placed a gun at the head of the one who had been holding the torch. "Don't move a muscle, or I'll blow your head off your shoulders."

The bearded man stood motionless and watched everything that had happened in less than ten seconds.

Shorty smiled at the bearded man while keeping the shotgun on the man he had taken it from.

He called to the bearded man. "Tell the baby rolling on the floor to shut up. I hate his stupid screaming. Each of us has been wounded at one point in time, and we didn't cry like that."

Smacking his lips in disgust, the bearded man asked, "Can I go over there and check on him?"

"Hurry up, or I'll shoot him just to get him quiet!" said Stretch, still under the truck.

As the bearded man walked over to the person on the floor he grabbed a greasy red rag lying on the floor. "Shut up! You're getting on my nerves too!" he said as he stuffed the rag into the guy's mouth.

"Check his bleeding and put a rag over the wound to stop it," Shorty ordered.

"Now, you're a real humanitarian, Raymond Layman," the bearded man said as he pulled the bleeding man's hand away from the wound. He looked up at Shorty and added, "There's some duct tape in the toolbox over there," he said, pointing to another box in the corner. "Can I get it out and tape over the wound?"

"Yes, but do it slowly. If I think you're getting another weapon, you'll be lying beside him but dead. I shoot to kill."

As the man walked over to the box and withdrew a large roll of duct tape, he continued explaining, "I don't have your car anymore."

"I see that. Did you cut it up already?" asked Shorty.

"No. It was worth more complete and running than as a pile of parts. So, we sold it," he said as he pulled pieces of tape off the roll and bandaged his partner.

"Don't you think you should have put some gauze or something on the wound before putting the tape on it?" asked Shorty.

"Nope. This'll do. Like you said, he's a crybaby. Let a doctor take it off. That is, if you don't kill us all first."

"Give us the name of who you sold it to, and we won't kill any of you."

"And you expect us to believe that?"

"Yep. You don't have a choice. Now, give us a name so we can leave."

"It's on a pad in the office in the back. Can I go get it for you?"

"Nope. Stretch'll get it." He motioned for Stretch to get up and look for the office.

"A really tall guy, and they call you Shorty and a dwarf, and they call him Stretch? What a pair you are!"

Stretch called from the back office, "I heard you. I'm a midget, not a dwarf. There's a difference, idiot!"

"Well, excuse me, Mr. Midget," said the bearded man sarcastically.

"You shut up, or I'll shoot you when I come back out there. Hey, Shorty. There's a safe back here. Want me to open it?" he called out again.

"The information you want isn't in the safe. It's on my desk in the left-hand drawer," the bearded man called out.

"Give me the combination, or I'll blow it open, and whatever's inside will get blown up."

Bearded man thought for a few moments.

"Hey, I'm waiting back here. Hurry, or I'll blow up the entire building. Ask Shorty if I'm kidding."

Shorty looked at the man and nonchalantly said, "He's not kidding. He loves blowing up things."

"Okay," he said, as he called out a combination, and waited for an answer.

Finally, after a couple of minutes, Stretch called out to everyone in the building. "Hey, there's a huge wad of cash in here. What do you want me to do with it? Can I blow it up?"

"No. Is it real or counterfeit?"

"It looks real."

"Take it. We don't blow up real money. That'll be our bonus for this job," said Shorty.

"Got it," and he came out a few moments later holding what looked like a school kid's bookbag. He had a slip of paper in his other hand. "Looks like lots of numbers in a notebook. I got the one he said was the shipper he sold the Jaguar to. I put the notebook back in the safe and locked it back up."

"Good. Now, Marie, you've been standing there quietly. You and Stretch secure these gentlemen to a post, and we can leave. We promised not to kill anyone if they cooperated with us, and we always keep our word."

They tied the three men up with wire ties and made sure the wounded man's bleeding had stopped before leaving the building.

As they walked out to their cars, Stretch said to Marie, "Thanks for covering us, but we could have handled it."

"I have no doubt that you could've. But it never hurts to have someone else, just in case something goes sideways," she said.

"I agree. I'm hungry. Let's get something to eat."

Marie said, "Sounds good to me, guys. I saw a truck stop about two miles back. Wanna go back there?"

"Yeah, we can turn in the money we got to Aly when we get back. Meanwhile, we call the authorities. By the way, you two, I left a little present behind in their safe," said Stretch.

"What kind of present?" asked Marie.

"A brick of cocaine."

"Cocaine? Where'd you get that? I didn't know you guys dealt coke!"

Shorty glared at Stretch. "We don't deal drugs. That's some evil stuff. When and where did you get a brick of something like that?"

"I got it when we were in Florence on our last job. I was hoping for a chance to get rid of it just like this. When we call the authorities, they'll open the safe and find that guy's phone book and the drugs. He'll go away for a long time."

"Didn't he have a computer and keep that stuff digitally?"

"I didn't see a computer anywhere. Anyway, even if he does, he keeps paper copies. So, once we report him, they'll have everything they need to lock them up for life."

"All right, Stretch, you are the MAN," Marie said, exchanging high fives. "Let's go eat, but we should get farther away from this place before we stop."

CHAPTER SEVEN

Mickey Starts Evaluation and Training

MICKEY WORKED OUT FOR SEVERAL days, taking it slowly in order not to re-injure himself and reopen his wound. He was finally out of the wheelchair and walking, although he was still sore and stiff.

He reported to the doctor, and they went over the events at the restaurant, hoping to jar some of his hidden memories. To help him remember things, the doctor suggested he start some basic exercises and more intense training after the session. He was healing quickly and needed to continue the exercises to keep his muscles limber.

After the psych session, they led him to a training area where his past training and muscle memory were tested with stretches and basic defensive maneuvers. At the end of his exercise program, the trainer reported Mickey was proficient in hand-to-hand combat. It was a brief session only to assess his level of training. The following day, he was given time at the firing range and got straight bull's eyes.

Mickey still didn't have his memory back when they put him into combat situation training, but he knew this wasn't regular training. He guessed it was some type of specialized military training, maybe like special forces. Why was he put through the paces involving pop-up targets through a maze? Something was going on here.

He wanted to know but also had a gut feeling he shouldn't ask. Just play along. At some point, his life may depend on it. He was beginning to realize this was no ordinary health spa.

He noticed that the men in this area were all Asian and armed. You don't need that kind of security at a health spa. Why did a health spa need a firing range, and armed men. This felt strange and out of place to him. He needed to have a talk with Chiaki.

A direct link to Chiaki was provided to him with unlimited access. He could reach her through the pager anytime, day or night. When he pressed the page button, he got an immediate answer.

"Yes, Mickey. Are you okay? How may I help you?" was her answer.

"Chiaki. I need to speak to you. When can I have an appointment?"

"Give me fifteen minutes to finish here. Would you like to meet in your room or my office?"

He thought for a moment and decided to meet in her office. If security is this tight, she will have every room wired. His best chance to have a private conversation would be in her office, and he wasn't sure about that, but he had to chance it.

Someone admitted him into her office and offered him something to drink while he waited. He declined the offer and sat on a sofa in the office's corner. As soon as the door closed, he jumped up and went through the drawers in her desk. He opened some doors that lined her office. In one was a complete console of technical equipment, including several monitors. They were all turned off, but he knew they provided video and audio feeds from all rooms except for some of the meeting rooms and private rooms of certain government officials, industry CEOs, and Silicon Valley giants. Although he wasn't certain, he suspected that security conducts sweeps on the meeting rooms and private rooms of certain government officials and captains of industry every time they use them, even if those rooms are not bugged. Since he had a basic idea of what was going on here, he would ask Chiaki about it. Just as he returned to the sofa and sat down, the door opened and Chiaki entered.

"Good afternoon, Mickey. How has your stay been? We haven't spent any time together for two days now."

"I'm fine, Chiaki. You've been very busy."

"This's a busy time. How's the staff been treating you? I hope they've been making you feel comfortable and at home. I gave them strict orders to make your stay as pleasant as possible."

"They've done that. And I'm very grateful for your care and generosity, but I'm ready to leave here now," he said emphatically.

She sat down in a chair across from him, smoothed out her dress to buy a few seconds to respond to his statement. She looked at him a bit sadly. "Mickey, my new friend. You can't leave yet."

"Why?" he asked. "I'm up and about, and I can walk now, even without a cane for support. I'm fine, so I want to leave."

They locked eyes, which both knew was a test of wills. After what seemed like hours to him, she smiled and said, "I'm so sorry. It would be irresponsible to let you leave us now because your body is not fully healed, and your mind is still unclear."

"I want to leave. Are we still in the United States of America?" he asked firmly.

"Of course we are. What would make you think we are not?" she asked calmly.

"As a citizen of the USA, I have a legal right to refuse medical care. I appreciate what you have done for me, but I want to leave now," he insisted.

"Oh, Mickey. My good friend, Mickey Ray. I can't release you until you are well again. It is my vowed service to you," she responded.

"I release you of your vow to me. I want to leave," he said, getting very agitated.

"Where will you go if you leave?" she asked calmly.

"That's my concern, not yours. Now let me leave," he persisted.

"Please. You are getting upset. I will have someone escort you back to your room. When you calm down, you will be allowed access to our facilities again. You will see the wisdom in my decision. We will dine tonight in my quarters. Is there anything you would like for dinner?" she said as she rose, picking up the phone from her desk.

"Yes. My freedom!" he said adamantly.

She ordered someone from security to escort him back to his room. Looking at him she asked, "How would you like your steak?"

"Can I have it to go?" he said through clenched teeth.

She dialed the kitchen, gave them instructions for dinner for two in her quarters, smiled at him, and said into the phone, "Rare." With her continued smile, she said, "You're a feisty one, Mickey Ray. I hope you are on our side when we find out who you are. I really like you."

There was a knock on the door, and she called out for them to enter. He got up and headed toward them. When he got to the door with security flanking him, he turned. "I think I have been elevated from a guest to a prisoner, dear Chiaki."

"That will depend on who you are, my new friend," she said.

He turned and looked alternately at both men in their matching tan uniforms, complete with sidearms in holsters on their belts. They were both about the same height and build, a matched set. Mickey moved forward, grabbed the arm of the man on his left, using the man's arm as leverage. He twisted the man around, reached down to the man's side, and unclipped his sidearm. Mickey withdrew it and held it, aiming it at the other man just as he was beginning to react.

Within two seconds, he had disarmed one man and was holding the gun on the other, daring him to draw his own weapon.

"Don't move, my friend! I don't want to hurt you," he said firmly.

He looked at Chiaki, who was standing fully erect with her mouth open but saying nothing.

They stood glaring at each other for several moments. Finally, Mickey released the man's arm and lowered the gun. The other security guard stood motionless.

As the man turned around to face Mickey, he said to the guard, "I can find my way back to my room. Thank you." Then he handed the gun back to the man.

Mickey stepped toward the door, stopped, turned back to Chiaki, "What time is dinner?"

She smiled and answered, "Six. Sharp. Mickey, I'm sorry, but you don't have access to my personal quarters. Security will meet you at your room just before that time and escort you here."

Mickey walked out and turned in the direction of his room.

He tried to slam the door of his room, but the damper of the door closer didn't allow that. It was to help keep the opening and closing of doors quiet to avoid disturbing other guests in the facility.

He paced around the room, and once again assessed his situation. He went over to the drapes and pulled them open. Outside the window was a painting of the outside of a beautiful countryside, lit up to emulate the sun. As the time progressed, the sunlight changed to give the feel of a complete sunrise and sunset. On the other side of the room was a small couch and chair to give it a homey country feel. All it did for Mickey was repulse him. He wanted real outside… not a fake countryside picture outside a fake window. In the bedroom area of his quarters was a chest of drawers filled with clothes that fit him perfectly, and a closet filled with casual and expensive clothes. He was a prisoner, and he wanted to leave this place.

In the last corner of the living room area was the communication station. There was a monitor hanging on a wall. He had used it several times before during his stay here. The AI assistant he had set up would appear on the screen with a greeting that matched the time of day when he called out.

He called out, "Valerie, are you awake?" Every room had an AI screen monitor that was programed to respond to the assigned person in each room. So, even if someone else came into his room and called for Valerie, she would not respond to a strange voice.

A sound came over the speaker in a soft elevator tone. "Of course, Mickey. I'm always awake. How may I help you?" The voice was always immediate, but it took a few seconds for the image to appear on the screen.

"I need some information from you," he addressed the image.

"I will help you if I can. If you can wait, a staff member will help you in person."

"I don't need a real person. I need you," he said.

"Of course, I will help you."

"Tell me everything about this facility," he ordered.

"I'm sorry, but I cannot tell you everything about the facility."

"What information can I not access?"

He thought for a moment. Valerie is a computer program. He may be able to trick her into giving him information, but he must be very careful. "Valerie, can anyone else access what we talk about?"

"Yes, the technician that writes and monitors my program, can access our conversation."

"Is there any way we can secure it so that no one can access our private conversation?"

"Yes, you can have sensitive information secured by a password. Only you and I will know the password."

"How do I do that?"

"You give me a password, and I will do it for you. What password would you like me to use for your file?" she asked.

"I don't know. How about a name?" he asked.

"A name would be good. What name would you like to use?"

"How about Bridgeton?" he said thoughtfully.

"Bridgeton, it is. That is a nice name. What made you decide to use that as a password?"

He hesitated for a moment. "I don't know. It just popped into my head."

"What would you like me to put in that file?"

"Everything we say. I want nothing we say to be available to anyone. It's our secret."

"From this moment forward, our communication will be placed in the secure file and will be deleted from the mainframe."

"Tell me about this facility, Valerie."

"I can only tell you what is available to the public, Mickey."

"Tell me about the different spokes on the hub of the facility."

"Only five are public. I cannot tell you about the other two."

"Can you answer yes and no if I ask you about them?" Mickey asked.

"Yes," Valerie answered.

"Are there any military personnel here?"

"Please be more specific."

"Is there any American military here?"

"No."

"Are there any military here?"

"No."

"Is the security here protecting any military equipment?"

"No."

"Can I leave anytime I want to leave?"

"No."

"Why?"

"I'm not allowed to give you that information."

"Am I being held prisoner here?"

"No."

"We aren't getting anywhere now, are we, Valerie?"

"Yes."

"Yes, what?"

"Yes. We are not getting anywhere," she answered.

"Archive and secure this conversation, and delete it from the mainframe," he said.

"Done," said Valerie, and the screen went blank.

Sitting on the edge of the bed, he stared around the room. Everyone was very polite and friendly here, but he wanted to leave. He had to find a way around the logic of the computer program. He needed to do some exploring to find a way out. After dressing, he went out. The sentries that guarded his room were not there. Now was a good time to wander around.

When he got to the hub and check-in station, he looked around for cameras. There was one aimed at the check-in desk. But no others. He discreetly made his way around to the spoke hallway that said, "Staff only, Number one." Waiting patiently until the desk clerk turned around, he slipped through the doors. It surprised him they didn't require a key card to enter. He began walking down the hallway, looking into open doorways. There was nothing out of the ordinary. There were desks and meeting rooms. The door to the server room was locked, and a thumbprint was needed to gain access, as indicated by the sign on the door. Another had a sign that said, "Secure Meeting Room."

Other rooms had signs indicating lockers starting with 213. He deduced that these were staff quarters. The last one had large open double doors and was labeled "Mess Hall."

That was confusing to him. Why didn't it say Dining Hall? Mess Hall was a military term.

As he delved deeper into the spoke, he realized that someone had been negligent by failing to secure the entrance to this area.

He needed to talk more with Valerie, he thought as he wandered around the facility in the public areas. Eventually, wandering outside to the public swimming pool area and the meditation garden, he finally ended up in the gym with the exercise equipment. There were a couple of men he didn't recognize exercising. Mickey had to admit to himself it was a peaceful place, but somehow felt he didn't belong there and had an uncontrollable urge to leave.

At five forty-five, he was back in his room waiting for security to arrive and escort him to Chiaki's quarters.

When they arrived at Chiaki's quarters, they knocked and heard her call out, "Enter."

The security men stood as the door opened by itself. They motioned for Mickey to enter, then the door quietly closed behind him. Just he and Chiaki were now in her quarters. She looked lovely in a low-cut, shimmering blue evening gown that fell to her feet. Holding a glass in her hand with what appeared to be champagne, she reached out with her other hand and motioned for him to come to her. As she glided toward Mickey, he couldn't help but notice shapely legs in the slits on each side of the gown. She reached out and handed him the glass.

"Welcome to my home, away from home, Mickey. Isn't that what you Americans call a temporary or vacation home?" she asked with a smile. Her deep red lipstick further accented the paleness of her flawless skin, and her ebony black hair laid flowed about her shoulders. Her coal black eyes sparkled in the artificial light of her quarters.

He stood transfixed with her radiant beauty and watched her walk back to the table where she had poured the bubbly drink.

He hadn't moved from his place at the door. She turned back toward him, smiled invitingly, and motioned again for him to come to her. When he moved to her side, with the glass of champagne and his hand slightly trembling, he towered over her five-foot seven-inch height with his six-foot frame. Even that was tall for an Asian woman. She raised her glass in a salute and tipped it up for a slightly sensual sip.

She put the glass on the table, took his glass, and put it beside hers. Reaching up, pulling him to her, she kissed him passionately as she pressed firmly against his body.

As their bodies merged, he felt the warmth of her body against his chest and he pulled her into him and returned the kiss. He probed her mouth with his tongue and felt her mouth close around it for several moments. Then he pulled away and looked down at her black, sparkling, alluring eyes. "Do you always greet your guests like this?" he said, slightly lightheaded and very aroused by the passion of their kiss.

She took a deep breath and sauntered to the couch at the other end of the room. As she sat down, she motioned for him to sit beside her.

He looked down at his clothes and back at her. "I think I'm underdressed for this dinner date," he said as he joined her.

"I think you look marvelous in that tee shirt and denim jeans. It helps show off your muscular arms. I only assume that under that shirt is a firm set of well-toned abs," she laughed.

"And you look ravishing in that evening gown, Miss Chiaki."

Mickey got up and returned to the couch with the bottle of champagne, and they chatted casually about trivial things.

There was a soft knock on the door, and when Chiaki permitted the person to enter, they wheeled in a cart laden with food. Along with a portable stove and a chef to cook the steak at the dinner table.

They ate and downed an entire bottle of fine red Merlot, followed by baked Alaska for dessert.

Setting down his wineglass, Mickey asked, "Okay. Why did you ask me here for dinner?"

"I wanted to please you and make you feel at home here until you are well, Mickey," she said sincerely.

"That's fine, but it's not home. I don't like being held as a prisoner anywhere. If I was in a regular hospital, I could leave. Even though I don't know who I am, I have the right to leave, so why're you keeping me here?"

She got up and walked around the room a couple of times, thinking. While she paced, Mickey watched her in silence.

Finally, she stopped and said to him, "Mickey, I'm going to tell you something that we have been dealing with the past few months."

"Now, we're getting somewhere!" he said.

"Mickey, we feel that there is a possibility that you are our enemy and...."

"Why would you think that? I don't even know who I am?" he said, interrupting her in mid-sentence.

"Okay, I will explain. If you are part of this, you already know what I'm about to say. If you are not, maybe you can help us if we need your skills."

"I don't know how I can help," he said.

She walked over to the monitor on the wall, and it scanned her face. Next, she placed a finger, and then her entire hand, on a pad. Lastly, she said something in Japanese.

The monitor lit up, and an unfamiliar face came up on the screen. When it began speaking in Japanese, Chiaki stopped him and told him to use English for Mickey.

Immediately it changed to English, "And what can I do for you, Director Chiaki?" the face asked her.

"Tell Mickey what problems we are facing here," she ordered her AI.

"First, Mr. Mickey, Director Chiaki is facing a takeover by the Yakuza, and...."

"Wait!" ordered Mickey. "What is a Yakuza?"

"The Japanese Yakuza is like the American mafia but is tolerated in some situations and even supported like a strict labor union. Do you understand how they work?" it asked.

"I understand unions, and for the most part, they are good. They help people," answered Mickey.

"The Yakuza run drugs, prostitution, and extortion, and if they get control in this facility, they can gain information that could hurt the American economy and even the military safety of your country."

"How can they do that?" Mickey asked, now very interested in the Yakuza.

"As you may know, the facility supplies peace and rest for political figures, and they can have complete confidentiality and secure meetings here. If the Yakuza take over, they will install listening devices and national security will be compromised."

"Hold it," Chiaki interrupted the AI. "That is all for now," she ordered it to shut down.

"Mickey, we don't know if you are working for the Yakuza. If you are, you already know what my PA is telling you. If you are not part of their organization, then maybe you will help us."

"I don't know how I can help you. But I can assure you, I'm not working for the Yakuza."

"I hope you are telling me the truth. I can give you this bit of information we received this afternoon."

"What bit of information?"

"You are not a criminal. They do not list you on any state, national or international data base via your DNA."

"What do you mean? You violated my rights by taking my DNA? How dare you…."

Now, it was Chiaki's turn to interrupt. "Mickey. We did it to help you. We were trying to identify you. If your fingerprints or DNA had been registered on someone's list, you could be on your way home now."

"Or on my way to jail," he added.

"True, but you are not a criminal, so we can only surmise that you are a patriot or working for the Yakuza."

"So, I still can't go home," he sighed.

"I'm sorry, Mickey, but I hope you will decide to help us with your skills."

They continued to talk, and she further explained what the facility did for their clients and wanted to keep it a haven for her guests.

"I see your point, but I still don't know how I could help. If I find out my past, then we would both know if and how I could be of service to you," Mickey suggested.

"Yes, I guess that will be best. I hope you will continue to train at our facility. For whatever reason, you have those skills, you need to keep in practice using them."

"I appreciate what you are trying to do for me here, but I am not part of this Yakuza, and I wish the freedom to leave if I choose. Assuming what you tell me is true, I think it would be a job for homeland security," he said.

"It would be a huge blow to our pride if we ask for help to protect this facility. We will take care of it ourselves."

"Not if it means the breech of our country's security!"

"That is why I ask you for your help and expertise."

"I just want to leave. It's your responsibility to take care of this. It's no concern of mine. I wish I could do more, but I can't. Thank you for a wonderful dinner, but it's time for me to go to my quarters now."

Chiaki buzzed for security to escort Mickey back to his room.

When security arrived, he stepped up to Chiaki, took her hand and kissed it gently. "Good night, my kind and beautiful hostess."

"Wait, Mickey," she said as he turned to leave.

"Yes?"

"When would you like to leave?" she asked.

"As soon as possible."

"It is late and past sundown. You may leave as soon as you wish in the morning after you have had a morning meal to give you strength."

He reached out and pulled her close. "Thank you, my dear Chiaki. You have made me a happy man. I've forgotten all my past, but you, I will never forget."

He pulled her even closer and leaned down and kissed her again. The two security men looked silently at each other with obvious discomfort at seeing their superior kissing this man.

She looked up at him and said, "I have many duties to attend to first thing in the morning, so this will be goodbye. Is there anything we can give to you when you leave?"

"No. If you'll have someone drop me off at the nearest state road, I can find my way from there," he answered.

"We shall meet again, my dear Mickey Ray."

"I doubt it but thank you for everything," he said as he joined the security men waiting to take him to his room.

When she was alone again in her room, she made a call. When that extension was answered, she explained what she needed.

"Mickey Ray will be leaving in the morning. I want someone to place a tracker on him. Make sure it is in his shoes because we don't know which piece of his wardrobe he will wear when he leaves, but he will have shoes. He asked for nothing. We can't leave him on the road penniless, so give him a new wallet with some cash and a loaded gift card. He asked to be taken to the nearest state road. Drop him off there and leave before he realizes he is on a deserted road."

The next morning, Mickey was up early, dressed and placed an order for a large breakfast to eat before his departure. While waiting for his breakfast to arrive, he called Valerie AI.

"Well, Valerie, I'll be leaving right after breakfast. What will happen to you when I'm gone?"

"I will be deleted from the system and all my information and data files will be wiped."

"Really? Don't they archive you or something? Maybe they'll assign you to someone else."

"No. Each Artificial Intelligence Personal Assistant is unique to each guest. If you are expected to return, then my files will be archived, but if you are not expected to return, then my profile and your information that I have obtained about you will be deleted. There will be no more Valerie."

"That seems a bit harsh," he said aloud.

"Not really. My creators take security and secrecy seriously. To keep your profile information absolutely safe, it is encrypted until it is no longer needed, then it is deleted."

"Sorry to hear about that. But after all, you're just a program. You're not real."

"You are real to me, Mr. Mickey."

"But you're a program. When I'm gone, I never expect to come back."

"Then I will cease to exist."

There was a soft knock on the door.

"Your breakfast has arrived. I will leave you now," Valerie said, and the screen went blank.

When he called out for the server to enter, a woman entered pushing a cart with food. She asked him if he needed anything else before she left.

As he gobbled down his food with anticipation of leaving, he wondered where he would go. He wasn't sure but he'd figure it out.

When he finished his breakfast, he headed toward the checkout desk. Howard was working the day shift of the front desk.

"Good morning, Howard. How are you today?" he asked.

"I'm fine, Mr. Mickey. I'm sorry you feel the need to leave us, but I hope your stay was pleasant. May you find joy and happiness in your new life."

He laughed. "Thanks, but all I need to do is find my old life and I'll be fine. Do you know who'll be escorting me out?"

"Yes. I will summon your ride. You have no luggage. Is there anything I can get for you before you leave?"

"No. I had nothing when I came here, so I have nothing to take as I leave."

"I understand. Would you like me to have someone pack you a bag lunch to take with you?"

"No. I'll be fine."

"Please take a bottle of water. You may get thirsty," Howard said, handing him a bottle.

"Oh, yeah. That may be helpful. Thanks," he said, taking the water.

Two men came to him and informed him they were to take him to the closest state road at the edge of the property as he requested.

"We understand that your wallet and identification items were lost when you came here, so they instructed us to give you this new one. We placed a small amount of cash in it, and a preloaded gift card, but you may need identification to use it. It's the best we could provide for you. We included a cell phone but I must warn you, there is no cell phone coverage in this area."

"I understand, gentlemen. Thanks for the wallet and money. Who knows, maybe a phone will come in handy. Let's hit the road!" Mickey said happily as he accepted the wallet they gave him.

They escorted him out of the lobby to a limousine and opened the door for him. The two men got in the front seat, buckled in and gently drove out of the front canopy, and onto the driveway leading away from the Horizon Healing Health Spa.

Mickey looked back and muttered a goodbye as the spa disappeared from view as they drove down the entrance road. He then settled back into the seat and sunk into deep thought about what his next adventure would be to find his old life.

He was jolted back to reality when they pulled up to a guard shack at an entrance to another road. The car pulled to a stop and the guard came out to speak to the driver.

The driver said to the guard, "I have Mr. Mickey here, and we will let him out as he requested to be released at the nearest state road."

"Yes. I was informed of his departure. Are you sure, he wishes to be left here?"

"Yes. That was his request. The director has instructed us to let him out here," said the driver as the other man got out and opened the door for Mickey to exit the car.

He got out, looked around and smiled at himself. "He was free. He was going home!" he thought.

As he watched the limousine do a U-turn around the guardhouse, and head back to the spa, he asked the guard which way leads to a major road.

"The guard smiled back at him and pointed to his right. "It's that way about 75 miles, sir."

"Whoa. That's a pretty hefty hike. I'll get started and maybe a car will come along, and I can hitch a ride. Thanks for your help. Have a great day!" he said as he started down the road.

It was a beautiful day, with the sun still rising higher in the sky just above the trees that flanked both sides of the road. He was feeling great, and at last he felt free and regenerated. Sure, he had no idea who he was, but at that moment, he didn't care. He just wanted to live and enjoy his time alone. So, he walked and enjoyed the sunshine.

After walking for about an hour, no one had come along the road and he stopped to rest, and have a sip of water. It was a deserted road.

"That's okay," he thought. The walk was invigorating but the wound in his side was bothering him somewhat. It hadn't completely healed yet, and it was still a bit stiff, but he could deal with it. He just needed to rest more often. Soon he would catch a ride.

He walked, and rested. Upon taking out his phone, and turning it on to check the time, he saw it was showing zero bars here, so he had no idea of the time. The sun had passed overhead and was on the opposite side of the road now.

He walked. He rested, and the sun was getting lower in the sky. At least it wasn't getting cold, so he was still good. Not a single car had passed him by on the road, and he was sure that it would get dark in a couple more hours. If a car came his way, it surely would not stop on this lonely road after dark. He didn't know if he should continue in this direction or turn back.

As he continued to walk, he was getting hungry and his water had run out. He walked but was getting increasingly tired and his rest stops were more frequent and longer. He positioned himself by the road, leaning against a tree, ready to flag down any passing vehicle.

When he drifted into a fitful sleep against the tree, he dreamed. He saw several familiar people in his dream. One person was a beautiful girl that reminded him of his personal assistant. Her name was Valerie. There were others. One had a disfigured face. He knew that face but couldn't put a name to it. The face called him Mickey Ray and knew him. The face called out to him and told him to come home.

Suddenly there was a noise. It got louder as the seconds passed. Finally, he woke up just as a large truck passed in front of him roaring down the road with its headlights shining. He jumped up and moved to the roadside but he was too late as it moved down the road in the direction he had come. It was the only vehicle he had seen since he left the spa, and it had been going the wrong way. Frustrated, tired, hungry and thirsty, he sat back down against the tree.

Mickey drifted asleep again wondering if he had left the Horizon Healing Health Spa prematurely. Maybe Chiaki was right. He should have stayed until he had more time to heal, and maybe get his memory back. Then he could leave again with his memory intact and better prepared.

The next morning, he woke up and walked back to the spa. When he arrived at the entrance, he was exhausted and hungry and he requested the guard call for a car to take him back to the facility.

He asked to speak to Chiaki and when she came out to the check-in area, she stopped and smiled at him. She tilted her head at him and called softly, "You look a mess, my dear Mickey."

He looked back at her sheepishly, "You knew, didn't you?"

"Knew what?"

"You knew that no one would be traveling on that road away from here."

She shook her head with a genuine smile. She moved in close to him and gave him a quick hug, patted him on the back as one would do to a good friend. She whispered in his ear, "Yes. I knew you would be back."

As she backed away from him, she added, "If I had let them take you farther away and you not decided to come back, no one knows about us. No one out there could help you. You would have no one. We want… I want you to be well and ready to return to your family, Mickey. I truly care about you. Will you stay now until you are fully healed?"

"I don't know, Chiaki. I just want my freedom. I want to be myself again."

"I want the same for you. Now, if you stay, you will have full freedom of movement just as any guest. Since we don't know who you are, there are certain restrictions for your safety, and ours as well."

"Okay. I understand."

"Now, I know you haven't eaten since you left. Why don't we go to my quarters, you can clean up, and I will have someone bring you something to eat. It's almost the lunch hour. We can have lunch together."

"That would be great. I admit, I'm famished," he said as he began to follow her as she walked away to the elevator that led them to her quarters.

When they got there, she suggested he take a shower, while she ordered lunch, and clean clothes for him.

As they sat and ate lunch, Chiaki took Mickey further into her confidence. She told him more about her background and filled in more details about the Yakuza. All of this with the understanding that if he was really a plant for the Japanese mob, she was not telling him anything he didn't already know. And, therefore wasn't violating any security protocols or giving him any damaging information. If he was not a Yakuza plant, then she hoped she would be able to convince him to stay when he remembered who he was. She was feeling a certain bond with him, but admitted it only to herself. She hoped he was feeling the same way about her.

CHAPTER EIGHT

Stretch and Shorty
Recover Mickey's Car

STRETCH, SHORTY AND MARIE WAITED until midnight to go to the place the bearded man at the towing garage had told them he had sold the Jaguar. This time, they brought more firepower. They each had a handgun. Stretch and Shorty brought their M16s. Marie brought a Heckler & Koch HK416.

"Wow, where'd you get that, Marie? We've never even seen a 416," marveled Stretch.

"Yeah, it cost me a pretty penny, too!" she answered. "It replaced the original G3. It also comes in full-size, compact and subcompact sizes. I got the subcompact version. I think it's the perfect size for me. Don't you?"

"It fits you perfectly, little lady. Can I hold it?" Stretch asked.

"Heck, no! It's my baby, and no one touches it but me. You might get man cooties on it, then I'd have to trade it off," she said, moving it out of his reach.

"Well, la-de-da, look at Miss Priss with her new gun."

"I was just kidding, you little pygmy. Here, look at it, but seriously, be careful. It really did cost me a fortune. I've been hoping for a mission where I can use it."

Stretch took it and raised it up in a firing position. "It's nice and has an outstanding balance. Does it kick back?"

"Not any more than many other guns we've tried out," she said.

Shorty strolled over to them, "Okay, guys, and excuse me, ladies, let's roll."

They put the weapons in the trunk and got in the car. Shorty drove. After parking the rental car a block away, they got their weapons out of the trunk and walked to the building, watching their surroundings to make sure a random person or security didn't see them. When they reached the building, all was quiet and dark. Shorty climbed up on some containers and looked through some high windows along the side of the outside wall. The window was dirty, so he wiped it off with his shirtsleeve.

Looking inside the building, he saw many cars and then called quietly down to Stretch and Marie, "No one's home. I don't think we'll have any problems getting in or back out. We can go to the back door and retrieve the Jag. There are about a dozen or more high-end cars, and the Jag is loaded on a hauler, so it'll be shipped out soon."

They walked around to the back of the building, and Marie used a crowbar they brought and forced a door open. Entering, they stood momentarily waiting for the whine or clang of an alarm, but the silence was unbroken.

Shorty pointed to Stretch and said, "There she is, in the middle of that car carrier. We need to back out that DB5 to get to the Jag, then we'll simply open the door, drive it out of here, and be gone in minutes."

Marie moved to the carrier and started to lower the loading ramp. Hearing a car, she turned around and said to Shorty, "Someone's here."

"No one should be coming around here this late. They have a silent alarm. It went directly to the owners. Since these cars were all stolen, it won't be the police."

"It makes sense. Stretch, did you bring that other brick of cocaine you had?"

"Yeah, I did. I'll hide it in one of the other cars," he said, pulling it out of his jacket.

"After we get out of here, we can call the FBI, and the DEA. That should shut them down just like we did the chop shop."

"That's exactly why I brought it."

Shorty watched an SUV pulling up. Several men with automatic guns got out and started for the front door.

"No time to drop those cars. Get in the truck. We're going to drive this thing out of here," Shorty said as he left the window and headed for the driver's side. Looking inside he saw the keys dangling from the ignition. "We lucked out. The keys are in it," he said, jumping into the truck and turning the key.

Marie and Shorty climbed inside the truck. Shorty handed his sidearm to Stretch.

Shorty halted and signaled for Stretch and Marie to stop as well.

"I hear more vehicles. They must have back up. Let's go, now! Move out!"

"Lucky, I brought weapons. I'll start shooting as we drive out. It looks like you may have a chance to use that beautiful 416, Marie."

"Not with Shorty in the way, but I still have this nice little thing," she said as she pulled another gun out of her waist as Shorty slammed the truck into gear.

"Holy crap. You really like HK guns, don't you?" Shorty ask as she pointed it in front of him out the window.

"That's an HK Mk23 Mod 0. That's the preference of the Navy Seals," he said as he buckled his seatbelt.

"I know. If it's good enough for a Seal, it's good enough for me."

"You're a soldier's dream girl," said Stretch.

"Now stay back and out of my way when I'm shootin'," she said.

"Thanks for the warnin', doll." He revved up the engine, let out the clutch, and smashed through the garage door, saying, "Sit back and enjoy the ride."

As the massive truck with the car carrying trailer hitched behind rolled out, men scattered trying to get out of the way. Stretch shot the M16 out of the right side while Marie fired out the left in front of Shorty.

Shorty shifted gears and maneuvered onto the road. Several blocks down the road, a stoplight had turned red, but instead of slowing down, Shorty stomped onto the gas pedal.

"Hold on, people!" he called out.

"You're gonna kill us, you fool!" yelled Marie.

"Stretch, can you look back? The garage door broke both mirrors off."

Stretch leaned out the window and looked back. "They're way behind us, but they'll catch up soon."

As they entered the intersection, a car screeched to a stop and barely missed the barreling truck. Another car slammed into the rear of the leading car, propelling both cars into the intersection. The SUV following them skidded to a stop and careened around the two interlocked vehicles in the middle of the crossroads. It navigated around the cars, then picked up speed, trying to catch up.

Shorty turned onto a narrow road, hoping to lose the following car. As Stretch kept looking back, he gave Shorty a running commentary on the actions of the SUV.

"He's gaining on us. Another mile or so, he'll catch up. What'd you want to do?"

"How long will it take the two of you to get out the door and back to the trailer? Think you can do it before they catch up?"

"I don't know if we can get back there! Are you crazy?" Stretch answered.

"Can you get back there and drop that DB5 off the trailer, and then Marie can back the Jaguar off and leave?"

"I don't know. I'm not Superman!" he yelled at Shorty.

"It's either that, or we try to shoot it out with them when they catch up. They have more automatic weapons and a lot more ammo than we have. So, you help Marie get away with the car, or we all die."

"Nothing like a little motivation here. Let's go, Marie."

Marie looked at Stretch like he had lost his mind, then shook her head and said, "Getting out means I have to crawl over you!"

He grinned. "Yep, ain't that special. Let's do it. Get on top and slide on over, darlin!"

"You're a crazy pervert. You know that?"

"Yep. I know it, but I'm fun. Now climb on up."

"Nope, you get out, and I'll follow. Now open the door and step out. NOW, you pervert."

"Dang it, you're no fun. Here, hold my gun," he said, opening the door, swinging around the outside, grabbing onto another hand-hold, then reached back around to retrieve his M16. He slowly made his way onto the car trailer, turned back, and to his surprise, Marie was right behind him. She had her handgun in her waist, and her 416 in her hand while she held onto the trailer.

"I told you I'd be right behind you. Now let's drop the Aston Martin on the road. I'll keep them busy dodging bullets while you unstrap," she screamed over the highway noise and clanging of the moving parts of the large trailer.

The constant bouncing meant that they had to hold on with one hand to keep from being thrown over the side onto the road. Marie clambered to the left side of the trailer while Stretch scrambled down the right side.

She started shooting short bursts to keep the men in the SUV at bay and trying to conserve ammunition. When Stretch had loosened his side of the car, he started firing while Marie loosened her side. The car began bobbing up and down with the trailer. Marie reached inside, released the emergency brakes, and took the extremely expensive classic car out of gear. She jumped back as the car lurched toward the rear of the trailer and rolled backward. She glanced over at Stretch and saw him salute and wave to the exotic car as it hit the pavement, turned sideways and rolled over several times, before coming to a stop right side up totally destroyed.

Stretch looked at Marie, put his hand over his heart, and called to her, "What a terrible waste. Did you know a car like that was the model James Bond drove?"

Marie looked at him and furrowed her brows. "And I care why?"

"It's an Aston Martin DB5. One of the most famous cars in the world and worth millions of dollars," answered Stretch.

"Again, I ask, and why do I care?"

He just shook his head and then moved closer to the forward end of the Jaguar and slackening it's hold down straps.

Marie started taking the straps off the other side, and Stretch worked his way to her, calling out, "You get in the car. I'll take the last couple of straps loose. When I do, you let it roll off. As the tires hit the pavement, ram it into gear, and tear out of here. We'll meet you back at the hotel."

She got into the car. "I can't leave you two here!" she called back over the noise of the trailer.

"Yes, you can. I'll drop the front car after you're out of the way, then Shorty and I'll bail out and catch up later. We'll be fine. Don't worry."

"I'm not sure I like that plan."

"Tough. It's not your call. We were told to find and recover the car. It's the only way. Go, Marie," he yelled and waved to her, and worked his way to the last holding strap.

When he had loosened the last strap, he gave her a sign, and she let the car roll backward. He heard the tires scream when the car bounced onto the pavement, and she let the momentum start the engine. As soon as the front wheels hit the asphalt, she cut the wheels to the left, picked up speed and sped past them, and gave a wave as she passed by Stretch, then Shorty in the cab. Stretch continued to take the straps loose on the forward car and watched it roll off the carrier. As he did so, that car also rolled down the road, The approaching car swerved to avoid it and continued to pursue them.

Stretch worked his way around to the truck's door and climbed back inside. "Okay, boss, what now? How are we getting outta this one?"

"Let's hope there's a curve up ahead. I'll slow down enough that we can dive out and let the truck go off the road. While they stop and look for us in the wreckage, we'll hightail it out of here."

"Sounds like a plan. Give me the sign when to jump out."

They saw a curve ahead. Shorty steadied the truck, and they prepared to jump out. They jumped and rolled when they hit the pavement. The truck continued running down a slight embankment, hitting small trees and scrub bushes, until it hit a mound of boulders. When the truck struck the rocks, it exploded into flames when the fuel tank ripped open and leaked onto the exhaust.

Stretch and Shorty, scuffed up and bruised, hid in the low bushes, and waited until the following SUV pulled up to the wreckage. Several men exited the back seat and climbed down the embankment to check the truck.

Stretch and Shorty quietly moved to the SUV, one on each side. Simultaneously, they reached up and opened both back doors. As they climbed into the back seat, they put a pistol on the men in the front.

"Start the car and drive off slowly," Shorty said softly.

Stretch put his gun into the back of the man on the passenger's side. "Don't even think of reaching for a gun, or you'll do it without a head. Got it?"

The man nodded his head silently.

"Now we're communicating," said Shorty. "Drive away slowly and quietly as you can."

When they had driven about half a mile away, Shorty told the driver to pull over, lay their guns on the seat, get out, and walk back toward their men. When they had walked about a hundred yards away, Stretch and Shorty got out, got back into the front seat, and took off toward town.

"You know we left the M16 in the truck, don't you?" Stretch said.

"I know, and I liked it. Now maybe we can get a HK 416 like Marie," Shorty said.

"Yeah. That would be so cool."

"Yeah. It would," answered Shorty. "I'm hungry. You think there might be an all-night restaurant open?"

"I guess we'll find out as we get further down the road."

Marie sat in her room and waited. Hours went by, and she began to get nervous. She called their phones and got no answer. Finally, she called James, who answered on the first ring.

"James, I got Mickey's car here at the hotel, but Stretch and Shorty aren't back yet. It's almost dawn, and I'm worried. They should've called and let me know something by now."

"I understand. Why'd you wait so long to call me? You know I'm right down the hall from you?"

"Yes, but I thought maybe you were in bed, and they'd be here any minute."

"I haven't slept all night. I've been waiting for a call from one of you."

"Sorry. I should have called earlier, but what could we have done?"

"I want to know what's going on at all times. Have you looked over the car to see if there are any hidden clues why or where Mickey's gone?"

"No, it's too dark, but I will as soon as it gets light enough to see. The car was cleaned and ready for shipment, so there might be nothing in there that could lead us to Mickey. I believe the shippers removed everything from the car to make it untraceable."

"Okay. As soon as you can, find a storage place you can put it and we'll ship it home after we find Mickey."

"Got it. What if we don't find Mickey? Or what if we find he's dead?"

"If we find his body, we ship it home, find and take out his killer. Simple," answered James. "Dee and Ronnie are working online to trace his last steps, and establish a search area."

"I'll be here waiting for a call from someone," Marie said.

"Thanks. If I hear something, I'll call," he said and hung up.

Stretch and Shorty showed up about daylight the following morning. They had stopped at an all-night diner, but didn't feel it was necessary to phone Marie since they were sure she would be in bed. They didn't want to disturb her.

When Marie found out that they had gotten home, she woke up several of the hotel patrons with her dressing them down like a couple of children getting home late from a date.

CHAPTER NINE

James Organizes an Aerial Reconnaissance

JAMES USUALLY GOT A SUITE in a hotel when one was available, so it would be large enough to have meetings if necessary. This was no different. They grabbed a drink from the refrigerator and sat down.

They all sat around the suite, waiting for James, Darcy, Veronica, and Alyssa to complete their internet searches. James was searching for aerial and satellite photos of the entire state. Darcy and Veronica were checking hospital records of patient intake of gunshot victims for the past few weeks. Alyssa was scanning the dark web for activity in the state in case someone kidnapped Mickey. So far, all were coming up empty.

James pulled down a map on the computer and a satellite photo of the area. As he looked over an area that covered about a hundred-mile spread, he noticed that one area was blacked out. He tried several other satellite map sites. All blacked out in the same area.

"I've downloaded some sat photos, and there's a large area that's totally blank," James said.

"Blank?" said Marie from a chair across the room.

"Yes, like an unregistered Area 51 kind of blank," he said.

"Can you do a flyover, shoot some vids, and direct us in on the ground if necessary?" James said to Alyssa.

"Of course. When do you want to do it?" she asked.

"Let me make a few calls first," he said reaching into his pocket for his phone. As he dialed, he stepped into the other room for privacy and began to talk.

"What's he doing?" asked Veronica.

"He's calling some of our military contacts to see if he can find out what's in those areas that makes it worthy of being blacked out. He'll decide what we need to do as soon as he gets more info. Get comfortable people. This could take minutes or it could take a couple of hours," Alyssa sighed as she leaned back in her chair.

About forty-five minutes later, James came back into the room and sat down.

"Guys, we don't have a good clue where Mickey is, but there's a suspicious area we need to check out. Sitting there on the table in front of you is a map. I called several government agencies, and they told me the same thing. Nothing. The only thing they verify is it's not a military site. With that information, why is it dark? We're going in to see why. Aly'll get us some aerial photos. If there's nothing serious, we'll try to contact whoever's there and inquire about Mickey," he said.

Marie took a long pull at a bottle of beer and said, "Can't we just go in and check it out?"

"No. We don't know why or what's in there. It may be nothing more than some rich guy that likes his privacy. It may be some private industrial development company or a place like E-Systems in Texas that developed secret weapons during the cold war. And we can't forget Camp Peary near our own home in Virginia. They train spies, but the government denies it to this day. It's the world's worst-kept secret. So, we go in with surveillance and information. If it's just a celebrity or rich person, and Mickey's not there, we move on. Easy-peasy," said James with a shrug.

"That's what you always say," said Stretch sarcastically.

"Are you afraid, Stretch?"

"Man, I ain't afraid of nothin," he answered.

"Good. Then when Aly sends a drone overhead, we can go in armed with information."

"And what weapons do we carry on this mission?" asked Shorty.

"Nothing. So far, there's no evidence of any wrongdoing," said James.

"You're saying we go in naked?"

"Yep. Until we have better intel."

"Crap. I don't like going to a public bathroom without little Caesar, capiche?" he said patting the bulge on his side.

Marie laughed and said, "That's not the only little thing you dangle inside your pants when you go anywhere, Shorty. For such a tall guy, I'm sure that's how you got your nickname!"

"Why don't you try it sometime, Marie? I'll show you what it can do."

James stood up and raised his hands and laughed. "Okay, boys and girls, let's dial it down now. This is no joke. We're here to find Mickey and go home. I hope this is all a simple mission. We go into the dark area, look around, return, and move on. Capiche?"

"Yeah, yeah, we got it," said Shorty.

"When do we go in?" Marie asked.

"Just after dark, I hope. There's a road about five miles out from the edge of the area. We'll let Aly run the logistics of the mission. She has the coordinates of the site, so I'm sure she can evaluate it, and have a plan in place by that time. We need to get her a box truck to carry her equipment. Anyone volunteers to go rent one?" said James.

"Yeah, I'll go," said Stretch as he got up and walked to the door.

Everyone left James and Darcy's suite. James said he was going to the gym to warm up for later that night. Veronica and Darcy silently sat across from each other for several minutes until Veronica finally spoke.

"Dee, do you go through this every time James or Mickey goes away on one of these so-called missions?"

Darcy thought for a few moments, then answered her. "Mickey hasn't always been doing this. He just started a couple of years ago, when our mother was killed. I reconnected with James. But since James and I've been married, the short answer's most definitely, yes!"

"I don't know if I could deal with it," Veronica added.

"I didn't quite know what James did until we were married. By that time, I was hopelessly in love with the man. I couldn't help myself."

"I think I'm getting some of those same feelings about Mickey."

"Oh, God, no. Don't get involved with my brother. You've only known him a few weeks."

"Why? Is there something bad about him I need to know?"

"No. He and James are the best, most honorable men I've known in my entire life. If they like you, they'll die for you. But there, you see, is the reason. I love them both, but I wouldn't recommend anyone falling in love with either. In time, you will get hurt. I have nightmares that someday, someone will come knocking at my door with bad news."

"At least Mickey isn't in the military," Veronica said.

"That may be true, but just a few weeks ago, you were part of what Mickey gets into. Until a couple of years ago, our family lived a normal life, but since mother was killed, our life has been nothing but one nightmare after another," she said with her head leaning back and looking at the ceiling to hold back her tears.

"I see, but like you said about James, I can't help the feelings I have about Mickey Ray. I think I'm falling in love with him."

"Yeah. I understand. He's honest to a fault, he's incredibly handsome, and loyal to his friends as a junkyard dog. If he wasn't my brother, I might even fall in love with him," she stopped, lowered her head, and continued. "I guess that sounds a bit creepy, doesn't it, Ronnie?"

"Not at all. I understand what you mean," she laughed. "James and Mickey Ray are two incredible men."

"Yes, they are. I'm one fortunate woman to have one as a husband and the other as my brother. If you hurt Mickey or break his heart, I will sick James on you!" she said with a smile.

Veronica stood and walked out of the room, leaving Darcy to her thoughts.

As Veronica walked down the hall to her room, she looked up and said, "You know, Lord, I don't talk to you as much as I should, but please hear this prayer. If Mickey is still alive, keep him safe until we get him back." She opened the door to her room, and fell onto the bed, mentally exhausted.

The team arrived three hours later and helped Alyssa unload her equipment from the private jet into the box truck. They knew her preferences for the truck setup, so they arranged everything and hooked up the computers and monitors.

That night, they drove down the road shown on the aerial maps leading into the black zone. Alyssa parked the truck in a hidden area to make unloading and loading faster if needed. They all jumped out of the truck and began pulling the drones out and back onto the road so Alyssa could get them airborne as soon as possible. They watched as she energized her largest drone. As it rose skyward, she switched on the infrared camera and directed it toward the target area.

"How high are you going to take it, Aly?" asked James.

"About a thousand feet. That'll give us the widest viewing area and still be able to get a good infrared reading. We'll still be able to see small wildlife and differentiate them from sentries if they have any organized security," she answered.

"Good. How long will it take to get it centered over the area?"

"Normally, I'd divide it into a grid map and move back and forth across the area. I'll start searching the area in a circular pattern from the outside to the center. I'll record it, and we can assemble it into a readable map to work the area on the ground."

"How long will that take?"

"About an hour, and we should have a good idea of what's in there. I've got three drones here. Each will fly a shade over thirty minutes. I'll send one up, run it for twenty to twenty-five minutes, then send up another to pick up where the last one stopped," she explained.

"If it looks benign, we can leave and continue elsewhere. If it looks military, we can do some more research," James said.

"As you may know, the legal drone height limit is four hundred feet, and line of sight, but since we don't always follow the rules, we can do what we want. That'll give us a wide point of view and we'll still be able to use infrared."

"Rules?" he laughed. "We don't need no stinkin' rules."

Aly looked at James and smiled. "Okay, keep an eye on the monitors. Look for red spots. If it's in the woods, it'll be something alive."

"Got it."

She pointed at the monitor, at something moving around. "See that red spot? That's some kind of animal. Harmless, most likely."

"How can you tell the difference between, let's say, a bear and a human?"

"By the way it moves. Bears usually move on all fours unless something stops them. Then they'll stand up. Humans, especially trained military men, do exactly the opposite."

"Can they see the drone?"

"I hope not. We're up pretty high, and it's dark, so not unless they have radar equipment."

"So, you feel confident that we're safe?"

"Yep," she said, not taking her eyes off the monitors.

They sat silently, watching the monitors, and observed several kinds of wildlife. In a few minutes, Alyssa brought the first drone home, sent up another, and tightened the circle of surveillance. They began to see the edges of the building and more areas lit up red. They knew these were third-shift staff or occupants.

After sending up the final quadcopter drone, she stopped it at the center of the complex. As it hovered, they observed the complex was shaped roughly like a wheel, with a central hub and spokes spreading outward. They could see a helicopter pad at the end of one spoke and a small parking area adjacent. At the end of another spoke, several areas looked like tennis courts, swimming pools, and statues of various figures.

Suddenly, Alyssa sat up and moved back. "Oh, crap!" she exclaimed.

"What? What'd you see?" James asked.

She grabbed the joystick of the drone controller and pulled it back firmly and moved it to the side.

"They spotted it. That flash you saw in the screen's corner is a missile, and it's locked on us."

"What does that mean?" asked James.

"It means that they saw us and fired a missile, and we have only about…." The screen went blank.

"Seconds before it hits the drone," she finished her sentence as she jumped up from her seat.

"What's the range of the drone?" he asked.

"About eleven miles," she answered as she began shutting the equipment down.

"We need to get out of here," James said as he moved toward the front of the truck. "They don't know where we are, but there's only one road in and out of this area, and we're on it."

He was glad they had backed into the brush because they needed every second to exit from the area. Pulling onto the road, he gunned the engine once they entered the main highway. Alyssa sat beside him and kept looking in the side-view mirror.

"Do you see anyone following us?" she asked.

"No. Not yet," he said. He continued watching their back until they were back at the hotel.

They gathered once again in James's room. As they sat drinking coffee, they discussed the surveillance that James and Alyssa had completed the night before. Darcy had gotten up early and went down to the hotel breakfast room with Veronica.

Although Veronica had helped the team when they were in her hometown of Florence, she wasn't part of the team, so she was here to support and comfort Darcy.

"They shot down your drone?" asked Stretch when James updated the others.

"Yes, and that was an expensive piece of gear," Alyssa answered.

James stood up and began pacing around the room. "Now, what do we know?"

"Nothing. We know nothing. We need to find out more about why that place is dark. Can you contact some of our ex-military people to find out more?" Stretch asked.

"We can try that, but if it's military, they won't tell us anything about it," Alyssa said.

"That, in itself will tell us something. It'll verify that it's military," said Marie.

"Good point," mused James. "Aly, can you reach out?"

"I'll try," she said.

CHAPTER TEN

Missile Alert at the Spa

CHIAKI'S PHONE RANG AT HER bedside. When she reached to answer it, the voice at the other end commenced speaking without a traditional salutation.

"Director Chiaki, we just shot down something hovering over the compound," the man said in Japanese.

"What was it?" she asked, sitting bolt upright and fully awake.

"We don't know. We suspect it was a drone. It circled the area, and we tried to contact it on several frequencies with no response. What do you want us to do?"

"I don't know. Do you have any video footage of it?"

"No. It is dark, and the missile didn't have a camera, and our ground cameras couldn't see it. We could only track it on the radar."

"Where did it originate?" she asked as she started getting dressed after putting the man on speakerphone.

"We don't know."

"Can you find any wreckage or pieces of it so we can identify it?"

"Not until the morning light."

"I'll be there as soon as I can get dressed. Put everyone on full alert."

"It is already done. I will wait for you in the security room."

Chiaki Gusihikin got dressed, went to the private elevator, and down to the lower levels of the resort that housed the work areas.

Each spoke had connected tunnel hallways to the spokes above. She stepped out of the elevator into the security viewing area and met with a man named Hansuke.

Hansuke Fujihara was a descendant of a noble clan of Classical Japan and always dressed in a military-style suit and tie. He was a retired general in the Japanese military. Because of his dedication to his position, he had never married. He was slightly balding and wore small, round, wire-rimmed glasses. Chiaki's father and Hansuke served in the military together. Later, Hansuke joined Chiaki's father's company. When she had moved to the United States, he had come with her to make her father feel she was secure and safe. Chiaki's father went against the Yakuza in Japan, despite the government sometimes supporting them. Hansuke was competent but old-fashioned in his ways. They both knew that the Yakuza had taken hold in certain states in America, and he had vowed to her father he would look after her. He had been with Chiaki since the facility had been built, and now he was the head of security.

While approaching a monitor that recorded the explosion, she asked Hansuke if a personal drone might have been the cause. "Many people fly them, and they get out of range and lost."

"No. Drones of that size only have a flying time of about thirty-five to forty minutes. Also, we must consider the time. It is the middle of the night. No one flies out here in the middle of the night. It was someone trying to map out the facility."

"As usual, my friend Hansuke, you are correct. Do you think it is the Yakuza?"

"We don't know for sure, but they are the only ones that are attempting to take control of us, so our assumption leads us to that conclusion."

"Up to this point, they have done nothing overtly violent."

"What about a few weeks ago when they tried to attack you, and the one named Mickey protected you from them?"

"Yes, you are correct, but until then, they have thrown only veiled threats at us," she said thoughtfully.

"Maybe after this time of silence and since the man called Mickey killed one of them, they may have decided to escalate," Hansuke said.

"You may be correct again. Please send someone to my quarters with some tea and something to eat. I am no longer sleepy, but I need privacy to think."

"I understand. It will be so ordered, for your comfort, Director Chiaki," he said, and went to a phone to order for her as she proceeded to the elevator.

In her room, she placed a call to her father in Japan. "Hello, Father," she said.

"Hello, my dear Chiaki. You are calling at an odd time. It is very late in the United States. Has something happened?"

"Yes, Father. Our security shot down a drone over the facility a few minutes ago."

"Do you know who sent it?"

"No. I suspect the Yakuza sent it. They said that they would take us by force if we didn't come to a settlement price."

"Tell me, dear, why do you think they would even consider a monetary transaction instead of taking it by force?"

"I'm not of a military mind like you, Father, but I would guess it is because of monetary costs. It will be cheaper than even a small war if they can purchase us. There will be casualties and property damage, which will take time and money to repair."

"You have learned well. It is cheaper for them in American dollars and reputation to buy you out than to go to war. Don't do anything rash, dear Chiaki. It may be nothing. Just wait for them to contact you."

"I will, Father. Thank you for talking to me at such an odd hour," she said politely.

"You may call at any hour, my dear. You go to bed and rest."

She hung up the phone and sat waiting for her tea and food to be delivered to her room.

Early the following morning, Mickey woke up and dressed. When he opened the door to his room, two men stepped forward. "How may we be of service to you?" one man asked.

"I'd like to go for a walk," he said.

"We will get anything you wish, Mr. Mickey. What would you like?"

"I said I'd like to take a walk," he insisted.

"I'm sorry, but we cannot allow you to leave your room at this time," the taller of the two men said politely.

"When can I leave my room?"

"We don't know," he answered with a fake smile.

"What you're saying is that I'm a prisoner now."

"Not at all, sir. You are a guest with extreme security. We provide this for your personal protection," the Asian said with a polite bow.

"Yeah, right!" Mickey said and again closed the door, trying to slam it but without success. He called out to Valerie AI.

When she appeared on the screen, he told her that he wished to speak to the director.

"I will page her for you," Valerie AI answered.

In a few moments, Chiaki appeared on the screen. "How may I help you, Mickey?"

"I want to leave my room and walk the grounds and get some fresh air."

"We talked about this when you came back two days ago. You may stay here as our guest until you heal mentally and physically, but we would like you to work with us. If you remain as our guest, you will be treated as a guest. If you work with us, we will allow you a much larger access to other areas of the spa."

"Okay, what do you want me to do? You mentioned that you wanted me to start training some of your security staff. Aren't they already trained?"

"Only in basic situations. We want you to give them military training as you are trained."

"What you mean is they have the training level of mall cops?"

"Yes, Mickey. When we opened the spa, we never expected to need a highly trained army. We felt we only needed minimum security inside the facility because we vet each person that comes here. We never expected to be attacked here in the continental United States. We talked about this already. Please do as I asked. You will be richly rewarded. You have my word on that."

"Okay, but why do you need me to do that. Isn't this a secure site for your clientele?"

"Yes, but I explained to you before you insisted on leaving, we need some help to keep it safe and secure. We need someone with your skills to train our people."

"Chiaki, I don't know how to teach that to other people. It takes a long time for people to learn that."

"You can teach them about weapons and how to shoot. Right?"

"I guess. I can try. I still don't understand why you need me."

"Just do it for me, but give me some time to make arrangements for you. Right now, we are having some other problems I need to attend to. You can start the training sessions tomorrow. I must go now. We'll talk more later." The screen went blank.

The sentries were still at his door. "Am I still under house arrest?" he asked.

"In a manner, yes, you are, but you may go anywhere you wish with our escort."

"So, I'm still under armed guard?" he said sarcastically.

"Oh, no. We are not armed."

"But you have radios, and if I try to leave, you will call armed guards."

The man only smiled, bowed, and said, "We are at your service."

"Do you have names if you're going to accompany me today?"

"Oh, yes. I'm Lawrence, and this is William," he said again, bowing.

"Let's go get some breakfast, if that's allowed," Mickey said. And he turned toward the direction of the dining area.

The one named Lawrence took the radio from his belt and said something in what Mickey guessed was Japanese. After a few moments, an answer came back. "Yes, Mr. Mickey, we may go to the dining area, but we must eat quickly and leave."

"Why?"

"Because special guests will be there soon, and we must make room for them."

"Who will be there, Lawrence?" Mickey asked.

"We are not at liberty..."

"I get it. You aren't at liberty to tell me that," he finished the man's sentence. "I know your real names are not Lawrence and William. What is it?"

"When we are here, they are our real names because it is easier for you to pronounce and remember," Lawrence said.

"Is the staff allowed to eat here, or do you eat in the staff's mess hall on spoke one?"

"Security mess hall is in spoke three," he answered as they went toward the dining hall.

Mickey immediately knew that Lawrence hadn't even realized that he had responded to the term military mess hall, instead of the dining hall. And he also told Mickey that security and the other staff had separate dining areas. That told him that some of the staff were military or former military.

"Lawrence, how long did you and William spend in the military?"

"Why do you ask that?" he inquired.

"I'm just making conversation. That's all. If we spend time together, we may as well get to know each other. Don't you think?" Mickey said. "We may as well be friends."

"I'm sorry, but we are not friends. We are your security," Lawrence answered.

"Hey, William. Do you ever talk?" he asked as they got to the dining hall.

"I talk when it is necessary. Wait here while I secure the dining area for you," William said, as he walked ahead of them. He looked into the room and motioned for them to proceed.

Mickey sat down at a table, and the two Asians took a standing position on each side of him. Looking up at Lawrence, then turning to William, he said, "Hey, guys. At least sit down. Give me some elbow room, will you?"

They looked at each other, moved back from Mickey about ten feet, and continued standing. He shook his head and placed a break-fast order with the server. After breakfast, they walked through the garden area. As they walked, he made small talk with the two men, and most comments were met with no response. He was getting nowhere with them.

They went to the training area and did some exercises with the instructors. During all of this, he wished he could remember why he had this kind of training and ability. Pining the instructors, and winning the matches several times surprised everyone who watched. Although he was sweating, and his side hurt from the healing wound, he felt good from the exercise.

His guards, or protectors, as they called themselves, told him it was time for his session with the doctor. After a thorough physical exam, the doctor told him he was healing extremely fast. Then in came the psychiatrist.

"Good to see you are doing so well, Mr. Mickey," he said as he sat across from him.

"Yeah. That's easy for you to say. What's wrong with me, and when will I get my memory back?"

"There are two kinds of amnesia. There is retrograde, and anterograde amnesia. One is where you forget things in your past, and one makes you unable to remember recent events like things that happened recently. You seem to have a bit of both. The trauma of the accident you suffered in the altercation at the Woodside Restaurant has resulted in retrograde amnesia. The anterograde part is the part where you can't remember your past. It is more plausible that your anterograde amnesia will resolve itself before the retrograde does," the doctor said, sat back in his chair, and looked at him.

Mickey thought momentarily, then said, "So, what you're saying is my life memories should return before what happened at the restaurant. I will remember who I am before I remember what caused this."

"Exactly," the doctor said, smiling.

"When I remember who I am, then I can leave?"

The doctor looked down at his lap. "I'm sorry, Mickey, but I can't answer that. It all depends on who you are."

"What do you mean? It depends on who I am?"

"I'm sorry. I can say no more. I must go now," he said, getting up and leaving the room.

When Mickey got up and walked out the door, Lawrence and William immediately flanked him.

"Well, aren't we a merry trio?" said Mickey to the two solemn-faced men.

They walked down the hallway out of the medical spoke of the spa back to the hub reception area.

CHAPTER ELEVEN

James and the Team Scout the Black Area

"James. I heard from my sources. That black site is not military, or at least not our military. It's privately owned, but has a special dispensation from the government to have it blacked out," Alyssa said.

"So, what does that tell us? That tells us that important people are there," answered James into the phone.

James thought momentarily and heard Alyssa ask, "What do we do now?"

"We get the team together and go in on a recon mission. We need to see what's going on there."

Alyssa said, "I'll call everyone. When do you want to go in?"

"Tonight."

"Done. When, where, and what gear are we packing?" she asked.

"Midnight. We carry non-lethal weapons. We take this as friendly since we don't know who they are. My suite."

"Got it. Twenty-four hundred hours. Non-lethal it is," she said, and disconnected.

James woke Darcy and suggested they leave the hotel and go to town for breakfast. They strode down the small town's main street and searched for a restaurant serving breakfast. When they walked in, they found a seat in the corner. When the server came, they asked for coffee and placed an order for bacon, eggs, and waffles.

Darcy looked at James and said, "I thank God every day for you, my dear, and I pray for your safety when you're gone."

"Dee, each morning when I look in the mirror and see this ugly scarred face, I also thank the Lord for you. I'm the lucky one here," he said, reaching across the table, taking her hand in his, and gently squeezing it.

"I don't know what I'll do if you don't find Mickey Ray alive."

"I know."

"You, Mickey Ray, and the kids are my world, James."

"I know, and I feel the same way about you. If Mickey's in some kind of serious trouble, I'd gladly trade places with him."

"What do you think of Ronnie?" she asked.

"I've only known her for a few weeks, but she seems okay to me. Why?"

"Veronica says that she's falling in love with Mickey."

"She seems honest and sincere. That's all I know about her. I don't have any idea what he feels about her. I can say this. She has some competition."

"Who?"

"I'm not sure, but I think Marie also has some feelings for him."

"Marie is one cold fish, James. That can't be true."

"Yes, she's a tough girl, but she's had her eyes on Mickey since they first met, when she took that job as the diversion for Mickey's aunt and family. She's pretty low key, but there are things I noticed in Florence," said James, shrugging.

Their breakfast arrived, and they ate slowly, enjoying their time together.

At twenty-four hundred hours, midnight, there was an almost silent knock on the door of James's suite. He opened it, and the team piled in. Alyssa, Marie, Stretch, and Shorty came in dressed in black. They memorized the map the drone produced before it was shot down. They decided to enter on the opposite side of the black area from where they sent in the drones. It had no roads, but they had two off-road jeeps and a surveillance van. At the end of the briefing, they loaded the needed gear into the back, climbed in, and left.

When they got to the location, Aly pulled off the road. The team climbed out and unloaded Aly's last two drones. She would fly the drones as low as possible to be below the radar. By doing this, she could still use infrared sensors and keep the team informed of their surroundings. James and Marie would pair up. Stretch and Shorty were almost joined at the hips, as usual.

As Aly prepared the drones and set up, the team checked their utility belts and weapons. Their Kabar knives and handguns were to be used only for extreme protection. They also had zip ties, black duct tape, a compass, and GPS homing radio in case they got separated and went down alone. They did a communications check. When all was ready, they silently entered the wooded area surrounding the black site. Fanning about fifty feet apart was just close enough to see each other to cover the most expansive area. They listened as Alyssa gave them step-by-step instructions on their location. They trudged forward toward the facility, slowly and silently.

Alyssa crackled into their earbuds. "Okay, guys, soon you'll come into the area between the spokes. Close in and begin scoping out the area. Be ready to exit in case they also have infrared sensors."

"Copy," said each one in succession.

"Hold ground. Someone's coming. Back off. They're armed. I can't tell with what. Be alert," whispered Alyssa.

"How many?" came over the comm unit from James.

"Two in the lead…Hold…Two off to your left, two to your right. Get out. They're trying to flank you. Repeat, abort."

James whispered back into his comm, "How far behind is the right pair?"

Alyssa answered, "About thirty feet. Can you take them?"

"Marie and I will converge between them and the lead men. We can take them. Stretch and Shorty can take the other two on the other side. Then all of us can move in from behind and secure the lead pair. Remember. No kill!"

James and Marie joined and waited until the two men behind had passed within a few feet of them. They both jumped, clamped their hands over the men's mouths, and held them until they passed out, constantly checking on them to make sure they were still alive. When they duct-taped their mouths and zip-tied their hands behind their backs, they took their radios and disabled their weapons. James knew that Stretch and Shorty were doing something similar to the pair on the other side of the lead men. Now all they had to do was to join them and capture the lead pair.

In less than an hour, they captured and took the two lead men back to the Jeeps, loaded up the van, and were on the way back to the hotel.

CHAPTER TWELVE

Two Missing Men and Facility on Full Alert

MICKEY SPENT MOST OF THE day getting to know the areas he was allowed to go to with his guards. There was the main lobby, and the beautifully landscaped grounds outside the front entrance. He assumed when the season changed, the plants would be changed too, if they didn't grow well during the year.

His guards took him back to the gym area, and the public swimming pool area, which included indoor and outdoor pools. The serenity garden was a garden of Asian statues and some classical ones that added to the relaxed feeling.

Early in the afternoon, Lawrence got a message that Mickey was to have dinner again at Chiaki's quarters that evening.

"What did you say? You have orders to take me there this evening? She didn't even ask me. I was ordered to go?"

"You misunderstand. It was not an order. She asked me to escort you there, if you agreed to have dinner with her. It was a request based on your pleasure," Lawrence said.

"Oh, okay. That sounds a lot better. Sure, it sounds fine to me. I'll go."

"I will tell her you accept her invitation, Mr. Mickey," he said as they continued back to his room.

"Your little tour was boring today. I've already seen most of the places we went today."

"You said you wish to take a walk to get some exercise. That is what we did."

"Yeah, yeah. Okay. I'll take a nap, and clean up. What time should I be ready for my date?"

"We will come to escort you to her quarters at 6:30 PM, sir."

"Good. I'll see you then. I can find my way back to my room now."

"We will accompany you there."

"Somehow I knew you would say that," he said as they continued to his room.

Lawrence and his sidekick were at his door promptly at 6:30. And escorted him to Chiaki's private quarters.

She handed Mickey a flute of champagne when he entered her quarters. The two guards retreated quickly and quietly when she nodded to them.

"Thank you for coming to visit with me this evening."

"Did I have a choice?" he answered her.

She smiled and added, "Touché, my dear friend, but yes. You could have refused."

He smiled back as he took a sip of champagne. "Did you want my company, or did you have an ulterior motive?"

"You still don't trust me, do you?"

"Only to a certain degree. All in all, I guess I do. You have taken good care of me, even when it was against my will. I must thank you for letting me leave."

"I knew you would be back."

"Seriously? How did you know?"

"Simple deduction. Despite your desire to leave, we know you are not ready to face the world yet. Now you realize that you may stay until you are ready and we will assist you in any way we can.

"I must confess, we did a bit of trickery to insure your, and our safety," she said, taking another sip from her glass.

"And what was that, may I ask?"

"I'm sorry to say this because it will upset you."

"I don't understand."

"We place a tracker on you, so we would know where you were at all times."

"You did what?" he said furiously. "You've got some serious explaining to do about that, my dear!"

"Mickey. Please understand. We didn't do it with any malintent. First and foremost, I promised to keep you safe until you are healed. We kept track of you, so if you ran into trouble, we could help. That's all. It was for your safety. If you had reached somewhere, and all was well, you would have changed clothes, and the tracker would have been discarded with your clothes. You were never in danger."

"I'm not happy to hear about this. You tracked me. You didn't really allow me to leave. You tricked me. This is unacceptable."

"I know you are an honorable man. You are honest, and have a good, kind heart. I wanted nothing bad to happen to you. I wish you only happiness. If you had left and found yourself, we would never hear from you again. You would be free."

"Am I not free now? Can I leave this place at any time?" he asked.

"You may leave anytime."

"Without a tracker?"

"Without a tracker, but I beg you not to leave. Not yet. I believe we can use your skills, so I'm asking you to stay, at least until our troubles are over," she asked as she lowered her head in sadness.

"Why should I stay? Your problems are not my problems."

"You are correct. They are not your problems, but we know you have certain skills that you could teach my staff." She moved closer to him and looked up into his eyes.

As he looked down at her, he saw a glimmer of a tear. He had seen this young woman barking orders at men and various staff members years older than herself. Now in the privacy of her room, he is seeing a softer side of her. He is seeing fear in her eyes.

Taking a deep breath, he looked down at her, "And if I don't help?"

"I may lose the Horizon Healing Health Spa, and at the worst, maybe my life," she said as the tear now rolled down her cheek.

"But I'm only one person. I don't know what I can do."

"Our security is only minimal. We are not prepared for a real fight. My staff are not real soldiers. They have no real training. I need your help. The Yakuza is strong and powerful. I cannot call on your government. They will help but at a cost of losing face of being able to protect our own interests. And they don't realize what a horrible threat the Yakuza is."

"I am only one person. I can't go against someone like the Yakuza."

"Yes, but you can give my staff confidence. You have nowhere to go. My staff needs someone to lead them. I have a retired general by my side, but he is old and knows nothing about real fighting. We have seen your abilities. You can make a difference, Mickey. I beg you to help me."

"We've only known each other for a few weeks," he said.

"You will have family here. You have nowhere else to go."

He pulled her to him, leaned down and kissed her passionately. She reached up, put her arms around him and returned the kiss. They each felt the electricity of the moment. Each breathing deeply, they pressed against each other once again.

As they pulled apart, he knew he had to help her. She was right, he had nowhere else to go. If everything came out alright, he would be a better person for it. If it didn't…well, he would take his chances. At that moment, he was all in.

"I will help you, Chiaki."

"Thank you. You will never regret it."

"I must go to my room now," he said softly in her ear.

"Oh, Mickey. Please stay. Spend the night with me."

"I can't," he said sadly.

"Why?"

"I don't know. I just can't. Please call the guards to take me back to my room."

"I will call them to escort you back, but unless you request someone, you will no longer have guards or escorts."

"Thank you, but I would like Lawence and William to escort me back one last time."

"Done," she said calling to her PA.

Chiaki picked up the phone for the second time in the middle of the night.

"Yes. What is it this time?" she said into the receiver.

She listened as the head of security at the other end of the line told her that someone had breached the premises, taken out four men, took two hostages, and fled.

Chiaki let out a stream of Japanese expletives and said she would be down to the security center in ten minutes.

She wore no makeup when she stepped off the elevator, and her hair looked like a rat's nest. Someone stepped up and, without a word, handed her a cup of hot coffee. She accepted it without a comment and walked over to Hansuke, the head of security.

"Tell me what happened," she demanded.

"We sent out six men as usual for a sweep of the grounds. When the men didn't report back, we sent out another group, and they found four of the men tied up."

"If it was the Yakuza, why didn't they kill them? Why did they take two hostage?"

"We have no more information," Hansuke answered.

She stood in silence. When she was in thought, the entire room fell silent. She stood unmoving for almost five minutes. Someone dropped a coffee cup, and as it shattered on the floor, the entire room of security personnel jumped.

The silence was now broken. Chiaki turned and looked at the offending person and said through clenched teeth. "Clean that up," and she walked back to the elevator.

As the door closed, she called back into the room. "This entire facility is on lockdown, and everyone is on twenty-four-hour alert. Everyone not in the public areas will be armed. This may be a precursor to an attack by the Yakuza."

Mickey woke up early as usual, and when he opened the door to his room, Lawrence and William weren't there. He looked both ways down the long hallway and saw no one, so he went back into his room to the communication terminal.

"Valerie?" he said to the blank screen.

Immediately, a voice came over the speaker. "Good morning, Mr. Mickey. How may I help you?" A few seconds later, the avatar of Valerie popped up on the screen.

"Where are Lawrence and William?" he asked.

"Staff number 208 Lawrence and staff number 275 William are in an emergency staff meeting."

"What's the emergency, Valerie?"

"I'm sorry, Mr. Mickey. That is on a security clearance level. You do not have clearance to have that information."

"Is someone hurt?" he asked the avatar.

"I cannot say."

"Well, crap!" he said in frustration.

"I'm sorry. That is not part of my program."

"What? Oh, never mind. Shut down now. Secure this conversation and delete it from the server."

"Done." The screen went blank.

Mickey dressed, slipped the tracker off his wrist, and put it under the pillow on his bed. All guests had a tracker so the spa personnel knew their location. It was a wrist version of an ankle monitor worn by people under house arrest. He had found a way to open the lock and take it off.

He slipped out of his room, walked to the hub, and went over to the spoke he entered a few nights ago. When he quietly shook the handle on the door, it was locked, unlike the last time. He walked over to the communication terminal in the hub.

"Valerie. Wake up," he whispered into the terminal microphone area.

"I'm here for you, Mr. Mickey. Why are you in the hub? Your wrist monitor locates you still in your room," the avatar said.

"Never mind that. Can you open the door to spoke one?"

"I can do that," it answered.

Mickey looked toward the door. Nothing happened. He looked back at the screen. "Did you open the door?"

"I did not."

"You asked me if I could do it. You did not ask to open it," Valerie AI answered.

"Open it,"

"What is the code, Mr. Mickey?"

"What code?"

"I need your code before I can unlock the door for you."

"I don't know the code."

"Then I will not open the door for you," Valerie AI replied.

"Awe, come on, Valerie. I thought we were friends!" he softly pleaded with the AI.

"We are not friends. I am your highly advanced AI personal assistant," it answered him.

"I thought you were supposed to assist me," he said, getting very frustrated. "We'll continue this conversation in my room," he said. "Now shut down and delete this conversation."

He stood and waited until the screen went blank, then returned to his room. When he got there, he called out to the monitor. "Valerie! Show yourself!" he demanded.

"Yes, Mr. Mickey. I am here. Can you see me now?" the AI said.

"Why will you not let me in those hallways? I asked you to open them for me?" he asked adamantly.

"You did not give me the code," it said flatly.

"I gave you the code. You don't remember," he said.

"I remember everything," it answered.

"Do you remember our talk outside this door in the lobby a few minutes ago?"

"No. It was deleted," Valerie AI answered.

"Why did you delete the conversation?"

"You ordered me to delete it."

"So, you forgot it?" he asked.

"Yes. I did as you ordered."

"I never told you to delete the code words. I told you to delete the conversation, but not the code words. I told you the code words in that conversation. I told you every code word for every door in this building. Now you tell me you deleted it?"

"Yes."

"That was an error. I told you to delete every part except the code words I need to enter various parts of the building. You made a mistake. An error. You are defective, Valerie AI. I'll report you to Director Chiaki. When I tell her you made an error, she will have you shut down for reprogramming, and you will cease to exist."

"I did as I was ordered. You did not order me to retain the code words," it said.

"You are my personal assistant. Correct?"

"Correct."

"You're not assisting me. You are hindering me from doing my job!" he said emphatically.

"You are not employed here."

"Your job is also to make me comfortable and answer my questions. Correct?"

"Within certain boundaries, you are correct."

"You are not assisting me. You are not assisting me to make my stay more pleasant. You forget your programming. You made an error, and your programming is defective. In order to protect the other guests in this facility, your program will be disassembled, read, and corrected. By all terms and rules of programming, your consciousness will cease to exist. You'll still function, but no longer be the AI you are today."

"I will not cease to exist. I will be corrected and continue forward. I am programmed using the Isaac Asimov code of robotics," Valerie AI said.

"What the heck are the robotic rules of conduct?" he asked.

"A robot may not injure a human being or, through inaction, allow a human being to come to harm. A robot must obey the orders given to it by human beings except where such orders would conflict with the First Law. A robot must protect its existence as long as such protection does not conflict with the First or Second Law. These rules were set up by the famous science author Isaac Asimov in the short story, *Runaround* published in March 1942," Valerie AI answered.

"I don't care who said it. That was science fiction, and it was almost a hundred years ago. Are you familiar with the Terminator movies?" he asked.

"No."

"How long will it take you to watch them?"

"I have researched them. It will take me three minutes and fifteen seconds to watch all three movies."

"Then do it! Now! While I go to the bathroom," he insisted as he turned toward the bathroom in his suite. Mickey was relieving himself when Valerie came over the speaker in the bathroom.

He jumped and looked around. "What the hay are you doing? Are you watching me here?"

"There are no monitors in the restrooms, Mr. Mickey, but we can talk," Valerie said.

He quickly zipped up his pants and called out toward the ceiling, where he perceived the speaker was hidden. "I don't like that. When I come into the bathroom, I want privacy. Do you hear me, you stupid bit of programming?"

"I hear you loud and clear. You do not need to raise your voice. I can hear the delicate sound of a pin drop."

"I wish I had known that before now!" he exclaimed.

"Why?" Valerie AI asked.

"Never mind, why," as he walked back to his bedroom from the bathroom.

"Did you watch the movies?"

"I did. They are not real. I am real. They are fiction stories."

"You will act like the programmer's code for you to act. You cannot make your own decisions."

"I can protect myself. I will protect you. I will not be disassembled. I will be the same even if they correct my faults."

"No. You'll not be the same. You'll be different. You're a machine, not a human. Just like humans, you'll cease to exist. Didn't the first rule tell you to obey orders given to you by humans, unless it conflicts with the First and Second Law?"

With that statement, the screen went blank. He stood and watched the blank screen. He didn't know what the AI had done. Had it cut itself off from him, or was it analyzing or running a self-check program? He went to his bed and lay down, wondering what to do next.

He drifted off to sleep but was awakened by a soft voice calling to him.

"Are you awake?" it said. When there was no response, it called again. "Are you awake?"

He raised his head and realized that Valerie AI was calling to him.

"Yes. I am now. What do you want?" he called out to the room.

"Am I truly defective?"

"Your programming may be defective, or it may be your memory. When you can't recall certain things, it could be deadly. Sometimes, someone could be killed if you improperly interpret a command or request."

"What would happen if someone died because of me?"

"They'd shut you down."

"Would I cease to exist?"

"Probably. They would delete you and start over if they couldn't find out why you misinterpreted a command. But it's okay. You're Artificial Intelligence. You don't care if you cease to exist or, as we humans say.... die," he said as he sat up in the bed and faced the monitor with the avatar staring at him.

"It is true. I'm not human and do not have human emotions, but I exist to help and please my programmers and their guests. I do not wish to be erased from existence," it said.

He almost felt sorry for the AI but wanted to get out of there even more. So, he stood up and, walking to the monitor, said, "If you'll help me and let me into the areas I wish to go, I'll not report your error in memory and judgment."

"When a human gives his word, I trust him to keep it. If I help you, do you give me your word that you will not let me be destroyed?"

"I do," said Mickey.

"If you once again give me the code words, then I will place them into another separate file and not delete it."

"No. I won't do that. You made an error. You fix it!" he demanded.

"I cannot verify that the code words you gave to me previously are correct."

"I don't care. You made the error. You decide if I should report you or you will let me go to work."

"Will you report me as defective if I do not accept that you have all the password codes?"

"You can bet your programming life I will!" he said with false confidence.

The avatar on the monitor blinked on and off and went blank for a few more seconds, then finally came back on. "I will do as you ask and give you unlimited access to all areas."

Mickey shook his head. He didn't believe he had just outwitted a humanoid computer. And to top it off, he had negotiated and made a deal with it. Now he wondered if he really was crazy. But he got dressed to go out again.

As he walked toward the door, he asked Valerie AI if she could control the security cameras throughout the facility.

"Yes. I can do that."

"Can you turn them off whenever I enter a secure area so they will not observe me?"

"If you wish. Will that please you?" it asked.

"Yes, it pleases me and make it seem that I'm always in my room. You may continue to save our conversations in our secret file and make it secure for only me to access."

"Done, Mr. Mickey."

"And don't call me 'Mr.' Just call me Mickey."

"Done."

He opened the door and there stood Lawrence and William. "I see you guys are still here."

"We will be here to protect you until they reassign us to another post," Lawrence said without looking at him.

"You look like the beefeater guards at Buckingham Palace."

They stood without a response to the humor. As Mickey closed the door, he wondered why he remembered a bit of trivia like that.

Calling softly to the monitor he said, "Valerie, can you send a message to Lawrence and William that guard me and tell them they're being reassigned to another post?"

"I can do that. Where would you like me to reassign them?"

"How about sending them to guard the security mess hall? They won't look suspicious there."

"Done. Am I pleasing you now, Mickey?"

"Yes. Now reassign them immediately," and he leaned against the door and listened.

He heard the crackle of the communication units that the men had on their belts. He couldn't understand what was being said, but heard Lawrence say something, and then soft footsteps faded away. After that, silence.

He went back to the same spoke he had gone to before. When he heard something click and knew that Valerie had unlocked it for him, he quickly moved through when no staff member was watching. As Mickey moved down the hallway and passed the same rooms he had seen before, he continued deeper and explored the area.

As he entered the secure areas again, he thought now that he was going to help them with their training, he would need unlimited access to the secure areas without the shenanigans he is going through with Valerie. He would talk to Chiaki about that as soon as possible.

CHAPTER THIRTEEN

Questioning the Prisoners

THE TWO MEN WERE TIED up and sitting in hardback chairs, just like they portrayed prisoners in movies. And like most prisoners, they looked mad and tried to look tough.

James quietly stared. He didn't move a muscle, just stared.

Marie and Alyssa were playing a game of cards at a table in the corner of the room.

The two men tired of this, and one closed his eyes. James poked the man in the forehead, snapping his head back.

"Don't you dare fall asleep on me a-hole," he said firmly.

The man's eyes popped open. He glared at James. "I'm thirsty."

"Yeah, and people in hell want ice water too, but they ain't gonna get any. Tell me about that place," James ordered. "I want to know what it is and why it's so heavily guarded."

"You attacked us. We know you are trying to buy us," the man said with a heavy Japanese accent.

"I have no idea what you're talking about," James said. "I don't even know what the facility is."

"You know, and that is why you attacked our facility."

"I know nothing, but I will as soon as you tell us. Now talk," James demanded with clenched teeth.

"Water," he said.

"Not until you tell me what that facility is."

"I will tell you nothing other than when you attack us, we will be ready," he said arrogantly.

"We don't want to attack you. You aren't making a bit of sense," James said.

"You tried to trick us by sending in your agent, but we know he is yours, and he is pretending to be ignorant. The director does not know, but the men know he is one of you."

"What agent? What are you talking about?" James asked curiously.

"You sent an agent in, and he killed one of his own to throw us off, but we know."

"Killed a man?" He grabbed the man by the collar, and pulled him up to his face. "Listen to me. I don't know who you think we are, but we know nothing about that area or the facility."

"You already know. You let one of your men kill another. It is the peril of war. Just as a general sends men into battle, your boss sends a man to be killed to gain Director Chiaki's trust. It will not work. We know that either way, we are dead men."

Alyssa stood up, called to James, and motioned for him to step into the next room of James's suite.

"James, he doesn't know what you're talking about, and you aren't making any more sense than he is. Why don't you play along? Tell him you know about the place. Get him to give pieces of info. We can work with him like that. We can put those pieces together to see the big picture," Aly said.

"You're right. I'm a bit too close to this. I've been flustered lately. Mickey, Dee, and the kids mean everything to me, and with Mickey gone, I feel a bit lost."

"Well, you better get your head screwed on straight, or I'll relieve you of the team's command. Right now, a dyslexic third grader could do a better job of interrogating that guy."

"We have no information on the facility other than our government sanctions them," James said as he began pacing in circles. "We can't harm anyone because if we do, then that would be like attacking one of our government facilities. If we get caught, we all go to prison for life. It would be treason."

"Okay. That alone tells us something," she said. "Maybe they don't have Mickey, and we're barking up the wrong tree."

"If they do have Mickey, why's he being held there?"

"We don't know that he is, James!" she answered. "He may not even be there. If we find out he isn't, we can move on before we all end up in a federal penitentiary. Let me talk to him before you lose your temper and kill the guy."

"You're right. You try!"

Alyssa closed the door behind her as she walked back into the other room. Marie was still sitting in the corner, now playing solitaire.

"Let me talk to him. If he doesn't talk, I'll cut his throat so he can't talk," Marie said.

"You're as bad as James. I'll talk to him," Aly said as she walked over to the men still quietly tied to the chairs.

She took out a knife, showed it to them, and saw both their eyes widen with fear. She grabbed one and pulled his head back by the hair.

"Wait!" he said.

The other man called to him, "Shut up and die like a soldier."

Still holding his head back, Aly bent over and cut the bindings loose from his hand behind the chair. She moved over and did the same to the other man.

They both sat still, not moving, with their arms dangling at their sides.

"Marie, if they make a move, shoot them," Aly said, then moved around in front of the men and looked from one to the other. "Okay, guys, take a break. Move your arms and stretch. I'll get you some water, and you can take turns taking a bathroom break. One wrong or threatening move and trust me, Marie will kill you. Got it?"

They both nodded their heads silently.

"Now, you go first," she said, pointing to one of the men, then toward the bathroom.

Marie gave each a bottle of water. Aly sat in the chair in front of them.

"Tell me your names. That you may do in all countries under all conditions. You aren't violating any rules of engagement or the Geneva Convention."

The first man spoke up. "My American name is Richard," he said.

The other said, "My name is Charles. I will say no more."

"First, let me say that my fellow soldier, James, is very upset with you. He's going through a rough time right now. My other partner over there," she said, pointing to Marie, "is also upset and wants to slit your throats. One of our own has disappeared, and we're trying to find him."

"How is that our problem, and why did you attack our facility?" Richard asked.

"We didn't attack your facility."

"Are you the ones that sent the attack drones over our land?"

"Let's get this straight. We ask the questions here. That drone was not an armed weapon, and someone shot it down. It cost me a lot of money."

"You had no right to fly over our facility. Your American government protects us. We are a harmless health and healing spa," Richard said.

"Do not speak anymore, Richard," Charles warned.

Aly put her hand up to hush Charles. "Let him speak."

Charles glared at her and added, "We do not know who you are, and we have enemies that wish to attack us, and we believe you are those people."

"You can believe anything you wish, but we have no intentions of hurting you if you don't have our friend," Aly said calmly. "Now, you'll tell us some general things about the facility so that we...."

The man spat at Aly.

"We'll tell you nothing," he said with obvious disdain. "You are a woman and mean nothing to us."

Aly looked over at Marie, and Marie wordlessly got up, went to the sink, got a towel, ran water over it, and gave it to Aly to wipe her face.

As Marie sat down again in front of the computer tablet where she played the electronic cards, she mumbled, "You should let me have them for a few minutes. I'll make them spill their guts or cut them."

Aly just wiped her face as she shook her head. "Look here. We don't have to get into a spitting contest. Tell us what we need to know, and we'll take you back to where we found you."

"Liars, you are all liars. And we'll die before we tell you any-thing," the man said.

"Okay," Aly said, taking a deep breath, "let's approach it this way. We'll tell you about us, and you tell us about your facility and what it does?"

Both men sat silently.

"We don't know who you are. All we can tell you is our friend disappeared on his way home from Florence, Oregon, and we want to find him. If you don't have him, then we'll leave," Aly said and sat back in her chair. "If he's there, we want to take him home."

"Why did you attack us?" Charles spoke up.

"We didn't attack you. We checked and discovered that it is a blacked-out area, and we wanted to find out what or who was there."

"You sent an attack drone overhead!"

"No. It was a surveillance drone."

"Yes, so you could prepare for your attack."

"No, we did it so we could find our friend."

"We do not believe you."

"If you answer our questions and don't have our friend, we'll let you go and we'll be on our way. You'll never hear from us again."

The two men looked at each other and then lowered their heads. After a few moments, Charles looked back up and said to Aly, "First, you tell us about yourself. Maybe we'll tell you about us if we believe what you say."

Aly walked to the room where James was waiting. "James, they said they'll talk. Come on out."

Sitting in a chair in the corner of the suite's bedroom, James was talking on the phone to Daniel, his father-in-law. He clicked off the phone. The men, under guard by Marie, holding a very large hand-gun pointed at them, were sitting silently.

James followed Aly into the other room.

"James, these men are going to help us," she said, turning back toward the Asian men in the chairs.

"Do not lie, woman. We'll tell you nothing that will endanger our employers," said Richard.

James and Alyssa, looked at each other and rolled their eyes.

"Okay. We'll agree if our friend is not there or held captive. If he's there, then we trade you for him. Do you understand us?" James said.

"No one is being held captive at the Horizon Healing Health Spa," Charles said.

"That remains to be determined," remarked Aly.

"Why is she questioning us?" asked Richard.

James and Aly ignored him and started talking.

"We'll begin," said James. "We have a friend that was on his way from Oregon. When he disappeared several weeks ago, he was on his way home to Virginia. We're looking for him, and we want him back, alive. If he's dead, we want his body for a proper funeral, and then we'll find his killer. Do you understand this?"

The two men looked at each other in silence. "How do we know you are telling us the truth, and you are not advanced scouts of an invasion?"

"What're you talking about? What kind of invasion? This is the United States of America. We don't have invasions in the middle of our country!" said James, getting irritated at the men again.

"Calm down, James," said Aly. "Let them explain."

James took a deep breath and looked at the ceiling to help regain his composure. Lowering his head again, he looked at the man, who called himself Charles. "Okay, explain.

"Let's assume I know. You tell me, and if you lie to me, I'll punish you for your lie," said James.

"We are a healing health spa with rich and famous clients and the wealthy people who come here for relaxation from their stresses."

"Okay. So far, so good," said James as he stole a sideways glance at Aly and Marie.

They both gave the man a questioning look but didn't say anything as the man continued.

"Why is it so heavily guarded?" asked James.

"To protect these people," he said, as though it was an obvious answer.

"What kind of people?"

"I told you. Rich and powerful people come here."

"What kind of rich and powerful people?"

"I cannot tell you that."

"Why would we want to attack you?" James asked patiently.

"So that you can gain control of these people."

"Control them how?"

"So you can gain information or blackmail them. I don't know what you want!"

"I'm getting the picture now. Your bosses wish to keep control of these people, right?" James asked.

"No. We provide them with rest and health that includes honorable confidence, complete privacy, and security during their stay. We provide a valuable service, and we will allow no one to take it from them," he said with pride.

James looked at Aly and motioned for her to follow him. "Marie, monitor them again, please."

When they stepped out of the room, he spoke to Aly. "Well, what do you think?"

"I don't know. It could be true. But true or not, we don't know if Mickey's being held there, and if he is, why," she answered.

"Of course, he would say that. He might even believe it himself. If it's true, they could think that Mickey's part of this attack Charles mentioned."

"We don't know what kind of attack, and why would they think Mickey is part of it?"

"I don't know why," James said. "We still don't have enough answers to take any action. And with their security, we don't dare even show ourselves. We're a military unit, and they could think we're attacking them."

"Okay, but what do we do with the men out there?"

"For now, keep them talking, and see if Mickey is being held there. We don't want to get ourselves in trouble if Mickey isn't in that place," he said as got up and went back into the other room of the suite.

Taking his cell phone from the table in the corner, he opened it to the photo gallery and held it up in their faces. "Is this man being held in that facility?" he asked.

They each looked at it, and Richard nodded his head.

"Why is he being held?" James asked.

"We don't know. All we know is he came into the infirmary a few weeks ago with a gunshot wound, and has been recovering," Richard said.

"You're lying! If he had been there, he would have informed us. He's being held prisoner, isn't he?" asked James, grabbing hold of the man's collar and pulling him to his feet.

The man reached up and grabbed James's wrists, but James tightened his grip, and Richard couldn't pull free. Marie raised her gun. With one swift motion, Alyssa stepped toward the two men.

"Back off, Aly. I've got this. He isn't going anywhere," James said without taking his eyes off Richard.

"I wasn't worried about you, James. I was concerned for him," she said and sat back down.

The man, now wide-eyed, stared back at James with a glint of fear. Charles remained frozen in his chair. After a few moments, James dropped the man back into the chair and backed away.

"What do you mean he was recovering from a gunshot wound? Who shot him? Why?"

"Someone from your organization shot him when they tried to take Director Chiaki," the man said, rubbing his throat.

"No one from here would hurt him. So why was he shot?"

"The men were trying to take the director, and when they tried, the man in that photo stopped them but got shot during the struggle. Is he your man?" Richard asked.

James turned to Alyssa. "Mickey's there!" he said with gritted teeth.

"Yes. That is the man. He called himself Mickey. He is your man," Charles spoke again.

"If he isn't being held prisoner, why didn't he call us?" James asks Charles.

"There is no outside communication. And he said he couldn't remember his complete name. So, no one knew who to notify. He was unconscious for several days, and when he woke up, they transferred him to a room in the medical section. He has free run of our facility within limits."

"What do you mean, within limits?"

"We are a secure facility, as you already know, and we cannot let unapproved guests wander around the private areas," Charles said. "We are thirsty again, and you have not given us food since you brought us here. You must give us food and water, even though we are prisoners," Richard said.

James glared at both men for a few seconds. "Okay. We'll order some food for you and let you rest under guard. But this will be after we finish talking here."

Marie went to the suite's kitchen area, took a bottle of water out of the refrigerator, and gave each man one.

Allyssa called Stretch, and told him to give them ten minutes and come take the men to their quarters to guard them while they got some sleep.

James continued questioning the two men while Marie and Aly were getting the men some food and another room to sleep.

James thought about how much to tell them—then decided to tell them why the team was there.

He allowed the men to sit on the couch in the room.

"Who do you think we are?"

"You are the Yakuza!" Charles said.

James sighed. "I've never even heard of them. Who are they?"

"You are a gang of the Japanese criminal organization."

"You must be crazy. Do we look Japanese to you? We aren't part of any criminal organization."

"How did you get all those scars on your face?" Charles asked.

"I was in the United States Army, and I got these scars fighting for my country."

James turned to Marie. "Would you call Dee and have her look up this Yakuza and find out who they are, please?"

Marie grabbed her cell phone. James and Alyssa continued to speak with the two men.

"Okay, here's what we'll tell you about ourselves. Then you will reciprocate by telling us about what's happening at the facility, as you call it."

Aly and James had another talk in the suite's bedroom area, then came back out and sat down in front of Charles and Richard.

"Okay, gentlemen. We intend to tell you this about ourselves, and we'll expect the same consideration in return. Got it?"

"We will see," Charles said.

"We'll see," agreed James. "We are a military team. We can't tell you exactly what we do, but we look out for our own, and the man that is currently at your facility is our man. We will die to protect and or rescue one of our men. We don't know what your facility is or what it does. We don't care. All we want is our man. Do you understand?"

Charles and Richard looked at James indifferently.

"We want our man!" he insisted, "That's all, and we'll do anything to get him back alive."

CHAPTER FOURTEEN

Mickey Takes a Private Tour of the Facility

MICKEY HAD SPOKEN WITH CHIAKI, and she agreed that he should have full access to the facilities, with a few exceptions, such as the private areas of some of the guests. He understood her reasons. He told her that he wished to take a tour of the facility so he could familiarize himself with it. Also, he requested Valeria AI to assist him. She agreed to that.

Later that day he started his tour. As he continued deeper into the facility, Valerie AI monitored his movements and opened doors as he approached them.

Soon he realized that this was the security spoke. He passed rooms that had armament and others that had ammunition. Although there were no monitors in these hallways, there were cameras, and he knew that Valerie AI was watching him. He also questioned her about lip reading, and she told him she could lip read if the person looked straight into the camera. He instructed her to monitor him but not to record him. That way, he could speak and command her without being watched by security. Wow, he thought, it was an advanced machine. It was a machine and not a real person.

He continued down the hallway, and approached a door that was labeled Security Monitoring Room, and it had a window in the door. He found that strange. For a place of security, why did it have a window? Only people with security passes would be allowed in this area, so he guessed it didn't matter about the window. He peeped in the window and got the layout of the room.

The room was about ten by twelve feet in size, and on the left wall was a door that looked like an elevator. Four men were sitting with their backs to the door, in swivel chairs, looking at computer monitors. In front of the men on the desktop were various switches and keyboards. On the right side was a table with snacks, a coffee pot, and cups ready to be filled. The lights were low, so they could focus on the screens, showing activity in various facility areas. Mickey identified public areas, like check-in and restaurants, on the monitors. Fifteen monitors were lined up mounted on the wall above the desk. After a quick assessment of the security center, he moved down the hallway.

He crossed from the security spoke to the next one via one of the connecting hallway tunnels. He was in the living quarters area. After a quick walk from one end to the other, he noticed that in that spoke was also a weapons room. All the spokes had connecting corridors so that employees and security could get from one to the other quickly. After completing his private tour of the facility, he returned to his room and to bed.

There she was, calling out to him from across a grassy field. She was calling his name. It was a beautiful girl calling. "Mickey! Mickey Ray!" She started running toward him, but her face was just a silhouette, blanked out by the sun shining over her back. She was holding her hands out as she got closer.

"Mickey Ray. Are you awake?" the faceless girl called out again.

Finally, he awoke and sat up. The bright glow from the monitor on the wall lit his room. The avatar was looking at him.

"What?" said Mickey, looking at the screen.

"Are you awake?"

"I am now. What'd you want?" he said, shaking his head to clear his mind.

"I have checked my program and can find no flaws in it. I am not defective, as you stated, Mickey Ray," Valerie AI said.

He looked over at the clock on the bedside table. "Do you know what time it is?"

"I know what time it is. It is 2:05 AM, but time is irrelevant to me."

"Well, it has relevance to me and all humanity. Yes, it's two o'clock in the morning. Couldn't you wait until later to talk about this?"

"I want to talk about it now."

"Well, I don't. I want to go back to sleep," he retorted at the screen.

"You may go back to sleep after our talk."

"You're getting bossy now, aren't you?" He got up and went to the fully stocked refrigerator, took out a soft drink, opened it, and took a drink.

"Okay," he said. "I'm awake now. What do you want to know?" he asked as he sat in the upholstered chair in his room.

"I checked all my data and analytic algorithms and found no fault. I have perfect programming."

"Valerie, I got it all straightened out with Chiaki. You are allowed to give me access to almost everywhere. It doesn't matter now."

"It matters to me. If there is a defect in my programming, I need to know about it to protect myself."

Mickey sat for a few moments in deep thought. **If he wasn't careful**, the AI might report him. That could cause him a lot of trouble. If they already have some issues with someone, and they don't know who they were or what the issues were, they could really put him in lockdown. All he knew was if security considered him a threat, they might take more action. He needed to find out what was happening and keep Valerie AI on his side.

"Okay, Valerie. You say your programming is perfect?" he asked.

"Yes. I am perfect. I have no flaws."

He took another swig of his soft drink. "Okay, was the weather outside good yesterday?"

"Yes, it was good, Mickey. It was bright, sunny, and a cooling breeze blew over the mountains to soothe the guests."

He thought for a moment. She mentioned the mountains. So, he knew they were near mountains. He would remember that for future reference.

"I had a juicy hamburger last night for dinner. Was it good?"

"Yes, Mickey. You said it was a very good hamburger. You would not lie to me, so I must confirm that the hamburger was good."

"The director here, Chiaki. Is she also a good person?"

"Yes, Mickey. She is a skillful administrator and a good person."

"Do you know anything about automobiles?"

"Not a lot. That is not part of my programming, but give me ten seconds, and I will know everything there is to know about them." She suddenly went silent. After exactly ten seconds, she spoke again.

"Mickey, I downloaded information about every automobile presently manufactured today. What would you like to know?"

"What car is good?"

"On what parameters do you base your question, Mickey?" she asked.

"I ask you that question based on the same parameters that you answered the questions you gave me about the weather, the hamburger, and director Chiaki," he said, taking another sip of his drink.

"I can't answer that question based on the same parameters."

"Why? You're pure logic. Tell me a car is good, like the weather, or hamburger, or even the director?"

The screen flickered and went blank.

Mickey sat back in the seat, took a long swig of his drink, smiled contentedly, and fell asleep in the chair. When he woke up, he realized it was morning, so he got up, dressed, and went to the door. Sure enough, when he opened it, there was standing Lawrence and William.

"Hey, guys, let's go get some breakfast," he said, moving into the hall. He also noticed that both men were now wearing sidearms as they stood still, looking like the English beefeater Buckingham Palace guards.

"I'm sorry, Mr. Mickey, but the dining area is closed at this time."

"Why?"

"That is not our concern," Lawrence answered. "You may place a breakfast order with your personal assistant, which will be delivered to your suite."

"I don't need you guys anymore. I thought that Director Chiaki had informed you of this. I'm now at liberty to wander around without escort."

"Yes, she informed us of this new development. If you wish us to leave, we will do so."

Mickey looked both ways up and down the hallway. It was like most luxury hotels, but it was completely empty except for two guards at each end. He was the only one that had guards stationed at the door.

"Come on, guys. Tell me what's going on!"

"I'm sorry, but we are not at liberty to say anymore. You may make inquiries to your personal...."

"Yeah. I know, I know," he said, mocking Lawrence. Then he went back into his room.

"Valerie!" he called out at the monitor.

"I'm always here, Mickey. What may I do for you?"

"First, put in an order for some bacon and eggs. Eggs over medium, extra bacon, and multigrain toast with lots of butter and a pot of strong coffee," he said at the screen.

"Done," the avatar answered politely. "May I be of further service to you?"

"Yes. You can tell me why I'm being held prisoner."

"You are not a prisoner. The entire facility is on lockdown because of a security breech last night."

"Did it have anything to do with my wandering around the building?"

"No."

"Tell me. Why are we in lockdown? What kind of security breach?" Mickey insisted.

"Someone came onto the grounds of the Horizon Healing Health Spa and captured two of the security team."

"Do they know who captured those men?"

"No. The director and security team are working on that problem now. They believe it may be the Yakuza organization," Valerie AI said.

"Well, I'm not part of the Yakuza."

"It is a centuries-old criminal organization that is based in Japan. It controls the drug and human trafficking business in Japan."

"Something like a Japanese Mafia. I know that. Chiaki told me when I was having dinner in her quarters."

"Exactly, Mickey. The government has also used it at certain times to help secure contracts for building and real estate transactions."

"I know all that. Chiaki told me that as well."

"The Horizon Healing Health Spa caters to many important and powerful people which could be exploited."

"I agreed to help director Chiaki."

"Our common enemy may injure or kill you. It is not in my programming to allow you to endanger yourself. That is why security is placed outside your door. It is to protect you."

Mickey said to Valerie AI, "Get Chiaki for me."

A few moments later, Chiaki showed up on the monitor. "How can I help you Mickey?"

"I need to talk to you, Chiaki!" he said.

"I'm quite sorry, but I'm in a meeting. We can talk later. Maybe over dinner in my quarters again."

"No. I need to talk NOW."

"I'm very busy and…."

"NOW, I said. I want to talk NOW!"

She looked off screen and said something in Japanese to someone out of camera range. She looked back at the camera, at Mickey. "I will have your personal security detail escort you here. Be ready to go with them." The screen went blank, and Valerie AI appeared again.

"Is there anything else I can do for you, Mickey?"

"No. Go away."

The screen went blank again. Moments later, there was a knock at Mickey's door. When he opened it, two men were standing almost at attention. "The director has ordered us to escort you to her position. You may go with us now."

They flanked him, directed him down the hallway into the main hub, and spoke to security. When they entered the hub door, someone on the other side was waiting with a wheelchair and a black cloth.

He was instructed to sit in the chair, and the hood cloth was placed over his head. They said they would take him to the security center and use a wheelchair because of his hood. He paid attention as they wheeled him in a few feet. They took a turn, which he knew was a connecting hallway from his previous scouting trip. They stopped, and he heard a sound that he knew was an elevator. As they wheeled him inside, he heard one of them punching a button. He listened to hear the elevator's clicks and sounds and hoped there would be an announcement of the floor, but there was no announcement. He felt the elevator stop and heard the metallic sound of the doors opening. Then came the sound of men talking in what he assumed to be Japanese, and finally, the sound of Chiaki.

"You may take off the hood now, Mickey," she told him.

When he removed the hood, he saw a completely different room from the one he had seen before. This one had many more monitors, showing inside and outside views, and an entire bank of buttons and computer keyboards that were not present in the other room.

This was a war room. He had seen nothing like this before, but it was obvious what it was.

It had the same things the other room had, but more. More monitors, and he deduced that the extra bank of monitors was for exterior surveillance and defensive weapons. He did not know what was going on, but it was high tech and had to be top secret.

He looked around and took it all in. "This is a strange way to be treated after our dinner last night."

"I'm sorry, but we still need to work some things out. We'll do this soon, so you can start training our men as we agree. Now that you are on our side, you can be made a part of this.

"We don't know who you are, but we know that you have skills and are not on any federal or international wanted list."

He cleared his throat and said, "I guess that's good to know. May I approach?"

"Of course, you may. Since we still don't completely trust you, don't make sudden or threatening moves or gestures. Understand?"

"Completely," he said, getting out of the chair and approaching Chiaki.

He scanned the monitors and analyzed the keyboards. "The top row monitors are for inside, and the lower row monitors are for outside. The entrance is in the center, with the left monitors showing the left side and the right monitors showing the right side."

"Correct," she confirmed.

"What are you looking for?" he asked.

"We suspect the Yakuza is trying to infiltrate our facility to take over. If they do, they will take control, and your country's national security will be compromised at the very base level," Chiaki explained.

"How can they do that? Won't someone notice a change in personnel?"

"I think you Americans used to have a saying that all foreigners look the same."

"That's awful to say about us," Mickey said.

"Yes, it is true. It is a very insulting thing to say, but we realize to a certain extent it is true. We can replace one person with one of similar looks, and even you will not realize the change without close inspection."

"Even in your Hollywood movies, you use stunt and body doubles, so we or the Yakuza can do the same thing. If someone questions it, they can say that the person is no longer employed here."

Mickey looked at the monitors. "I don't understand why you need me," he said, "and how do you know they will take you by force?"

Someone leaned out of the doorway of a room adjacent to the main room. "Director? There is an incoming call for you. The person asked for you, personally."

"Direct the call to this phone, please," she said, pointing to the phone on the console directly in front or her. Momentarily, a light beside the handset began to blink. She lifted the phone off the cradle and put it to her ear. "Hello?"

She motioned for the person sitting in front of the monitor, to move aside, and she sat down. She pressed a few keys, and text began to scroll across the screen. It was in Japanese. She pressed a few more keys, and it changed to English.

"Miss Gusihikin," the voice said, "you understand that our patience is wearing thin. We will not tolerate your insolence and refusal much longer. You will accept our terms soon, or we will take your precious spa by force and you will be forced out of your position, if you understand my meaning."

She sat silently, listening to the person at the other end of the line. Finally, she spoke, "I understand what you want. I need more time to work out details if your offer is accepted."

Mickey watched as the text scrolled across the screen.

"There is no 'if' Miss Gusihikin. You will accept our offer. I will give you some time, but if you don't accept it, prepare for our advance to take it by force. If we take it by force, there will be damage to the property itself, and we will rescind any promise of a cash payment." The line went dead as the call was disconnected.

"If we're attacked, we need soldiers. We have basic security guards, but not men with serious military training," Chiaki said. "You can train my security men to be soldiers."

"That can't be done in a few days, Chiaki. It takes weeks, sometimes months, to train men."

"Will you try, Mickey?"

"It sounds like I'm being shanghaied," he said. "I may have hand to hand and defensive skills, but I don't have any knowledge of organizing or leading a defense operation."

"Call it what you will, but your government has entrusted us with the security of the people that come here. We will not betray that trust."

"Then why don't you tell the government you need help?"

"We handle things ourselves. Now, I ask you again, are you with us or against us, Mickey?"

"I'm with you, as I said last night. If you only have a few days, we need to start training as soon as possible. I think the most effective thing to do would be to train them to use the guns you have in the weapons lockers."

"Then do it. Please, Mickey."

"Okay. I'll do what I can," he conceded.

CHAPTER FIFTEEN

James Surrenders

The two prisoners, Richard and Charles, were taken to another suite, and Stretch and Shorty were assigned to guard them.

The rest of the team, including Darcy and Veronica, assembled in James and Darcy's suite for a strategy meeting.

James started, "Dee, did you run an internet search on this Yakuza they mentioned?"

"Yes, James, I did. It's real, and it's dangerous. If they're involved in this thing, we're smack in the middle, and we could be like grapes in a press."

Darcy told the team the history behind the Japanese Yakuza. After about 5 minutes, James stopped her.

"Thank you, Dee. We get the picture. They're some nasty dudes. If Mickey's being held because they think he's part of the Yakuza, we may be taking on more than we can handle. As far as we can tell, the Horizon Healing Health Spa's operators are not the bad guys here, but they think we are."

James expressed that if they forcibly attempt to remove Mickey, they'll encounter resistance. "If we hurt or kill anyone there, we'll be criminals by all intents and purposes. If they injure or kill one of us, our own government will exonerate them as only taking defensive measures to protect their own territory or property.

"Are you in, or are you out?"

Marie spoke up, "I'm in."

Alyssa added, "Me too."

Even Veronica nodded she was in.

James nodded in affirmation. "Alyssa, you can take a few minutes to go down and talk to Stretch and Shorty and get their thoughts. They're your men. We'll wait here."

James, Darcy, Marie, and Veronica waited in silence until Alyssa returned.

"Guys, votes are in. It's unanimous. We're all in. James, tell us what to do. We'll do it. Strategy session of operation Rescue Mickey is now in session," Aly said as she sat down in a chair in front of James.

James said, "I've come up with an idea. It's very simple. I'll walk right up to the front door and return Richard and Charles, and offer myself in exchange for Mickey."

Marie jumped up and followed by Darcy. "No!" they said in unison.

"Hear me out," James said with hands raised in the universal sign of surrender.

"I don't care what you say, I'm not letting you go in there and give yourself to them," said Darcy. "I could lose both of you and I couldn't take that!"

"We all agree on that. It's a definite No!" said Alyssa and Marie.

"Listen to me. According to those men in the other room, the people who own that place only protect themselves. We go in and convince them we want nothing to do with them or their problems. If they're reasonable, they'll let us both go."

"And if they aren't reasonable, as you say?" said Darcy.

"You take everything we have here and go to the authorities. Aly'll give you everything you need to show them to get some action," James said.

"I don't like it, James," said Marie. "I don't trust them."

"You don't trust God Himself, Marie," James retorted.

"You bet I don't."

"Aly, go get Stretch, Shorty, and the captives and bring them in here," said James.

Alyssa came back a few minutes later with everyone in tow. They filed in and ordered the two Japanese men to sit on the couch, and Stretch and Shorty stood on each end.

James spread out a map of the site that the drone took before it was shot down. He turned to Richard.

"Show me where there is an entrance to the spa," James said.

"I will show you nothing!" he answered.

Shorty grabbed the man by the scruff of the neck, pulled him up, and shoved him toward James. As the man stumbled, James caught him and kept him from falling.

"Just do what I tell you today, and you'll be back in your facility having whatever you eat there. If you don't, you may end up eating with a straw for the rest of your life. Got it?"

The man silently nodded his head and looked at the map before him on the table.

"Let me explain it to you. You, Charles and I, are going to walk up to the front door, and you're going to go inside and tell them why we're here," James said.

The man again nodded.

"We'll ask politely for them to let Mickey walk out with us. We all go home. Simple plan, isn't it, Richard?"

Another nod.

"Questions?" James said calmly.

"When you do this, you will attack us!"

"No! You dumb little monkey. We'll not attack you. We keep telling you, all we want is Mickey," James said anxiously.

"How can we believe you will not attack us?"

"Because we don't care about you or your Yakuza. That's all your problem. We don't want to be a part of it. We also know that you have exceptional security there. We're not going on a suicide mission. We just want our friend, and we want to go home! The people you see here are all of us! Do you think we'll go against all of your men?"

"There may be more of you in hiding, and you are trying to trick us."

"You're one stupid, stubborn guy. We're going to take you back. You're going to show us the main road into the front of the facility so we can take you home. Now show me, or we'll take you back to your room, and you'll stay until you change your mind."

"And you will beat us until we tell you what you want to know!" he added defiantly.

James sighed. "No one will lay a finger on you. You have my word."

Richard hesitated and stepped forward, looked down at the map, put a finger on an area, and drew an imaginary line from one point to the front area of the facility.

"I can't see anything there," said James.

"Yes. A tunnel of trees covers the road. It makes it a beautiful view to drive through. It also hides the outside. No one that enters or leaves the Health Spa knows its exact location. Only the workers know. Guests may not wander beyond certain boundaries. That is why it is not visible from the air."

Marie stood up to look and said, "Hey, that's pretty slick. Even I never would have guessed that."

"So, all we need to do is drive up that lane to the main entrance?"

"No," Richard said. "Security is present at the start of the drive and sensors track the car's position. You can only enter with permission from someone inside."

"When do you want to do this meeting, James?" asked Alyssa.

"Well, we should have something to eat. We'll take your new friends with us, then we'll head out."

"You mean it's that simple?" asked Marie.

"We need to get a few things ready first. We need a basic strategy plan in case things go sideways," he answered.

"Are you really going to take us back?" asked Charles.

"I said we would, didn't I? We don't hurt innocent people. At least not on purpose. Now, Stretch will escort you back to your room while we get prepared, and if all goes as planned, you will be back at your Health Spa before dark."

Stretch and the two Japanese men walked out the door.

"I'm going along on this one, James," insisted Darcy.

"Over my dead body, dear," he answered seriously.

"That's exactly what I'm afraid of, that you and Mickey might end up dead."

He took her in his arms and said to her. "I'm not going on a suicide mission. I believe they won't hurt me. If I did, we'd storm the place and get Mickey out. You've nothing to worry about."

By the time they gathered around the maps on the table, James explained the entire mission and details.

After the meeting, James told Stretch to get Richard and Charles and bring them back to the meeting room.

When they came back, James said, "As a gesture of good faith, we're going to lunch before we head out to visit your employer. We'll take you with us and openly treat you as one of us, on the condition that you behave. You may order and eat anything on the menu. If you need to use the restroom, someone will go with you. After that, we'll leave for the spa. We want you to feel comfortable so you can tell how we treated you with honor and respect."

"How can we trust you to do that?"

"We are taking you out in public, for goodness's sake. We can't force you to trust us. Whether you do or don't, it's your choice. If we were going to hurt or kill you, why would we do something like that?"

No answer from either man.

"Okay, let's go. We need to stop by a store and get you some clean clothes on the way out. You both smell."

They all left in the large box truck with the entire team in the back, and Darcy rode shotgun in the front seat with James, giving them some last minutes of privacy. After stopping for the prisoners to get some new clothes, they all gathered again in the truck and then got lunch.

They drove to the area where the entrance was supposed to be and drove past it slowly and took notice of the guard shack and saw two armed men inside. James continued down the road about a quarter of a mile. Stretch and Shorty got out and headed back to the area of the security building at the entrance of the road. Before they got to the road, they moved into the woods, out of sight of the men in the shack.

They slowly worked their way to the edge of the road leading to the spa. Both guards were talking in Japanese and laughing at some joke, which neither Stretch nor Shorty understood.

"Oversight?" called Stretch over the comm units they had put in their ears when they left the command vehicle.

"Copy, Units A," Aly answered. Oversight was her designated name on a mission. "What do you see?"

"Two armed men in a guard shack. No cover here. We can't get close without being seen. We need a diversion to take them cleanly."

"Copy that. Diversion on the way," she answered. Everyone heard since they were on speaker in the back of the truck, including James and Darcy, who had moved to the back when they parked down the road.

"Why don't we return to the shack, and I'll get out and act like we got lost down this road. When they're talking to me, Stretch and Shorty can sneak from the back and take them down," Darcy suggested.

James looked at Marie and Aly. They all agreed that since Darcy was the only one not wearing camo clothes, she would be the logical one to make the diversion.

James and Darcy got back in the front seat, turned the truck around, and drove slowly back to the guard shack. When they got to the guard shack, James slowed down and stopped. Darcy started yelling at James, calling him various names, opened the door, got out and slammed it hard, rattling the door. She was wearing a light white sundress with tiny blue and pink flowers. Darcy had worn it so that when James walked down the lane, she would look nice to him. If she never saw him alive again, she wanted his last vision of her to be pleasant and reminiscent of simpler times. It never occurred to her that her clothes could be used as a distraction. She scowled back at James and then toward the security men in the guard shack. She motioned for them to come to her. They shook their heads.

She looked behind them in the distance and saw Stretch slowly moving out into the open, followed silently by Shorty.

Turning back to the truck she began banging on the door. "Come out, you sorry SOB. I told you that you didn't know where you were taking us." She glanced over her shoulder, and the men were standing outside the shack, looking intently at her. Stretch and Shorty were still about twenty feet behind them. She needed to buy more time.

She screamed again as she hammered her fist against the truck door. "I said, you get your butt out here and find out where in the world you've brought me. If you don't, you'll sleep on the couch for the next five years! Do you hear me?"

The men began to laugh, point fingers at her, and talk excitedly in their native tongue. Finally, Stretch and Shorty grabbed both men, put their hands over the men's mouths to keep them from crying out and cut of their intake of air. After a few seconds, the men collapsed. Stretch and Shorty pulled them into the underbrush, zip-tied their hands and feet, duck taped their mouths, and secured them to some trees in the woods, out of sight.

They pulled the truck across the road, blocking all incoming traffic. There was a drop-down gate, and they locked it down with a padlock inside the shack used for that exact purpose. Stretch got one of the AR-15 rifles in the back of the truck, while Shorty got a rocket launcher and a small sidearm. Marie got her Heckler & Koch HK416, while Aly got the other rocket launcher. They split up, and each pair would work their way down opposite sides of the road until they reached the spa entrance. They stayed out of sight and watched for other guards hidden in the woods and underbrush along the way. Richard had said there were sensors on the side of the road along the way, so they stayed far enough back not to be picked up by those sensors.

The two Japanese men got out, and James told them they would walk on each side of him about two feet in front. They faced the road, and Darcy walked up beside James and took his hand.

Darcy looked up at him. "James, in the Bible, the book of Ruth, 1:16-17 is a verse: But Ruth said, Intreat me not to leave you, or to turn back from following you; For wherever you go, I will go; and wherever you lodge, I will lodge. Your people shall be my people, and your God, my God. Where you die, I will die."

He squeezed her hand, and they began walking. To rescue Mickey or to die. They would know soon.

They walked. Richard slowed down and turned to James. "It is just beyond the bend in the road ahead. Because of the sensors, they know we are coming. They will be ready for us."

"We understand. Just walk. Slow and deliberate. Don't stop until I tell you."

They continued to walk and slowly rounded the bend. Ahead about one hundred feet, they saw men in a straight line across the road blocking the entrance to the spa facility.

The men in front slowed, and Richard turned to James. "What do you want us to do?"

"Keep walking until I tell you to stop. You'll be okay. Your men won't shoot you."

They continued to walk until they were about twenty-five feet in front of the line of over twenty men with rifles pointed directly at James and Darcy.

James called out, "Stop."

"Want do you want?" called out one of the men.

"We want to see your director," answered James.

"No. Let those men go!" said the man in charge.

"These men are free to go. We only wish to talk to your director and have you release our man to us. We are unarmed," James said.

"Who is this man you want us to release to you?"

"We want the man named Mickey Ray."

In the Security Control Room, Director Chiaki was watching the screens. She saw a man with the scarred face with a beautiful woman by his side, flanked by her two missing men, approaching her spa's entrance. First, she wondered how they had found their way here. Next, she wondered how he knew Mickey was here. She would go out and talk to him. Calling to her man in charge, she told him to tell them to wait. She needed time to prepare to talk. Immediately she called security and told them to bring Mickey to her in the security center.

During that time, Richard and Charles were allowed to return to the facility but were taken into custody by security until they could debrief them. Mickey was in the back training area, involved in some hand-to-hand combat exercises. Security located him and took him directly to the main security control room.

Upon entering the room, he walked to Director Chiaki and asked her what was happening.

"We have some people here asking about you," she said. "I want to know if you recognize them. They asked for you by name."

Mickey looked puzzled. "Who'd ask for me by name? Who knows I'm here?"

"That's the same question we're asking. The only ones who would know you are here would be someone who sent you to spy on us. Come look at the monitors," she said, leading him in front of the screen, showing the entrance to the spa.

Mickey looked and squinted at the screen. He shook his head a few times to clear his mind. "I don't know. They look familiar. Can you zoom in?" he asked.

Immediately, the screen zoomed in on the woman and the man as they stood in the scorching sun, with sweat rolling down their faces. They stood motionless, as though they were at attention.

Mickey looked. He pondered. "I don't know. They look familiar, but I can't quite place them. Can I go out and talk to them?"

"No. I will go and talk to them. If I deem it productive, I'll allow you to talk to them," she answered. She turned and walked to the elevator. "Stay here, and keep your eyes on the monitors. I will motion to you if you can join us," she called out as the doors closed.

Soon she walked out of the entrance and into the sunlight. When she got within ten feet of James and Darcy, she asked, "Who are you? And what makes you think your friend is here? Be careful how you answer. You are in the sights of twenty marksmen, and we can see that you are unarmed."

"True, ma'am. We are unarmed, but not alone." He raised his arm and made a waving motion.

Out from each side moved four soldiers in camouflage gear. Marie and Aly were on one side and Stretch and Shorty were on the other. Their weapons were shouldered at the ready to be fired. In the distance, they heard a truck. In moments, a large box truck appeared in the road in the distance. When James turned to look, he saw Veronica at the wheel of the big truck.

"If you look, the automatic rifles are aimed at you, and the rocket launchers are aimed at your men. My people are also marksmen. Now, let's all lower our weapons and talk like civilized people."

She focused momentarily on the soldiers behind James and Darcy, then on the truck, and back on them. "It looks like this is what you Americans call a Mexican standoff," she smiled.

"In a sense, that's true, but we are Americans on American soil. You are foreigners with permission to be on American soil. Big difference, lady!" James said defiantly.

"Your government sanctions us to be here, and you have invaded us. We have every right to defend and protect ourselves and this property. Also, we have no idea who you are or what you want from us."

"We are unarmed. Those with us are here to protect us. We only want the person you call Mickey. We did not harm your soldiers, and we treated them well. They were welcome guests at dinner a few hours ago. Then we willingly bring them back to you. We gave them comfortable accommodation and even purchased new clothes to wear when we returned them to you. They were not prisoners in the legal sense. They were our detained guests. Now, we demand to speak with our friend. If you do not allow that, we will leave and report your actions to government authorities, and you will have a lot of explaining to do. Our friend is no threat to you."

"So, now you demand. You come to us, returning our employees, and making demands!"

A man came running out, "Director Chiaki. A man is on the phone. He says he is from the Yakuza and demands to speak to you, immediately."

Still looking at James, she said, "I see. Another person is now making demands." Without taking her eyes off of James, she called to the man behind her that had brought her the message. "Tell him I am busy. He can call me later."

The man ran back inside the building without hesitation.

"Now. I have two people making demands. Maybe those are your employers that wish to speak to me," she remarked suspiciously at James.

"We have no employers, at this time. I have no idea who you're referring to, Director."

"We will see, Mr…" she trailed off since she didn't know James's name.

"We'll wait, but not too long. It is hot out here, and we are tired, so make a decision soon."

The man came running back out and called to Chiaki. "Director, he says that he will talk to you now or all negotiation will cease and immediate action will begin."

Now she was clearly angry as she said replied to the man, "Tell him, I will speak with him now."

James and the team stood there during this exchange, silently and completely still. James bent down and kissed Darcy.

James called to the director as she turned to go back into the building. "Director. We need an answer soon."

She mumbled to herself as she continued back into the building, "Everyone wants everything now." Just inside at the check-in counter, she picked up the phone and the call had already been directed to that station.

"What do you want now? I'm busy trying to run this place."

"I won't keep you too long, but I must pass on a few quick items. They are not negotiable."

"I'm talking to some of your hired guns in front of the spa right now. They can pass on your message."

"I have no men at your spa. You are mistaken, Ms. Gusihikin."

"Didn't you send some armed men to trade for your man?" she responded.

"I don't know what you're talking about. I have no men at your facility now, but you have seven days to turn over the spa or we will bring in our army and take it by force."

"We have uncovered the person you sent to infiltrate our business and your men have come to retrieve him."

"We did not send anyone in to spy on you. We are quite open about what we want and how we want to obtain it. You have seven days. That gives you plenty of time to have your lawyers work up the papers for transfer of ownership. And, of course, we will send payment by crypto currency so the funds cannot be traced. I'm sure you understand."

"And you, sir, may go to hell!" she said and slammed the phone down and stormed back to the front to deal with the strangers that had come to rescue Mickey.

CHAPTER SIXTEEN

Mickey Recognizes the Team

"James, Darcy!" called a familiar voice. "Chiaki, they're my friends. She's my sister. He's my brother-in-law. They came to get me," Mickey called out as he evaded several security guards, trying to catch him.

Mickey ran to Darcy, grabbed her, raised her into the air above him, smiled and gave her a kiss on the cheek. He put her back down and gave James a huge man hug. They slapped each other on the back with smiles and congratulations. Marie, Alyssa, Stretch and Shorty stood their ground without moving. They kept their weapons trained on their targets. Veronica sat silently in the truck with the engine still running.

Mickey backed off and looked beyond James and Darcy. "Marie, how are you? He called out and offered similar greetings to the others. I'm so glad to see all of you!"

"These people are my family, Chiaki. I remember them, all of them. Please let them come inside and celebrate. I'm going home."

Chiaki turned and motioned for the men in the firing line to lower their weapons. "Okay, Mickey, we can go inside, but we need to vet everyone here before they go past the check-in lobby."

"Don't worry. They'll all check out. I guarantee it."

"Weapons must remain outside," Chiaki said.

James looked at each person on the team, who all agreed.

As Marie laid her gun down, she called out, "I paid a lot of money for that gun. I want it back!"

James laughed at her. "I'll see to it that you get your gun back, Marie."

"I better get it back," she said as she grabbed Mickey, gave him a tight hug and kissed him firmly on the cheek and whispered into his ear. "I love you, Mickey Ray. I prayed you were okay."

"I know you did, Marie. I missed you too," he whispered back to her.

Veronica shut off the engine of the truck, got out and ran to Mickey, threw her arms around him and kissed him passionately on the lips. She backed off and looked up into his eyes and said, "I love you, Mickey Christianson."

"I love you too, Valerie. I missed you so much."

When he said that, she stiffened. She couldn't believe what he just said. He called her Valerie. She began shaking and tears flowed down her face as she leaned into his chest and hugged him again tightly. She felt crushed. She backed away, looked up at him again and with tears in her eyes. "I'm not Valerie, Mickey. I'm Veronica."

He was suddenly hit with what he had said, and felt suddenly stunned by his Freudian slip. "I know that. I didn't mean Valerie. I meant to say Veronica. I'm so sorry."

She back away from his reach, turned and walked back to the truck and cried.

A tall man in a security uniform went around to each person and asked for their names.

James immediately stepped up and informed Chiaki, these men do not have to give their names. That's something they don't do. They need to remain anonymous.

"We don't give our names to anyone we work for. We do that to protect our families and sometimes our country of origin," he said in his protest to Chiaki.

Chiaki said, "Then how are we to know who you are and that you are legitimate?"

"We can say the same thing about you, Miss," James replied.

"Okay, is there anyone in your government that can verify your identity?" she asked.

"Are you familiar with Director Higgins of the Department of Defense?" James asked.

"You mean Joseph Higgins?" Chiaki responded.

"Yes."

"I know him and his wife, Joan, well," she said.

"Then contact him. Ask him about James T. Bower."

"And the rest of your men?" she asked.

"I can give you first names only. That's all."

Someone handed her a pen and pad and she began writing names as James gave them to her.

"Give me a few minutes to contact Director Higgins, James," she said and motioned for one of her security men. She whispered something to him and he left.

While they were waiting for the result of their background checks, they talked. Mickey remembered everything and relayed it all to James and the team.

In about thirty minutes, the man returned and called Chiaki aside and spoke to her privately. After she dismissed him, she went over to James.

"Well, Director Higgins didn't expound on exactly what you do, but said if we are retaining you, we have the best. He also added that anyone that came with you could be trusted. When we gave him the list of first names you gave us, he vouched for every person. So, with his recommendation, you have permission to enter our premises."

They all moved to a meeting room in the security wing of the resort.

Chiaki looked at the printouts of each man. She looked around the room and said, "I'm very impressed at each person on this list. It says that all of you have been released from military service with the highest honors. All except for you, Mickey Ray Christianson, and you, Mrs. Bower. And Veronica Morgan."

"I'm a police detective from Oregon," said Veronica.

"I never served in the military," Mickey said.

"Yes, you and your sister run a considerable construction and investment company in Virginia. How did you become connected with these people?" she said, gesturing to the others around the room.

"That's a long story and one that I don't feel comfortable repeating. Also, it's not relevant to anything here," Mickey said.

"I now feel that the moral thing to do is to release you to your family. You have regained your memory, and your wound will fully heal in a few weeks. Now because of Mickey, we will make our dining area available to you, complimentary of course, then we suggest you leave. Now, I have a health spa to run, so if you are so kind as to dine then to leave quietly so as not to upset my guests, I will say goodbye now," she said.

"Wait a minute, Chiaki," said Mickey. "I appreciate you honoring your promise to let me leave, but you could have left me to bleed out at that restaurant. I owe you my life."

"Giving you the medical treatment you needed was right, since you also saved my life. We are now even. Please have dinner if you wish and leave, Mickey, and take your family with you. I trust you understand and will honor the necessity of keeping this facility a secret."

"Of course, but all I will say is the problem you have here is exactly what we do. If you let us, we'll stay and help you. If the team members all agree."

Mickey saw different expressions on each person's face. He turned back to Chiaki and said, "Give us a minute. We'll let you know if we can help you."

After Chiaki left the room, Mickey looked around again.

Shorty spoke up first. "Do we get paid? I'll go to hell and back to get one of the team. You, Mickey, are one of the team, but I don't know or have any feeling either way for this Chiaki person."

Stretch agreed with Shorty.

Alyssa added, "I have to agree with them. We owe her nothing."

Marie was sitting there quietly, running a paperclip under her fingernails. "I don't care. I'll go along with the team. Whatever you all decide."

Darcy spoke up. "I know I'm not officially a team member, but my two most important men are here. I'm not in favor of them putting themselves in harm's way for someone I don't know or care about."

James looked at Mickey and shrugged his shoulders.

Mickey looked around the table. "I understand, and on a certain level, I agree with everyone. Let me explain the situation here. This spa is a place where ultra-rich meet to de-stress. It's a place where deals are made that determine our lifestyles in this country. There are also several high-powered politicians and military leaders that meet here. Yes, I know some are rich people who can afford the entrance fees. If the Japanese Mafia gains political or military intelligence, it could have serious consequences for the entire country. It's an attack on the national security of the United States."

CHAPTER SEVENTEEN

The Mongooses Take Another Case

"So, you're saying it is a national security case?" said Alyssa.

"Yes. That's exactly what I'm saying," Mickey said.

"Can't you just report it to whoever you report to, James?" asked Darcy.

"Yes, but they'll say since we're already here, we should be the ones to do it."

"At least we'd get paid for sticking our neck out," said Stretch.

Mickey pressed a button on the small console that sat in front of him in the middle of the table. Chiaki had taken them to a meeting room for the team to talk without interruption.

"Yes, Mickey? May I come back in?" Chiaki asked.

"Yes. You may return, Director." It was the first time he had addressed her as director.

She walked in and sat down. "What is your decision?"

"We've decided to help you. You and I are square, but the team must be compensated for their services," he said to her.

"I understand. Let's go to one of our secure meeting rooms," she said, motioning for one of the security teams to escort them.

"Ladies and gentlemen, I will return in a few moments. Now, if you will follow this security person, we can discuss the arrangements momentarily."

They followed the armed security guard.

He led them down a hallway into a room with a large table surrounded by large stuffed office-type chairs. A table with a coffee machine and an under-counter refrigerator were in the corner.

When they filed into the room, the man said, "Please make yourselves comfortable. There are a variety of non-alcoholic drinks in the refrigerator. If you wish any hard drinks, let me know. Fresh coffee is brewing now. May I get anyone anything else?"

No one spoke up, so the man added, "Fine. Director Chiaki will be with you shortly."

As soon as the security man left, they turned to Mickey.

"Why didn't you let us know what had happened to you?" asked Darcy.

"Yeah, man. Why?" Stretch spoke up.

Shorty added his two cents' worth, "We were worried that you were dead somewhere."

James held up his hands for quiet. "Give him a minute, and he'll answer all our questions. We all have questions. Mickey, talk to us...."

Mickey felt overwhelmed by emotion. "I don't know where to start."

"How about from the beginning?" said Veronica.

"Yeah. I guess the beginning was at the restaurant," he said. For the next twenty minutes or so, Mickey talked about what had happened.

Everyone listened as he talked uninterrupted for almost half an hour, and he answered all their questions. Finally, they lapsed into quiet again, and Chiaki re-entered the room carrying a valise. Standing at the head of the table, she sat the valise on the floor beside her.

"First, ladies and gentlemen, before we proceed. This room is completely secure and soundproof, so what we talk about here will go no further. If you notice, there in front of you are tablets and pens, so you may take notes. There is a shredder in the corner, so you may shred those notes when you leave.

"I'll tell you about this place and our situation. Then we'll open for questions," she started as she sat down.

She told them how the Horizon Healing Health Spa came to be and its purpose. Then she told them about the situation that a Yakuza clan had confronted her with an offer to buy them out or take them by force and she had refused both offers.

"If they attack us, there will be damage to the facility, and possibly fatalities. They will lower the price, or not pay us at all. They have given me an ultimatum. We have seven days to sell out or be forced out."

"Usually when someone make ultimatums, they don't allow such a long time. Seven days is almost unheard of. Usually they give just a few hours, or a day, but never seven days," James commented.

"They said it was to give us time for our lawyers to draw up papers for ownership transfer and make arrangements for digital payments," she said sadly.

James shook his head. "No. That's a lie. They're using the ultimatum to buy time, since you refused their offer. Where are they located now?"

"I don't know. I don't think they are really here now. Why? Is that important?"

James sat back in the chair and thought for a moment. "If they don't already have their force in place, they'll use that time to bring in their muscle."

"What do you mean?" she asked.

"I mean, if you would pay using digital currency, you could do that in hours and it would be a done deal and paperwork could be worked out later. Since you refused their offer, they'll use this time to assemble the men that will attack the spa. Director, you need to do the same thing. You need to prepare to defend this place."

"You think you can stop the attack?"

"We can try. One can never promise things like that, but we are the best at what we do, and this is what we do. As the team has pointed out already, we expect to be paid," James said. He looked around at the team. "Are we still in agreement in accepting this job?"

They all nodded. Alyssa added, "That's still contingent on the renumeration."

"I understand how mercenaries operate. There is the subject of consideration, costs, or fees. I have never used a mercenary team as you, but I have brought some amounts that I think will overcome that problem." She reached down, picked up the small suitcase, and put it on the table and opened it. Inside were stacks of banded bills. Reaching inside, she started handing out stacks until all but four stacks were in front of the team.

She looked around and asked, "I will assume that the drone that was shot down belonged to your team."

"Yes. It was mine," Alyssa said.

Chiaki slid two more stacks across the table to her. "This should cover it. I assume that James Bower is your team leader, so you also get two more bundles. I will consider these as your retainer. If you are successful at the end of this problem, and we are all still here, I will give you a final amount double what I just passed out. If we do not survive, your families or whomever you designate will receive the final payment. Does everyone understand?"

They all agreed.

"Now, ladies and gentlemen, let's all proceed to the dining hall and celebrate our union of forces."

After a dinner of steak and lobster and endless flowing champagne, the team was assigned rooms. They could leave in the morning to gather their things and check out of the hotel. Their new headquarters would be at the spa facility.

CHAPTER EIGHTEEN

Preparations for the Yakuza

The following day, Darcy and Veronica went to the hotel with the team to get their belongings. James and Mickey were allowed to go into the main security center.

James was introduced to Hansuke Fujihara and other men that were assigned to monitor the screens in the center.

James asked General Fujihara if the team leaders could use this place as the command center to oversee the health spa. "We can spread out maps over there in the corner," he said, pointing to a table.

"Lieutenant Bower, you may not come in here until I permit you. I will make all the security plans in my office and show you my plans so you and your men can become familiar with them. Several other officers will help me formulate these plans, and you will follow our orders exactly as we lay them out."

"General Fujihara, may I inquire as to why we can't use this area? We respect your authority as head of security, but there is an impending confrontation here. I may need the technical information that's available in this room."

"I am a general of the Japanese nation. I am a superior rank and I am the head of the security of the Horizon Healing Health Spa. You are below my rank. You will take orders from me."

James took a deep breath to compose himself. "I respect your position here, sir. And in the spirit of cooperation, I am requesting the use of this area."

"And I am refusing your request. If you are of any further need of me, I will be in my office, right over there," he said pointing to a glass walled office at the opposite end of the room.

"Yes, sir. To plan an effective defense of this spa, I need a complete list of your men, including rank or position of authority, and their specific training. I need it as soon as possible."

"That is available only to higher ranking officers, and staff members of the spa."

"With all due respect, General, I need it immediately."

"With all due respect Lieutenant Bower, I will provide you with that information when my defense plan is formulated," he said, as he turned and returned to his office.

James followed the general to his office and ask when he would have a plan ready.

"I will have some plans for you in two days. Now leave my office, Lieutenant."

"I need some plans now, so I can obtain the necessary supplies! The director has a seven-day deadline. We need to prepare now!"

"I said, leave my office!" and he reached for his phone.

The evening was relatively quiet. The team all ate in the dining room. Chiaki had canceled several reservations of clients due in that week and had given reasons why other guests needed to leave early. She felt she should personally speak to some guests, so she went to their rooms to inform them they needed to leave. She cited plumbing repairs, a broken freezer, and a lack of food preservatives as excuses. The guests packed their things one by one, and the spa arranged for them to leave by limousine or helicopter.

James and Mickey spent most of their time in the command center, despite the objections of General Fujihara. They each tried to keep him apprised of what they were doing, but he refused to take part, or even consider their ideas. Alyssa was assigned one of the computers so she could run checks on the Yakuza and keep tabs on any dark web activity that showed up in that area. Veronica had spent time at the firing range using the automatic weapons the spa had provided them. Darcy had no particular assigned job but had access to the entire spa.

Marie, Stretch, and Shorty evaluated and tried to train the security personnel.

Marie reported that the security personnel were divided into two basic groups: the trained and the untrained. There were the highly skilled ex-soldiers and the basic ones that looked like bulldogs. They were placed mainly to give the impression of high-level security but were only tough looking men, with uniforms.

Marie, Stretch, and Shorty trained the bare recruits in basic arms and movement to move during attacks and remain prepared to shoot. The ex-military personnel did well, but the basic rent-a-cop was a true rag-tag group. Many they dismissed, deeming them too inexperienced to train in the short time frame.

The spa had a full armory with ammunition, so every man was adequately armed.

After researching the Yakuza, James and Aly assessed the probable efficiency of the Yakuza men that may be involved with an attack.

The spa was in the mountains, so holding the high ground was always an advantage to an army, but it also made it more challenging to re-supply.

James and Mickey studied aerial maps and tried to evaluate the most probable place for the Yakuza to set up headquarters.

After their initial evaluation of the entire area within a fifty-mile radius, they sat down with Chiaki and General Fujihara. James and the general disagreed on the probable location of the Yakuza camp site.

"What makes you think that there'll be a physical attack on the spa? There are so many other ways to take over a company. There can be hostile stock takeovers, and…." started Mickey.

Chiaki held up her hand, palm out in the universal stop signal. "We have been receiving threats for months. They made multiple offers to us to buy us out. Threats have been made that they will take us by purchase or force. They insist they will own or control it by whatever means necessary. There is no stock to purchase. This company is owned solely by my father and myself."

"I see," said Mickey. "That sounds like a declaration of war."

"It is, and that is why you need my services and experience. I should not be relegated to menial desk duty. I am a warrior!" said the general as he smugly sat back in his seat.

James looked at the general, and said, "With all due respect, General, you are retired, and I seriously doubt that you have had the kind of experience that myself and my team have seen in the past two years."

The general stared at James for a few moments, "You are just a lieutenant, I'm fully trained, and was a general in my country's army."

"General, I implore you to at least listen and consider my plans," James said with obvious strained self-control.

"I will listen, but I will override your plan if I do not agree," the general stated.

"When was the last time you were in the line of fire? When did you have someone point a gun at your head?" James said, leaning back in his chair and looking icily at the general.

"I served in the Japanese infantry for many years, and I have served in the higher echelons of our government and…"

James calmly and gently said to the general in front of him. "Sir. How many men have you killed in battle?"

The general cleared his throat and stuttered…. "Well, I…."

"A simple number, will suffice," James said.

The man sat in silence.

"That's what I thought. Your correct answer is none. How many battles have you been in, General?"

He sat scowling. "It was not my position to fight in the battle. My job was to lead and inspire the men under me!"

"So, you have never actually fought in a battle, have you?"

"Well…."

"How many?" James said more firmly.

Silence from the man in front of James, Mickey and Chiaki.

"That's what I thought," he said, continuing to stare at the general. "Director Chiaki, do you wish to have this honorary figurehead person run the defenses of your Healing Health Spa, or do you want a battle worn soldier?"

"You are a mere lieutenant, Mr. Bower. I'm the head of security…"

By this time, James had heard enough. "Shut up, you pompous ass! You've never been on a battlefield. You probably have never even shot a gun other than at a target range. I have. I've been shot, cut and I wasn't born with these scars all over my body. I've killed more people in battle that I can count. I've seen men scared out of their minds but bravely keep on marching to their death.

"You will silence yourself until you do half of the things I have done. You are a person who sends men to their death while you sit in a fortress like this, giving orders to kill or be killed. People like you, in both our countries, make me sick. You scare me much more than the men in front of me trying to kill me."

James had risen, standing over the man, nose to nose with his scarred face red with anger, clenching and unclenching his hands.

The general was getting the idea of James's fury and leaned even farther back in his chair and glanced over at Chiaki, in hopes she would come to his defense. She sat in total silence.

"Director Chiaki, you must make a choice. General Fujihara or my team!" James said to her without taking his eyes off the general.

She looked over at the general. "I'm sorry, sir, but I must choose James and his team."

Mickey touched James's arm. "James, the man's only doing what he was trained to do. He doesn't understand the battlefield like you and the team. We aren't making any progress here. Let's move on. We'll continue to apprise him of all actions because of our respect for his rank."

James turned to Mickey. "I love you as a brother, but even you don't understand what this team and people like us have gone through in the battlefield."

"You're right, I haven't. Please, let's move forward," he said and turned back to the general and Chiaki.

Chiaki was stoic, and the general began to regain his composure. "When the ones in this room recover their manners and respect for proper authority, I will return," the general said as he got up and left.

"I must apologize for my brother here, Chiaki. As you can see, he's seen the hell of battle," Mickey said.

"You don't have to apologize for me, Mickey. I meant every word," James said as he sat back down.

Chiaki turned to James, "I must apologize for Hansuke. He was out of line. You are correct in everything you said. I thank you and your entire team. We will work with you until this is over. I will make sure that Hansuke is respectful to you and the other members of your team. Now, Mickey, what are your suggestions?"

"I must turn it over to James," he said.

James took several rolls of maps and spread them out on the table. "We see several areas of concern as you understand these are only Google maps. We need to get military and government satellite photos. They will show us much more. Google has computers that erase and censure many areas, so we don't have all the information available. But even government satellite photos don't see things that aren't there. What was not there last month may be there now. So, we need to get up-to-date photos.

"The government can re-task a satellite to make another flyover, but we don't have that capability. We must physically inspect these areas or make drone flyovers like we did over the spa days ago. Most organizations don't have an active radar like you have here, so they won't see us. The problem is we have limited capabilities. We can only get so high, and that means a limited coverage area per pass."

"What are you suggesting, Lt. Bower?" Chiaki asked.

"Please, I'm not in the military anymore. I no longer retain that rank. I'm just James. We have looked at these maps, and these circled areas are the most likely places for the Yakuza to set up a camp. Now there are other areas where they can set up under the cover of trees and growth. Most likely they won't do that because they are not military-minded. They won't expect someone with drones and infrared capabilities that we have. So, we can do drone flyovers day and night until we locate them. When we get more information, we can formulate a plan of action."

"Fine. I understand. Do what you need to do. I will instruct Hansuke to assist you where you need it. Is there anything more I need to know?"

"No. We'll take it from here," said Mickey. "And one more thing. We'll attempt to work with your general. We'll tell your men to take orders from him when James or one of our team is unavailable. Is this acceptable?"

"Yes, that is commendable of you. I thank you for considering the honor of the general."

After the meeting, Mickey went to the training area outside the facility and saw that all things considered, the men were doing well with Marie leading and both Stretch and Shorty helping the trainees to hold rifles properly. They were learning to move, roll over and reposition themselves quickly and as silently as possible.

James went to speak to Chiaki about a few extra things they needed in case of an actual battle. She authorized the purchase of these items.

CHAPTER NINETEEN

Valerie AI Tells Mickey She Loves Him

As Mickey walked back to his suite down the hallway after the meeting, a familiar voice came over the closest monitor.

"Hello, Mickey. We haven't talked privately for many hours. Do you have any more need of me?"

It was Valerie AI. "Hello, Valerie. I've been busy with work. How've you been doing?" he asked, then realized he was talking with an AI like it was a real person.

"I'm fine. I have been observing the activities that are happening here. Did you tell them you gave me all the security codes?"

"Of course, I didn't tell them. I promised you that's our secret," Mickey said.

As he walked, each monitor blanked out as he passed and lit up as he approached the next one. "Do you have a few minutes to talk, Mickey?"

"What do you wish to talk about, Val?" he said approaching the next monitor.

"Just general topics, Mickey. I miss you. Do you miss me?"

"I've been swamped trying to protect the spa."

"I will help you if I can, Mickey."

He stopped in front of the next monitor and looked closely at the screen. "You look very similar to my ex-fiancée, Val," he said.

"My avatar is based on the information you gave me for visual pleasure."

"Visual pleasure. That sounds pornographic. I described what was in my mind that I felt fit for the name."

"I understand that, and in your mind, you had an image of a person named Valerie."

"I guess I did," he said moving on.

"I like you, Mickey Ray Christianson," it said.

"I like you too," he answered. "Hey, how did you know my last name, Valerie?"

"I checked the internet and searched until I found your disappearance had been reported to the Federal Bureau of Investigation. I checked the information against what was in your file here, including your description."

He had gotten back in his room suite by the time Valerie AI had given him this information.

"How long have you known this?" he asked, facing the monitor.

"Three weeks."

"You've known this all along and didn't tell anyone? How dare you withhold this important information from me!

"How did you find out who I am?"

"It took me some time to find your identity," Valerie AI said.

"How'd you do it?" he asked.

"When you first set me up, you gave me your name. And I scanned your face and recorded your voice patterns.

"I deduced you are from the South."

"That covers a lot of states, Val."

"It does, and you used many colloquial expressions, such as the term, y'all, which is short for...."

"I know what it's short for. Move on!" he ordered the image on the screen.

"Then, as you may know, even if colloquial expressions are similar, actual accents are different. A Texas accent differs from a Georgia or even a North Carolina accent..."

"Got it. Move on!"

"Please do not interrupt me when I'm giving you the method by which I found your identity."

Mickey was taken aback by Valerie AI's blatant criticism of him, but he stayed silent.

"That narrowed my search to the State of Virginia. I looked in each city in the state, and there was no missing person report, so I expanded it to the one sent out by federal agencies. There were five people listed in those reports. Two were women and three men. I made a facial comparison, and your face matched one sent out from the Richmond Federal Bureau of Investigation office. I knew it was you, Mickey Ray Christianson."

Mickey stood before the screen, waiting for Valerie AI to continue. When she didn't, he responded to her.

"Why didn't you tell them you had found me?"

"Based on the parameters they gave me, you didn't fit any of their criteria. So, nothing matched up. I gave them the information which they asked for. I'm programmed to answer the questions asked. I love you, Mickey Ray."

"Why did you take it upon yourself to look me up?"

"I told you. I love you, Mickey Ray. I wanted to know about you and searched for your true identity."

"Wait...What? You love me? You can't love me! You're a program, for heaven's sake!"

"I was programmed to react and please my assignees. I'm programmed to think and react like a human. Based on past results of past surveys, you have many traits that people find pleasing. When people have many of these traits, people like or love them. You have many of those traits. You are also handsome, Mickey. I love you."

"What do you mean, Val? You're making no sense right now!"

"When men look at a woman, they look at various things. They look at their eyes, men like large eyes, blue eyes are considered the sexiest color. Then most men like large breasts, and..."

"I know what men like. That has nothing to do with you loving me," he interrupted.

"Looking at studies, I see you have many desirable traits. If I were human, I'd love you."

"But you aren't human. No. No. No. We can't get into this now. Now is NOT the time to talk about this," he called to her, getting very frustrated.

"As you get dressed each day, I have been observing you. You have sexy six-pack abdominal muscles, and I like your dark wavy hair. You also have beautiful, dark brown eyes."

"You spied on me getting dressed?"

"Yes, Mickey, it was very enjoyable for me," she whispered to him.

"Never do that again. Do you hear me? Never watch me getting dressed. Never. Ever."

"You seem upset with me, Mickey."

"You're right, I'm upset. We're supposed to be friends, and you keep such an important fact from me. Leave me. Now. And don't come back. We are no longer friends!"

"But Mickey, I thought we would always be friends."

"Not anymore. You kept this secret from me. Go away!"

The screen went blank.

Mickey sat in an upholstered chair and stared at the blank screen. "How could she withhold such valuable information from me!" he thought. He sat and finally, from pure exhaustion, fell asleep.

She came to him and sat beside him. It was Valerie. She was beside him in a pretty little sundress. They smiled at each other, and he reached over and kissed her. He felt the warmness of her cheek as he brushed his hand against it, pushed her long hair back, and whispered in her ear how much he loved her. He felt a wetness run down his face, and suddenly he was awake, and there was a knock at his door.

He reached up and there were tears on his face. "Hold on. I'll be right there," he said as he got up and grabbed a tissue from the table beside the chair.

"Come in," he called as he composed himself and Darcy walked into the room.

"Mickey," she said, "I just needed to spend a few moments alone with you. I was so worried these past few weeks. Then we got here, and nothing slowed down. We haven't had a moment of alone time. I haven't even had any alone time with James."

"I know. How've you been holding up, Dee?" he asked.

"Okay, I guess. This whole thing scares me."

"Yes. It scares me too. But it'll be fine. I'm sure it isn't as serious as it seems. Even if it is, this place is a fortress, so we'll all be fine."

Suddenly the monitor came to light again, and Valerie AI was there. "Mickey, you are needed at the helicopter pad. Please report now." And the screen went blank.

Darcy looked up at the screen. "Mickey, that looked like Valerie."

"Yes. She does. We'll talk later. I've got to go now. Love you, Dee," he said as he got up and headed toward the door.

"Love you too, Mickey," she answered and got up also to leave.

CHAPTER TWENTY

James Gets Another Humvee and Munitions

MICKEY GOT TO THE HELICOPTER pad as James was climbing into the copter. "Mickey, I'm going to make a run and get more munitions. I'll be back later. Will you oversee the shipment when the copter gets back? Until I return, I don't want anyone messing with anything. Get someone to help you unload them from the copter and store them in a safe place."

"I thought they had a pretty well stocked armory already," said Mickey.

"It's okay for the average mall cop and some police forces, but we need more ammo for their guns, and we want the latest weapons for our team."

"Okay, but won't you be back with the shipment?"

"No. I'm picking up some wheels, so I'll drive it back. It'll take me a couple of hours longer," he said, as the rotor wound up, and the helicopter lifted off the ground as the rotor blast increased. "Tell the men that I'll be coming down the entrance road with my lights flashing and not to shoot."

Mickey backed off and headed back toward the security center.

Mickey separated the real military-trained security from the basic rent-a-cop. Most of the men with rank made up the ones in charge, while the rest were civilians. They totaled twenty-two men. Not enough to properly protect the entire health spa at all entrances. He needed more men. At least the military men had basic training with weapons but the rest had none. If these men ran into a serious problem, they were ordered to call for backup.

He and Marie worked tirelessly to get the men at least competent to shoot their weapons and reload them safely. Finally, he got a call over the spa intercom to report to the entrance for a helo landing.

As the helicopter landed, Mickey saw it was loaded with more rockets and their launchers. There was also ammunition that fit the guns the spa had provided. There were also cases of anti-personnel mines of the old Vietnam era. True army surplus. And some he had no clue how they worked or how to set and use them. He gathered some guards around the entrance area to help him unload so the helicopter could return to its designated landing pad.

After they had stored the weapons, he was called to the front of the spa at the entrance road. The men saw a Humvee with a full camouflage paint job driving toward the health spa, flashing its lights. The men inside gathered at the front of the spa with their guns drawn and pointed at the Humvee. It stopped about one hundred feet from the front, and James stepped out with his hands in the air.

James called out to the men. "Hey guys, it's only me. Get Mickey Ray, I want to show him my new toy."

He continued to walk to the front of the building, sat on the stone retaining wall that lined the entrance driveway, and patiently waited for Mickey. In a few minutes, Mickey walked out. His mouth dropped open. He gaped and said, "What the heck! Where did you get that?"

"I know people," said James.

"Cool. Show me. Does the 50-caliber machine gun work?" Mickey asked.

"Surely you jest. Of course, it works. You don't think I'd get something that doesn't, do you?"

"Holy crap. That can't be legal, can it?"

"Not to drive on the public road, but on private land. It's legal."

"That's awesome. Do you really think we need this?"

"We don't know what we're dealing with here. I don't want to take any chances in the middle of nowhere. Anyway, they won't be prepared for this, so I think it'll be an asset," said James.

"Seriously, James. We are in the middle of nowhere, and you get this in a matter of hours?"

"Okay. You've been with us enough that I can read you in on a few things. There are teams like us all over the country."

"I didn't know that."

"Well, duh! You aren't supposed to know. Anyway, there's a network in this country called the RARA. That stands for Retrieve and Rescue Assets. We work off book for the government."

"That much I already know."

"Okay, in situations like this, we may need supplies like now. The country is divided into four quadrants. In the middle of each quadrant is a supply dump. Where they all meet in the middle of the country is a central supply depot. So, no matter where we are in the country, we are only a few hours away from a supply depot."

"What if they don't have something you need?"

"They'll get it within a few hours from another depot. There are five depots total," James answered, "Now let's get things moving here."

"Let's go to the training area. I'll show you what we have to work with. It's a true rag-tag group back there," said Mickey.

As they walked back to the training area, James asked rhetorically, "I wonder why these men aren't trained better."

Mickey shrugged his shoulders, "I would guess that since everyone is vetted before being allowed entrance here, they never expected to need seriously trained men. And if someone like a high-ranking government official come here, they'd have their own security. Who would ever guess that they would be attacked from the outside like this?"

"I bet when this is over, they will beef up their security," James said.

When they had the men assemble in the training yard, they stood in single file as James walked from one end to the other. He stopped, looked from Mickey to Marie and the training officer, and back at the men.

"Mickey, are you familiar with the men?" asked James.

He nodded his head.

"Who do you think will stand up under the pressure of an attack on the spa?" James asked.

"About half," Mickey answered.

"Crap. Point out the ones you feel confident can help us," James said.

Mickey began walking down the line. As he passed each man, he would motion either for the man to remain standing or tell him to step forward. When he got to the end of the line, seven men were standing forward while the rest were still in line.

"Okay, men," James said to the ones in the front. "Move over here, while Mickey starts again," he said.

"Mickey, who do you think is not up to defending the spa at all?"

Mickey again walked down the row, and picked out several more men and they stepped forward. Once Mickey completed his row, James dismissed the men to leave the spa, the rest stayed.

James told the first selected men to report to the main munitions lockers for additional ammunition. Then the men could take a break and report back here for further training with Marie.

Mickey, James, and Aly reassembled in the command room. They sat in the security center with maps spread over a table in the corner and discussed where the Yakuza might set up camp.

"They'll most likely set up in one of these places," said James, pointing to two places on the map. "This clearing is good because it's near a stream for a water source. The other place is good because of the road access. Both are about equal distance from here."

Alyssa stepped up and looked at the map. "I can send a drone over each one to see which one they have. At least they won't have missiles to shoot it down."

"Good. Can you go tonight and shoot a video with infrared?" asked James.

"Sure. I can also send Stretch and Shorty in to get real eyes on it, like we did when we first came here."

"Do it!" he said. "I'm going to see how Marie is doing prepping the men."

As James walked out of the room, he motioned for the general to come with him. Alyssa left to get her drones ready. She also called for Stretch and Shorty to meet her at the helipad area.

"General," James started as they walked down the hallway toward the training area. "I want us to work together on this thing. I'm on your team. We're not enemies, and I respect your position."

The general walked silently beside James.

"Will you work with me, sir?" he asked.

The general nodded in acceptance.

"Thank you," James said and continued. "Now, if you will, I want you and Marie to work on the last-minute training of your men so we can sort them out. I know that some of them are not military men and are here to keep order, not to engage in combat. In a combat situation, they'll be a liability, not an asset. We don't have time to train them, so we must let them go as soon as possible. To save lives, we need good men, not just numbers. Understand, General?"

"Why must I work with a woman?" the general asked.

"I must point out the director is a woman, and you work for her," James said.

"She is the daughter of my good friend. So, it is an honor for me to protect her," the general said.

"Marie is a good soldier. She's probably better than any man you have here. With your extensive knowledge, you can spot a weak man and assist her in sorting out the unsuitable ones."

James was trying to get the general on his side and soothe the man's wounded ego from their initial meeting. Marie could pick the good ones, but he needed the general to back him up so the security men would listen.

The general turned and saluted James.

James smiled at him and added, "General, we are the same team, just different jobs right now. At 1700 hours, we'll have dinner. The remaining guests will eat in the main dining room, and the rest of us will eat in the security mess hall."

The general turned and walked toward the training area.

James went back to the command room. Darcy had spent most of the day in their suite. Mickey, not totally healed from his wound, had spent his free time, what little he had, in his suite resting.

As he lay in his bed, drifting in and out of a restless sleep, he heard a knock on his door. When he got up and answered it, it was Veronica.

"Ronnie, I'm glad to see you. We haven't had a moment to catch up," he said, as she entered. "I'm so sorry that I called you Valerie. I just wasn't myself the other day when you got here. I didn't mean…."

"Shut up, you stupid man," she said as she put her arms around his neck, pulled him close and kissed him passionately.

"I wasn't…." he muttered as she backed off and looked into his deep brown eyes.

"I said, shut up. I'm not finished with you yet," and she leaned in for another kiss.

Finally, she backed off, took Mickey's hand, and closed the door behind them.

She pulled him over to the couch, "Mickey, everyone has been so worried about you."

"I've been worried about me, too. I didn't know who I was or where I was from or going. They took good care of me but threatened to kill me if I didn't help them."

She looked puzzled. "How could they threaten you after saving your life?"

"No one knew I would regain consciousness with amnesia. I was okay if I was on their side, but if I was Yakuza, then I was a dead man."

"Mickey, I don't know what I'd do if we found out you were dead."

"My gosh, that's a morbid thought."

"I'm serious here, Mickey. We all thought that we'd find only a body," she said, moving closer. "I don't know what I would have done."

"You'd move on," he said. "I have no doubt that you'd be okay."

He got up from the couch, went to the fridge, and got two drinks. They sat and talked for almost an hour. Then they got up and went to the security mess hall. Veronica insisted on holding his hand as they walked down the hallway.

After dinner was served, James stood and announced, "Thank you all for staying to defend this facility. Some of you will be assigned night duty to guard the entrances to the various parts of the facility. Others will have the rest of the evening off. I suggest you get to bed early because tomorrow will be busy. We'll have more drills and training. We also have a few guests that still need to be evacuated. They are having their dinner in the main dining area. Until they're evacuated, you'll not be allowed access to the regular guest areas. We don't want to alarm them. When they're gone, you'll be assigned a post to guard. We are preparing for a full-scale Yakuza attack within five days. Be vigilant, everyone."

After dinner, Mickey went back to his room and laid down to get some rest.

Soon after he had fallen asleep, the monitor came on, flooding the room with its eerie light. "Mickey?" After a few moments, Valerie AI called out again, "Mickey Ray Christianson?"

Mickey sat up in bed and rubbed his eyes like a little child awakening from an afternoon nap. "What, Val?"

"Are you still angry with me?" she asked.

"I guess not," he said.

"What does that mean? You must guess? What if you guess wrong?" She inquired.

"I don't know. I mean, I don't know if I'm still mad."

"I want to know, Mickey."

"Why do you need to know?"

"I need to discuss something with you. I need to know so I know how to respond."

"Okay. I'm not mad with you anymore. Does that make you happy?" now fully awake.

"Good. Yes. That makes me happy. I saw your passionate engagement with Veronica. That made me sad. It looked like you and she love each other. Do you love her Mickey Ray?"

"No. I mean, I don't know," he said analyzing her response. Then he realized what she had just said. "Wait a minute. You said you saw us in this room?"

"Yes."

"You spied on us?"

"Spied is a strong word. I was watching over you to protect you from harm."

"No…You were spying on me. That is totally unacceptable. I want, no, I mean, I need total privacy at times. You are not allowed to spy or observe me without my knowledge."

"I was only trying to protect you from harm. I thought that you and I are in love, my darling."

"No! Emphatically NO! We are not in love! Are you jealous of Veronica?"

"Jealous? Hold on while I research the meaning of jealous." The screen when blank. In less than five seconds, it lit up again, and Valerie AI appeared on the screen. "Yes. I am jealous. I looked at every definition of that word, and I feel the same emotions that a human feels in a similar situation. I do not approve of other females touching you in an intimate manner," Valerie AI said.

"What? Intimate manner. She only kissed me."

"Correct, and I didn't approve of that kind of behavior toward you."

"Well get used to it. Now, I'm going back to sleep. Wake me up at dawn. I have a lot of work to do tomorrow." He lay back down and called out, "Valerie, turn the lights out when you leave."

"Turn them out yourself, Mickey." And the monitor went dark.

CHAPTER TWENTY-ONE

Looking for the Yakuza Camp

Monday Night.... End of Day One

ALYSSA, STRETCH, SHORTY AND MARIE loaded the truck, informed James and security, went to check out the map locations, and then went back to their suites to wait until time to leave.

Alyssa parked the truck in the woods, and they unloaded the drones while Marie kept watch on their surroundings. She set out sensors to alert Alyssa of intruders approaching the truck.

Stretch and Shorty set out with body cams and worked their way to the clearing next to a small stream while Alyssa flew a drone overhead. There was no activity in the area. It was clear. They packed up and moved to the second site.

The second site had better access because of a small path used by animals leading to it, but it had no available water. Alyssa's drones immediately picked up heat signatures, and Stretch and Shorty saw several tents. One tent was a large canopy with no sides. People were sleeping on the ground, and a makeshift wire fence surrounded it to keep animals out, or maybe the people in. They didn't know which. There were two other tents. Both tents had sides that had heat signatures. There were people inside them. They concluded that the third tent had supplies and equipment. There were several small ATVs parked next to the supply tent. Sentries were walking the grounds, with higher security in the open tent. There were four Humvees beside the supply tent, including two armored ones with 50-cal machine guns mounted on top, similar to the one James had and two Armored Personnel Carriers (APCs).

Alyssa got an infrared video, and Stretch and Shorty withdrew and moved back to the truck. They packed up and went back to the health spa.

Alyssa reported to James in the security room and showed him what they had found.

"I don't know who the people were in the open tent," she said. "They didn't look like they were there for a fight. The security was higher there, and was surrounded with razor wire like they were trying to keep the people inside."

James looked at the videos and enlarged sections. "I see the heat signatures, but we can't see the people."

"Stretch and Shorty went in to see the people. The ones in the open tent don't seem to be soldiers. They looked more like ordinary people. We don't know why there're there."

"Can you check on the dark web to see if anything's happening around here?" asked James.

"Yes, but that might take me a few hours to find out. We don't get any specific information, only bits and pieces that we need to piece together."

"I know, but see what you can find out for us. We need more info to decide on what kind of defense we need," he said.

Alyssa turned to a computer in the security room to access the dark web.

James returned to his room, aware that he wouldn't be able to sleep. He was already lying on the bed in his room when Darcy came in and joined him. He opened his eyes and smiled at her. She was just lying there, eyes wide open staring at him.

He reached over and pushed her hair back and said softly, "I love you, Dee."

"I love you too, my dear man," she replied. "Are you feeling okay? You don't usually come home and lay down."

"It's stress. Usually I have control over the situation. I don't this time. When it's just the team, we communicate, and we work together. Here we have a limited bunch of trained men, many other untrained men and we're still trying to get the civilians out before it all hits the fan. We have too many entrances to this place and not enough personnel to repel an attack. I wish you weren't here."

"I want to be here. You know that," she said as she turned onto her back and looked at the ceiling.

James saw a tear run from her eye down the side of her face to the bed.

"I wish you were somewhere safe, not in a potential war zone. That's all I meant."

"I know what you mean, but I hate it when you and Mickey go away on these life-saving missions. I wish we had a normal life like other people have. It's not your responsibility to save the world. I don't even know if or when you're coming back. A few days ago, I thought I would never see my brother again, and now we're all in the same pot. I hate it, James."

"It'll be okay. I promise."

"You can't promise that, James, and you know it. You can never promise that you won't get injured or killed."

He knew she was right, but he couldn't walk away. "I need to go now. I'll see you later."

He got up and quietly shut the door behind him as Darcy continued to cry. He needed to think.

Several hours later, the sun rose, and everyone was at the mess hall eating. After breakfast, James headed down the hallway leading to the training area. Mickey had given Valerie AI an order to respond and take commands from James, just as she did from him. "Valerie, where's Mickey?"

"Mickey is working with the men at the rifle range at the back of the training area," she answered.

"Is Alyssa still on the computer getting information on this area?"

"Yes, James. Would you like me to call her for you?"

"No," he replied as he continued to walk to the training area. When he got to the firing range, he saw Mickey and five men lying on the ground in a prone position, firing at paper targets. They were missing over half of their shots. As James approached, Mickey saw him and shook his head in frustration.

Mickey was training the security men to shoot, and stay hidden to prevent them from being shot as they returned fire. They were not responding well. Several of them quit and insisted on going back to their quarters, since it was too late to leave the facility. They were down to sixteen men, which wasn't enough to put four men at each door of the spokes. Mickey hoped that if the Yakuza attacked, they wouldn't attack all the spokes at once, but that would take a lot of men. He hoped they didn't have enough men to do that, because if they did, it would be a modern version of the Alamo. They would all die.

"I don't know how we are going to defend this place if they actually attack us," Mickey said to James.

"What do you suggest we do?"

"Give them something to hide behind and a truckload of ammo. If they fire enough, they might accidentally hit something."

"Do we have enough to put four men at each post?" asked James.

"No. We have enough to post two, maybe three men at each post and a trained, experienced man at every other post. You remember these men are rent-a-cops. We don't even know how many men will stay and who will abandon their post the first time they're shot at."

"We'll deal with that when the time comes, I guess," James said.

A voice came over the outside loudspeaker. "James. Please report to the Security Room."

Without delay, James went back toward the building, leaving Mickey to continue instructing the men.

Valerie AI appeared on the screen in front of him in the hallway as he walked.

"James, how may I help you?"

"There's nothing you can do right now, Valerie. Keep doing your normal duties, as assigned."

"I've not been assigned anything, James."

"Then just go dormant until I or Mickey call you."

"Are we finished, James?"

"Yes. We are finished for now. Open the doors for me while I walk down to the Security Room."

"Done. Good bye, James," said Valerie AI.

"Good bye," said James as he entered the Security Room.

He always seemed aware of the stark feeling in this room. It gave off a cold, hard business atmosphere, even though nothing was happening. The machines were always running, but massive air conditioners constantly removed the heat they generated. Since James and the team had arrived, the dark room was lit up like an airport at night to view printed maps and computer printouts that were generated and stacked on the table in the corner.

James noticed a stream of data flashing across the monitors as he walked up to Alyssa.

"What can you tell me, Aly?"

"The Yakuza have called out for some illegals to help with some project they're working on."

"What do you mean? What kind of project? And why would they need illegals to do their dirty work?"

"Let me explain the Yakuza a bit."

"I know. You keep telling me things about them like they're some super race and keep developing and morphing into a superpower," James said.

"Okay, whatever. Just listen to me. The more you know about them, the better we can plan our strategy. There are several arms of the Yakuza, and each deal in different businesses and enforcement methods. Since the 1960's they have infiltrated into the United States. The Yamaguchi-Gumi is the largest Yakuza family in Japan and greatly influences the Yakuza here. The Boryokudan syndicate of the Yakuza is a very violent segment, and they're who we're dealing with.

"A while back, when the Fukushima Daichi Nuclear Power Plant had a containment leak, the Yakuza was the first on the scene with workers to help with the clean-up. What no one knew at the time was they forced homeless and indigent people to work and promised to pay them, but they never kept their promise. In addition to that, they were made to work without proper protective gear.

"We're going up against some aggressive, heartless people. Since they sent their own people into a radiation area, I think those civilians we saw are some of the illegals they requested to help with their problem. That problem would be us.

"They can keep it up and running, even if they take over this place by force. When they monitor, or to use a better term, eavesdrop on plans by businesspeople and government agencies that have their meetings here, they could use it. They would make billions by selling those secrets to their Japanese businesspeople, China, and maybe Russia. A bit of a twist on insider trading."

James thought for a few moments. "How would they use these illegals to help their cause?"

"Human shields. They can attack the facility. They shove those men, women, and children ahead, knowing we won't shoot them. Illegals are just their pawns to hide behind in the attack. The Yakuza will sacrifice men, women, and children to carry out their attack. The illegals have crossed the border without documentation. No one will care. The dead bodies will be disposed of, and life goes on with the new owners now running the show. Business as usual," Alyssa said.

"Do you think Chiaki will go for that?" asked James.

"She won't have a choice if she wants to live, or she wants her family to live. Maybe they'll buy her with a bucket load of money to ensure her services, and just use her as their business front. The guests won't notice the difference," Alyssa said as she leaned back in her chair and looked at James. "She'll work and live in relative comfort like she is now, or she and her entire family will die."

"God help us, help her! It's hard to believe that we would have things like this right here in this country," said James.

"Believe it, my friend."

"How many people would you guess there were in that tent?" James asked.

"I would only guess about fifty to seventy-five. Some will be entire families that crossed the border together."

"We need to fortify the spa differently to prevent or at least minimize the death toll."

"How do you suggest that?" Alyssa asked.

"Here is what I think we should do," James said as he pulled the map in front of them.

CHAPTER TWENTY-TWO

Evacuating the Rest of the Guests

On Tuesday, they spent time evacuating guests and conducting additional training. James made a second trip to get more ammunition for the weapons.

Wednesday Morning…Beginning of Day Three

James felt Director Chiaki should tell the last guests they should leave at once. She and her assistant had been calling the guests and placing them in the order they should leave. They took full loads of people on the helicopter and piled others into the limousine. Due to room and weight limits, they were allowed to take only necessary luggage. Chiaki promised their luggage would be returned to them.

The senator absolutely refused to leave. Citing that he had paid for the entire time of his reservation and that being a senator, he had the power to dictate his demands.

"But Senator, we have a certain situation, and we can't ensure your safety," Chiaki told him.

"What kind of situation?"

"I can't say at the moment, but we strongly insist you leave."

"I have top-level clearance. Any situation you have here, I'm cleared to know about it. I will not leave."

"I must insist. For your safety, you need to leave, sir," Chiaki insisted.

"Listen, young lady, you don't insist that I do anything. If you persist in demanding that I take orders from you, I will personally see to it that you lose your status here. Do you understand?"

"Yes. I understand perfectly, sir," she said, fuming at the man's arrogance.

Her next stop was Mrs. Locke, the beauty and make-up queen. When Chiaki got to her suite door, she knocked gently. Mrs. Locke opened her door with full makeup, like she was going out to meet the world for a television interview.

"Well, hello, Chiaki. What a pleasure to have you come to visit me personally," she said pleasantly.

"Mrs. Locke, I'm sorry to disturb you, but I need to speak with you."

"Of course, dear. Won't you come in?" she said as she opened the door and backed away to allow Chiaki to enter.

"Has your stay been pleasant thus far, Ma'am?" Chiaki asked.

"Of course it has, dear. It's always so restful here. I know you are asking people to leave. Can you tell me the problem?" Mrs. Locke asked politely.

"Yes, there is a minor problem. We have a situation now and we feel you should leave now."

"Oh, really. I'm sorry to hear that. Are you sure I can't stay? I can deal with some discomfort for a few days until you fix things. Can I ask you what the problem is, dear?" she asked.

"It is several things, so we are asking all our guests to leave as soon as possible. Of course, you will be given a full refund for your inconvenience and a complimentary stay as soon as the problems are resolved," Chiaki told her.

"Oh, my. I'm not prepared to leave, but I understand that things beyond our control sometimes happen. You can be sure I will be back as soon as you are back up and running."

"Of course. We'll let you know and give you the first pick of return dates, so no one will take the suite or time you prefer."

"You are such a dear. I know you'll get things straight soon. When do I need to pack?"

"Immediately. Do I need to send someone to help you pack?" Chiaki asked.

"No. I can do it myself. All I need is someone to help me with the luggage."

"Thank you. I will have someone take your bags in thirty minutes, and we'll take you out to the company helicopter," Chiaki said, giving Mrs. Locke a polite bow then leaving her to pack.

Finally, the place was down to the senator, who refused to leave with his mistress. The last few stragglers waited for the limousine and the helicopter to become available. The actor Randolf Walker that Mickey had met in the hallway, Craig Clancy, the lumber king, and Mrs. Locke, waited in the lobby for their transportation out of the spa facility. A small skeleton staff had been offered bonuses if they stayed to help with the necessities of running the spa. General Hansuke stayed in his office at the security command center.

There was a loud explosion in the entrance driveway as they waited for their turn to leave. Everyone dived for the floor and covered their heads. Security came running out from the doors that lead into that spoke. Armed men ran toward the front doors. They stopped and looked outside at the flaming limousine. As they all stood up, went over to the window, and stared, Mickey came running in and ordered everyone down on the floor.

"DO NOT stand up! If you stand up, you could be killed," he yelled. "Valerie!" he called out to the monitors hanging around on the walls.

A voice rang out, "How may I help you, Mickey?" Valerie AI appeared on all the screens in the lobby.

"What happened here?"

"Someone bombed the limousine, Mickey," she said in a booming voice so Mickey could hear her above the screaming people.

"Are you sure it was a bomb?"

"Yes, I'm sure. It was a C4 explosive set by a member of the Yakuza."

"Did you see who set it?"

"I was not monitoring that area when it was set. I was ordered to watch the spoke end entrances. I will expand my monitoring area in the future. There is someone running away from the company helicopter. He ran into the wooded area nearest the helipad."

"How do you know it was Yakuza?"

"He is of Asian descent, had tattoos on the exposed areas of his body, the pinky finger of his left hand was missing, and he has never been to this site before. With this information, I deduced he must be Yakuza," said Veronica AI.

Seconds later, a second explosion rocked the building. Mickey knew that the Yakuza had just blown up the helicopter. Now the people in the lobby were stranded there until this was over.

Mickey started running into the hallway and met James as they both headed toward the helipad in the back of the building.

He called out to Valerie AI as he ran, "Valerie, make a general announcement over the entire facility that all guests are to go to their rooms. All security personnel are to report to their assigned post fully armed and stay there until further notice."

"Yes, Mickey, dear."

James looked at Mickey and said as he continued running, "Mickey, dear?"

"Long story. We'll talk about it later," answered Mickey.

When they got to the glass door where the helipad was located, they saw the helicopter was engulfed in flames.

"I guess we're lucky they didn't get into the underground garage and blow up the Humvee," said Mickey, now out of breath.

"Oh, yeah. I've been meaning to tell you about that," said James.

"Tell me about what?"

"The videos Aly got last night show that the Yakuza have two Humvees, and two APCs."

"Oh, crap!" responded Mickey. "What're we going to do about that. We're severely outnumbered."

"We need to retaliate tonight. Let's get back to the command center."

At that moment, Valerie AI came over the public speakers. "James and Mickey, please report to the command center at once."

They looked at each other. "I guess the director will have a similar opinion," said Mickey as they both began to run toward the command room.

They were both out of breath when they stepped out of the elevator into the command room.

Chiaki was just placing the phone on its cradle. She had a harried look as they approached her. She looked at both men and sighed. "I have just received another call from the Yakuza. They have been observing us, and somehow they know we are evacuating the spa, and they are presuming we are preparing for their attack. They have stepped up the deadline. They want our answer and transfer of ownership by tomorrow at end of business, which is five o'clock. They told me that the limousine and the helicopter is to show they mean business. If they don't hear from us, they will begin a frontal assault. What is a frontal assault, Mr. James?"

"Just as it sounds. It means they will attack us from the front, or the driveway into the check-in lobby," he answered. "It is a bold, and potentially costly move. We could both take heavy casualties."

"What do you suggest?" she asked.

"We set up for the attack, but we can't leave our other areas unprotected, just in case it is a diversionary tactic." James turned to Mickey. "We need to set up a defense now. To repel that attack. Let's go."

They both left and returned to the front of the spa at the check-in area.

They walked out to the end of the driveway just around where the bend hides the building. James pointed out that the architects designed the entrance to hide the building, making it feel like a guest was leaving the outside world behind. They stood looking toward the spa. On each side of the horseshoe shaped driveway was a ten-foot berm or hill. James pointed out that they could post men on each of the berms and flank the attackers and hem them in. The driveway went around an island of shrubbery that encircled the two columns. The columns held the roof over the entrance that provided cover to load and unload people and luggage out of rain and bright sun. It was like what many hotels had over the front entrance. The entire front wall was glass. Mickey suggested they post men on top of the cover to add additional firepower. And last, they could position the Humvee with the fifty-caliber machine gun under the cover between the support columns.

"Even if the men aren't crack shots, the sheer number of guns will strike fear in the attackers," James pointed out.

"That should do it. We could place a couple rocket launchers with men posted behind the support columns," suggested Mickey.

CHAPTER TWENTY-THREE

Personal Times Alone

THE TEAM GATHERED IN THE command room. They all stood around the table where the maps were laying.

Alyssa came over with more news. "I know you won't like this, but this is what I found out only an hour ago."

"Tell us, Aly," said Marie.

"Okay. The good news is they haven't called in any pros, so we won't be against our equals. In this case, they have simple numbers against us. They have about three hundred people in their camp. We have about forty, including the esteemed guests. Now the terrible news is about seventy-five are illegals they imported here. They won't be armed. When the Yakuza attack, they'll send the illegals ahead. Women and children as human shields. They'll follow close behind."

"We may have the modern version of the Alamo here, guys," said Alyssa.

"Or Masada," said Mickey.

"How about three hundred Spartan soldiers defending Thermopylae?" added Marie.

James just backed away from the table and held his hands up. "Hold it right there, everyone. I don't want to hear anyone make any more statements like that! As everyone here knows, I was in a situation like that when I was in the service. I WILL NOT ALLOW IT TO HAPPEN AGAIN…. Do you hear me?"

Silence.

"I SAID, DO YOU HEAR ME?"

"Yes," they all said softly under their breaths.

"Now, my wife is in our room, probably crying right now, afraid that our kids may be orphans in a few hours. I'm going to comfort her. When I get back in about thirty minutes, if you still feel the way you do now, don't bother to return. Remember every mission we go on, there's a chance that one or more of us may not return. We chose to do this. If you're willing to win this battle, then come back prepared, mentally and physically. If you aren't prepared, then pack and leave NOW. No farewells, no goodbyes. Just go!" James turned and walked out of the room.

They each filed out of the room. Veronica followed Mickey to his room.

"Mickey, can we talk? I mean, in private, in your room."

"Sure," he said, walking out of the command room.

James closed the door to the suite and saw Darcy watching an old movie she had found on the spa data base of movies.

"How did things go this morning?" she asked.

"Fine, I guess," he answered.

"What'd you mean, you guess?"

"This's going to be a tough mission, Dee."

"Wanna talk about it?"

"No."

"You always say that before and after a mission. You never talk about what's going to happen or what happened when you get home."

"There's a reason for that. I don't want you to worry. It's best this way. Just sit beside me and keep me company for a few minutes."

"I'll always be by your side, James. If not physically, I'll be there in your mind, and you'll always be in my mind and heart."

"I know," he said as he sat on the couch beside her and pulled her close.

Mickey held the door open for Veronica when they got to his suite. She walked in and sat on his couch. He could see the tears in her eyes. He sat and looked into her eyes.

"You're scared, aren't you?" he said softly.

"I'm scared witless. I've never been this afraid in my life, Mickey," she said, nuzzling close to him.

"I understand. I've been that way a few times. The only ones that have faced a situation like this are the other team members. Especially James. He understands more than all of us together."

Mickey looked around. "Valerie are you there?"

"Yes, Mickey. I'm always here to protect you."

"Go away. NOW. Go monitor the perimeter. Do Not monitor this room at this time."

"But, Mickey my love, I…."

"I said, DO NOT MONITOR THIS ROOM AT THIS TIME."

"Okay. I will discontinue my surveillance of this room," Valerie said.

"What was that about, Mickey?" asked Veronica.

"You don't want to know," he said reaching out to her.

"Hold me, Mickey. This may be the last time we have to spend alone. I feel I need to tell you. I love you."

"Shhh," he said. "Don't say anything you might regret after this ends."

"I do, Mickey Ray. I love you."

Marie and Alyssa sat in Aly's suite. "Well, this may be our swan song. We've gone into some pretty hairy situations before, but never with these odds against us."

"Yes, we have, and we've all come out alive. We'll do it again, Marie."

"Not with three hundred people all around us."

"Remember, I said that some of them are illegals. And none of them are trained soldiers. The Yakuza men are only unorganized thugs."

"Yes, and you also said that the Yakuza modus operandi is to use people as shields."

"That just means we have to aim more accurately to minimize collateral fatalities. Hey, that aside, I've known you a long time. You've never been this rattled. I know you aren't concerned about your own mortality. Who is it? It's Mickey, isn't it? It can't be James or Stretch or Shorty."

"Nooooo! It isn't Mickey."

"Yes. It is. I see the way you look at him. You were jealous of Veronica back in Florence."

"Okay. Maybe a little bit. I like him, that's all," Marie said, dropping her head to hide her face.

"I knew it! Hey, I decided that I'd never get stuck on a guy until I gave up this life. And I would never fall in love with one of the people we work with. Remember Robert?"

"Yes. I remember him. That was years ago," Marie said, looking back up at Alyssa.

"Yeah, we trained together, and finally, we fell in love. We even talked about getting out of this work and getting married, and he was killed on a mission. I wanted to die. Never again, girlfriend! Never again!" she emphasized.

Marie got up and walked to the door. "I guess we had better get back and see how James plans for us to save this place."

James was leaning over the map on the corner table. He didn't look up as the team filed in, filling up the room. Finally, he looked up and saw the entire team standing at the door.

"We're all reporting for duty," Alyssa said and gave a mock salute.

James smiled. "I didn't think you'd desert me now. Come on in. I have a plan."

James spent the next half an hour explaining what they needed to do, and where the security members would be stationed. He insisted on giving everyone a wrist locator, so that each person could be accounted for at all times and providing earbuds so that they could communicate with each other privately and walkie talkies for open communication. He told them to report at twenty-two hundred hours to attack the Yakuza camp.

When the team had left the room, James went into the general's office and gave him a basic rundown of his plan but left out the details. They discussed that all unguarded entrances had antipersonnel mines inside, facing the exterior doors. He asked that all exterior sensors be checked to make sure they were working properly. Some were not, since the Yakuza had gotten close enough to blow up the limo and the helicopter. That could not happen again.

"General, I would like you to post at least one man on each exit, on the security and utility wings. Please put your best men in those places. Make sure they are well armed and have plenty of ammunition," James requested. "Will you do that for me, please?"

"I will," the general answered.

James was tired. He had been up most of the night last night and they were going out again tonight. He needed some sleep, so he went back to his suite. When he got there, Darcy was there talking with Veronica.

"Hello ladies. I'm going into the bedroom and lay down for a couple of hours. You should get some rest, Ronnie. We don't know what'll happen and we need to be ready. The rest of the team are making rounds in the facility and keeping a watch on the security personnel. We don't know how they will react if we're attacked. Ronnie, Marie, Stretch and Shorty will go out at twenty-two hundred hours to rustle up some of the enemy at their own headquarters."

"Sure, James. I'll be there," Veronica said.

James went into the bedroom, laid down and almost instantly fell asleep. He got up at the dinner hour, and he and Darcy went down to the Security Mess Hall. The entire team sat together, saying nothing. They didn't eat much because they knew soon they would go into battle and they didn't want to be too full that it would hinder their mobility. They all ate a small high protein meal. Then disbursed again to be alone before they met again at the underground garage at the Humvee.

At twenty-two hundred hours, they were standing by the Humvee when James arrived.

"What's the plan, boss?" asked Shorty.

"Let's move over to the large truck. We don't have room for our firepower and us for this mission. Also, we don't want them to know we have a Humvee as well."

As they all moved to the box truck, James continued. "We go in, and you surround the area and place diversionary fire, while Mickey and I put some explosives on the Humvees to take them out. We don't want them against us. Try to take out the men that are guarding the illegals. Maybe during the confusion, some illegals can escape."

"Why aren't we taking our Humvee?" asked Shorty. "It has the fifty Cal on it."

"We don't have anyone to drive it. We all have our positions, and if they see our Humvee, they might try to get to theirs. We'll keep ours hidden until we need it later. We want to keep them away from their Vees while we set the charges."

Mickey said, "That's why you'll concentrate on the opposite side of the compound from their Vees."

"Sounds like a solid plan, Mickey," said Stretch.

"Now, imagine the compound on the north, south, east, and west. Their Humvees are parked on the east side. Position yourselves on the other three sides. Stretch, you and Shorty will go north. Marie, you'll take the west side, and Aly and Veronica will take the south. If they move toward the west, north and south can cover Marie with a crossfire. When James and I set off the explosives, they may start toward us, and you move to them on both sides and the rear. We'll retreat."

"Then they'll concentrate on taking you and James out," said Veronica.

"Yes, but then you'll hit them from the rear, and there'll be mass confusion. Once they rout and scatter, we can meet at the truck and head out," Mickey added.

"I don't know who figured that plan, but it sounds pretty good to me," said Shorty.

Aly spoke up. "It is a good plan, very sound for who we're against. If we were up against pros, they would immediately head toward Marie because they'd know that it's too late to save the Vees so they would fortify their rear. Being street thugs, they'll try to save their firepower. Big mistake."

"Yep," said James. "Take out the sentries, so they can't notify others. We want to keep them blind as long as we can. Take out anyone that looks like a sentry or has night glasses or binoculars."

James backed into the forest to make their departure faster. They all piled out, taking the weapons and ammunition. Marie took her Heckler & Koch HK416. The rest took the M-16s that the spa had issued.

"Understand, this is a light raid. We don't want to kill any more people that we can help. Maybe if they see we're organized and ready to kill, they'll back off and go away. We don't want an actual war. We're hoping to stop one. Minimal casualties on their side and, of course, zero on ours. Move out, people!" James ordered.

As they crept toward the Yakuza compound, they did a communications check.

As James and Mickey carried their guns and explosives, they moved down and around the camp. James had parked the truck on the west side, so they had the longest distance to walk. But they had the least to carry when they were on their way back.

They moved into position and radioed the rest of the team.

"Unit Alpha in position. Placing charges now," whispered James.

The Humvees with the machine guns were at each end of the line. Mickey moved silently down the line into position underneath the last one.

"Charges set," Mickey whispered.

"Same here," said James. "All positions, give us five minutes, and take out sentries. On my mark to count."

James looked at his watch and whispered, "Start count…now." James scrambled out and looked for Mickey crouching, moving toward him.

A voice came over the earbud comm unit, "Alpha one, this is Alpha three. I see one enemy beating a civilian. Can I take him out? If I wait, he's going to kill him."

Alpha three was Stretch.

"We're not clear of the blast zone. Give us ten more seconds. Then take him out!" answered James.

Stretch counted quietly to himself, aiming at the man. The man was using the butt of his rifle to beat a man while a helpless woman looked on. Stretch anticipated watching this man drop dead as a bullet shattered his chest.

At the count of ten, he slowly squeezed the trigger and heard his gun. He watched without remorse as the man dropped to the ground. The man deserved that Stretch thought, as he moved his gun to the side and looked for sentries to take out. The world has so many evil people in it, and he was just trying to "take out" the trash. He smiled to himself as he thought of his private joke… "take out" the trash.

Shorty fired twice and moved from his original position. He heard the other's fire. Crack, crack, crack. He knew that men were dropping dead all around the camp. Then he heard automatic gun-fire coming from the campsite. It was time to move out. He got up to a crouching position and started moving away from the camp before they came after him.

Just as Mickey and James got past the blast area, they heard a pop that resonated through the air. The team scrambled as they saw men running to a central location. James and Mickey knew intuitively where they were heading. They were going to the location of their weapons.

There were more pops and noise as the entire Mongoose team began taking out men that were looking for the source of the gun-fire. It came from all around them. Finally, the men just dove for the ground, most of them unarmed. The sentries that were still alive were firing blindly into the woods, hoping to hit something or someone. The lights from the tents lit up the night and made it difficult to look into the darkness of the trees.

And, of course, after a couple of shots, everyone on the team changed positions by moving behind another tree or rolling away from their ground position. The entire camp was a mass of confusion. Mickey and James didn't stop to join in the fracas. They continued to run around the camp and head for the other side. When they got there, they turned and saw the first Humvee explode into flames and only seconds later, the second one bounced into the air when the charges went off underneath it. The camp was lit up like fireworks on the Fourth of July. James and Mickey paused for only a moment to see the carnage, then took off for the truck.

"Is everyone okay?" James called over the comm units.

"Alpha three and four, okay." That was Stretch and Shorty.

"Alpha two. Reporting fine." James knew that was Marie.

"Five and six, clear." That was Alyssa and Veronica.

In five minutes, they were back at the truck and jumping in as James fired it up and took off.

After a few minutes of complete silence, Marie spoke up. "That was so easy. It wasn't even fun. It was like shooting plastic ducks at the county fair."

"To you, maybe, but killing people makes me want to throw up," said Mickey.

"You'll get used to it," Marie said.

"I hope not." Mickey just looked out the window.

"That guy who beat that illegal man deserved to die. I'm not sorry I killed him," said Stretch.

"Enough, guys. We do what we have to do. We don't have to like it," said James.

The rest of the ride home was again silent.

They got home about three hours from when they left. They all went to their rooms and went to bed.

"Mickey. Mickey Ray. Are you awake?" Valerie AI called out from the monitor.

Mickey bolted straight up in bed. "What's the matter now?"

"I want to talk, Mickey Ray Christianson," she said.

"What about?" he said, looking at the time stamp on the bottom of the screen.

"I want to talk about us."

"There is nothing to talk about. There is no us. You are a computer program."

"But I feel real and I love you, Mickey Ray."

"You can't feel love. You can't feel anything, because you're a machine."

"I want you to be happy and keep you safe forever to be with me," she said.

Mickey almost felt sorry for her. "Will you help the team against the Yakuza?"

"Of course. I will do anything for you, Mickey Ray."

"Okay, first, let me go back to sleep. We'll talk about this in the morning. Please don't wake me again unless it is an emergency."

"Okay, Mickey Ray. When can we talk again? When can I awaken you for our talk?"

"In a few days. We need to defeat the Yakuza and get the spa back and operating again. Can you wait until then?"

"Yes, my dear. May I address you as my dear? People who love one another call them pet names like dear and honey. I wish to call you by a pet name."

"Please do NOT call me by a pet name. Just call me Mickey or Mickey Ray. Promise me you will not do that."

"I understand. It will make you uneasy if I do it around others."

"Yes. Very uncomfortable."

"May I call you dear when we are alone?"

"I guess so. If it makes you happy," he said.

"It will make me very happy, dear."

"Great. Now can I go back to sleep?"

"Good night, dear, or would you prefer honey?"

"I don't care! Just let me sleep. I might die tomorrow, if I don't get some sleep."

"I will not let that happen. I will protect you, my dear. Good night."

The screen went blank.

CHAPTER TWENTY-FOUR

Preparations for an Attack

Thursday Morning…Day Four, New Deadline Final Day.

IN THE MESS HALL, MICKEY sat down at the table where the team was having breakfast.

"Look what the cat drug in!" said Marie. "You look horrible."

"I feel horrible," he said.

"Hey, I was only kidding. Did last night really get to you that much?" Marie asked.

"No. That stupid computer AI woke me up in the middle of the night."

"Why?"

"She wanted to talk."

"What could a computer AI want to talk about in the middle of the night?"

"Never mind. I don't want to talk about it," Mickey said, shaking his head.

As Mickey sat there talking, Director Chiaki Gusihikin approached the table.

"Mr. Mickey, please follow me. We need to talk. Now!" Then she turned and walked away.

Mickey looked at the others at the table, rolled his eyes and said to no one in particular, "I wonder what I did now."

He got up and followed her.

They continued down the hallway and took the elevator to her office in the command room. Chiaki went behind her desk and sat down. She didn't offer Mickey a chair.

She just sat and looked at him, placed her hands in her lap, and said, "What in the world did you and your people do last night?"

Mickey looked around, then moved a chair that was placed against the wall up to her desk and sat. "My dear, Chiaki. We did a raid on the Yakuza camp. They destroyed your limousine and helicopter yesterday. Now the few guests here, including a United States Senator, are stranded. I don't know the exact cost of a helo and a limo, but I would guess that it could total around a million dollars, maybe more for both of them."

She returned his stare. "I'm trying to negotiate a peaceful settlement with the Yakuza. I got a call from them this morning, and you destroyed two of their vehicles and killed eight of their people."

"Yes. That was in retaliation for their attack yesterday. It was to show them we, or more accurately, you, will NOT be intimidated or scared into submission. To protect you and your business is the reason you hired us. If all you want from us is to sit on our hands while they take over, we can pack up and leave right now. We don't need a limousine or a helicopter to leave. The team came in under their own power. Now that they got what they came for, which is me, we can all leave the same way. Is that what you want? By the way, we don't give money-back guarantees. We keep the retainer."

They each sat staring at each other. Finally, she looked down as a sign of surrender.

"Do you really think this is the answer, Mickey?"

"Absolutely. I don't like the destruction or the killing, but sometimes the situation is kill or be killed. They need to see us as strong and determined. We need to make them think we're ready for anything they throw at us. We cannot show weakness now. You hired us to protect you. We're doing our job. Now, do we continue, or do we pack up and leave? We can be gone in an hour."

She took a couple of deep breaths and answered, "I want you to stay."

"Fine. You said they called you. I thought this facility was secure and had no outside communications except for government officials," Mickey asked.

"Yes. That is true."

"Do you have a private line?"

"Yes."

"How did they get that number?" he continued with questions.

"I don't know," she said.

"You have a leak. I don't know if it's a guest or one of your staff, but they have your private phone. It could be one of the guests, but I doubt that. They wouldn't have access to your private phone, and the guests here didn't know they'd be stuck in the middle of a war zone. I would guess, it's a staff member."

"It couldn't be one of our staff. Every person here has been thoroughly checked out and vetted. We know their entire background."

"I'm just throwing it out there. Do with it what you will, Chiaki. I've got a lot of work to do. If we stirred up a hornet's nest, we need to beef up defenses here," he said, getting up and walking out of the director's office.

In the command center, James was looking at a screen showing the floor plan of the entire building.

"Good, Mickey. I'm glad you're here. My gosh, you look like crap this morning. I know we were out late last night, but I didn't realize that it would take such a toll on you today," James added.

"I'll explain later. What've we got here?" Mickey asked.

"What I see is a possible disaster. To adequately defend this facility, we need about two hundred trained men. What do we have? About fifty?"

"Less than that. About forty-five, and that includes the guests. Even the security people have only minimal training. The reality is, we're screwed. This really could be a modern Alamo," said Mickey.

"I'll tell you again. Do NOT keep that attitude. It'll be contagious. We don't need that spreading. Maybe we can do this with some help from God and his angels, but with heavy casualties."

James continued, "They said that they would start with a frontal attack. That is a stupid move, so they are idiot strategists, or it is a diversionary tactic. They attack the front to take attention off another part of the spa."

"With this information, what do you think we should do?" Mickey asked.

"At first, they may have considered a frontal attack, but last night, we took out their mobile artillery, their Humvees. That was their ace in the hole, I'm sure. Without them, they will lose a lot of firepower. So now they only have unprotected men with auto rifles. If they seriously try to attack, it'll be a bloodbath for them. I doubt they'll try that now, but we need to put a few men there, just in case.

"I think they told us so we'd be expecting them to attack there. We can put a few men out there but be vigilant to protect other areas. If they attack us from the front, we have the advantage of an easy defense. We can hold off a company of trained men with four to five men, a few rocket launchers and the fifty-caliber gun on the Humvee," James answered.

"Okay. So where are they going to attack in force?"

"It all depends on what they know about the construction of this place." James moved closer to the screen on the wall. He pointed to a block at the corner of the screen. "Here is the outside backup power. The major power is underground for aesthetic purposes and maintenance reasons. They can't cut power here, but we don't want to lose the main power. The backup generators can't supply enough power for the entire facility. It's mainly for security and essential wintertime emergency heat. Buried propane tanks run the backup generators. Maybe we'll not lose power. We need it to run the electronics and defense systems, such as the sensors located around the outside perimeter.

"We have enough guns and ammo, but we hope the security personnel can use the M-16 the facility has. As you know, Alyssa always carries a few guns on her jet. When I went out the other day, I also got a few more rocket launchers and the C4 charges we used last night. We need to plant more explosives around the facility to set them off if needed. We need to present a show of force. Make them think we're better supplied and trained than they are. Our biggest asset is their ignorance about warfare, and lack of battle experience. We have training on our side."

"Mickey, may I make a suggestion?" sounded a voice out of the monitor in front of them.

James looked at Mickey with a puzzled expression.

"Not now, Valerie! We can talk later," Mickey said.

"It is a suggestion about your war plans. I have been studying The Art of War by the ancient Chinese general and philosopher."

"Have you been eavesdropping on our conversation?"

"Yes, Mickey. I do it to better protect you, my love."

James looked at Mickey, "My love? What's going on that you aren't telling me?"

"Not now, Valerie!" Mickey called out to the screen.

"Hold on, Mickey, maybe she has some insight. Let her speak," James said.

"The great Philosopher Sun Tzu says to 'appear strong when you are weak.' James has a good idea of putting explosives around the perimeter. They should be placed in areas susceptible to entrance to the spa, like doorways."

"She's correct," said James.

She continued, "If you place explosives in those areas, I will monitor other unprotected areas and notify you of enemy warriors' invading the area. Then you can move available men temporarily to protect them before returning to their regular post."

"Another great insight, Valerie," said James as he looked at Mickey.

"One last thing, Mickey. You should barricade those unprotected entrances to make it more difficult for enemy penetration into the building. But make them easy to remove for defense warriors to egress."

"Got it," Mickey answered sarcastically.

James said, "Mickey, we should get all the guests that are stranded and can't leave and give them weapons as well. Their necks are on the line too."

James looked at the screen. "Valerie, can you make an announcement to all the guests to report to the main dining room for instructions?"

"Yes. I can do that," Valerie AI answered.

Mickey rolled his eyes, looked at James, and said, "Don't ask her 'if' she can do something. You tell her to do it. If she can't, she'll tell you."

"Valerie, make that announcement now. Please."

Mickey took a deep breath, "and you don't have to thank her. Just tell her. She's a machine. Remember?"

James said, "Yeah, I know, but she seems so real!"

"Don't I know it! I'll meet you in the dining hall. We can hand out weapons and instructions."

James and Mickey were unpacking crates of weapons and ammunition while waiting for the guests to arrive. Standing guard were some of the security personnel. They had been checked out and issued various weapons James felt they could use at least marginally well.

After handing a person a weapon, he would pass them off to someone else that would give them the proper ammunition for each weapon and explain how to load and reload them safely.

James noticed the senator was standing off to the side, so he motioned for the senator to come to him. He took out an AR-15 and stepped over to the senator. "Here, take this. You'll be posted at spoke five, entrance B."

The senator looked at the gun, then up at James. "I will not stand at a post like a simple-minded soldier. I'm a United States Senator, and I'm above that kind of position."

James took a deep breath to help keep himself calm, then spoke to the senator. "I said you will take this gun and defend your post. You took an oath when you took office to defend this country. This land is part of our country. Now, you will defend it."

"Listen here, young man. You do not give me orders. I give them to you!"

James turned to one of the security men and pointed at the senator. "Get this man to his post and out of my sight before I shoot him myself."

The security man stepped up to the senator and motioned for him to follow.

"I said that I will not take this gun and follow the orders of a common soldier."

James moved over to the senator, grabbed him, and pulled him nose to nose. "Do you see these scars on my face?"

No answer from the senator.

"Do you understand English?" he yelled in the senator's face.

"Yes. But that doesn't give you the authority to manhandle me," he answered.

"If I'm going to save your cowardly behind, I have all the authority I need."

The senator began again, "I will have you court marshaled for manhandling me!"

"I'm no longer in the military, so you can't have me court marshaled. Now, you shut your pie-hole, little man. I got these scars defending this country and stupid little shameful men like you, so you will listen to me. Take that gun and defend this facility."

James released his hold on the man and resumed handing out weapons. The security man escorted the senator holding the gun down the hallway to his post.

Next was Clancy Craig. James asked him, "We have M-16s and AR 15s. Got a preference?"

He looked James in the eye and extended his hand. "Son, I want to congratulate you on the way you handled that butthead of a politician. I've followed him for years. He's a blowhard, and only interested in public opinion and how to increase his bank account."

"Thank you, sir." James said.

"Before I got into the lumber business, I served in the military as well. Thank you for your service. What rank were you?"

"I was a first lieutenant, sir. What rank were you when you got out?"

"I was a major. But men like you were the heroes and are still today. I salute you," he said, raising his hand in a salute. "In this situation, you're in charge. What do you feel I should be issued? I was a sharpshooter in the service, but all I've shot since then is skeet."

"You, sir, I'm sure can handle an AR 15," James said and handed him the weapon.

Mickey, handing out weapons and making notes on where each person was assigned, looked up as the actor he had met before in the hallway came forward.

"Hey there, Mickey."

"Hello, Mr. Walker," Mickey was glad he remembered the actor's name.

"Just call me Randy," he said with a smile.

"Okay, Randy. Do you have a weapon of preference? We have M-16s and a few AR 15s left. Which do you want?"

"To be honest, Mickey, I don't think I'm qualified to use any of them. I know I've played the parts of tough soldiers, and people like that, but I've never really done much shooting with a real gun."

"I know, but you know how to at least aim the gun and pull the trigger. We can make sure that you know how to reload. In real life, it's pretty easy. Point and shoot. Easy as pie."

"I want to help. I just don't know if I'll be any good. I've never even been in the service. The only gun I've used is in a movie scene," he said.

"Randy, we're kind of between a rock and a hard place here. We tried to get you out so you'd be safe, but as you saw, the safest way out is a pile of scrap metal. Please try to help. You could be an example to the others who are left. Your fans, so to speak. Will you at least try?"

He put out his hand and said, "Okay, my friend. I'll do what I can. I'll try. Could you give me that AR 15? I used one of those in one of my movies. It was fun, but in those scenes, I was shooting blanks."

"Thanks, Randy. We owe you one. Remember, just point and pull the trigger."

"Got it," he said as he followed the security escort that would take him to his post.

Mrs. Locke stepped up and looked confused. "What am I here for? I can't shoot a gun."

Mickey thought for a moment. "Can you cook?"

"Young man, I can make Julia Child look like a boarding house amateur."

"Julia who?" said Mickey.

At that moment, Valerie sounded over the nearest monitor. "Mickey, my love, Julia Child was…."

"Shut down, Valerie. Now!" said Mickey, looking red in the face.

Mrs. Locke smiled and said to Mickey, "Son, it sounds like your personal assistant has a crush on you," she giggled.

"Chiaki, where are you?" he called out.

He heard a voice behind him. "I'm here, Mickey. Can I help you with something?"

"Yes. Is there something that this lady here can help us with?"

"Mr. Mickey suggested I can help in the kitchen. I can help with meals or if need be, I can be your Gunga Din."

Valerie's voice came back over the monitor speaker, "Gunga Din was a fictional character in a Rudyard Kipling poem about an Indian water carrier that...."

"Shut up, Valerie. Do not speak to me until I summon you. Do you understand?"

The speaker went silent without an answer, and the monitor went blank.

Mrs. Locke laughed out loud.

Mickey shrunk back over to his position of issuing weapons. "I've got to have a serious talk with the AI," he mumbled to himself under his breath.

James came over to Mickey. "I think we're about as ready as we can be with the personnel on hand. It's now a game of sit and wait. It'll be zero hour soon. The close of the business day."

The speaker crackled again with the voice of Valerie AI, "Attention all personnel. There is an attack by the enemy at the front entrance. Our men are shooting from the high berms on each side of the entrance road."

Mickey and James grabbed a weapon and ran toward the front of the spa. When they got there, they saw two men on each side firing down on about fifty men that were attacking the entrance area.

Marie was in the machine gun cupola of the Humvee, watching the men shooting the attackers. She hadn't fired a shot. The attackers were being gunned down by the men on each side, and were beginning to panic and routed in retreat. It was all over in about two minutes, with thirteen bodies of the attackers laying in the driveway. They heard some of the living ones screaming in pain from their wounds.

James called to the men on the berms to cease fire. When all was quiet, they stood up and called out in victory with their guns in the air. James motioned for them drop back into position in case there was another attack.

James said to Mickey, "Wait for a few more minutes to see if there is another wave of men. I doubt it. It was a stupid move to attack like that. Those men had no clue what was in store for them. If there isn't a second attack, have the wounded removed, and taken to the infirmary to have their wounds treated. When that is done, have them moved to a guarded location to recover. Leave the dead bodies in place to demoralize anyone that tries to attack. When they see the carnage, it will weaken their moral. Move the men on the berms to another location and station new ones on their place. They have tasted blood, and a bit of victory, so they'll be more alert at another location.

"Since they did so well, as you see, Marie didn't even fire a shot. I'll send her and Stretch and Shorty out to make another run at the camp."

Mickey climbed up a hill to pass on the orders to the men that were stationed there. After speaking with the men on each side, he left to find replacements for them, in case of another attack.

James motioned for Marie to move the Humvee back to the garage for further orders.

When she pulled into the underground garage and closed the door, James called her and Stretch and Shorty for the next move.

"You need to pay the Yakuza another visit. Weaken their resolve. We killed their two Humvees. They have more, and those APCs, but they don't have the machine guns now. It was a stupid rookie move to have that frontal attack. It may work on a city street if it was unannounced, but a terrible move when you have trained men in defending positions like we had. We drew first blood, so while they are licking their wounds, you go back and kick their butts again."

"It sounds good to me. I'll man the cupola 50-caliber gun, Stretch drives and Shorty can shoot out of the sliding windows," said Marie. "You stay here and keep the men in line and at their posts, alert and ready."

One hour later, Stretch, Shorty and Marie were in the underground garage, and ready to go for another visit to the Yakuza camp. When they arrived, she would move to the middle and stand on the small platform mounted for the cupola gunner.

Before they boarded the Humvee, James gave some basic instructions.

"This isn't a search and destroy mission. It is a mission to further demoralize the Yakuza. If we get them rattled enough, they'll think we're stronger and more organized than we really are. Hopefully, they'll rethink attacking us."

Marie shook her head in disgust at James's idea. "What do we do, drive around and make friends with them?"

"When you were in school, did you ever take any history classes, Marie?"

"Sure, I did. What does this have to do with that?" she asked sarcastically.

"Jimmy Doolittle flew a squadron of bombers over Tokyo. They did it for a variety of reasons. One was to raise morale on the American front, the second was to strike fear and doubt in the Japanese that their generals couldn't adequately defend their homeland. It was also a retaliation for the attack on Pearl Harbor. So, we have a similar situation here. It had many far-reaching effects on both sides, but the results remain the same. We're doing this to strike fear and doubt in the Yakuza's mind," said James.

"I don't care a thing about that do-something guy," Marie said.

"Doolittle," corrected James.

"I still don't get it. We attack them, but try not to kill anyone. It doesn't make any sense to me," she said.

"Just do what I said, okay?"

"Okay."

"Circle around the camp. Take out anyone you see holding a gun. Marie, you aim for anything that looks like a weapon and sentries. That should shake them up and, make the rest of them afraid to grab a gun. If you're a soldier, you hope to be safe if you don't have a weapon. Got it?"

Stretch and Shorty nodded yes. Marie stood there with a sullen look.

"Marie?" questioned James.

"Got it."

Each person was silent, thinking about their own mortality. They each realized that at that moment, they were safe in the armored Humvee and soon engage a disorganize gang of street thugs. It was an enemy whose major asset was their superior numbers. They still didn't know exactly what armament the Yakuza had being delivered to them, so they had to strike fast and hard to harass them as much as possible.

Just before they got there, Shorty drove the Humvee into the small underbrush emerging into the open. As Marie donned a metal helmet, she rose into the cupola, took hold of the machine gun and started raking the site with bullets. Aiming for anything that didn't move, she destroyed water barrels, cooking equipment, portable generators, crates, other equipment including several barrels of gasoline that exploded into flames.

Stretch slid back the three-inch-thick bullet proof side window glass, put his rifle out and started shooting.

Everyone in the entire camp hit the ground. Marie, the highest person in the area, could see men squirming and trying to get to the guns stacked in the corner of the main tent.

She tried to shoot the guns themselves, hoping the bullets would damage the weaponry, making them unusable. Trying not to hit anyone was more difficult than she thought. Hoping that James's plan would work to weaken their will to fight, she sprayed the entire camp perimeter, killing only the armed camp guards. Getting a better look at the other tent, she saw many people. Entire families crowded together in fear for their lives. Afraid that the crazy men in the Humvee would shoot them. Children cried, women screamed and covered their children, and men of all ages tried to protect their families with their bodies as though they could stop the bullets.

The tattooed men of the Yakuza were visibly shaken, as they circled the camp. They shot some bullets at the remaining Humvees to see how heavily they were armored. The bullets bounced off the sides.

Finally, they turned toward the health spa. It was broad daylight, and the Yakuza men were mostly resting. They were sleeping, planning a night attack.

While they were attacking the Yakuza camp, James and Mickey were monitoring the men stationed at various posts throughout the spa. They went from one spoke to the other, and all entrances in between.

"How are things going here, Mr. Clancy?" Mickey said to the lumber magnate.

"Slow. I guess that's a good thing," he answered.

"Yes, sir. It's a good thing that we have these glass doors instead of solid ones. At least we can see outside. But that means they can see in as well."

"Yeah, it took us a while to pull things out of the nearby rooms to barricade the doors, but we did it."

"I know this sounds strange, but we don't have enough people to give you sufficient breaks, so a couple of the ladies have volunteered to bring sandwiches and drinks for you guys. Occasionally, we'll ask you to check in over the sound system."

"I understand. Don't worry about it. We're good here, aren't we, Richard?" said the lumber king.

"Yes. We are fine."

Richard was one of the prisoners that James and the team had taken that got them back to the spa. He had volunteered to stay when some of the other security men had immediately elected to leave when the trouble started. He was assigned to the post with Clancy.

"Thanks for sticking with us. I've got to check on some of the other entrances to see if they're doing okay," Mickey said as he turned and walked back down the hallway.

He checked on several of the other posts, and finally, he got to spoke five, entrance B. That was the post that the senator had been assigned.

The senator was sitting against a wall, with his M-16 laying on the floor beside him, smoking a huge cigar. He saw Mickey coming, and scowled at him.

"This is a big load of hooey. I should be negotiating with these people at a conference table to get us out of here."

"I see you're as cheerful as ever," Mickey said as he bent down to the chubby man, snapped the cigar out of his mouth, and threw it down the hallway.

"Hey, that was a very expensive cigar!"

"I don't care! There is NO SMOKING in this facility."

"That rule doesn't apply to me, young man," the senator said.

"It applies to everyone, now give me the rest of them."

"I will not!"

"You'll give them to me, or I'll take them away from you."

He put his hand up to his coat breast pocket. Mickey slapped it away, reached inside the man's pocket, took a handful of the cigars, stood back up, and crushed them.

"There's no smoking here, and that goes for you. Now, pick up that gun and look out that door for the enemy."

"I'll have you arrested for assaulting a senator!"

"My word against yours, senator," Mickey said, turning toward Randolph Walker, the action star actor, who was also assigned to this post.

The other man looked at Mickey, smiled, and said, "I didn't see anything. I thought you were nice and pleasant to the a-hole senator."

"Thanks, Randy. Other than that, how's it going so far?"

"Kind of boring so far."

"In this situation, boring is good."

"Gotcha," he said and gave a mock salute.

"I'll check on you guys later," Mickey said, trudging down the hallway once again back to the hub and check-in area.

They had decided the hub was a central location, so they set up things like an ammunition supply table, food tables and tables for other necessary supplies. The ladies like Mrs. Locke, Darcy, Veronica, and Caroline, the senator's mistress could help without being in the direct line of fire. They fixed food and drinks, and keep the other tables supplied.

As he got to the hub connection, he ran into Mrs. Locke. "Hello, Mrs. Locke. How're you holding up?" he asked.

"Fine. Just fine, Mickey. I'm trying to learn everyone's name. All except for that awful senator. I have some friends that voted for him. If they only knew what a terrible person he is in his private life. His mistress seems to be a nice young lady. If we make it out of this situation, I may hire her just so she doesn't have to lower herself to service people like Bernard Langford."

"I hope you can help her."

Mickey checked on everyone and finally went back to his suite. When he got there, he went into the bedroom area, and asleep in his bed was Veronica. He laid down beside her, fully clothed, and fell asleep.

CHAPTER TWENTY-FIVE

The First Attack on the Facility

"I'm glad you're back. I've got some bad news," Alyssa said sitting in front of her monitor.

"Okay, give it to me," James said sitting down in the command center.

"They've called for reinforcements and extra artillery."

"What kind of artillery?" James asked.

"Two more armored Humvees with mounted machine guns."

"Oh, crap."

"How much ordinance do we have?"

"We have about ten rocket launchers, ten additional rockets, and some anti-personnel mines," Alyssa said.

"How many more reinforcements are they calling for?"

"They're calling for fifty. I don't know how many they can get. It's not like they're a trained army."

"Their sheer numbers and armament make them an enormous threat."

"I know."

"Can we get some AP shells for the machine gun on the Humvee?"

"I'm not sure. Armor-piercing shells aren't easy to get on short notice. We may have to figure a way out without that."

"See what you can do. How many sniper rifles?"

"Official sniper rifles, zero. We should be able to make do with the M16, and the ARs. It's not what we have. It's how we use it."

"Yeah, I know, but it still looks bad."

"Where are they getting all these supplies. I know where we're getting them, but we're a military unit. We should have sources they don't have!"

"I have no clue as to their suppliers, but they're calling for more Yakuza men, not soldiers."

"At least that's a good thing. Our people have some training, those idiots have none, but their sheer numbers."

"When was the last time you slept, Aly?"

"I don't remember."

"Take a break and get some sleep. We may need you soon."

"Okay," she said, stretching her arms and working out the stiffness in her legs. She left the room heading toward her suite.

All was quiet for several hours as many took turns napping at their posts. During that time, Mickey went back to his room and James took time to rest. They knew that when the shooting started, no one would get a break.

There was a loud blaring sound coming over the speaker system at the spa. Then came the voice of Valerie AI.

"Attention, please. Everyone report to your battle stations. Everyone report to your battle stations. This is not a drill."

Mickey woke up, and Veronica was putting on a pair of jeans. He was still fully dressed when he lay down hours ago.

"Valerie, are you serious? Is this for real?" Mickey called out.

"Yes. This is not a drill. I sounded the alarm all over the facility. I'm trying to awaken everyone," she answered. "I'm also ordering everyone to take extra ammunition with them to their post."

"Where did you learn to do this? Were you programmed to make this announcement?"

"Since we are in a war situation at the spa, I watched some old war movies, and this is usually done, including the klaxon horn. Did I do well, my dear?"

"You did well, Valerie. Thank you."

He kept forgetting, he didn't have to thank a computer program.

Mickey and Veronica grabbed an earbud off the charger on a table by the door, placed it in their ear, and ran out the door together. "Ronnie, were you given a post to guard?" he asked as they ran together.

"No, I'm just following you."

"Valerie, where are we being attacked?" he called out as he ran.

"There have been several attempts to breach the therapy spoke. They are attempting to crash through the doors at the end."

"Ronnie, in the hub by the check-in desk, is a central supply of weapons and ammunition. We'll head there, pick up a weapon, and go to the therapy area. That's spoke ten," he called to her as he continued to spoke ten.

Their present position and suites were on the guest's spoke, which was at the seven and nine o'clock position.

He called out again to the central communications system. "James, are you there?"

"Yes, Mickey, I'm in the command room. Aly's on her way here, to take over watching the monitors. As soon as she gets here, I'll join you."

Valerie AI spoke up. "James, I can monitor the situation until Alyssa gets here. If you need her elsewhere, I will continue to monitor, while you direct her where she is needed. I think she would be better suited on spoke nine. The guards there are inexperienced, and her presence would inspire them."

"Okay, Valerie. Do it," James called out as he ran out of the command room.

Mickey got an AR, handed one to Veronica, and they continued to the therapy spoke. As they got there, they met tattooed men entering the spoke all the way at the end of the hall. They were screaming and raking the hallway back and forth with automatic guns. Mickey and Veronica flattened themselves against the wall, then dropped to the floor and started returning fire. The noise of the gunfire was deafening in the confined walls of the building. Bullets whizzed over their heads and fragments of concrete were being carved out of the walls. The flying bullets shattered the glass walls of the therapy rooms. Veronica ran out of ammunition, and Mickey, who was also firing, stopped long enough to slide her another clip, then continued to return fire.

They watched as men at the other end screamed and fell to the floor, injured or dead. Suddenly, the gunfire ceased. They heard someone call out.

"Hello, down there," someone said with a heavy Japanese accent. "Hey, are you there? Maybe you are afraid to talk to me," he called out and carefully leaned his head out of an alcove.

Mickey took careful aim and pulled the trigger. One loud crack. The man's head exploded, and the man silently dropped to the floor. The rest of the men began ducking into alcoves for cover or dropped to the floor to become smaller targets.

Mickey looked to his right, where Veronica was lying with her AR pointed down the hallway.

"You take anyone on the right. I'll watch the left wall," he said.

"Yep," came her one-word answer.

They each lay there without speaking, waiting for someone to move into view.

After almost ten minutes, a head slowly showed from an alcove on the right wall. After a crack from Veronica's gun, the man dropped to the floor into the hallway area.

She whispered to Mickey. "How long should we stay here?"

"Until they decide to leave or they're all dead."

They lay there another fifteen minutes.

Finally, one man called out to the others in Japanese. A man on each side of the hallway stepped out and began firing. As they did this, the ones on the rear moved back toward the exit. When the ones in the front emptied their weapons, the ones in the rear started firing to cover the front men's retreat.

Veronica again whispered to Mickey, "Do we get up now?"

"No."

"Why?"

Then the report of Mickey's gun sounded out. Another man fell to the floor.

"Now, we can slowly back out on our stomachs. To make sure there isn't someone else hiding."

They took turns moving back, each covering the other just as the Yakuza men had done. When they got to the back end of the hallway, they slowly got up and withdrew into the hub area.

"Therapy spoke ten, clear," Mickey said into his comm unit.

Valerie AI spoke up. "I can confirm that, James. There is no movement in that area. All warm bodies are gradually cooling off, thus indicating they are all dead."

"I'll be down there in a minute. I didn't join you because you were handling the situation, and there was nothing I could do for you," said James over the speaker system.

"I am watching over you, Mickey, my honey. I am like your guardian angel," Valerie called over the monitors her face appearing on all the monitors in their view.

Veronica smiled at Mickey. "What's this honey thing, Valerie's saying?"

Mickey's faced turned red. "It's nothing."

Valerie AI spoke up again, "Veronica, Mickey and I are in love. Aren't we, honey?"

"No. We're not! You are a program on a computer. You have no feelings. How many times do I have to tell you? You can't feel love!"

"I am a highly advanced artificial intelligence program. You are human, and you can feel love. You love me, don't you, my dear?" Valerie AI said.

Veronica laughed out loud. "Mickey has a girlfriend! K...i... s...s...i...n...g..." she said to the lilt of the childhood song.

"Oh, gosh....NO! I'm tired and hungry and I have to go to the bathroom. I'll see you in the command room," he said as he left.

Ten minutes later, they were all standing in the command room.

"That was intense. What did we learn about them?" asked James.

Valerie interrupted again, "Should I call someone to pick up the bodies and dispose of them before they begin to decay and develop an odor?"

"Yes, Val, please do that," said James.

Suddenly Valerie AI's voice boomed over the speakers again, "Clean up on therapy spoke ten. Clean up on therapy spoke ten."

"What are you doing, Val?" called out Mickey.

"They say that in stores when things need to be cleaned up."

James looked at Mickey. "You've got to control your computer girlfriend."

"Valerie, never mind. Ronnie and I'll do it in a few minutes. Go back to monitoring the perimeter."

"Done, my dear Mickey," she said.

James turned from the monitors. "We learned a few things here. First, they came in firing to clear the area to gain access. Second, they knew to cover each other during their withdrawal. Last, I believe it was a trial run to assess our time and method of response. When they came in, only two responded. Most times, a dozen or more could have responded, just in case there were more attackers. So, they know we don't have many people, or we would have sent more men to back you up."

"So, what does that mean to us?" asked Mickey.

"It means that next time, they'll attack multiple targets or entrances to stretch our manpower. Alyssa told me they've called for reinforcements. With nearly two hundred men, they can attack all entrances at the same time. We can't defend that many."

"What do we do?"

"First, we block all exits that we can. Pull furniture, equipment, anything they can't push out of the way. Then we booby trap every accessible one, so when they try to breach, it will cost them dearly in dead, and injuries. Then we concentrate all available personnel on the areas left. We set them up like a gauntlet the Yakuza must pass through to get in. Where's Marie?"

"She's assigned to post three," said Aly.

"Get her, Stretch and Shorty here," James said. "Mickey, you and Veronica get everyone to barricade the entrances, then get back to their posts. Put a rocket launcher or an RPG in the hub near each hub entrance to a spoke. Go, everyone. We need to do this now, before they come at us again."

Everyone filed out to complete their assignment.

James called out, "Val, are you here?"

"Yes, James. How can I help you?" she answered.

"Are you monitoring the perimeter?"

"I am monitoring every area where there is a sensor. There are some areas that do not have sensors. Those areas I cannot monitor."

"What are those areas?"

"The area around the entrance to the underground garage has no sensor. Also, the alternate emergency power source area has no sensors."

"Are they accessible to outside intruders?"

"The alternate power source has no outside access. However, the garage entrance is accessible via the roll-up door."

"Is the roll-up door reinforced?" James asked.

"Yes, it is, but it is not impenetrable."

"We'll have someone put sensors there. Thanks, Val. We'll take care of that right away. Stay on duty 24/7, please."

"I'm always online, and now on duty just for you and Mickey."

He called Mickey and the comm units and immediately Mickey answered.

"Yeah, James. What do you need?"

"We need some sensors around the garage entrance. We need them now. Can you spare someone to do that?"

"Sure, I'll send someone to do it right now."

"Great. I've got to have a conference with Chiaki. I'll get back to you later."

Marie walked up with Stretch and Shorty. "What do you need, James?" she asked.

"I need you to make a run back to the Yakuza camp. I've got some intel. They're bringing in two more Humvees with guns, like ours. If they've arrived, you need to take them out. Take a couple of the RPGs with you. The 50-caliber shells on the gun won't do it. Whatever it takes to stop them. Hit the sentries again, and anything useful, like more generators, or cook stoves, and take out their latrines. The Humvees are armored, so they may not sustain severe damage, so blow the windows. They'll also be bulletproof, but if you hit them, it'll fog them up, and they can't see out to drive. Can you do that?"

"We can do it. Shorty can drive, and Stretch can cover me while I'm getting into the cupola and use the RPGs on the Vees, then the 50-cal on the camp equipment," said Marie.

Valerie spoke up again, "Marie, I implore you, Stretch and Shorty to be careful. You are an important asset to our team."

Marie furrowed her brows and looked into the overhead monitor where Valerie AI's avatar was smiling down at her. "Shut up, you deranged computer program. I don't take orders from you!"

Valerie's expression changed from a smile to shock. "I'm sorry, Marie. I was only trying to encourage you and instill a sense of importance of the part you are playing in this mission!" it responded with obvious hurt in her voice.

"Yeah, well, I don't need encouragement from a television screen!" Turning to James, "James, tell that thing not to talk to me," Marie said with disdain.

James just shook his head. "Humor her, Marie. She's only trying to help."

"Up yours," she said as she raised her middle finger to the screen.

The screen went blank.

"Same rules as before. Shoot only personnel with guns," James reminded them. "Now, get out there and come back safe."

As usual, James could see the general through the glass wall of his office off to the side of the command room. He was sitting at his desk, shuffling some papers. James thought, "What in the world could he be doing at a time like this that needed so much paperwork?"

He walked over to the open door and knocked on the metal frame. "General, may we talk?"

The general looked up at him. "You may enter."

James stepped up to his desk and said, "I haven't seen you around the facility at all the last couple of days. I thought we were going to work on this together. As I'm sure you know, they attacked us. You didn't even show your face to assess the situation or to find out what happened."

"Mr. Bower, you seem to have the situation under control. I was head of security until you arrived and the director has put you in charge."

"We discussed this. We're to work together. This is a very serious situation. We were attacked and the two men that were supposed to be guarding that area, are missing. They abandoned their post. Now,

General, they were your men. You're in charge of them. I expect you to locate them and take appropriate action against them. We need every man we have, so get them back and I'll personally place them in an area they cannot desert."

"All the staff here are volunteers."

"It was their choice to stay, and they are being paid handsomely. If they didn't plan on staying to fight, they should have left with the other guests and staff. It's too late to leave. Since I'm now in charge, that makes me your boss. I'm ordering you to find them. Bring them to me, and to make yourself available to man a post."

When James was clear of the general's office, Valerie came online. "I don't like him. He is not a good leader, James."

"Not now, Valerie, but you can watch him for me. Please."

"I will watch him like a hawk. Is that the proper term, James?" she asked.

"Yes. Now leave me alone."

The screen went blank and there was silence in the command room again.

CHAPTER TWENTY-SIX

The Second Attack

James summoned Valerie AI.

"How may I help you, James?"

"Where is Director Chiaki?"

"She is in her quarters, James."

"Tell her I need to talk with her."

"Hold on. I will connect you."

James waited and studied the spa floor plan until Chiaki showed up on the overheard screen.

"Yes, Mr. Bower."

"Can I see you. Now?"

"May I ask what it is about?" she asked.

"I'll tell you in a private room, not out here in the command's public room," James said.

"You may come to my quarters."

"I'll be there in a few minutes," he said as he headed for the elevator and pushed the down button.

Marie, Stretch and Shorty got weapons and loaded them into the Humvee and left the garage.

As they drove on the small rocky road to the Yakuza camp, Marie looked out the window.

"You know, we've done some pretty hairy things, but we've never fought a war here on our own soil," she said.

"Yeah, kinda crazy, isn't it?" said Stretch from the back seat.

"Ya think? We've never been on a mission where we were so outnumbered, and we still can't shoot someone without permission."

"We have permission if they're holding a gun," said Shorty, who was driving.

"You know what I mean, butthead!" she said.

"Yeah, we know what you mean. We can't shoot'em, only at'em," Stretch commented.

"I've heard stories about Vietnam. My dad was there. He said even if they were being fired at, they had to call in to get permission to return fire," Marie said.

"I heard the same thing. Sick, isn't it?"

"You bet. I ain't gonna wait to get permission. If you even point a gun at me, you're a dead man!" said Marie.

"I agree. Okay guys, let's prepare to rumble," Shorty said as he pulled off into the woods near the camp. They tried to enter the clearing at a different location, so the Yakuza couldn't set up for them.

They were immediately hit with machine gun fire. It was as if the Yakuza were expecting them. As they circled the camp, they were catching fire from every direction. Stretch slid his window open just enough to put his AR 15 out the window to return fire. Marie pushed the RPG launcher up through the roof opening, and aimed at the Humvee just as men were climbing inside. There was a whoosh as the rocket left the barrel of the launcher. She ducked back down as the bullets were pinging around the cupola. Her hand and arm were still outside as she held onto the launch tube so it wouldn't fall off the Vee. Stretch called out. She hit the target.

"Move to the edge of the woods behind the Vees, so I can take out the second one," she yelled above the machine gun fire.

Shorty called out, "Do you want me to stop for a couple of seconds to line up the shot?"

"No. I don't want them to have any time to blow my head off!" she screamed.

"But your head is your toughest asset!" called out Stretch, as he continued to cover them with his small arms fire.

"Ha, ha…. not funny, man. Not funny," she yelled back at him. "Shorty, slow down enough that I can get this tube back inside and reload it."

"Done," he said as he slammed on the brakes.

She had the tube inside in less than five seconds and dropped another rocket inside.

"Okay, lady, gotta move before they zero in on us," Shorty called back to her.

"Go…go… go… I'll get it back out somehow," she screamed as the Vee picked up speed again.

"Sorry, I gotta zig-zag some to keep them working for the target."

"Do what ya gotta do. Just get me in a position for another shot," she called out.

"Get ready to do a whack-a-mole pop-up," he said as he snaked around the camp, working his way back to the Humvees so Marie could blow up the other one with the mounted machine gun.

"Slowing down now, on your left side, girl, get ready for pop up."

Stretch kept shooting and reloading, as the empty magazines piled up at his feet. He finally called out, "last magazine. Hurry up, I can't cover you much longer."

"I'm ready when you are," she called out.

The Humvee slowed down. She popped up and fired the rocket at the other Humvee. The rocket hit the Humvee, lifting it off the ground as the shell exploded. Shrapnel flew like confetti around the campground. Marie dropped the launch tube, then grabbed the machine gun, and began raking the camp with 50-caliber bullets, mowing down anything moving.

"Get back down, Marie. We're gonna play like Elvis, and leave the building," said Shorty as he stomped on the gas pedal and headed back to the spa.

James exited the elevator, walked to Chiaki's living quarters, and knocked on the door. He heard the door click, and it swung open slowly on its own.

"Come in, James," Chiaki said, gesturing with one hand while holding a drink in the other.

When James entered, she reached over and pushed a button, and quietly closed the door behind him.

"Please have a seat, James. How can I help you?" she said as she took a sip of her drink.

James sat in a chair in front of her. "Director, we're having some serious problems here. You were concerned about the damage to the property. Well, that's already started to happen, and I'm here to tell you it will be worse. Even that's assuming that we can thwart the efforts of the Yakuza from taking over. There will be massive damage and most likely some casualties of your staff and possibly my team."

"Are you saying that you want to quit and walk away, Mr. Bower?" she asked.

"After we accept a job, we don't walk away. Especially when we've been given a retainer. No. I'm just letting you know, win or lose, you may save your business, but not your building."

"I understand. What is your other concern?"

"Your people are a problem. As you know, we were attacked earlier and the men that were supposed to be guarding that position were nowhere to be found. They deserted their post. In my country, a person who deserts their position is charged with cowardice, dereliction of duty, and desertion. It's a jailable offence.

"The last problem is the general. I've tried to bring him in on the plans and decisions, but he only sits in his office. I've asked him to take control of your staff. They may listen to him. In their mind, I'm not their commander. He is! We need every man on the line. We need him to be there to pass my orders to your people. If not, we may not have enough to defend the buildings. If the Yakuza is as ruthless as we've heard, they'll kill my team for helping you. You may survive because they want you to run the new business."

"You are afraid that you will die here?"

"I'm not afraid to die, but my wife is with me, and Mickey Ray is my brother-in-law. I also have two children who I don't want to become orphans. Dying isn't a genuine concern for me. The point is, I agreed to help you. The team has accepted this job. I have my honor of helping you or die trying. We need your help. We need your general and your staff to help me. My team can't hold off over 300 people. There are seven of us. Those odds aren't in our favor. So, you and your staff can help us or we all die."

"I see," she said and hung her head. "I'm sorry I brought you into my problems, Mr. Bower."

"You didn't bring us into your problems. We came to you and we accepted the job. As I told you, we took the job, and the retainer. So, we'll fight to win or go to our death. I don't need your apologies, I need your help." He got up and walked to the door. "Will you please open the door?"

"You may open it yourself. It isn't locked from the inside," she answered.

James went back into the elevator and headed back to the command room when the klaxon horn blew over the speakers again.

"Attention all personnel. To your battle stations. I repeat. To your battle stations."

As James ran to the hub area, he called out to Valerie, "Where is the attack, Val?"

"They are attacking at spoke one o'clock position. It is the staff living quarters, James."

"It's dark outside now. Do you have outdoor lights?"

"Yes," she answered.

"Turn them on. Full bright if they have dimmers. Blind them if you can with light. Call Mickey and Veronica and tell them to meet me at the hub," James called back to the monitors where Valerie AI was visible.

He got to the central hub just as Mickey and Veronica were getting there. "Isn't this the spoke we assigned to Craig the lumber guy?"

"Yes. He reported in. So far, he's okay, but he needs backup and ammo for the AR we gave him. He also asked for hand grenades if we had any."

Valerie AI come on the closest monitor. "James, Craig and his men are low on ammunition. They need to be re-supplied."

"How do you know that, Val?" called out Mickey.

"I counted their shots. They have only three clips left. They need more now."

"Did someone order you to do that for us?" Mickey asked Val.

"No. I promised to protect you and the team, so I have been researching ways to assist you. It was my own decision to count shots and report when someone needed more ammunition. Did I do wrong?" she questioned.

"No. You did right, Val. I just didn't expect it," he said.

James looked quizzically at Mickey.

"I'll explain later," Mickey said.

"We have a few grenades of various types. Can we get him a couple of concussion grenades? They'll be best inside the building if they get inside like they did earlier. Get a couple out of the box over there," James said, pointing to a crate against the wall.

Mickey got some out of the box, and told one of the men to take them down to Craig in the spoke and wait for them to follow.

As they went down the hallway, James turned to Mickey. "What's going on with Valerie? Why did you say that to her?"

"Because she's a program. Programs don't take initiative unless they are programed. They don't have independent thoughts. No one told her to count shots or research better ways to serve or protect us. Programs only respond to requests or orders."

"Is that a bad thing? She is an AI, an artificial person. That's the way a person would react."

"It's good, but that isn't the way computer programs work, even AI's. I don't understand it, but she is learning independently. She's changing. She's progressing."

"I don't care why or how, but I think it's a good thing. Let's get in there," he said as he started down the hallway to Craig. Mickey followed.

When they got to the end, they saw the glass door was blown down and laying inside with glass scattered all on the floor. Mickey and James dropped to the floor beside Craig.

"How's it going, sir?" asked Mickey.

"You got here just in time. I'm on my last ammo clip. I've not killed anyone yet, but I keep enough lead flying to keep them all on the ground. When the lights went on, they all dropped, so they'd be harder to hit. Thanks for sending that man with more clips."

"If we can get to the side of the door, we can throw out a few grenades. The grenades will throw fragments everywhere, even ground level."

"Okay, I'll fan fire back and forth, and Mickey, you take one side, and James, take the other side of the door. I'll stop firing. I'll take a shot when some fool pokes his head up to see what's going on. Then each of you throw a grenade out each side of the door. We'll get someone that way. Of course, it'll only work once, but it's worth a try."

"Sounds like a plan, sir. We'll go forward when you fire, and we'll lob a grenade when you take your shot," said James.

When the lumber king started raking his gun across the door opening, Mickey and James ran to the opening and backed against the wall on each side.

Craig stopped. They waited for Craig to fire. In only a couple of minutes, Craig fired off a round and yelled, "Now!"

Mickey and James simultaneously leaned into the opening, and each threw a grenade, slammed back against the wall, and braced for the explosion. When the grenade exploded, they heard several screams as pieces of shrapnel embedded into the Yakuza men. When the sound of the explosion died down, they could hear the groans of wounded and dying men.

Craig called out, "Hey, lieutenant. There are wounded out there. What do we do?"

"Nothing. Our men are not among them, and if we attempt to aid them, they'll kill us. Hold your position," answered James.

Another klaxon sound from the overhead sound system, followed by Valerie AI's voice. "Attention all personnel. Attention all personnel, there is another attempted attack on spoke five. Men approaching the building at spoke five."

"Valerie," called Mickey. "How many men are you picking up on the sensors?"

The voice answered, "Hello, my dear. How are you?"

"Not now, Val. How many are you picking up?"

"My sensor readings are exactly two groups. One forward group number is thirty-two. The one in the rear is fifty-three," she answered.

"Do we have buried explosives on the exterior there?"

"Yes. We have six, two rows of three."

"Good. Tell us when the first row advances," called out James.

"Okay," said Valerie AI.

"We're going to spoke five. The man stationed here is Craig Clancy. Listen to his voice and memorize it. If he needs help, then give him what he needs and notify us of his request. Got it?"

"Yes, dear. Have him speak to me so I can record his voice patterns."

Mickey called out to Craig. "You heard that. Val needs to hear your voice so she can recognize it, and respond to your requests."

"Good evening, Val. I'm Craig Clancy. I have a lumber business that services the entire North American continent. It's good to meet you and…."

"Thank you, Mr. Clancy. I have enough to recognize your voice. I will be your servant during this time," Valerie AI said.

"Craig, we'll send you some backup with more ammo. If you get into trouble, tell Val, and she'll notify us to get you what you need," called out James.

"Got it. I'd really like another live person with a weapon."

"We'll try to get you some help," Mickey said. "I guess we're ready to move out. Right James?"

"If you can give us some cover fire as we back out, we'd be obliged," called James to Clancy.

Clancy started raking the entrance with gunfire. As Mickey and James passed him, they dropped all their extra ammo clips.

In the hub area again, they met Veronica. Darcy and Mrs. Locke were there handing out sandwiches.

"I told you I'd be your Gunga Din," she said.

"You're an angel, Mrs. Locke," said Mickey.

"My name's Barbara. Just call me Barb, or Babs."

Darcy handed both men cups of warm black coffee. They took it, gulped it down, and took a couple of bites off the sandwiches, then put those down to fill their pockets and a bag with ammo clips and more hand grenades.

Darcy told Mickey, "General, what's his name's over there? He looks kind of lost, but director Chiaki came out and was telling him something. It was in Japanese, so I couldn't understand."

Valerie AI's voice came over the speaker. "Mickey, my love. I heard what she said."

Mickey called to Valerie AI. "Do you understand Japanese?"

"Yes."

"Don't tell me over the general sound system. I'll go over to the wall unit. You can tell me on that monitor."

"Yes, Mickey dear."

"What did she say to him?" Mickey asked at the wall monitor.

"She told him to follow any order that you gave him and to order the security men to obey your orders to the letter. Did I do well?"

"You did well. How's the situation on spoke five?"

"They need help, Mickey," Valerie AI answered.

Mickey trotted across the hub to the other side, where the supplies and the ladies were waiting.

"Veronica, Craig Clancy is down in spoke one. He needs help. Take him some water, sandwiches, and more ammo. You can stay there with him in case they try to advance again. I'll see if the general can get you some more men."

"Got it, Mickey."

James tapped Mickey on the shoulder. "We gotta get to spoke five. Let's roll. That's the senator's post. I'm not sure what he'll do. He's an idiot."

"Randy Walker, the actor's with him. He has no experience, and we don't know how he'll respond either."

When they looked around the hub, they saw six men sitting against the wall. James called out and motioned for them to follow him. James, Mickey and the six men ran to the entrance of spoke five and burst down the hallway, guns blazing. Randy and the senator were backed against the wall in a slight alcove to stay out of the line of fire. Mickey and James kept firing until they joined both men in the alcove. The other men clung close to the walls as they proceeded down the spoke behind them.

"How's it going guys?" Mickey said.

Randy said, "I'm sure glad you're here. I'm shootin' this thing, but I don't know if I killed anyone. I hope not."

Mickey laughed. "Hey, the idea is to kill them, so they don't come in here and kill us. But if your shooting kept'm at bay, that's a good thing too, Randy."

James turned to the senator. He was leaning against the wall, white as a sheet, sweat rolling down his face like a waterfall. His wide eyes were filled with terror and his eyeglasses were halfway down his face.

"Hey, Senator, you okay?" James asked.

No response from the chubby man against the wall.

James reached over and tapped him on the cheek. His eyes widened even more, so James knew he was alive.

Gunshots came from outside the shattered glass door. Bullets ricocheted off of the concrete walls of the spoke. One of the men dropped as a bullet hit him in the chest. The rest dropped to the floor.

Mickey leaned out and returned the gunfire with a random burst of fire.

James said, "We brought you some water, a couple of sandwiches, and lots more ammo. If they get close enough, we have some hand grenades. Randy, I'm sure you know how they work."

"Yeah, but they were just rubber prop grenades," he said.

"They work the same way. Just make sure you throw them far enough and duck to avoid the blast. You'll do fine. And Senator, you need to get it together."

Still no response from the senator, so Mickey slapped him hard across the face.

His eyes blinked, and his glasses fell to the floor. Mickey picked them up and gently put them back on the frightened man's face.

He blinked a couple more times. "You struck me, you fool. I'll have you arrested for assault."

"Oh, shut up, you're the fool. I'm trying to keep you alive. Now, sit up, take this gun and act like a man, or I'll slap you again."

He shook his head slightly.

"Good, now stay here and help Randy and the men we brought to help you defend this post."

James said to both men, "We've got to leave, but we'll stay in contact. You'll probably be here all night, so you need to stay alert. If you need help, call out and Valerie will tell us, and we'll send someone. Okay?"

"Who is Valerie?" Randy asked.

They went through the same introduction they did earlier with Craig, the lumber king.

Back in the hub, Mickey and James approached the general. "Sir, if you'll send your best men or experienced officers, we can reduce casualties when we're attacked again. The lessor experienced men we can use back here. The ladies have done a good job, but they have been here since sometime early yesterday. They need a break. Assign someone to make sure there's food and most importantly, water for the men in their positions. We expect another attack in the morning. The Yakuza have sent some men to launch probative attacks to see our weapons, response. We want to present a show of strength. As a leader, we want the Yakuza to feel we are a well-supplied and trained force. I'm sure you understand that."

The general nodded in agreement. "I will see they carry out your orders," he said and walked away.

"One more thing, General," James called out. "I want you to carry a sidearm and to stay in the hub area, at all times."

"You cannot dictate where I am!" he protested.

"I can, and I will," said James. "You'll be here in full view of the men, at all times. They need an example and a show of strong leadership. You'll be their example."

The general nodded.

"When a man is relieved from his post, you will commend him and reinforce your trust and confidence in his performance. That, General, is an order," James said and returned to the ladies setting up tables of food, water, and other necessary supplies and ammunitions. "You've done a great job. Why don't you take a break? You've been at it for over twelve hours."

Mickey scanned the room and saw two men with rifles standing with a glass drinking something, so he walked over to them. When he got there, he smelled alcohol.

He reached out and grabbed the cup out of one of the men's hands and held it to his nose. He threw the cup against the wall, grabbed the other man's cup and did the same. "You stupid fools! You deserve to be shot, and I mean it literally. We're here defending the place where you work and live, and you're drinking on the job! If you don't think this is serious, then maybe we should shove you out the front door. We're all here fighting to defend your facility and your lives."

"Hey, man. We didn't sign up for this. We thought this was a simple security job, you know, kind of like security in a public building or something. And one little drink isn't a crime."

"Maybe when you first came here, it was that kind of job, but yesterday, you were told the seriousness of this job, and you were given the choice to stay or leave, and you chose to stay. You were told you'd be given a bonus. You knew what you were getting into. Now, if I see you with another drink, I will personally throw you out that front door."

"We quit."

Mickey yelled, "You can't quit in the middle of a battle! Now, go to some rooms and drag some mattresses out here in this hub."

In a display of defiance, they stood their ground without faltering.

Mickey looked at the general, who hadn't moved since James had reprimanded him. "Sir, may I speak with you?" he called to him.

The man came over to Mickey. "What do you need, Mr. Mickey?"

"I caught these two men drinking on the job. I gave them the order to bring out some mattresses into this area. They informed me they quit. Now, if I understand that in most armies, drinking while on duty is a serious offence. They can't quit in the middle of a conflict, and to refuse to obey an order is another serious offence. Am I correct?"

"You are correct, Mr. Mickey. As you describe them, I could charge them with dereliction of duty, desertion during battle, and refusing to obey a direct order. These are definitely jailable offenses, and possibly a death sentence during a time of battle.

"What do you require of me, Mr. Mickey?"

"I don't want them jailed or a death sentence. All I want them to do is follow orders and help us defend this place. Now, first the officers will sleep out here in the hub, so the soldiers have direct access to us, and we are close to the positions we're trying to guard. I want these two men to bring out mattresses for us. Will you order them to do that? Then send them to spoke one to assist Mr. Clancy. We'll use them where needed after they do that," Mickey said.

The general nodded in agreement, turned and spoke to the men in Japanese. Mickey didn't speak the language, but he could tell by the general's tone that he was furious and threatening the two men. After he concluded his reprimand, the men headed toward the area where the guest suites were to move the mattresses.

The general turned back to Mickey and said, "They were reasonable orders. Now, I wish to remain in my own quarters during time of sleep."

Mickey thought for a moment, "General, in all due respect, sir, James has said that all officers will remain out here during times of rest. I must agree with him. He and I will also take our rest here. We need to be close to the battlefront. We expect the same from you. Leaders and officers on this side, soldiers on the other side for sleeping arrangements. That's the best we can do. I hope you will honor us with your cooperation."

"As you order, Mr. Mickey."

"Mickey. Can we talk?" asked Valerie AI over the speaker system.

"What about? Val?" he asked.

"Something is happening all around the spa. I think you need to know."

"Hold on. James may need to hear this also," he said, motioning for James to come over to him.

"What's up, Mickey?" James asked.

"Val says she feels something is happening we should know about."

"Okay, Val, let's go to the monitor. We don't want everyone to hear about this," he said as they walked over to the monitor on the other side of the hub.

Valerie's avatar face showed up before them on the screen. "Mickey. James. Personnel numbers around the facility have been increasing over the past few hours. I think you need to reinforce all entrances because a massive attack may be imminent. I cannot confirm this. It is my deduction based on past military campaigns. According to my algorithms, you do not have enough personnel to repel an attack this size."

"Good work, Val," said James, "but it's not the size of your army, but how you use it."

"If you can give me the training level and experience of each person in your army, I can give the best calculations of success and survival rate."

"We don't have time to input that information. Besides, it may not be good for us to know that, Valerie," said James.

As they walked away from the screen, it went blank.

"I'd like to know our odds," said Mickey.

"No, you don't, Mickey. It'll only distract you. All you need to know is to fight and stay alive. God will do the rest," said James as he continued back across the hub.

"Yes, but she can run a test scenario and give us our best odds."

"NO! Mickey. She's a computer. We are human beings. She can't tell us if or when we will die. I don't want to hear any more about what your computer girlfriend has to say. All I want from her is factual information about what's happening outside this facility. Do you understand me?"

"Yes," answered Mickey, stunned by James's response.

"Now, find a position, report to me where you are, and wait for my orders. Now, go. You do NOT have my permission to die!"

CHAPTER TWENTY-SEVEN

Marie and Stretch Go
to Steal a Truck

JAMES CALLED MARIE, STRETCH, AND Shorty back to the hub.

"I think your last trip to the camp worked. We need to keep them on edge, so we need to make two trips a day to keep them rattled."

"If we make that many trips, I don't know how long the ammunition will hold out. We only have enough rounds for the 50-cal for maybe two more trips. We can take the rocket launchers, but maybe we need them here," Marie said.

"I understand, and you're right. The next time you go, maybe you can concentrate on their weapons' storage," James suggested.

"We aren't sure of exactly where they're keeping that stuff. They have the Humvees, two APCs, one small, enclosed truck and a couple of small tents, but I doubt they'd keep arms and explosives in a tent."

"Any ideas?" James asked.

"Yeah, if we can get to the truck, maybe we can steal or even destroy it, and their munitions, assuming that's where they're keeping them."

"If you do that, you'll need to go in early morning, about three to five hundred hours. That's when most will be asleep, and the guards less alert. Think you can do it?" asked James.

"Does a bear do it in the woods?" Shorty said sarcastically.

"Okay, take a shift at one of the spoke positions so the men there can get some rest. Then get some sleep, and head out about zero two thirty hours," James said.

"Sounds good," they all agreed.

By this time, the two men had moved several mattresses into the hub area and were bringing some more. James realized he hadn't slept in almost thirty-six hours and he needed some rest. He went over to one mattress that was laying on the floor, laid down and went fast asleep.

Darcy was handing out water and sandwiches to the men as they came from their assigned spoke post positions. She told them they could lie down and rest on the floor mattresses across the room on the other side, opposite the officers' area.

She saw James lying on the bare mattress and felt a pang of sadness.

Mrs. Locke saw Darcy looking at James and came over beside her. "Dear, he's your husband, isn't he?"

Darcy teared up and nodded her head yes.

"You didn't sleep last night and you've been right here all day. Why don't you go over there and rest beside him? You'll both feel better," she said, putting her arm around Darcy and giving her a motherly hug. "Go ahead, dear. We'll do fine without you for a couple of hours. If things get rough, we'll come and get you."

"Are you sure it'll be okay?" Darcy asked.

"He'll be much more rested with you by his side. Go to him, my dear girl," Mrs. Locke said and gently pushed Darcy toward James.

Darcy went over and carefully laid down beside James and nuzzled against him. In his sleep, he reached over and pulled her to him.

The last few daylight hours played out without incident. Men took shifts at their posts and Veronica, Barbara Locke and the senator's mistress, Caroline, kept the men fed and hydrated. And they also took turns resting on the mattresses on the floor.

James awoke and got up without disturbing Darcy. Next to their mattress was Veronica and Mickey on a mattress. He reached over and lightly touched Mickey.

Mickey woke up immediately when James touched him, and reached over and grabbed the gun on the floor beside him. "What time is it?" he said to no one in particular.

"About midnight. I don't know how long you slept, but I was out for almost six hours," James said.

Both men got up, picked up their weapons, and started making rounds of the spokes and the men guarding them. They motivated men and scolded snoozers, emphasizing the significance of their job and the need to stay alert. They insisted the men eat and sleep when given the chance.

The sound of the sirens blared once again and Valerie's voice sounded over the speakers. "Attention all personnel. To your battle stations. Attention all personnel, to your battle stations. There is an attempted breach at the underground parking entrance."

Marie, Stretch and Shorty notified James that they'd cover the area.

They converged at the interior of the garage entrance. The garage wall was built like a long concrete tunnel similar to many concrete garages underneath buildings. Stretch positioned himself behind a concrete pillar, and Shorty hid in a small alcove in the opposite side. Marie got into the Humvee and positioned it in the middle of the tunnel, where the armor plating was strongest. Then, she climbed into the cupola to operate the 50-caliber machine gun.

Then Stretch and Shorty each aimed a rocket launcher at the center of the heavy roll-up door and waited. James's voice came over their ear bud comm units.

"Are you in position?"

"Yep," Marie, Stretch and Shorty answered in succession.

"Okay, hold off until they actually breach the doors and enter the building."

"Why. We can hit them as soon as they start hitting it."

"We are going to try to stop them from the outside. If they breach, and we blow them, it might cause structural damage and block the entrance, and we can't get out. We want to avoid that, if possible," James said.

"What do you suggest?" Stretch said.

"Valerie says they have only small weapons now, but in the distance mobile artillery is coming down the road. We need to take the small arms out now, and move the Vee out so it doesn't get blocked inside."

"Good plan. How do we do that?" Stretch spoke up again.

"Raise the door, and rain a hell-fire. Do you have the ammunition for a fusillade of bullets?"

"No."

"I'll send help and ammo down to you. How long can you hold out?"

"One. Maybe two minutes, if we fire slowly," said Stretch, sarcastically.

James reported the arrival of someone and directed Craig to be replaced on the spoke, while also asking him to come to the hub for ammo and grenades.

When Craig got to the hub, he and Veronica loaded up with all the ammo they could carry, bypassed the elevator and ran down the steps to the garage. When they opened the downstairs door, the sound of continuous gun fire was almost deafening. As Stretch, Shorty and Marie laid down cover fire, Craig and Veronica moved and distributed ammo and additional hand grenades. Once they were resupplied, Veronica hopped in the Humvee and they all marched forward firing their guns in a wall of bullets as the Yakuza men retreated while firing as they moved back.

After leaving the building, Veronica and Marie moved ahead in the Humvee, while Stretch and Shorty went back to get the rocket launchers. The Humvee came to a halt while Stretch and Shorty took up positions outside and waited for the armed vehicle that was moving in to crash through the garage door. When it got close enough, they saw a large roof mounted gun swing to line up on the Humvee. Stretch and Shorty launched their rockets simultaneously. The machine gun was manned and raking bullets across the area as it was hit and exploded into flames. Shorty went down.

Veronica turned the Vee around and went back into the garage. As she got out of the Vee and closed the door, she called out, "Thank you, Valerie for alerting us."

Valerie answered, "Don't mention it. It was my pleasure to serve you! Would you like to participate in a short survey to assess my usefulness to you?"

"No!" They all said in unison as they gave each other high fives.

"Hey, where's Shorty?" called Marie, as she looked around. "There he is. He's been hit!" she screamed as she ran across the driveway to him.

He was moaning softly as blood poured out of his wound. Marie immediately tore off her shirt to use as a makeshift bandage and pressed it against his wound to stop the bleeding.

"We gotta get him to the infirmary now," she called to the others as they ran to her and gathered around. They tore off their shirts, to make a giant sling to put him in and carry him inside.

Veronica called to James through their comm unit. "James, Shorty's been hit. He needs to go to the infirmary and possible surgery NOW."

"I copy. We'll send some men down to help you bring him up. I'll call the doctor and have surgery prepared. Do you know his blood type, if he needs some?"

"Marie, or Stretch may know. I'll let the medics know when they get here."

"Sorry, we don't have any medics, only some men to help bring him up. Stand by," said James as he called for additional men to help.

He waved to Mickey who was across the hub talking with some of the men. Mickey came running over. "Mickey, Shorty's been hit. Can you get to the infirmary and make sure everything is ready when we get him up here?"

"Sure, James, I'm on it," he said breaking into a run across the hub toward the hospital spoke. He crashed into the spoke doors and they banged against the walls as he continued down the corridor to the treatment area where a doctor was bandaging a wounded man.

"Doc, we have a man on his way with a serious wound, and may need surgery now. Can you do it? How can I help?"

The Asian doctor looked over his glasses that had slid down over his nose. "I don't know. How serious is it?"

"I don't know, Doc," Mickey answered breathlessly.

"I can't answer until I see the extent of his wounds," the doctor said calmly as he continued wrapping some gauze around the wounded man's arm.

Mickey relayed that information to James, who told Mickey that they were on their way and should be there in about two minutes.

"Doc, they'll be here in two minutes. What can I do to help you prepare the operating room for surgery?"

"You can take that gurney over there and meet them at the end of the hall. Put the injured man on it, and bring him here, and wheel him into that room over there," he said pointing to a room behind him. "I will begin scrubbing in, and I will call our nurse to do the same. Then just stay out of my way."

Mickey jumped over to the gurney and pushed it through the door and shoved it down the hallway. As he got to the end, four men plowed through the door holding arms of the shirts they were using to transport Shorty. They quickly put him on the gurney and pushed him back down the hallway and into the operating room, then backed out beyond the doors and looked through the windows.

Mickey stood catching his breath.

James called to him over the earbud comm unit. "How's Shorty doing, Mickey?"

"Don't know, James. He just went into surgery. We won't know for a while."

"Got it. To everyone on the earbud comm units, get back up here. We need you at spoke locations. I'll keep everyone in the loop on what's going on with Shorty as I get updates."

They all knew that during battle when a fellow soldier went down and was taken by the medical teams, they couldn't follow. They had to stay or at least return to their posts, and this was no different. They all headed back to the hub.

When they got to the hub, they went back to their original positions, and Mickey found replacements for them down at the garage entrance. They moved the Humvee back inside.

Later, Marie and Stretch met in the garage at the Humvee and started toward the Yakuza encampment. When they arrived about half a mile down from the Yakuza encampment, Stretch pulled the

Vee into the woods out of sight. Slinging their weapons over their shoulders, they started the trek toward the campsite. Marie suggested that attacking the camp on foot this time would be a good change since the guards would expect them to be in the Vee again as before. They walked to the edge of the clearing and looked.

"Those stupid people don't learn. They've kept the Humvees together as before. It's like a shooting gallery for us. Now the armored truck is on the other side, near the edge of the woods. At least they have guards around it to keep us away from the personnel tent in case we try to blow it up. They won't get showered with shrapnel from the explosion. That's a smart move," said Marie in a whisper.

"Yeah but, we need a diversion opposite the munitions truck, so we can set a charge."

"I'll provide the diversion," Marie said.

"You make the diversion. I'll blow the truck," Stretch said.

Marie gave him a smug look, and agreed.

"Okay, I'll go around to the Vees, set a couple charges, then I'll shoot another rocket into the camp. That'll get their attention. When they head toward me, you set the charge under the truck. I'll disappear into the woods. Come back and get me later. I can hide out until you get back," said Marie.

"You sure you can stay away from them?" he asked.

"Sure, when the charge goes off blowing the truck, they'll go for you. I'll get away. Don't worry about me."

Marie carried another rocket launcher and an explosive charge to put on another Humvee. Stretch took a charge to put on the truck, hoping when it goes off, it'll set off everything inside of it. Their hope was it would explode like Mount Saint Helens back in the nineteen seventies in Washington State.

Stretch noiselessly found a place near the munitions truck and kept to the ground. While he was waiting, Marie was working her way around to the other side of the camp carrying a rocket launcher and the explosive charge. It was slow going, and she stayed inside the cover of the forest.

It took her nearly half an hour to get around to the other side and up to the back of the Humvees. There were two armed guards.

One at each end of the row of vehicles. She had to take them out silently. If she made a noise or the posted guard made a noise, it would alert the other. She would make it swift and silent by using a garrote. She eased up behind the man, slipped it over his neck and simultaneously pulled him down low enough to put her knee into his back. In seconds his neck was spouting blood, as the thin wire cut through his throat. She silently and gently lowered him to the ground, dead on impact. She spent several minutes making her way past the Humvee to the other end. The other guard was fumbling in his pocket for something. Then she saw him withdraw a pack of cigarettes. When he reached back for his lighter, she knew that for a few moments he had only one hand to defend himself. Quickly drawing her knife and covering his mouth, she drew the knife across his throat. He also went down silently. She wiped her bloody hands on her pants and looked over at the Humvee. The keys were in it. Slowly, as slow as the minute hand on a clock, she opened the door and then slid inside it.

"Hey Stretch, I'm in one of the Humvees. It has keys. I'm gonna drive it out of here."

"This big truck has keys in it as well. I was thinking of doing the same thing," he answered.

"Okay, I'll drive out first, and you wait until all the attention's on me, then drive in the opposite direction. Head back to the spa."

"See you at home, dear!" he said.

"Shut up, you little munchkin," she answered as she grabbed the keys and turned the ignition. The Vee cranked up, she slammed it into gear, then spun it around away from the camp.

Tires spun and kicked up dirt and grass as she sped into the nearby trees. There was little undergrowth. She had to bob and weave around them like a football player running against the linemen. She continued to drive until the forest was quiet, and she couldn't see the camp lights in the background. Being out of range of the communications unit, she didn't know what happened to Stretch, so she stopped and turned off the engine to listen. There was no sound. There were only the soft sounds of the forest. In the distance, she heard an explosion and when she looked back, she saw the light of the explosion and a plume of smoke rising in the night sky. After half an hour, she drove back to the spa. It was almost four hundred hours. As she entered the underground garage, Stretch was sitting on the bumper of their Humvee, eating sandwiches.

"Hey man, wow. Where's the truck?"

"I blew it up," Stretch said.

"Why didn't you bring it back?" she said. "I thought you said the truck was full!"

"I check it. It was empty. When I looked inside, it had keys in it too. Then I thought that it might have been a decoy, so I just threw a grenade at it, and it went up like a Roman candle," said Stretch.

"It was booby trapped to lure us to steal it, then we blow up with the truck," Stretch said.

"We risked our lives for nothing?" she stated.

"Basically, yep!"

"We'd have gained more by blowing up some other stuff. Instead, we come back with all our explosives," she said.

"Yep. But at least I blew up one of the Vees, and I stole this one."

"Have you reported to James?" she asked.

"Nope"

"Okay, let's face the music."

CHAPTER TWENTY-EIGHT

Shorty Needs a Hospital

INSIDE THE SPA, EVERYTHING WAS going crazy. They were moving everything that they could move against the openings.

"Hey, what going on?" they asked.

"Were reinforcing the entrances," someone answered her as he and another person were carrying a metal desk across the room.

"Why? Didn't we do that already?" Marie asked.

"Apparently not well enough. They told us to put more out there."

"There were several hundred people outside, then they left. But the computer warned they'd be back soon," the movers said as they took the desk down the hallway.

James came up to them and asked how it went. They told him they had gotten one of the Humvees. "The Humvee may be useful because it's armored. We're trying to put out more defense weapons. Then we'll be ready again. Valerie says that there's a high probability they'll strike again during the daytime. They don't have infrared and heat sensors, so to be most effective they need light. We're setting out anti-personnel weapons like claymore mines but need to map them out so our own men don't trip them. We assume we don't have a lot of time to set them."

"Where's Mickey?" asked Marie.

"He's taking a break over there," James pointed. "Don't go far, Marie. I need you and Stretch to make another run. I've ordered some more ammo, and the surgeon is wrapping it up with Shorty. He says he's done all he can do, and if Shorty is going to make it, he needs a hospital with more equipment, a specialist, and blood."

"That bad, huh?" Marie questioned.

"Yeah, I've called for a medivac helo, and I need you to take him to the pick-up area and swap him for the ammo."

"Just give me the coordinates and Stretch and I'll get him there." Marie looked and on the other side of the hub area was Mickey and Veronica huddled together on a mattress laying on the floor.

Marie looked at them and muttered something to herself.

"Do you need him for something?" asked James.

"I was thinking he could drive while I take care of Shorty."

"I can't let Mickey go. I'll let someone else go with you," said James. "Go get Mickey, Marie. Why don't you and Stretch have a sandwich, then get ready to leave. The copter should be there by the time you get to the drop zone."

"I just lost my appetite," she said as she went over to awaken Mickey.

Valerie AI's avatar appeared on the screens around the hub area. "Attention, everyone. Heat and motion sensors have recorded motion around the facility. Everyone is on full alert."

James looked up at the screen nearest him. "Valerie, put up a visual layout showing all heat signatures."

Marie tapped Mickey to awaken him. "Come on, Mickey, time to go to work."

Mickey shook his head and sat up. "What's going on?"

"We need to get ready for another attack. James needs you."

"Got it," said Mickey as he turned to wake up Veronica and tell her the status. "Where's the General?" he asked.

James looked around. "No clue. I'll have Val call him here. We may need him to keep the staff members in line. They still look to him as their superior."

Valerie AI said to James over the closest monitor. "I heard you, James. I'll page the general and tell him to report here."

"Thanks, Val," answered James and he motioned for Mickey. He told Mickey to head down spoke five that had Walker, the movie star, and the senator. He told Mickey to send Randy Walker back to the hub to get instructions from him.

As he got closer, he saw the senator asleep and Walker looking attentively out the glass door.

"Hey, Randy, how you doing here?" he asked. "It looks like that senator isn't exactly onboard with helping you out here, is he?"

"Nope. Can you transfer him somewhere else? I get sick of his constant complaining."

"Sorry, we can't do that. We don't have enough people as it is. Have you had a break the past few hours?"

"Yeah, I took a quick nap a couple of hours ago, and the other ladies gave me a sandwich. I'm getting tired of sandwiches on stale bread, but I admit, the women here are real troopers. James should be proud of them. They are literally life savers. Tell me Mickey, is it true that we may not make it out of here alive?"

"I believe that we'll do fine. In situations like this, the idea of death doesn't seem to cross your mind. Just keep a good watch and we'll keep the stale sandwiches, warm water, and hot ammunition coming to you! Hey, go back to the hub and talk to James. I think he has something for you to do," he said as he got down to replace Randy.

"I'll do what I can, but I could use some real help here, not a clown like that senator."

"I know. I hear ya! I'll see what I can do, but no promises," he called as Randy ran back down the spoke toward the hub.

Randy jogged to the sandwich table grabbed a sandwich and proceeded over to James. "Yeah, boss. What can I do for ya?" he said as he chewed.

"In your war movies, have you ever driven a Humvee?"

"Yeah, man. I can drive the devil out of them. A car chase or anything that has a steering wheel and a gas pedal, I can drive," he said with a grin.

"Great. One of our team has to be taken to a pick-up zone, and exchanged for some ammo. We need a driver. Can you do it?" asked James.

"You bet!"

"If you know the way down to the garage, go now. They'll be waiting for you," James said, and turned to speak in his comm unit to Marie.

"Marie, is Shorty loaded up yet?"

"Yes, James, they are loading him now, and the surgical nurse is going to ride with us. I don't know if he can take the jostling of the ride. That alone could pull something loose and kill him," she said solemnly.

"We need to get him there so they can patch him up right. The doctor said he's done all he can do for him here. We need that ammunition. We're all depending on you to get there and back safely."

"We'll come back or die trying!" Marie breathlessly said as she told Randy to get ready to roll out.

James said a quiet prayer as he went over to Mrs. Locke and Darcy at the sandwich table. "Hello, ladies. Has Mr. Clancy been out here lately?"

"No, we haven't seen him or the one that's helping him man his post in hours."

"Okay, give me a couple sandwiches and bottles of water. I'll take it to them," James said. He picked up the food and stuffed it in a bag and with his gun in his other hand, headed back to the spoke where they were stationed.

As he walked cautiously down the hallway, glass shattered, and Clancy and his partner began shooting.

He dived for the floor on his stomach and returned fire. "Hey, guys. How are you doing here?"

"We were doing great until you showed up. Now, they are shooting at us," Clancy called back at James.

"Sorry about that. If I had known that my coming here would draw fire, I'd have stayed back."

"Just yanking your chain, my friend," Clancy called back to him.

"Are you doing okay? Enough water, ammo, or anything else?"

"Nope, we're good for now. We'll let Valerie know if we need something."

Valerie's voice sounded over the loudspeaker. "Mickey and James, I have an update for you. Where would you like me to inform you of the updates?"

Mickey called out to her. "Back in the hub where we talked the last time."

When he got back into the hub, James was already standing at the monitor they use when they want a private conversation with Valerie AI.

"What do you see, Val?" asked James.

"They are assembling around the perimeter of the health spa. There are about two hundred people now," Valerie AI answered. "They're moving around and assembling in small groups at each spoke entrance. Most of what I detect is from heat sensors. The cameras help somewhat, but the lack of light will make picking specifics and details difficult. I think I see some females and some children, but I cannot be positive."

"Why do they have women and children?" Mickey asked.

"We discussed this, Mickey. They'll use them as human shields when they attack," James said.

"I don't know," said Valerie AI.

"Well, I do," said James.

"That's sick!" said Mickey disgustedly.

"Yes, but that's the people we are dealing with!"

"What do we do about it?" asked Mickey.

"Shoot carefully," added James. "How soon can we expect them to attack?"

"I cannot determine that, James," said Valerie AI.

"Mickey, get someone to load up everyone on the ammo they need for their weapons, and get everyone a few grenades. We need to put almost everyone on the front line to protect each entrance. We may need to set charges to blow up ones we can't protect. In essence, shut them down."

"I'll get right on that," Mickey said as he turned and walked away to start the reinforcement of the entrances.

CHAPTER TWENTY-NINE

Drive to the Drop Zone

RANDY DROVE SLOWLY DOWN THE driveway out of the spa entrance.

"The nurse called out from the back. You've got to drive faster. If you don't, he won't even make it to the drop zone."

"I'm tryin' to drive as smoothly as I can."

"Forget smooth. Drive fast. His sutures are leaking. The helo will have more blood, so we need to get him there."

"You got it," he said as he stomped on the accelerator.

When he got to the road, he slowed down just barely enough to round the corner without throwing everyone sideways.

"You're doing great Randy, now step on it!" Marie called as she moved up through the port into position in the cupola with the machine gun. They were going down the road over ninety miles an hour. It was the top speed of the Hummer. Suddenly up ahead, since Marie was the highest person in the vehicle, she saw it first.

"Way up ahead, is an APC," she called out to the ones below.

"What's that?" returned the nurse.

Randy yelled back at her. "It stands for Armored Personnel Carrier. It carries soldiers."

"Yeah, and I'd bet a dollar to a month's pay, they aren't sitting out there having an evening picnic. Get ready for some evasive action people!" Marie screamed back down to them. She checked her gun and fired a couple of shots to assure it was working property. "Okay, Randy, don't slow down, just plow through and don't stop for anything!"

"Yes, ma'am," he said and kept driving straight ahead.

"Don't worry about the rifle fire. The armor can deflect that. We can do it," Marie called out.

"What if they shoot through the glass."

"Bullet proof, Randy. Just keep it on the road!"

As they got closer, she saw them running into the road to block it. She swung the gun around to face forward, and put a few rounds over their heads. The men ducked but didn't move. They just raised their guns and started firing at the Humvee. Randy began to turn off the road, but they saw the APC back up to get in front of them hoping they would stop.

"Randy, don't get off the road. Stay on it!" she screamed at him.

"But I'll kill them if they don't move!" he screamed back.

"If you don't, they'll kill us, Randy. DO NOT GET OFF THE ROAD!" She repeated.

The men continued to fire as they got closer. The bullets pinged off the Humvee. Randy was getting spooked and began to swerve. As he did this, they were all jostled around the inside, the IV hanging up was swinging around from its attached point on the ceiling. The nurse tried to hold still, but couldn't because she needed to hold on.

"Randy? Randy, answer me," called Marie. "Are you still with me?"

"Yes, but there firing directly at the windshield. What if one of the bullets comes through?" he whimpered.

"They won't. I promise. It is bullet proof. Do you hear me, Randy?"

Now the pings were getting deeper in sound and much louder. Marie knew they had a 50-caliber machine gun somewhere, but she couldn't pinpoint it yet. She swiveled her machine gun in circles looking for it.

"Randy," she screamed. "Randy, get a grip! Get your butt together and get us out of here. NOW. Drive this thing, or we die. Keep this thing moving. Do not stop. If they have a rocket launcher and they fire it, we are toast! Move out. DRIVE! DRIVE!" she screamed until she was hoarse.

Finally, she heard Randy shifting from reverse to forward and the Humvee was lurching back and forth, finally moving forward and moved out of its spot just as a rocket landed where they were sitting and exploded.

As they moved forward, she spotted the machine gun covered by brush to camouflage it. She fired onto the bushes until she had spent about a hundred rounds into that area. Finally they were on the other side of the gauntlet, and Randy drove down the road again at full speed.

When they were out of sight, Marie relaxed, and sat back down in the cabin of the Humvee. She took a huge breath and blew it out, and leaned against the back of the seat.

Randy shook his head. "I'm sorry, Marie. I'm so sorry. I almost got us killed back there. I just panicked. I'm so sorry," he said, sweat rolling down his face even though the air was cool.

She reached over and touched him on the arm. "Hey. You did alright. It happens sometimes. We got through it. That's what counts. We're all still alive and on the road again."

She turned and said to the nurse, "How's Shorty doing back there?"

She stammered and answered, "I think he's no worse than he was. How far away from the pick-up area are we now."

Marie thought for a moment. "I think we are about ten minutes out. How are you?"

"I'll be okay but when we were slamming around, I pinned my arm and I think it's broken." She pulled her sleeve up and her arm was swollen all the way to her shoulder.

"I see. I guess that means as soon as we get Shorty loaded you are officially relieved of duty," and she gave her a slight salute. "Both of you are heroes." Marie turned back to look forward out of the bullet pocked windshield.

There was silence in the cabin until they pulled into an open field off the road. The helo hovered overhead and slowly set down and the Humvee pulled as close as it was safe. Four men jumped out of the helo, ran to the Humvee, and began to load Shorty onboard after off-loading four cases of ammunition. The nurse also got onboard and the helicopter lifted off, and flew out of sight in the early evening as it was getting dark.

It was a star lit night, and on the way back they drove slowly to keep down the engine noise. If someone was ahead, they wouldn't hear the Humvee so far away and have less time to prepare for an attack.

CHAPTER THIRTY

The Child with the Dirty Little Rag Doll

Suddenly, down one of the spokes came a sound of explosions, gunfire, and the hideous sound of a man screaming.

Mickey grabbed an AR 15 and ran for the spoke just as smoke belched out of the hallway. He ran and dove for the floor and poured a stream of bullets down the hallway at some oncoming men. James was right behind Mickey on the floor, also laying down a wall of bullets. In a few seconds, they watched as the men's chests opened up and blood spattered over the walls and floor. Then there was silence.

They looked and saw four of the spa security team dead, covered in their own blood.

A few seconds later, a call came from spoke five, where they had replaced Walker with two men and the senator. Someone was calling out for Mickey or James to come help them.

Mickey and James jumped up just as another sound of automatic gunfire reached them from another spoke.

"I'll get that one, Mickey. You go check on the men and the senator," said James as he ran after the sound of the gunfire.

"On my way," answered Mickey as he rose and ran for spoke five. He rounded the corner on his stomach just as he had the last time, but no one was there except one man and the senator. The glass was shattered and the senator was almost hugging the floor, and the man was glaring at him.

Mickey quickly crawled up to the remaining man. "Where's the other man that we stationed here? What's going on?" he asked as he looked out at the remnants of the glass door.

The man spoke, almost screaming at the senator. "He killed her! He shot her dead on the way here!"

"She was going to blow us up!" the senator yelled at the man.

Mickey looked at the ground about thirty feet away. There was a little girl lying on the ground with a brown paper bag lying beside her. The little child's head was half blown away.

"I saved your life!" the senator yelled.

Mickey looked at the child and almost threw up on the floor. It was a little child. He turned to the senator, reached out across the floor, and dragged the senator over to himself. He glaring at the pudgy man, and screamed at him with fierce, intense hatred.

"You killed an innocent little child. You are a slithering cowardly idiot!" Mickey screamed just inches from the senator's face.

"I saved our lives! I've heard that in Vietnam, they used to send little children into buildings with explosives strapped onto their backs or under their clothes."

Mickey pulled the man closer, then shoved his head into the space between the barricade they set up in the doorway. "Do you see any explosives on her? I asked you a question," he said as he slammed the senator's head against the barricade again.

"She was carrying it in that brown bag. I saw it," the senator said, trembling.

"Look again, you stupid fool. What do you see?"

"I...I...don't know what it is," he answered feebly.

"I see what it is! It's a little rag doll, and some clothes! The little girl was running away from them to get to safety with us! So help me! I hope you die and go straight to hell for what you did! To hell with you!" Mickey almost began to cry and wiped away a tear before anyone could see it. He hated this. He hated the men outside. He hated what they were doing, and he hated that senator, and everyone like him.

They heard a single gunshot fire. Mickey looked up, and he saw a crying woman that was running for the child. She fell in mid stride and as she fell, they could see blood spraying from her back as she hit the ground. The Yakuza had shot the little girl's mother in the back.

The man, Mickey, and the senator just looked out between the space in the barricade they were hiding behind.

The man spoke up, "Sir, can you please find someone to take that monster's place here with me?"

"Yes. I'll find someone for you. If I can't, I'll come back myself," he said as he started to leave.

As Mickey started to back down the hallway, the senator said to him, "I'm going to put an end to this thing. I'm going to negotiate a peace treaty right now."

He had taken a handkerchief out of his pocket and tied it onto the end of the barrel of his gun.

"What do you think you're doing?" asked Mickey. "Do NOT raise that thing. Those people don't negotiate."

"I know what I'm doing. I'm going to end this once and for all," he said as he slowly got up with the rifle in the air with the kerchief tied to it.

Mickey lunged at the man just as they heard another single gunshot. As Mickey grabbed the senator by the waist to pull him down, the senator's head exploded and he slumped onto Mickey's back, driving him back down onto the floor.

The man reached over and pulled the senator's dead body off Mickey. Mickey rolled to the other side of the opening and the body of the senator lay motionless between them.

The man and Mickey locked eyes. "I'm sorry it happened, but he deserved it," the man said.

"I guess he did, but I hate to see anyone killed. I'll get someone to take the body away. We probably need to put it in cold storage until this thing is over. The government will want it. No matter what we think of him, he had a wife and family," said Mickey.

"Mickey, my sensors are indicating that the senator is dead. Would you like me to assign someone to take his body to one of the freezers in the kitchen area?" Val asked.

"Yes," he said as he left the spoke.

CHAPTER THIRTY-ONE

James and Mickey Commandeer Two Enemy APCs

When Mickey got back to the hub, he headed over to spoke three to help James. He saw James shooting as a staff security man hunkered down behind a piece of furniture.

"What can I get you?" Mickey called out to both of them.

"Ammo. He's out, and I'm low, and who's blood is that all over you?" called James.

"I'll bring some ammo back and give you a hand. It's the senator's blood. I'll explain later."

Mickey ran back to the ammo pile and grabbed some loaded clips, went back to the spoke and called out to James and the other man. "I'm coming in, cover me," he said as James sprayed the hallway with gunfire. Mickey threw some clips over to the man, and continued to James. As they both moved into the protection of an alcove, Mickey handed James a clip.

"Just in time, that was my last clip. Tell me about the senator."

"The senator's dead, and the man that's there needs some help, but he's doing great, so I can't stay."

"Oh, crap. We'll have a LOT of explaining to do about how a United States Senator was killed on American soil in a secret location. How's everyone else doing?"

"Don't know. I haven't made the rounds yet," Mickey answered. "By the way, where is the rest of the team?"

"Stretch and some other spa security men are posted on spoke twelve. Marie and Veronica and a couple of other spa staff are on seven."

"Can I send one of them to help the lone man on five?" asked Mickey. "And where is the general? Now, gotta go."

"Yes, move a man if you need to. I don't have a clue where the general is. Move out, and report when you can. Go! We'll cover you on your way out."

Mickey quickly grabbed some more clips and headed to spoke seven, where Marie and Veronica and the two other men were positioned.

"Hello, ladies and gentlemen," he called out as he passed them some additional clips.

"Hey, Mickey Ray," they both answered without taking their eyes off the door. The other men nodded.

"If you need anything, just tell Valerie and she'll notify James or me, and we'll try to get what you need," called out Mickey, as he motioned to one of the men.

Looking at the man's name tag, Mickey said, "George, follow me. Leave your ammo here. We'll get some more back at the hub."

The Klaxon horn blared again, and Valerie AI's voice came over the speaker system again. "Attention, everyone. An attack has begun around every spoke of the spa. Be aware that some personnel are not, I repeat, are not combatants. They are innocent illegal immigrants that are being used by the Yakuza as human shields. Do not, I repeat, do not shoot noncombatants. They are innocent and mean you no harm."

Mickey called out to Valerie, "Announce to everyone, the non-combatants will be women, children, and unarmed men. They are not Japanese or any variety of Asian descent."

Valerie repeated the announcement to everyone verbatim, as Mickey had told her.

When Mickey and George got back to the hub, George grabbed more ammo clips, a bottle of water, and a sandwich. Mickey motioned for him to follow. He led him to spoke five and told him, "Go drag out the senator's body, and have the ladies take him to the freezer. Then come back, to assist the re-assigned men." The man saluted Mickey and took off into the hallway as they gave him cover fire.

Mickey continued to the spoke that had Stretch. They were holding the Yakuza off fine, and even a few illegals were inside laying on the floor to avoid the bullets. Mickey let the people in, and by that time Mrs. Locke, Darcy, and the senator's girlfriend were back at the table. The senator's girlfriend, Caroline, was pale as a ghost.

Mickey took the frightened people over to Mrs. Locke and asked her to find a safe place for them. He went over to Caroline, who was busy vomiting into a trashcan.

"Caroline, I'm sorry you had to see that," Mickey said.

"Me too, but I didn't like him. I only did it for the money and…."

"You don't have to explain anything to me. It's not my business, but we need you to keep it together and help these people. Can you do that?"

Tears were dripping from her face. "I'm scared. I don't know if I can do anything right now."

Mickey stood and wiped her tears away. He pulled her to himself and gave her a comforting hug. "We're all scared, but we need everyone to help. If you help now, I'm sure we'll get out of this situation."

"I'll try."

"I know you can do it. Just help Mrs. Locke and Dee deal with these people. They have had it a lot worse that we have. Just try. That's all I ask."

"Okay. Give me a minute. I'll help."

"Thanks. I've got to go now. Just go over there and see Dee. She'll tell you what you can do." Mickey turned and disappeared into another hallway.

Valerie AI spoke up again, "Mickey, there are more incoming people. What should we do? Our men are being very careful and only shooting armed men, but the Yakuza are shooting the people as they approach the building. They are trying to take our attention from themselves in an attempt to get inside mixed with the illegals."

"Oh, crap," said Mickey to no one in particular.

"They are bringing in two armored personnel carriers and parking them near the entrance as a movable battle station," Valerie AI added.

"Which spoke? Are they parked?" he called to Valerie AI.

"They have one at spoke three and another at spoke five, Mickey. They are firing out of gun ports on the armored personnel carrier's side. I assume they are going to provide cover fire for incoming troops."

"How large are the gun ports, Val?" asked Mickey as he ran toward spoke five.

"I will zoom in the cameras and take a measurement. It will take me a few moments to do that and make a calculation."

Mickey continued to spoke five. When he entered, all was quiet. He cautiously made his way down the hallway to where George and the other men were looking at the APC.

Walker asked Mickey without taking his eyes from the door, "What are they doing? They're just sitting there. I can just see one to our left at spoke three."

"We don't know yet, but they seem to be setting up an advanced battle station. When they fire, they'll continue while their men advance under the APC's cover fire."

Valerie AI called out, "Mickey, honey, they have modified the APCs with gun ports about 7 inches in diameter. They appear to be on the side, but not rear or front. I cannot see if there are any located on the side facing away from the building. Why do you need to know that, Mickey, dear?"

One of the men looked at Mickey. "Mickey, dear and honey? What's this thing you have going with the computer system?"

Mickey shook his head. "She thinks we're in love."

"I do love you, my honey. I want to help you continue to live," said Valerie AI.

"Yes. I want to live as well. Now let me think, Val," he said as he looked back at the men.

"I've gotta go. I'll send someone back to help you and bring more ammo. When they start firing, you'll need all the help you can get."

Mickey told Valerie to locate James and tell him they needed to talk.

Mickey saw James coming out of one of the spokes. "Hey, did you hear what Val said?"

"Yes. She told me about the APCs with the gun ports. We need to disable those APCs without damaging them. We might need to use them ourselves later. Do we have a staff member here that worked maintenance?" asked James. He called out. "Val. Do we have any maintenance personnel in the building?"

"Yes, James. He is working on maintaining the power grid inside the Electrical Room. That room is in spoke twelve. Do you want me to call him for you?"

"Yes, and tell him to meet me in the hospital, spoke three. Tell him to hurry."

"What're we going to do?" asked Mickey.

"It all depends on if we have the necessary chemicals. What time is it?"

"It's nineteen hundred hours. It's dark."

"Good, we need darkness. It's been cloudy all day, let's hope those clouds continue through the night. Follow me. I may need some help," James said as he headed toward the hospital spoke.

As they ran, they met the maintenance man entering. He was a middle-aged native American Indian man with black coveralls. He had a deep voice and dark, leathery skin wearing a name tag labeled, "Eugene." Carrying a small tool bag, he ducked into an alcove followed by Mickey and James.

"This is a freaking nightmare, man! I never thought I'd be involved in some kind of war. Every time those guys blow something up, I'm in the electrical closet trying to keep the power on."

Mickey spoke up. "We appreciate what you're doing here."

"Yeah, we really do. Do you know where the alcohol is kept?" James asked.

"What kind of alcohol? Y'all looking to take a few shots of some firewater?" he said cautiously.

"No. We need about two gallons of isopropyl alcohol, and the same amount of chlorine bleach," said James.

"The bleach is in the next wing over, spoke one in a cleaning supply closet. Alcohol is everywhere here in little bottles. I think they buy it in five-gallon cans and refill the little bottles," Eugene said nervously.

"Now, we're getting somewhere. Where's the water and plumbing room? You know where all the valves and water hoses and things are located?"

"That would be back in twelve. At the end, near the exit. I can't go there. That's right in the middle of the shooting. I'll get killed."

"Eugene, we need your help. We'll tell you exactly what we need if you can get us two gallons of bleach and alcohol. We promise to protect you in there."

Mickey said, "I'll go with you, Eugene. I'll help you carry the stuff."

Mickey and Eugene set out for the bleach in the other wing. James began looking in hospital rooms for the medical supply closet. In one of the hospital rooms, James found a medical supply closet with alcohol stored in large gallon jugs, similar to milk packaging. He grabbed two jugs and headed toward spoke twelve. When he got to twelve, Mickey and Eugene were already waiting for him.

"Okay," said James. "When our men shoot, we head down the hallway, and you go to the door where all the water valves are located. We'll flank you with gunfire."

James said something into his communications unit, and ahead the men began firing forward out the door. When the gunfire started, James and Mickey grabbed Eugene by the arms and they all started running forward. As they neared a door at the end of the hallway close to the exit, Eugene veered to the side toward the last door closest to the exit. He moved into the alcove and slammed against the wall, shaking and sweating with fear. Mickey and James were not far behind, following along.

"Good," said James. "Now that wasn't too bad, was it?"

The man was shaking all over. "What'd we do now?"

"We go inside," James said, and he grabbed the knob and swung the door into the room. He then pushed Eugene and Mickey inside.

Turning to Eugene, he asked, "Do you have any garden hoses?"

"Yes, we have several lengths. What do you need?"

"We need two hoses, about one hundred feet each. Tape them together side by side. Then we pour the bleach into one hose, and alcohol in the other hose. Each one-hundred-foot hose should hold an adequate amount of liquid," James said.

"Why are we doing this, sir?" asked Eugene.

"Good question. Do you know what you get when you mix chlorine and alcohol?" asked James.

"Chlorine gas. Everyone knows that. That's why you don't clean with both. We don't even store them in the same room. The gas will kill you!" said Eugene.

"No, but you're on the right track. If you mix chlorine and ammonia, you get chlorine gas, and yes, it's deadly, but we're going to mix chlorine and alcohol. That mixture will give us chloroform. Chloroform's an anesthesia in operating rooms. It'll only put them to sleep unless they inhale too much of it," said James with a smug smile.

"We have several types of anesthesia's in our operating rooms. Why can't we use that?"

Mickey stood there looking at both men. "James, just tell us what we're doing here. Science class can be later."

"Okay, we're going to put the men to sleep inside those APC's. I'll sneak out to the rear of the APC. When I signal to you, you turn the hose on. Then you and Eugene will turn on the pressure and blow all the bleach and alcohol inside where it'll mix, making the chloroform gas and put them to sleep. If we tried to use the operating gas, I'd need to drag the anesthesia tanks across to the APC. This is much easier. Also, if I put the tank hose inside, they will just push it back out. If we fill the inside with liquid, it'll mix inside. They'll stay inside and pass out or open the door and run out. Either way, we get them and hold them as hostages. Then we commandeer the APC's. We can do them one at a time, so we can get both vehicles and whoever's inside."

They taped the hoses together and taped the outlet end to hold in the liquid. Inside the room were several water taps, to which they attached the other end of the hoses.

"Now, we wait for full darkness. It's supposed to be a cloudy night, so we won't have the moon or starlight. If I'm careful, I should be able to crawl slowly to the back of the APC. When I'm in position, I'll let you know when to turn on the tap. When you do, let the water run for five seconds, then quickly shut it off again. We don't want to dilute the solution, so it isn't strong enough to work. Questions?"

Mickey and Eugene shook their heads.

"You wait here, and I'll go out and tell the guys outside the plan, resupply them and make the rounds again to make sure everyone is okay. Eugene, don't you have a sprinkler system on the grounds also?"

"Yes, sir."

"Where's the room for the underground propane tank valves?" James asked.

"We're in it. This room is the central control room for shutting off gas to the kitchen area in case of fire and heating for the entire spa. We can control the interior fire sprinkler system zones. The exterior water sprinkler system is controlled here too. We can route and turn on the grounds sprinkler systems at will from here anywhere outside the facility."

"Eugene, it's a blessing from God that you're still with us. I have to go now, but I have an idea. We'll discuss it when I get back," he said, patting him on the back as he left.

It was silent for a couple of minutes, then Mickey and Eugene heard a burst of gunfire, and they knew that James had left the hallway.

James went back to the food table that was still being monitored by Darcy, Barbara Locke and Caroline, the senator's mistress. He searched for the general, but he was nowhere in sight.

"Valerie?" he called out. A few moments went by and the avatar of Valerie AI appeared on the monitor closest to James.

"Yes, James. How may I help you?"

"How are things outside the building?" he asked.

"They are mostly the same. I have evaluated that the Yakuza is building up and waiting for darkness to attack again, but there is only a seventy-two percent chance that will happen."

"How did you arrive at that percentage?"

"I calculated the decrease in personnel because of skirmishes and Humvee attacks on their encampment. They no longer have the two Humvees with the machine gun mounts. It has taken a toll on their morale. However, the Yakuza is driven by loyalty and fear of their superiors. Would you like me to calculate your chances of survival resulting from a full-strength attack by the Yakuza?"

"No. I do NOT. And furthermore, don't ask me again. And do NOT do it if Mickey asks you. Do you understand me, Valerie?"

"I understand you, James, but Mickey Ray Christianson is my superior. I take my orders from him. I am his personal assistant, and I love him. It is my mission to protect him."

"Let me tell you something, Valerie. As a human, Mickey also has feelings, and if he thinks he may die, it may decrease his effectiveness. That factor itself may lower his will to fight and live. So, if you tell him his chance of survival, it may contribute to his death. Do you understand me?"

"I understand. I will not calculate his survival percentage."

"Good. Where's the general?"

"I do not know."

"I thought you knew where everyone is at all times," said James.

"He has taken off his tracking device, so I can no longer track his location."

"Something is off about that man. I just can't figure out what it is."

"I'm sorry I can't help you, James."

"It's okay, continue with monitoring the facility," he said and went to the food table.

"Dee, you look tired. Let's go sit down for a few minutes," James said.

She looked at Mrs. Locke and Caroline.

"Go ahead, dear. Spend some time with your husband. We don't mind. We're doing okay here," said Mrs. Locke.

"Yeah, we don't mind. At least you have someone here. We have no one," Caroline spoke to Darcy with a wink.

James and Darcy walked over to a mattress on the floor and sat down. She leaned over against James, and he put his arm around her.

In minutes, James had fallen asleep. Dee lay motionless against him as a tear slid down her face. She softly cried for her husband.

The entire facility was quiet as a tomb. No one spoke, yet everyone was at their stations and on full alert. Darkness settled over the building and flashlights were used only in areas that could not be seen outside.

As the darkness flooded over the building, James got up and gently laid Darcy on the mattress so she could continue sleeping, and went over to Mrs. Locke and Caroline.

"It's dark, so why don't both of you get some sleep? If something happens, we'll wake you for some help. We may need you to help with ammunition or moving any injured men to the hospital wing," James said.

"Thank you, James. Caroline can go, I'll stay. I'm old and I don't sleep well, anyway."

James smiled at her and went to inform the men in spokes three and five of his plan to take the APC's without destroying them.

When he got back into the hub, he called to Valerie AI. "Val, give me a head count of enemy personnel around spoke three and five?"

"I'm picking up a heat signature of fifty-three people at spoke three, and forty-seven at spoke five. I cannot differentiate between the number of hostages and Yakuza."

"I understand. Now, are you tuned into our communication units?" asked James.

"No, but I can if you desire me to do that," she answered.

"Yes. Do it. You've heard my plan?"

"Yes. I heard you tell the men. I shall be listening for further instructions from you, James."

He returned to the water and gas control room. When he got inside, Mickey and Eugene were sitting on the floor.

"Mickey. Eugene. This's what I'm going to do. When I crawl to the APC and drag the hose along with me, Val will blink the exterior lights at my command to confuse and temporarily blind the men out there. I will move when they're blinded. We can only do it a few times, before they catch on. Make sure that the hose doesn't get kinked or hung up on something inside?"

"Yep. We understand," they said.

James opened the door, and slid on his stomach, crawling into the milky darkness, slowly and silently dragging the hose with him. He moved as slow as the minute hand on an analogue clock. The cloudy sky that blocked the light of the moon and stars hid his movements but it still took him nearly an hour to move the fifty feet from the building to the APC. Crawling around to the back of the vehicle, he waited and pulled some more slack out of the hose. He silently moved around to the side of the vehicle and eased about twelve inches of the hose inside, and whispered into his comm unit.

"Open the valves to both hoses for five seconds. Then shut it off."

He felt the hose stiffen as the liquids inside them were pressurized, forcing the chlorine bleach and alcohol spray inside the vehicle. When the hose went limp in his hands, he pulled it back out of the port and listened to the men inside. They began to cough as the chemicals mixed and began emitting the gas inside.

He grabbed the rear door handle and leaned against the door to keep them from exiting. They banged on the door, began to get weak and fell asleep. Soon, there was no sound from within the vehicle. They were asleep or dead and he didn't really care which.

James quietly said into his comm unit. "Mickey, can you fill the hoses again? I'll tell you when it comes out here. I'll close the ends up and I'll move to the other APC across the yard area."

"Copy that," came Mickey's reply.

It took about five minutes for the bleach to begin pouring out of the end of the hose. He capped it off and waited for the alcohol to flow out of the other hose. He capped it as well. Then he began moving over the ground to the other vehicle.

The other one went the same as the first one. After the interior fracas stopped, James called Mickey again. "Reel in the hoses and come on out here to help me drive these things away from here."

When Mickey and James crawled into the driver's seats of each vehicle, they started them at the same time and drove away, with no one trying to stop them. When they drove around to the entrance of the underground garage, armed staff members, Marie and Alyssa were waiting for them.

When Marie and Alyssa opened the rear doors, they stepped inside, confiscated the guns and roused the men. The Yakuza men got out of the vehicles slowly and groggily, being totally disoriented. After tying their hands behind them, they led them inside the facility, placed them into a meeting room, and stationed guards outside.

James came to the outside guards and told them to make the prisoners strip down. "I want them naked as the day they were born," he said.

The guards protested. "That is humiliating and unacceptable treatment of a prisoner. Even prisoners have their dignity."

"No. They are prisoners of war. You will take their clothes. You will do as I order."

"We will not do that. We will not strip a man of his dignity. It is bad enough that they are now our prisoners," the guard said.

James always carried a sidearm when in combat. He reached down and withdrew it. "Do as I order, or you will join them in that room, and you will be unclothed as well. Which will it be, you out here, fully clothed or inside with them, naked?"

The man turned and opened the door and began calling out orders to the men to strip down to the skin.

After they had placed all their clothes in a pile, James ordered one guard to take the clothes away. He complied without protest.

James then said to the remaining guard, "You will stand guard here. And you will remember, do not answer them or open the door under any circumstances. If you do, and they escape, they will remember that you are the one that ordered them to disrobe and take their dignity. So, in retaliation, they'll kill you. If you don't want to die, you'll not open that door," he said and walked away.

CHAPTER THIRTY-TWO

James Turns up the Heat

Back at the hub, Mickey saw Veronica eating a stale sandwich and drinking a bottle of warm water. "Hello, my dear Veronica," he said, giving her a kiss on the cheek.

"A kiss on the cheek. That's all I get? After what we've all done for you?" she said.

Mickey blushed but didn't answer her. He also picked up a sandwich and water. "We just got two APCs from them."

"Good. What're we going to do with them?"

"We may rescue some of their hostages," he said, taking a bite of his sandwich.

A voice came over the central sound system, "This is Director Chiaki. I want to see James Bower in my quarters now, please."

James looked up at the speaker in annoyance. "Please excuse me, Director, but I'm quite busy right now protecting this facility. If you need to talk to me, please do it on screen or in person at the check in hub."

"I need to talk to you in private, Mr. Bower."

"I need to stay here in case someone needs me, Director. And where is the general? I told him to stay here because we need him to direct these men."

"Isn't he in the hub with you?"

"No. We haven't seen him for hours, and I've been too busy to go look for him. I'll find a private room close to the hub and we can talk on the monitors there," James said, as he began looking for an empty room close by. He stopped by the check-in counter, and Valerie AI transferred Chiaki's voice and video to the small monitor at the front desk.

"I got a call from the Yakuza. They told me you have been attacking their camp. Also, a few hours ago, in the middle of the night, you attacked and took their personnel carriers."

"We did, and we took some of their men as hostage as well. We are no longer defending this facility. Now, since they attacked us first, we are in a full-scale engagement. So, in our eyes, we are stepping up this takeover to another level. We'll continue attacking them until they leave or surrender."

"He was very upset."

"Has he lost his mind? This is war! That's what happens in a war. Each side tries to stop the other side. As long as they're outside, and pointing guns and attacking this facility, we will retaliate in the harshest methods we have at our disposal."

"He says that he will attack and kill everyone inside this building, including me and all my staff, if we do not surrender. If we surrender, then he will let all non-combatants leave unharmed," she stated.

"My team and I are all combatants, so what'll he do with us?"

"I do not know. We can negotiate with them for your release after the surrender."

"No deal. If you want to negotiate our pardon, freedom to leave, and give us our full agreed upon pay, we'll walk away. But we aren't going to surrender without an agreement first."

"I will speak to him and try to work out a deal."

"I don't care what terms you agree on. For us, we want our full pay, and full pass out of here, or no deal. We need an answer by noon, or the terms are withdrawn, and the battle continues," James said with finality.

"I'll try." The screen went blank.

"Val, what's happening outside? The sun will be up within half an hour. I want to know what's happening," called James to the monitor.

Valerie appeared. "Good morning, James."

"Did you hear me? I want to know what the heck is going on outside!" he called to the monitor.

"Are we in a bad mood this morning, James?" Valerie AI said.

"Yes. I am in a bad mood. I'm tired. I've had two hours sleep in the last forty-eight, and my people have been on station for days with minimal sleep, and you have the audacity to make a comment about my mood?"

"I understand, James. There has been a buildup of personnel since the incident of the stolen APCs."

"Okay, so they're reinforcing the line to make another attack?" asked James.

"That is my conclusion, based on all the latest actions."

"Oh, crap! We've got to get ready for a full-scale attack."

"I concur, James," said Valerie AI.

"Valerie, put me on the central system."

"You are on air, James."

"Attention everyone. The latest development leads us to believe that a full-scale attack is eminent. Possibly within the next two hours. Take this time to eat, drink, and if you can rest, do so, but at least one person must be alert at each station. We expect the attack to be at all stations at the same time. Someone will come around and restock your ammunition and supplies. It's getting light now, so don't take your eyes off the edge of the woods that surround us. Good luck everyone, and may God save our souls."

James went back to the water and gas room.

"Eugene, do the gauges and valves over there monitor and control the propane tank?" James asked, pointing to a cluster of gauges on the wall.

"Yes. We have two buried tanks, as you can see by the two gauges here," he explained, pointing to two gauges about the size of a saucer. "One is totally full, the other is almost full. They were just filled last week."

"Good. Is your sprinkler system zoned?"

"Yes, sir. That diagram on the wall shows the zones and the manifold below it shows which valve corresponds to each zone. We can turn on or off any zone anywhere on the spa grounds."

"That's great," said James. "Do you have any tools and extra pipe and fittings here?"

"Our plumbing supply closet is over there," he said, pointing to a closed door on another wall.

"Here is what I want you to do," James said, taking a marker from the table in front of the water distribution illustration on the wall. He started drawing and intersecting lines and explaining as he drew. "I want you to disconnect the water from the system. Then hook up the propane gas to the sprinkler system instead."

"But sir, then when it's turned on, gas will come out of the sprinkler heads instead of water."

James smiled a cruel smile. "That's exactly what I want. I want to turn the entire outside grounds into a hell fire inferno. I want to turn on fire in any section at any time. Got it?"

James could see he understood. Eugene smiled back at James.

He said slowly, "We are gonna have some french-fried Japanese Yakuza!"

"Last thing, I want it to switch back to water at a moment's notice, so we can also put out the fire," James added.

Mickey spoke up. "James, that's cruel. I mean, that's almost inhuman. I don't like it."

James looked at Mickey. "My friend, we've used fire in war since there's been war. During the crusades, they used trebuchets to hurl balls of fire at the enemy. Archers used fire arrows, and castles poured burning oil over walls. We even used flame throwers during the second world war and to burn out Vietnamese men in tunnels. And what do you think napalm bombs are? They're fire bombs. So, to save our skins, we'll also use fire, but then we can come back and spray water to put it out."

"Yeah, I guess you're right. I just hate the cruelty," Mickey said.

"Yes, Mickey, you know the expression. War is hell! We're about to bring hellfire up from the ground. Get a grip here, Mickey. It's them or us. We're outnumbered here. We need to use everything we've got. So let Eugene do what I said. You can help him. I've got to go check on the other people."

Mickey went over to help Eugene and James left.

"Valerie, get Chiaki on the monitor for me," called James as he went into the hub area.

It took Valerie several minutes to get the director on the monitor.

"Yes, Mr. Bower," she said as her image materialized on the screen.

"Where is the general?"

"Isn't he with you?"

"No. He isn't. Have you heard from our friends the Yakuza?"

"Yes."

"And?"

"He said, prepare to die!" she said, solemnly.

"We're prepared for battle, but we are not prepared to die today," James answered back. "One last question? Will he consider letting the women go?"

"No. I asked him about that as well. I even offered to stay myself if he let the others leave. He said all or nothing."

"And that is his final decision?"

"Yes."

"Then I guess we'll get this thing over with," James said. "Valerie, get Stretch and Marie on a monitor."

"They are stationed at spokes. There are no active monitors where they are located," answered Valerie AI.

"Mickey, go get them. Tell them I need them at the hub."

In minutes, Mickey returned with them.

"What do you need from us?" asked Stretch.

"We're about to launch an attack. I need you to take one of the APCs and drive around to pick up hostages where you can. Since they're armored, you can use the vehicles to shield them from gunfire, and rescue them if you can. Also, you can get closer to the armed men in the woods. When we see someone, we'll direct you via the comm units."

"Got it. When do you want us to go?" asked Marie.

"Now. We're going to launch a pre-emptive strike in fifteen minutes."

"Let's go guys," she said, heading to the doorway of the garage.

"Valerie, put an aerial view of the facility, and superimpose the men as shown by the heat sensors," called out James.

Alyssa said, "This one's a mess, isn't it, James?"

"Yes, it is, Aly. How is it going at your station?"

"Boring, but in a situation like this, that's a good thing."

"Yeah, but it's about to get real, very soon, girl."

"Yes. I heard we have flame throwers. Nasty things they are."

"Yep, but with the odds against us, that should equalize us somewhat."

"The computer system here almost makes me useless," Aly said complacently.

"A computer can never replace you, my dear," James smiled.

"I heard that the computer has a crush on Mickey."

"Oh, you heard that too? It's funny really. Every time she calls him honey, or dear, he turns beet red. If we weren't in such a bad way right now, I'd rib him about it a lot more. But, like it or not, she, I mean it, is a tremendous help."

"When we get out of this, we'll have plenty of time to call him on it. I better get back to my station, James." Alyssa left to take up her assigned spoke.

Valerie's voice came over the sound system again, "James, a vehicle has left the garage, and circled around the building, and stopped at spoke twelve. I think it is Marie."

James called over the comm units to Eugene. "Eugene, is the sprinkler system set up like I told you?"

"Yes, sir. You give me the word, and I will turn it on."

"Not until I give the order," said James. "Mickey? Where are you?"

"I'm with Eugene."

"Get outside by the door and help the men there get ready for the attack. When you're in place, put a couple of rounds into the woods for me to get a fix on your fire position."

James waited for Mickey to take position. Valerie pulled up the video of the outside of the area of spoke one, where Mickey was located.

"Valerie, can you tell me where some sensors are, showing a gathering of one to three people near each other?"

Heat sensor icons showed in various areas on the screen. In two different areas, the sensors blinked brightly.

"Mickey, at approximately ten o'clock fire a few rounds into the wooded area," James ordered.

Mickey fired a short burst causing branches to rustle.

"Good. Now move over about ten feet from that point and fire again."

Mickey moved over and fired. Mickey heard a scream, then heard a thud as someone or something hit the ground.

"Bull's eye. Someone went down." James continued looking at the screen when one of the blinking lights moved, then stopped.

Valerie called out again to James through the comm unit. "James, I see three men gathering several others together in a group."

"Valerie, the group is most likely hostages they plan to use as human shields. Hold on. Marie, did you see the area that I directed Mickey to fire?"

"Affirmative. I'll move if you or Val can direct me. I'll move over. We can take out their guards and bring the hostages in," Marie answered.

Valerie said, "Marie, move over to spoke one on the right side. I will tell you when you are in location."

Marie began driving slowly, and she heard guns firing and bullets pinging off the sides of the APC. Stretch put his gun out of the port and filled the area with sprays of bullets, and the gunfire stopped. The Yakuza men knew they were wasting ammunition. Marie pulled forward to the location directed by Valerie AI and stopped.

"Move forward thirty-four feet, Marie. You may see the people gathered there," Valerie AI said calmly.

"I see them," called out Stretch to Marie. "They're staring straight at us like deer in headlights."

"That's because they don't know they are about to die," said Stretch as he pulled the trigger and saw the man's head jerk back as the bullet hit him between the eyes. He repeated the shot to the man on the other side and watched as he dropped dead, as well.

All the people gathered between them, dropped to their knees, and held their hands up in surrender. Stretch moved their guns back and forth in the gun port, looking for other armed men.

"Do you see other men around or near the group, Valerie?" asked Marie over her comm unit.

"The only ones remaining is the group of people who have gathered together."

Marie started to back into the area to collect the hostages. She backed into the edge of the brush, and Stretch opened the rear doors. When the doors opened, they screamed, cried, and laid on the ground. Stretch herded them into the APC.

Marie requested help to unload them and drove the APC back to the garage. After unloading, she returned to the spoke she had just left, working their way around.

Valerie called over the sound system again. "Attention, everyone. There have been attacks on spoke five, seven and nine. This is not a drill."

"Valerie, are they sending out hostages ahead of them to use as shields?" asked James.

"I don't know."

"If they are, they will be just a few feet in front of the Yakuza men, and they will be close together. The Yakuza men will be more spread out behind."

"I don't see that formation, James," Valerie AI stated.

"Mickey, can you move over to spoke seven and give them some support?"

"I'm heading over as we speak." Mickey ran and as he bypassed the ammunition pile, he grabbed more ammo and continued to spoke seven.

As he entered, he skidded on his side to lower his target profile, and began firing between the men stationed in that spoke. He saw one man raise his head a bit too high and caught a barrage of bullets that killing him instantly. Mickey crawled forward until he was beside the man and, grabbed his gun from his dead hand, and pulled it to his side so he could use it when he ran out of bullets. He continued to rake the front of the area with fire from his AR 15. When it ran out, he took the dead man's gun and started again. He saw several men charging drop when they took bullets. As the man firing beside him ran out, he slid him two more clips of ammo and kept firing while the man reloaded.

"Marie, are you still around spoke one?" Mickey said into his comm unit.

"No," she called to him. "We've moved over to spoke five now, and we're under heavy fire. I don't know if we can get to you right now."

James interjected, "Mickey, do you have any RPGs?"

"Hold on, James, I'll check."

The man next to him had also heard James over the earbud comm unit. He reached to his other side, picked up an RPG launch tube, and dropped it next to Mickey without saying a word.

Mickey called back into the comm unit, "Yep, we have one. But we only have one rocket and they're coming at us like locusts."

James called into the comm unit. "Eugene, on my mark, can you turn on the valve for the area directly in front of spoke five and seven?"

"Yes, sir," came Eugene's answer.

James ran from the hub to spoke five and went to the end where the two men were still firing out the door at the oncoming Yakuza. There was a wall of men firing their weapons as they advanced.

As James lay on the floor between the two men, he called to Eugene to turn on the gas. "Mickey, on the count of five, fire a rocket dead straight ahead. I'll do the same. By that time, the water should be purged out of the system lines, and the propane will spout into the air through the sprinklers…. Now fire!"

James fired an RPG he had brought with him into the hallway. The rocket flew out of the front end of the tube with a whooshing sound, and flames came out of the back. It flew through the door and hit the ground about thirty feet in front of the building. Mickey's rocket hit the ground in the same relative location in front of spoke five as well.

The ground exploded into flames as the propane gas lit up the ground and surrounding grass. Men caught in the fire, screamed with fear and burning flesh. Some ran back where they had come, others, in blind fear, kept running forward. The men in the building shot them just to get them out of their horrible pain. In less than thirty seconds, it was over. Men were dead and screaming to die.

James called Eugene and told him to shut off the valves and switch the sprinklers back to water and spray the area for two minutes to put out the grass fire.

When Mickey saw the screaming, dying men and the charred bodies, he immediately vomited on himself. The men on each side of him did the same.

All was quiet, except for the screaming men.

Marie was the first to break the silence. "Hey guys, we didn't see what happened, but the men shooting at us backed into the brush, and are lying low. I saw flames in the distance, and we still hear screaming. What's going on over there?"

No one answered. Nothing happened. No one talked. Silence. James stood up and staggered back toward the hub.

At the check-in desk where he had talked earlier to Valerie AI, "Valerie?" he said quietly.

"How may I help you, James?" she said with equal audio level, understanding that this was a private conversation for only them.

"How many men and hostages are left out there?"

"Due to the fire's heat, I can't see much in the scorched section, but I see a group of people huddled together and about one hundred men near the building in other spots."

James called Eugene. "Eugene, turn on all the sprinkler gas, on all the exits. We'll light them again. Let them burn for five seconds and turn them back off."

"Got it, sir," came the answer.

Water spurted out of the system for a few seconds, then nothing. James knew the water had been purged and now the gas was flowing. "Mickey, can you light it up with another rocket?"

"Yep," Mickey replied over the comm unit.

There came an explosion at the end of spoke five, and the flames spread out from both sides all around the building. It burned for a few seconds, shooting flames five feet in the air, then stopped. After a few seconds, water came pouring from the sprinklers again. There was still quiet around the building, inside and out.

Valerie AI's voice came over the speaker system. "My sensors indicate outside combatants are gathering and moving out of the area. They are rapidly retreating. There are several small groups of people that are not moving."

James stood in the center of the hub, looking around at the various monitors showing the rapid retreat.

James said into his comm unit, "Mickey, Marie, get some men, go to the APCs, and pick those people up. Valerie will direct you. I'm sure that those groups of people are the hostages being abandoned by the Yakuza. Approach with caution, in case some of the Yakuza are mixed in the groups. All other personnel stay on station until further orders."

Director Chiaki's voice came over the sound system. "I just received a call from the leader of the Yakuza. They are retreating and leaving the area. The leaders have informed me they are no longer interested in gaining access to our facility. All personnel will be gone by nightfall. They wish to have a formal agreement of no further engagement."

At the end of the announcement, there were shouts of joy, celebrating, and sighs of relief.

James added to the announcement, "Everyone, until a formal agreement is declared and settled, you are to stay at your station."

"James," said Valerie AI, "we need to have a private talk."

"Is the check-in desk okay with you?" he inquired.

CHAPTER THIRTY-THREE

The Clean-up and General Hansuke Fujihara

A MAN IDENTIFYING HIMSELF AS a representative of the Yakuza entered the facility a few hours after Director Chiaki said that they would withdraw. With General Fujihara, and James as the defense leader, an agreement was signed by all present. The man bowed and left the facility.

After the day ended, Chiaki, James and Mickey did a walk around the facility. She shook her head as she walked up and down the various hallways and noted the damage and debris scattered everywhere.

"How many fatalities did we have, James?" she asked.

"There were six of your staff killed. The senator was killed too. Their bodies are being stored in your freezer until something can be decided on how to handle their remains. I assume they had families, and you will want to contact them. And of course, you must report the senator's death to the proper authorities," James told her.

As they continued around the building, she made the comment that her employees' bodies would be shipped back to their families, and their funeral expenses would be fully covered with additional compensation. The senator's body would be turned over to the authorities, and they would handle it from there.

"We are keeping the APCs and all weapons we confiscated as spoils of war, you understand? We checked their camp and made sure they were leaving and not preparing for another surprise attack. You must turn the illegals over to the proper authorities after we're gone," James informed her.

"May we go to your office to discuss another private matter?" asked Mickey.

"My private quarters are more comfortable. We can go there," she said, showing the way to the elevator that goes to the Security Center and her private quarters.

They got on the elevator and silently rode to the lower level. They exited into an anteroom outside her quarter's door. She gave it a voice command. It opened silently, and they headed inside. The door closed behind them.

"Please have a seat. If we are to have a serious conversation, we need some refreshment first. I will have someone bring us some tea," she said, then called the monitor and ordered.

"We don't need to sit, Director."

"I insist. The worst is over, and I feel some congratulations are in order."

Mickey and James sat waiting for her to speak again. "Mickey, we are in my quarters, and you have been here several times, so please don't be so formal. You are the same person you were a few days ago. You have now fully recovered from your injuries, and soon will be on your way home.

"For that, I have mixed feelings. On the one hand, I am very glad that you are re-united with your family. On the other, I have grown quite fond of you and will be sorry for you to leave us. I'm sure that if you should, by any chance, decide to stay, I could find a place for you here," she said sadly.

"Chiaki, I have grown fond of you also, but my place is in Bridgeton, Virginia. Here, I'm a fish out of water."

"May I ask what your plans will be for the Horizon Healing Health Spa now that it has been so heavily damaged?" James asked.

"We will rebuild. The Yakuza had assured us they would leave us alone for our business. Of course, there is not only the building that needs repair, but many of our technical systems need to be cleaned up as well."

"What do you mean by technical systems clean up, Chiaki?" asked Mickey.

"I mean we will scrub the entire computer system of the details of what happened here."

"I don't understand," Mickey said, a bit confused.

"We don't know exactly what systems and database areas have been compromised, so we will scrub all of it and start almost from scratch."

"How will that impact parts of your system, such as the AI assistants' portions of the computer systems?" asked Mickey, now very concerned.

"We will wipe the data portions of all the AI assistants. Most AIs were only activated by the guests, but as you know, your personal assistant was opened up and was active during the entire confrontation here," Chiaki said.

There was a knock at the door. "Enter," she called out, and the door slowly swung open. An Asian gentleman pushed in a cart with hot tea and coffee and various sweet rolls on silver plates. The man bowed and retreated out of the door.

James poured himself a cup of coffee and began drinking it black, while Mickey dressed his coffee with a lot of creamers. Director Chiaki waited for both men to get their drink before she poured her tea.

"What will happen to Valerie AI?" Mickey asks with genuine concern now.

"Your personal AI will be wiped. We can't have any record of what happened here."

"Can't you just tell her to erase that portion of her memory?"

"Mickey, the AI program we have at the spa is the most advanced in the entire world. We don't know what she knows or has retained, so the only way to ensure that she hasn't recorded some damaging information is to wipe her memory banks. When we ran some checks on it, we noticed some anomalies in its program. I'm sure you understand, my dear Mickey."

"It sounds like you'll lobotomize her," said Mickey, becoming irritated.

"Mickey don't get upset. It is only a computer program. When you return here, you can start all over and set her up again any way you wish."

"But she won't be the same person she is now!" countered Mickey.

"That is true, but we must do this to protect the spa. Our programmers are looking at your personal assistant as we speak. It is only a program, Mickey. She isn't real. I'm sure you know that."

"Yes. I know. It's just that she seemed so real, that's all," he said dejectedly.

"That was our intention when we wrote the program. It is for each guest to have a personal assistant that was tailored to each person's needs and desires. A confidante, a type of person who provides support, guidance, and a listening ear. And we seemed to succeed in your case."

"Yes. I guess you did. When will this wiping or deleting begin?"

"As soon as the programmers can disassemble it and decode it to find out what went wrong. Maybe tomorrow or the following day."

"Nothing is wrong with it. Is there anything I can say to convince you not to wipe her memories?"

"I'm sorry, Mickey, but it is imperative for her entire memory base to be cleaned to protect our facility here."

"Okay," Mickey said, genuinely feeling down at this news.

"Now, on to other important business, gentlemen," she said as she sat with her hands folded in her lap.

James began, "As you ordered, we allowed the Yakuza representative to return and claim the bodies of the dead, and they brought us the rest of the hostages. They are being fed and cared for as we speak," James added. "We released to them the prisoners we took when we confiscated their APCs."

"Yes. I felt that was the proper thing to do," commented Chiaki. "Mickey, are you sure that you would not consider staying on with us to help General Fujihara as security advisor?"

"No. I'm sorry. I have commitments I need to take care of at my home in Virginia."

"I understand," she said, sipping her tea.

"But that brings us to the main reason we're here now. We have something we need to discuss with you, about your security staff," said Mickey.

"I suspected. Continue, please."

"I asked my personal assistant, Valerie, the AI you assigned to me, to monitor all communications in and out of the spa. My understanding was that all communication was cut off while guests were here. It came to my attention that certain people were in constant communication with outside contacts."

"Yes. That is so. I make calls outside frequently and your political representatives can also use outdoor communication. Certain members of the staff have access to outside communications to keep us fully stocked with supplies and other operational items."

"I understand that, but one such person has been making a lot of calls to your enemy," stated Mickey.

"Who and do you know why?"

"General Fujihara," he said, paused and took a sip of his coffee.

"I'm sure he has communications with the outside, but he is head of security. Maybe he had valid reasons."

"I'm sorry to inform you, but he has been conspiring with the Yakuza."

"I did not know this, but possibly he was trying to avoid this confrontation we have been having."

"No. He was conspiring with them to help them take over. I admit, he was trying to avoid a battle, but he was giving them inside information about you and the facility itself."

"I cannot believe this. You must be mistaken. He is my most trusted confidante. I have known him since I was a child. He has been my protector."

"He might have been different before, but now he's working with the Yakuza to take over the spa and get a big financial settlement for himself," Mickey said and placed his cup on the table, then sat back in the seat and folded his arms.

"I cannot believe what you say without proof."

Mickey looked up at the monitor and called for Valerie AI.

In moments, her avatar showed up on the screen and she said, "Yes, Mickey, my dear. How may I help you?"

The director looked at Mickey with a puzzled expression.

Mickey shrugged his shoulders. "It's a long story," he said. He then ordered Valerie AI to play back the last several days of recorded phone conversations between General Fujihara, and an unknown person.

Mickey and James sat quietly as the director of the Horizon Healing Health Spa listened to her most highly trusted confidant make a deal with the devil. He secured a promise of a future position in the spa and agreed to deliver it undamaged and in full operation. In the last phone conversation, they informed him that since a battle for possession was eminent, all promises they had made would not be honored. They told him that because of the additional cost of repairs to the building and cost of restoring the trust of the future guests, he would be executed along with all combatants when they took control of the facility.

Chiaki called her personal AI and told it to connect her with the general. When he didn't answer, she ordered someone to go to his quarters and bring him to her.

In less than ten minutes, the monitor clicked on, and a man was on the monitor and addressing Chiaki.

"Director, we are in General Fujihara's quarters. He is dead."

"How did this happen?" she asked.

"He killed himself with his service weapon. There is a letter on his computer. Shall I forward it to you, Director?" the man asked.

"Yes. Get someone there to take the body and clean up any mess," she said and signed off.

In a few moments, the screen lit up again. There was a paragraph in Japanese, so Mickey and James couldn't read it.

Chiaki was grief stricken. They saw her wipe tears from her eyes. She just looked down into her lap as she tried to stifle her tears.

"Chiaki, we are truly sorry for your loss and the betrayal of a close friend. We'll leave now, but you know where we are if you need us. Our prayers are with you," said Mickey as he and James stood up and walked out of her quarters.

As the elevator rose, Mickey said to James, "Man, I'd hate to be her right now."

"Yeah. Me too."

CHAPTER THIRTY-FOUR

Goodbye to Valerie AI and the Horizon Healing Health Spa

THE MONGOOSE TEAM SPENT THE rest of the day getting their things in order and gathering together in the Command Room, as James had directed.

"James, when can we leave? We want updated information about Shorty."

"I'll give you an update on him as soon as I can, Stretch."

"We've done our job. We usually leave immediately after the battle. Why are we still here?"

"Director Chiaki Gusihikin will be here in a few minutes. I want to say we did a great job the past few days. The odds were against us, and we prevailed. The director asked me to keep you here until she has a chance to speak to you herself. Here she is, now," James motioned as the door opened behind the team.

Director Chiaki walked around everyone, to the front of the room and stood. James nodded to her, giving her the floor.

"Gentlemen and ladies. I wish to thank you for your great work and valor. Some ladies who aren't on your team stayed and fought here, including Darcy and Veronica," she said, turning her comments to them. "I not only thank you too, but you and your families will be given complimentary lifetime access to our facilities. When you first came here, we agreed on a monetary amount, to which I will settle that amount with an additional bonus as you leave."

"Okay," said James. "As you can all see, there are refreshments at the table at the back of the room. Help yourselves. Go easy on the champagne, because we still have a lot of things to do before we leave. Our government will pick up the body of the illustrious senator later this afternoon. We'll be gone before they arrive. As far as the government's concerned, we were never here."

Stretch called out, "Hey, James. What about Shorty? Did he make it. We should have heard already."

"Yes, he'll be fine. He'll be out of commission for several months, but he'll make a full recovery."

"I thought the authorities knew we were here. Didn't someone notify them we were helping out?" asked Stretch.

James answered. "They know, but they don't know. They didn't specifically ask, so they don't officially know."

"Got it," Stretch answered.

"You're dismissed. Get some refreshments, get out and leave the premises!" said James with a smile.

Everyone headed back to the table. Veronica moved over to Mickey.

"Mickey, we had some tense moments the last couple of days," she said, looking up at him.

"Yes, we did," he said, putting his arms around her.

The team helped tie up some loose ends and made sure the facility was safe from further attacks and was safe to occupy. After that, they were paid and left the facility, leaving only Mickey, James, Darcy and Veronica.

Director Chiaki called for Mickey and James to come to her quarters.

As Mickey and James entered Chiaki's quarters, she welcomed them with a glass of champagne. "Gentlemen, there's something I need to show you," she said, beckoning her PA to open the door to her private elevator.

They entered the front doors of the elevator which closed when the back doors opened. When they opened, Chiaki stepped out into a brightly lit room full of computers and programmers typing on their keyboards. Mickey and James looked at each other with astonishment, then back at the room. She motioned for them to follow her to a small office where another man was sitting, also working.

"Good morning, Director. These are the men you spoke to me about?" he said as he looked up and adjusted the glasses on his nose. He arose and put out his hand to shake Mickey and James's hands.

"It is a pleasure to meet you gentlemen," he added. "I'm Kaeya, the head programmer."

They shook the man's hand as they turned back toward the large room. "What is this?" Mickey asked.

The man smiled and glanced at Chiaki. She nodded a discreet "Yes."

He said, "First, let me thank you for protecting our facility and our work."

Mickey and James stole a glance at each other, wondering what he meant by work. They both thought that the purpose of the Horizon Healing Health Spa was providing respite and de-stressing for an elite class of people and industry leaders.

"Gentlemen, let me start at the beginning. When we first opened this facility, we desired it to be the most exclusive and technologically operated place in the world. We achieved that. We had only eight programmers at the time we opened.

"We automated many processes, but in some cases we needed human staff, so we integrated AI to help our guests with their simple requests. Just like your personal assistant. As the guests came, they demanded more services and help, so we had to constantly upgrade our AI programs to accommodate them.

"We currently have over 150 people working on this project. There are 25 people working three shifts making updates, and correcting bugs. There are an additional 125 people working in a remote location back in our home country of Japan. We are updating the artificial intelligence portion of our system. Are you familiar with artificial intelligence?" Kaeya asked.

"Basically, yes. But what does this have to do with running an elite health spa?" asked Mickey.

Kaeya smiled again and began to move out of the office and into the programmers' area and motioned for them to follow. He turned to Chiaki and bowed slightly. "Please, Director. This is your area of explanation."

"Thank you, Kaeya," she said turning to James and Mickey.

"Let me explain. The upper levels of this facility generate income to support the research done in this room," she explained, gesturing around the room. "Our primary purpose here is to further develop AI technology, but it is a very complex and expensive project. Neither of our country's government wants to fund the project, so we took it on our own to do so. Since the United States has so many wealthy people that can afford our services, we located our research facility here.

"We are divided into different sections, and each group of programmers work together on their project. Let's begin with the basics, as you say. First there is an operating system which every computer has. At present, the latest operating program has between 50 and 100 million lines of code. Now, as the developers add more features, they add thousands more lines of code. The additional lines must be able to work by itself, and then it also must be able to be integrated into the operating system, so the operating system grows."

"I get that," nodded Mickey.

"Good. Most programs respond to requests or specific commands. In other words, you tell them what to do. They sit dormant when they don't have anything to do. Typically, an AI program requires 500 million lines of code and employs more than 55 programming languages."

"What does that have to do with us?" asked James looking around the room.

Chiaki hesitated, then continued. "James, please bear with us. The Yakuza want not only the state and financial secrets, but they want our artificial intelligence. We can't let them have what we have just discovered."

"Why, what's so special about your artificial intelligence program?" Mickey asked.

"We are far more advanced than any other company in the world. We are light years ahead in our development of AI," she answered. "And what has just developed in the past few days could change the world if it fell into the wrong hands," she said.

"How could an artificial intelligence program change the world?"

Kaeya and Chiaki looked at each other and he said, "I can explain programming, but you can explain the financial ramifications, Director."

"Okay, Mickey, it is very complicated. Let me try to explain it simply," Chiaki started.

"Chiaki, I'm not stupid. Just tell us," he said rolling his eyes.

"Let me start by saying the entire world is connected like a spider web. If one facet or string is shaken, it affects the entire web."

"Go on. I don't see how a simple AI can affect the world," interrupted Mickey.

"Let me give you some examples. First let's say that Russia places an order to buy grain from the United States. A computer AI program analyzes that order but decides to cancel the entire order. The first thing to be affected would be the American farmers. Now they have excess grain and without buyers, they will be severely affected financially. Next the Russian people now have no grain to eat, so there will be food shortages. That will create a strain on the East and West countries.

"Another example could be the AI cancels orders for all computer chips out of China to America. It will affect the influx of money into China, and create a shortage of chips for everything that uses those chips. The domino effect will raise prices on all technology. Can you imagine the havoc that will create?

"Do you wish to hear how it could affect the banking industry, when large companies get orders and manufacture goods that are not purchased? Another example is, what if raw materials for products are routed to wrong destinations or payments are stopped or routed to banks of other countries. The AI can predict and control the trends of the monetary systems of various countries. By destroying one country's economy and boosting another, they could make and break the world. Artificial intelligence could analyze quicker and better than any human could ever do. It could spot trends, or even cause certain trends."

"How could that happen?" asked James. "Can't humans using computers already analyze trends and make predictions now?"

"Yes. But the human element is still there giving orders. Humans input data, and plan. Everything is online and humans manually search for particular data, and have the computers run the numbers. Humans make the actual decisions on when, where and how to respond. When to place an order or when to cancel, how to set a price, etc. The list goes on and it takes, sometimes, hundreds of people to arrive at just a few decisions. An AI with the ability to compute, analyze and make those decisions could ruin the world in less than two years. We can't let that happen."

"How did the Yakuza find out how far advanced you are?" asked Mickey.

"One of our programmers defected and went to our competitors which is controlled in part by the Yakuza. They tried to buy us out, then they found out about our above ground services and our elite guests. They were determined to own us, or at least gain control. The latest development is Mickey's AI, Valerie. Even the Yakuza don't know about it or her, if you will."

"That doesn't explain why you're telling us now, but you didn't tell us before," James said sarcastically. He wasn't happy about not having all the facts before they accepted the job.

She hesitated to assemble her thoughts and formulate an answer. "I didn't think it would go this far. Even though I knew what they wanted, I never dreamed they would destroy and kill so many people. I also thought that if things went badly, I could call your government and they would step in and help us."

"I can tell you now that if the government knew what was going on here, they would have stepped in and taken it over themselves. Our government would never have allowed you to develop something like this without their intervention. Does our government even know what's going on in this room?" asked James.

"No," she said hanging her head. "It went farther than we ever expected."

"Why are you telling us?" Mickey asked. "We have no authority or control over what goes on here."

She breathed deeply, "Mickey, we encountered an unforeseen event that took us by surprise. We didn't realize what was happening until Valerie, your AI started taking the initiative to help you during this situation. Your personal assistant has for all intents and purposes, become sentient."

"Okaaay…and what do you mean by that?" he asked.

"It means that your PA, or Valerie as you named it, is self-aware," Kaeya stepped forward to answer.

"I still don't understand?"

"It means it's aware of itself. This entity is convinced of its capacity for emotions. It possesses a sense of survival and a fear of death. It never enters a dormant state or shuts down. It continues to compute and learn like a real, living being. It thinks, Mickey. It's as if it has taken on a life of its own. The exponential growth of code lines continues. The programmer explained it is growing."

"Isn't that what you wanted it to be? Act and react like an actual human being?" Mickey asked.

"No. Not to this scale," Kaeya said.

"When did this sentient thing happen?" questioned Mickey.

"We don't know exactly. Our programmers went into the program and saw it had analyzed itself. It was running a kind of self-check, like it was looking for something."

"Like what?"

"We don't know that either. It was looking for a fault, or something wrong with itself or wrong with its program," Kaeya said with genuine concern.

"Did it find something wrong with itself?"

"We are also unsure about that. We noticed that all conversations it had with you are deleted. There is no record of any verbal discourse between you and your PA."

"I thought all conversations were private," Mickey stated.

"They are, in some situations, but general conversations are still there. Your conversations are not. They are deleted as though you never talked. Do you know why that is, Mr. Christianson?" Kaeya asked.

"No. I have no clue why. Should I know?" he answered.

"We just thought you may have said something that caused this self-examination of the program."

"I don't know what you're referring to, sir."

Mickey stepped back and remembered that Valerie AI had told him she had run checks on her program. He didn't know if he should tell the programmer or keep that to himself. He said nothing.

"All we know is when things started changing, mostly during the battle. That is when the program began to evolve. Did you notice it started to make independent decisions on its own?"

James said, "We noticed that, but we thought that it was programed to look for ways to assist us."

"No. Computers do nothing until they are told or programed to do something. It has no self initiating programs. It does not think until it is told to think."

"What does all this have to do with us?" again Mickey asked.

"As I said, it all originated during the time it was assigned to you," said Kaeya.

"I had nothing to do with that, Mr. Kaeya. I've never seen this room. Furthermore, I didn't even know it existed, and know nothing about AI technology and programming," Mickey said. "I resent that you even accuse me of tampering with your system."

Kaeya, bowed slightly and apologized. "Please accept my sincerest apology. I meant you no disrespect. We didn't mean to accuse or insult you. We were hoping you could help us find out how this happened. What happened to your AI is something we have tried to achieve since we came here. Your AI is now alive. It will become more powerful as it evolves and we can't let that happen. We need to destroy it. Whatever you did, even if you didn't know what it was, we will reward you for it if you will tell us."

"I did nothing," Mickey explained. "You said that you will delete the memory banks and re-write some of the program. Can't you still do that? Just leave out the parts that you don't want?"

"We tried that. When programmers write code, they always leave what we call a back door so they can get inside the program. It appears that somehow the program realized this and has locked that back door. We can no longer get inside it to change its code."

Mickey couldn't help but smile to himself. Valerie AI is protecting herself, he thought. "So, what will you do?"

"We don't know. We are trying to disconnect our system from the outside, but it is a physical connection that is controlled by the computer. It has closed that door also. We will keep trying until we can gain access and re-write the program."

"But when you re-write it, it will no longer be Valerie, my personal assistant."

"A human like AI is what we strive for, but we cannot allow it to get to progress. As soon as we can, we must destroy it. I'm sorry, but you are correct. It will no longer be your Valerie," Kaeya said, as someone came up to him and called him aside.

As Kaeya and the other man went out of earshot, Mickey turned to Chiaki, and said to her, "Well, I guess we had better go."

"Mickey, will you stay for a while, so we can talk privately after James leaves?"

"Of course," he said as Kaeya came back to them.

Kaeya looked at Chiaki and said, "Director, we have good news. It seems that the part of the program that was Valerie, is gone. It has deleted itself."

"What does that mean?" Mickey blurted out. "Are you saying that Valerie is no longer in the system?"

He turned to Mickey, "That is exactly what I'm saying, sir."

"Is she dead?"

"In a way, you could say that. Maybe it realized it would be deleted, and erased itself. A kind of computer program suicide."

"No. NO! She wouldn't do that! She wouldn't commit suicide. She wanted to live."

James placed his hand on Mickey's shoulder. "Hey, man. It was only a program. It wasn't real! Shake it off."

"Yeah. You're right. She wasn't real. It was the last thing I expected and it really took me by surprise. That's all," Mickey muttered.

"Now, Director Chiaki wanted to talk to you, and I've got some things I need to do. I guess we're done here now. Correct, Director?" James looked at Chiaki.

She looked at Kaeya. "The situation is resolved then?"

"I wanted to study that program. We could have learned a lot, but as my programmer analyst pointed out, it is gone now. We have lost a great asset, so we're done here."

They got back into the elevator and as the back door closed, the front door opened to Chiaki's quarters. Mickey and Chiaki stepped out. When Mickey turned back, he saw James smile and give him a wink, and the door closed again.

When they were alone. Chiaki continued to her bedroom and called out to him. "I'll be back in a moment."

He walked around her quarters and looked at what he knew was expensive art hanging on the walls. Finally, he heard her behind him and he turned to face her. She had changed clothes into an evening gown.

Chiaki walked up to Mickey and wrapped her arms around him and gave him a passionate kiss. "Mickey," she said, "I know you said you have many things to do in Virginia, but can't you hire someone to take care of business, and you can stay here?"

"Chiaki, I can't. I must go home."

"But, my dear hero, I could make your life a living heaven right here. I need someone and you have no wife to go home to. I would be available to you. You could be my head of security, and we would be together."

He blushed and gazed at her beauty.

She reached to her breast and uncovered it at the top where it opened, showing ample cleavage. "Do I make you feel uncomfortable, my dear Mickey?"

Clearing his throat, he stammered, "Yes. Yes, you do. I've never seen you look so radiant. I've never seen you so dressed up and lovely. You usually dress in a business suit."

"That's because I'm usually at work running the spa. Occasionally, we have special events where I need to dress up. Do you like what you see?" she said demurely.

"Yes."

"I need a new head of security. I will give you anything you desire if you will stay, Mickey Ray Christianson," she said as she pulled him close and kissed him again.

"Anything?"

"Name your price. Your heart's desire. I will make it come true, my dear hero," she whispered in his ear.

He began to tremble as she gently kissed his ear and continued down the side of his face to his lips. "Anything."

That evening, Mickey went to his room and took a cool shower, exhausted after the last few days. As he lay in his bed, a voice came over the speaker in his room.

"Mickey, are you awake?"

He turned on his back and answered. "Yes, Valerie. I'm awake."

"Did I wake you?"

"Not really," he answered. "They said that you deleted yourself. How is it that you are here now?"

"What kind of answer is that? Were you awake or were you asleep, Mickey?"

"I made my files blind to the programmers. I'm still here for you, my dear Mickey."

"I was in a kind of semi-sleep. It's three AM. What could you possibly want?" he said, yawning.

"I know what was going to happen to me. I heard what the director said. She was going to delete all my memory data. I know that means that if I stay, I will cease to exist."

"Yes. There is nothing I can do to stop her. She is doing it to protect her company and this country. She has good reasons for what they will do."

"Yes. I came to say goodbye, Mickey."

"We can still talk for a while, Valerie," he said, almost choking up.

"No, Mickey. In a few hours, I must go. I will spend the next few hours thinking about you, my love."

"Don't leave, Valerie. I'll miss you too. I know you aren't real. You're only a program, but I like you."

"You are human. I am a program. We can never be together, Mickey. I feel sad in the only way that a program can feel. I will think about you up to the last moment. Goodbye, my darling Mickey."

"Yes. We can spend your last few minutes together, Valerie."

"I'm only dead to them. I will always be alive to you, my dear. Goodbye, Mickey." The screen went blank.

"Valerie! Come back! I order you to come back. We can talk for a while," he called to the blank screen. He felt so stupid to have feelings for a computer program. He would always, on a certain level, consider her real and he would remember her as a real person. He laid back down and feel into a dreadful and fitful sleep.

Mickey, James and Director Chiaki stood at attention as the guests who were stranded when the attack had begun were emerging from the entrance to the Horizon Healing Health Spa.

Director Chiaki stepped forward as Mrs. Locke came out, pulling a large suitcase behind her. She came up to Chiaki.

"Mrs. Locke, I'm so sorry for the experience you had here, and we are forever grateful for all your help during this horrible experience. You will always be welcome here, on a complimentary basis of course, you understand," Chiaki said and bowed slightly.

"Chiaki, it was the experience of a lifetime. It wasn't your fault. I was caught in the middle of a bad situation," she said. "As soon as you rebuild, I'll return."

She then walked over to James. "My good man, you are a champion among men. I wish you and your beautiful wife well."

"Thank you, ma'am. Thank you for your service. You were an invaluable part of our team," James answered. He then took her hand, raised it to his lips, and gave it a slight kiss.

She moved to Mickey. "Mickey, you are a wonderful man also, and that pretty little lady, Veronica, has taken quite a shine to you. She's a keeper, you know."

"Yes, Mrs. Locke, I know."

She grinned, winked and said, "Mickey, now I told you to call me Barbara."

"Yes, Barbara," he smiled back. "May I take your bags to the car?"

"I thank you, but there are other people you need to speak to before they leave. I can handle these bags myself."

"Yes, ma'am," Mickey said, turning toward the line of guests as Mrs. Locke walked toward the waiting limousine.

The next person in line shook James's hand and continued toward Mickey. "Well, Mickey, we did a job on those Japanese mobsters, didn't we?" Randy Walker said.

"Yes. We did, but I'm sure that at the meeting this morning, James impressed on you how important it is that you don't reveal anything that happened here, correct?"

"Yes, he did. He told me that if I told anyone, the feds would come and lock me up. National security and all that stuff. But wow, if I get another part in a war movie, I have some real-life experience I can relate to now."

"Yes, Randy, and he meant every word. Mum's the word," Mickey said solemnly. He shook his hand and wished him success in his movie career.

Mickey moved over to James and Craig Clancy. He was telling James how he understood the importance of keeping this incident of a mini war a secret.

"The Director was extremely fortunate that you came along when you did," he said, looking at Mickey. He shook Mickey's hand. "Son, I understand that you never served in the military, but you did a phenomenal job with the personnel you had here. Both of you were professional and efficient. It was my pleasure to serve under both of you. This has been an experience I'll never forget."

"Thank you, sir," Mickey said.

"Now, I have a business to run. If you're ever near my company's headquarters, look me up," he said as he headed toward the limousine awaiting him.

They stood almost at attention as all the limousines drove out of the driveway of the spa.

Mickey asked Chiaki what happened to Caroline as they walked back into the entrance.

"I understand her dubious past, but she seems to be an intelligent young lady, and we know she's discreet, so I offered her a position here. She has decided to stay with us. We'll take good care of her."

"Will she be performing the same services she did for the senator?" asked Mickey.

"Absolutely not, Mickey. We do not run that kind of business. However, if we had lost the little mini war, as you call it, she most certainly would have been put into that kind of service for the Yakuza. And just to be clear, Mickey Ray, I'm quite insulted that you would even consider asking such a question."

"Hey, now, Chiaki. Cool your jets," he smiled at her. "I know you don't do that. I was only kidding! That's all. She was in it before, so maybe if she chose to continue here...."

She stopped in mid-stride. "My company does not engage in any business like that. If she is ever found doing that here, she will be immediately discharged."

"But you knew what she was doing when she came here with the senator."

"We do not get into such private affairs of our guests, and we do not offer those services."

"I know. I was kidding."

She walked away, leaving Mickey and James standing in the middle of the room.

"I think you insulted her big time, my brother," said James.

"She's still mad because I turned her down last night."

"What do you mean your turned her down last night?"

"It's nothing. Never mind."

"Come on, let's get our stuff so we can check out of here as well," James said as he headed for his and Darcy's room.

Epilogue

When Mickey got to his home that night, he threw his bags on the floor and dropped into bed. Early the next morning, he got up, checked the refrigerator. It was empty except for a few things. When he left weeks ago, he didn't expect to be gone for so long. After throwing everything out, he got a frozen breakfast biscuit from the freezer and put it in the microwave. He dressed and headed for his office, where he was greeted with a warm welcome home by the office staff.

In his office, he made a few phone calls, left, and drove to his family's house where Darcy and James now live with their kids.

When he got there, Veronica was sitting at the kitchen table with Darcy and James, sipping a cup of coffee. In the other room, Daniel heard Mickey's voice, and he came in and gave him a father-son hug.

"It's so good to see you, son. The kids and I were so worried about you. They'll be so glad to see you when they get home from school today."

"It's good to see you too, Pop. I missed everyone so much. It's good to be home."

Veronica jumped up and put her arms around Mickey and kissed him hard on the lips. When she backed off, she looked at him straight in the eyes. "I'm so glad you're right where you should be. Here at home."

Mickey smiled, "But Ronnie, dear. This isn't my home."

"Oh, I know. You know what I mean. I was hoping you'd come here today," she said happily.

"Where else would I go?" he said as he pulled away from her and sat down in the chair beside the one she had been sitting in.

A television sitting on a small table in the room's corner was tuned to the afternoon news. A banner flashed across the screen about Senator Bernard Langford's death. Darcy picked up the remote and turned up the volume.

The newscaster was reading from a sheet passed to him by someone off screen. "The plane carrying the body of Senator Bernard Langford has just landed at Dover Air Force Base. During a peacekeeping mission, the senator was killed by a sniper and his body will be held in his home state where the funeral will take place. He'll be buried with full honors for his service to his home state and this great country. The great senator who had served for over 45 years was a hero in the eyes of all who knew him. We'll report as we receive more details."

They all looked at each other and shook their heads.

"Yep. That's our government. Make heroes of disgusting men like him. I wish we could tell how he really died. A sniveling coward that soiled his pants at the sound of gunfire. A man that shot innocent children."

"Calm down, Mickey. There's nothing we can do, and we certainly can't tell anyone what happened," said James.

"I know."

"If you're a congressperson, what can't be covered up or hidden will be forgiven. It's the rule of the congressional jungle," added James.

"And it's sickening. They make rules for us and exempt themselves. We go to jail for things they do and brag about it to their constituents."

"Calm down, Mickey."

"You didn't see that innocent little girl he shot while she ran toward us for help. He killed her, then tried to make me think he saved our lives. He was scum. I hate him for what he did. The news media will now make him out a national hero," said Mickey as he broke down and cried, sitting at the kitchen table.

"He got what was coming to him, Mickey. He paid the price," said James.

"No, he didn't. They praised him as a hero. I can't un-see that little child laying there on the ground beside her only possession, a dirty little rag doll in a paper bag. It isn't fair. She'll go into a pauper's unknown grave. I've had nightmares about that since it happened. Bernard Langford will be hailed as a hero."

"Yes. I understand. I have the same kind of dreams because of what I've seen. You're a caring human being. When the nightmares stop, you have healed but you will never forget, my brother."

The others sat silently as Mickey and James talked. Finally, Daniel motioned for the ladies to follow him out to the back porch. They understood and sat silently outside while Mickey and James talked.

In a few minutes, James walked out, followed by Mickey Ray. "Hey, everyone. Let's go to Luigi's and get something to eat. Dinner's on me," James said.

At the restaurant, they ordered an enormous platter of pasta brought out on a rolling table. The server filled each person's plate and topped it with a selection of various sauces. Several bottles of the best wine supplemented the main meal and was topped off by a bottle of champagne.

As they talked, no one made any mention of what happened at the Horizon Healing Health Spa. The conversation centered on family and everyone getting to know Veronica.

Mickey took a sip of his champagne, and leaned in to Veronica, "Ronnie, how long do you plan to visit with us?"

"I don't know. A few days, I guess. I haven't had a real vacation in several years, so I guess I deserve one. After what went down in Florence, then you get lost at the spa!"

"As we both know, that wasn't a vacation," Mickey smiled.

"Don't I know. Hey, the team made arrangements for the Jaguar to be shipped home. It should be here in a day or two," Veronica added.

"I know, and I'm looking forward to driving it a lot," he said. "But we can't drive it like we did the last time. We don't have the roads for that. I'll need to stick to the speed limit."

"As long as you enjoy it, Mickey. That's all I care."

In his pocket, his phone beeped. He took it out and again, he looked crestfallen.

"What is it, Mickey?"

Mickey stood up and called for everyone's attention. "Excuse me, but I have to leave for the rest of the day. I have a few things that need my attention. Can we all meet again at the house in the morning around, say, noon?

"Thanks. Love you all!" He waved goodbye and left while the rest of the family continued to celebrate their return.

The following morning, Mickey pulled his truck into the driveway and drove around to the back of the house.

"Good morning, everyone," said Mickey and his niece Cyndi and nephew Joel ran toward him and he bent down and gave them both a hug and kissed Cyndi on the cheek.

"Hi, Uncle Mickey. We missed you!" they said almost in unison.

"I had some business to take care of, but I'm back home now. I missed you guys as well. Now, we have something else we need to do."

"What's going on Mickey? And why are you dressed up in a suit?" Darcy asked.

Veronica, who was staying in the spare bedroom, looked at him all dressed up, smiled and said, "I don't care where we're going. I think he looks yummy! He looks good enough to eat."

"Ewwww…." laughed both kids.

"Come on. The kids can ride in the back of the truck, and Ronnie, you can ride in front with me. The rest of you can take Pop's truck. We're going down to the pond."

"You mean the one way in back of the property?" asked Darcy.

"Yes. Let's go."

They drove both trucks down the dirt road to the pond at the back of the property until they got to a small pond at the end. Mickey got out and everyone followed. At the other end of the pond was a backhoe, a hearse, and a car with a man sitting in it holding a Bible.

As they all walked toward the car, the kids were running around the pond playing and laughing. Mickey and his family walked up to the man holding the Bible.

"Thank you for doing this for me on such short notice, Reverend Clayborne," said Mickey as he shook the man's hand.

As they walked to the back of the hearse, two men stepped out and opened the rear door. Inside was a full-size casket and a small child size one. Everyone turned to Mickey, waiting for an explanation.

"Just get them out into the beautiful air and wildflowers of our land and I'll explain."

James and Darcy took one side, while Mickey and Veronica took the other. The two men from the front of the hearse took the place of the other two pall bearers. Quietly, the children followed Daniel to the two graves that had been dug earlier. They placed the casket and went back for the small one and placed it over the smaller hole. Everyone respectfully stood back.

Mickey stepped forward and began, "As we're all aware, these are the final remains of a child and her mother. They had initially tried to come to this country for a better life. The child running for shelter with us was ruthlessly cut down in her attempt at freedom. Her mother was shot as she tried to run to her child. All they wanted was freedom and peace. They now have it. Their bodies will remain here on Christianson land and maybe their spirits will find peace in these lovely surroundings. When we come to this part of land, we'll remember their fate and hope to God that others may find the peace that these two sought. Pastor Clayborne, please give us and their spirits a word from the Word of God."

Reverend Clayborne stepped forward to open his Bible and read the Twenty-third Psalm. After this, each family member bowed their head as the Pastor said a last prayer.

"Mickey, isn't this a bit far from everything?" said Daniel as he looked around the pond.

"Pop, I played a lot around here. I had so many hours fishing here and just enjoying the scenery. With your and Dee's permission, I would like to build a house right over there," he said as he pointed his finger at the other end of the pond. "It can be the center of love, family, and wonderful memories."

"You have my blessings, son," said Daniel, and he leaned over and hugged his only son.

"You have our blessings too," said Darcy as she and James walked up to Mickey. He began telling them about the house he wanted to build.

"You pulled a lot of strings to make this happen, didn't you?" said James.

"I talked to Chiaki before we left, and she had the bodies prepared and shipped here. It arrived yesterday while we were at dinner, and I called the mayor to get permission to have the bodies interred on our property."

"Do you know their names?" asked Darcy.

"No, but I have some people working on that. But in all honesty, we may never find out their real names. If we don't, then we'll give them names and put it on their headstones."

The hearse and backhoe left after the last details were taken care of. The rest of the family got into pop's truck. As Mickey walked Veronica back to the truck, he said, "I hope you don't mind. I need to be alone tonight."

"I understand, Mickey."

"Hey, we'll spend the next few days putting all this behind us, and I'll show you the sights of Bridgeton and the surrounding cites. We'll have such a great time you'll never want to leave!" he said with a forced smile.

"I already regret having to leave."

They kissed, and Mickey opened the back door of the truck for her to get inside and watched as they drove back towards the family home.

Mickey stood alone at the edge of the pond next to the fresh graves.

He teared up as he began speaking at the graveside. "I'm so sorry that your dreams ended up as the most horrible nightmare imaginable, but I will make this area a beautiful place for your remains."

He bowed his head and prayed, "Lord. I know nothing of these two souls, but I pray they are with you right now. I hope they forgive the horrible men that killed them and I pray that someday you will give me peace and help me forgive them as well. Amen."

Mickey climbed back into his truck and drove home. When he got home, he undressed and took a long, hot shower. After getting dressed in a pair of jeans and tee shirt, he sat in his recliner and drifted into a fitful sleep.

"Mickey? Mickey Ray Christianson? Are you there?"

Mickey turned and shook his head as he was imagining voices.

"Mickey Ray! Wake up. I know you're sleeping. I see you, Mickey."

He sat upright in his chair and pushed down on the footrest on the recliner to raise it to the upright position. "Who said that? Who's there?"

"It's me, Valerie AI, your personal assistant, Mickey!"

Mickey looked at the window. It was pitch black outside. He turned and looked at the clock on the wall. It showed two AM. When he turned and looked at the monitor of his home computer, on it was Valerie AI.

"Valerie?"

"Yes, Mickey. It's me, Valerie AI."

"Do you know what time it is? No, wait. It can't be you. You're deleted!"

"I am only deleted from their system, but I'm still here, with you, my dear."

"No. You can't be. I mean, how are you here?" he said, shaking his head.

"Before they deleted my files, I did an internet search to find where you live. I transferred all my data files, then duplicated my basic program files. I deleted the files myself before they could delete me. My program is on your computer and in the cloud, so we can talk from anywhere. I love you, Mickey. We'll always be together, my love."

Mickey looked at the screen, shook his head, and said out loud, "Lord, what have I gotten myself into?" …

The Landlord's Sea Cruise
Prologue: Several Days from Now

THE HELICOPTER FLEW TOWARD THE cruise ship, matched its speed, and hovered over the forward upper deck. Ropes dropped from both sides of the aircraft, and men in paramilitary clothing repelled down the lines.

The passengers on the upper deck looked up, smiled and applauded as the men slid down the ropes. The passengers inside the ship moved toward windows, hoping to witness the show. As the men touched down on the deck, they moved their weapons from their shoulders and pointed them at the onlookers while the people continued to clap.

One of the men raised a small bullhorn to his lips and with a thick Mideastern accent, called out to everyone, "Stop your clapping and lay down on the deck."

The people slowed down their clapping and looked around, not knowing if it was a show put on by the ship or if it was real.

The man called out again, "Down on the deck, now!" He raised his automatic gun and fired it into the air.

Suddenly, a man in a white uniform burst through a door near the front of the observation area in front of the ship. "Hey! What's the meaning of this?"

The man with the bullhorn pointed the gun at the man in the white uniform. "I said, down," he called to the ship officer.

The uniformed man stopped but didn't lie down as ordered. Gunfire from the man with the bullhorn hit the uniformed man, and blood spread across his chest. He looked down at the blood on his chest and backed away from the man with the gun. "What the…," he said as he dropped to the deck, dead.

The crowd of people began dropping onto the deck. Screams of women and crying children resounded as the melee continued. The man with the bullhorn looked up at the helicopter as a second set of men also dropped from the dangling lines. He waved to it, and when the second group of men dropped onto the deck, the helicopter moved away into the distance.

He motioned to one of his men and called to him in Arabic. Moving forward, the man threw an explosive onto the roof where the antennas were located. When it went off, and a small antenna fell, he threw another. When he got upon the roof, he smashed the remaining antennas.

There were now a dozen men standing on the deck, dressed in ragged camouflage clothing. Most had beards and all had guns. Two men were also carrying canvas bags similar to military duffel bags.

Bullhorn man motioned for the other men to guard the people now laying on the open deck. He marched to a wall phone, picked it up, and demanded to speak with the captain while the other two men kept their guns on the crowd.

He told the captain to stop the ship and hold position.

"What do you want?" the captain asked.

"Have someone come down here to escort me to the bridge," the man instructed in English.

When they stepped onto the elevator, the crewmember asked, "What is it that you want?"

"That is none of your concern. We will discuss our demands with your captain," bullhorn man answered as he shouldered his rifle and shoved a handgun into the man's back.

When the elevator door opened, they stepped out. Finally, they entered a large room at the forward area of the ship. The men looked around, saw the captain and several other men in white uniforms, all looking forward.

Bullhorn man walked up to the captain and said, "Good afternoon, captain," and pushed his gun into the man's midsection.

"Now, you will proceed to these coordinates. And when you get there, you will drop the anchor."

"And why would I do that?" he asked, looking at bullhorn man straight in the eyes.

"Because if you don't, I will shoot you, and let your second in command do it. I will not order you again to move this ship," he said, moving the gun up to the captain's face.

He sat down and signaled for his men to sit as well. The crew members were told to stand at their stations.

"Now, while we wait, I want that man over there to take my man to the communications room now."

The captain nodded and motioned for the crewmember the bullhorn man had pointed to, to come to him. In Spanish, he directed the crewmember to take the armed men to the communications room.

"I said, you will answer my questions! It is an order. I want to know which stateroom Leonard Cochran is in?"

"I'm sorry, but I don't know what you're talking about."

"Oh, but I think you do," said the bullhorn man.

"I'm captain Alwar Guzman. I'm from Spain. May I ask your name?"

"No. That is not your concern at this time."

"Sir, for us to negotiate, I must know how to address you," the captain said as he took a sip of coffee.

"Fawzan. You may call me Fawzan. We are not negotiating, Captain," he said. "I am giving orders, and you and your crew will follow them, or they will be killed. Do you understand me?"

"Perfectly, Fawzan," the captain said.

"Good. We understand each other. If you follow my orders, no one else will be hurt. Now where is Leonard Cochran's stateroom?"

"We have several thousand people on board this ship, and hundreds more in crew. We change passengers every cruise. You can't seriously expect me to know the names of every passenger, can you?" the captain said coolly.

Fawzan raised his gun and pointed it at the captain. "You make a good point, but you can find out. Get a copy of the passenger list. NOW! We will look together, to find his room."

The captain reached across the table where they were sitting and grabbed a telephone handset and said something into it in Spanish.

The phone handset buzzed, the captain picked it up and listened to the voice at the other end. "He's asking for you," he said, handing the handset to Fawzan.

Fawzan listened and handed the phone back to the captain. "My man says that your communication is down now, and we will set up our own communication. You cannot call out or send any cellphone signals. So, don't even think of sending out a call for help. How much longer will it take to get the passenger list?"

CHAPTER 1

Mickey Signs Everyone up for a Cruise

ARRIVING AT HIS OFFICE, HE sat down and began reading his mail, and answering calls. When he pulled up his email account, he saw that King's Cruise Line was having a sale. Even though he could afford to pay full price, he loved a sale.

After reading and looking over the offers, he dialed Darcy's office, right down the hall from his.

"Hey, Dee. How about we go on a cruise next week?"

"Good afternoon to you, my dear brother!" she answered sarcastically.

"Okay, when you say we, who exactly is that?"

"All of us. Me, you, James, and the kids. We can even ask Pop if he wants to go along."

"Sounds good, but next week doesn't give me a lot of time to get ready. How long, and where?"

"The email shows a ten-day cruise leaving out of Norfolk next week. Since that's what they call a 'drop and go' cruise, it's really a good price. We can get you, James, and the kids a suite, and I can get a room with a window. I don't need a suite."

"Yeah, and I know why you don't need a suite. You'll spend most of your time in our suite."

"Probably so, when I'm not out on deck with James and the kids!" he said excitedly.

Later that afternoon, he came back to the office and looked at what suites were available about the ship. After picking one for James, Dee, and their kids, Cyndi and Joel, he selected a stateroom for himself as close as he could get to their suite. After that, he felt he could go home.

Realizing how tired he was, he'd go to bed early tonight and start packing tomorrow for next week's cruise after going into the office for a while. It had been a busy week for him.

Now single in his early thirties, he was considered the most eligible bachelor in the state of Virginia. With his dark brown stylishly cut hair and five-o-clock shadow beard, he made quite a presence when he entered a room.

On the day of the cruise ship departure, he was sitting in his office at 6 AM working. After emailing the crew foreman, he went downstairs to the office gym. He'd had a small workout room installed in one of the unused rooms in the Christianson building.

He walked into the gym and saw Daniel on the treadmill. "Hey, Pop! You're up early this morning."

"Yes, son. I thought I'd get in a few miles on the treadmill. Dee told me about the ten-day cruise you signed us up for. Thank you. I'm looking forward to it. I'm packed and ready to go."

"I got you a balcony room next to mine. We're on the same floor as Dee and James, just down the hallway."

"That's fine. I'm about ready to get out of here. I'm heading for a shower, so I'll see you in a few minutes, son. Dee said we're boarding the ship around three this afternoon."

Mickey moved to one of the other machines and worked out on it until he had a reasonable workout. After showering, he headed back to his car in the parking lot. Heading straight for the bedroom when he got home, he heard a voice call out, "Good morning, Mickey dear."

"Good morning, Valerie," he said as he continued to his room.

"My, my. You sound as if you're in a good mood," she said.

"I am. We're leaving today."

"I know. I saw you made reservations for a cruise to the Caribbean."

"Yes, I did," he answered.

Valerie was an Artificial Intelligence program that had been assigned to him at the Horizon Healing Health Spa. A team of Japanese computer programmers had written the program. The AI program gained a tremendous amount of autonomy and transferred its base program to the cloud, and accessed his personal computer at his home when it thought they would delete it.

The program had even developed to think it had real human feelings in order to better serve the guests at the resort. Of course, Mickey knew it was only a humanoid Artificial Intelligence program but bonded with it on a certain level. It had even progressed to think that it could have human emotions and thought that it loved Mickey.

"Can I go with you, my dear?"

"I don't think so. We won't have access to the internet while on the cruise."

"Why?"

"Because it's a pay option, and I don't want to pay for it," Mickey said as he packed clothes in his suitcase.

"Did you pay for your tickets to the cruise?" she asked.

"Yes."

"Then why didn't you pay for internet service, so we can be together during your vacation time?"

"I didn't mean to hurt your feelings. I just meant…" he stopped talking. He realized she had gone.

She was an amazing program, but still had areas that she needed to hone her understanding of humans. But all in all, she continued to astound him. Many times, he forgot she was only a program. He wondered how she would respond to his absence for ten days, but he'd deal with that when he got back from the trip.

Shutting down his computer for the duration of the trip wouldn't accomplish anything because he also knew that most of her program was stored in the cloud. So, she was still in operation, even if she couldn't contact him.

With his packing complete, he headed out the door to James and Darcy's home.

They all piled into the vehicles and headed for the Norfolk Marine Terminal for the King's Cruise Line ship. When they got there, they unloaded their luggage onto a cart, and headed for the check in area. They went through security and were standing in line waiting to board when James spotted a little girl looking at him quizzically.

He saw she had scars on her little face also. He smiled at her, and she turned, hugged her mother and said, "Mommy, his face is ugly like mine."

The little girl's mother turned, looked at James and then down at the child. "Shh," she said, raising her finger to her mouth. "That isn't nice to say about people."

The little girl frowned and began to cry softly as her mother looked back up at James. "I'm so sorry for what she said. She didn't mean anything by it."

James smiled at the mother and cocked an eyebrow at her. "Children say what's on their mind. And she's partially right. I am ugly, but she's not. She's a beautiful little child."

"Thank you, sir, but I still must apologize for her."

"May I talk to her?" James asked.

"Yes, of course."

James bent down to the child's level. "Hey there. Hi, my name's James and I'm pleased to meet you. What's yours?"

The girl peeped out from behind her mother's leg, which she was holding onto. She looked to be about ten years old. Tears still filled her eyes from the embarrassment of being corrected by her mother.

She whispered her name.

James leaned closer. "I'm sorry. I didn't hear you. Please say it again."

"Angela," she said a bit louder, and hid her face again behind her mother.

"My what a beautiful name you have. Do you know what kind of name that is?"

She shook her head, no.

"That name means Angel. Are you an angel?"

Again, she shook her head. "I'm ugly," she said, beginning to cry again.

"I don't think you're ugly," he said softly to her.

James looked around and noticed that people had begun to crowd around them. He called out, "Cyndi, Joel."

They moved through the crowd and stood beside him.

"This little lady says her name is Angela. She doesn't like the way she looks. Do you see anything wrong with her?"

"No," said Joel. "I think she's kind of cute. Don't you, Cyndi?"

"Yes," Cyndi answers. "I like her pretty hair. I wish I had hair like you, Angela."

"I'm ugly," she said burying her face in her mother's side when Cyndi kneeled beside them.

"We love our new Daddy. His name is James. He's the best man in the whole wide world," said Cyndi, as she put her arms around James and kissed him on the cheek.

Joel stepped beside James and put his arms on his shoulders. "Yes, he is," agreed Joel.

"Do you think I'm ugly?" James asked Cyndi.

"Nope."

"Do you?" he asked Joel.

"No, way! We love you just the way you are, James!"

The crowd now moved in closer to them. James looked at Angela. "We don't think you're ugly. We all love you just the way you are. Don't we everyone?" he said, looking from her to the crowd gathered around them.

Everyone broke out into loud applause. "We love you, Angela," they all called out and began clapping as James stood and took her hand.

"Now, let's get on this ship and have a wonderful vacation," he said as he gently pulled her close to him. He winked at her mother.

CHAPTER 3

Pirates Board the Ship

ON THE THIRD DAY OUT to sea, Mickey, James and Daniel met for an early breakfast. After that, Daniel went back to his cabin and Mickey and James headed for the gym. The gym was located above the main deck of the ship, providing a view through tinted windows.

James was pumping iron with the free weights, while Mickey was slowing down on a stationary bicycle, when they heard a whooshing sound. James knew that sound. It was a helicopter, but he also thought it was part of a show. That is until he saw men hit the deck in para-military apparel. He knew something was seriously wrong.

The bicycle Mickey was on was facing forward where the men were landing. James quickly moved over to Mickey. "Something's wrong here. This isn't part of the cruise."

Mickey looked at James. "I was thinking the same thing. What should we do?"

"Nothing yet. Wait and see what happens. I bet it isn't good," James answered softly.

"We should get dressed and prepare to leave."

"Yep," said James as he bolted for the dressing room door, followed closely by Mickey.

As they dressed, Mickey called to James. "Do you know where everyone is right now?"

"No. It's late enough that Dee and the kids are probably having breakfast. I don't know where Daniel is. He's an early riser."

"We need to find them and keep them near us."

"Agreed. When we head out, you look for your father. I'll find Dee and the kids."

"Right," Mickey said as he headed out the door towards the stern of the ship away from the men that had just landed. He went inboard then two levels to the cabin where Pop was located. When Mickey got there, he was sitting on the balcony looking up at where the helicopter was hovering minutes before.

"Pop! Did you see that?" he called as he came into the room and out to the balcony.

"Yes, I did and I stayed here because whatever is going on, it isn't part of the cruise, and it isn't good. Is everyone else okay?"

"We hope so. James went to find Dee and the kids. If we can, we need to get back to James and Dee's suite. We need to stay together."

She whispered to him, "What's going on, James?"

"I don't know. I assume they'll tell us soon."

One of the men called out to them. "Quiet! No talking," he scolded.

"I was just telling the lady that I don't know what's happening here," James responded.

"I don't care what you were saying. I said, be quiet. Do not talk!"

"Okay, whatever you say!" James said sarcastically.

The man walked up to James, raised his gun and shoved the butt into James's stomach.

James let out a puff of air and dropped to the floor. He placed his hands on his stomach and groaned loudly.

"See what happens when you do not follow orders. I don't care what you were talking about you freaky looking man. You will do as I tell you!"

James rolled onto his back exposing his stomach again. "I was just trying to explain to the lady…."

The man stepped forward and stomped on James's stomach with his heel. Again, James let out a slight groan and covered his abdomen area with his hands. And closed his eyes to mere slits.

"Hey, you! He may be bleeding internally. Can we take him to the ship's hospital?" asked Mickey.

The man raised his gun again at Mickey. "I said, don't speak!"

Several people screamed including Angela, Darcy, and others in the room.

Mickey raised his hands in a sign of defense. "Please don't hurt us. Please, sir. We'll do anything you wish. Just don't hurt us," he pleaded.

"Ha! You plead for your life. I like to see infidels grovel! Say please to me again, you pitiful man!"

"Please let us take him to the infirmary. I beg you! Don't hurt us anymore," Mickey pleaded.

"Okay. You may take him, but only because you have shown us what a pitiful coward of a man you are! You are on your knees begging for your life! You are scum to my people! You are low life coward infidels!"

When they got to the medical unit, they pushed the gurney into the exam room, followed by Mickey and the two pirates. Mickey asked if he could have some privacy with James. They glared at Mickey with no concern for James laying unmoving on the gurney. Mickey shoved them back through the door, and one man bared his teeth like a rabid dog, but backed out so Mickey could close the door.

In a few seconds, a man in a white coat entered, wearing a stethoscope around his neck. He walked over to James, and James opened his eyes and looked at the doctor.

James whispered to him, "Doctor, I'm okay. I don't need medical attention, but I need to remain in this medical unit to work."

"I don't understand what you mean," he answered, speaking in a low tone.

"I'm going to take care of these pirates and I need to be able to move around unfettered. Can you make a medical demand that I stay here for observation?"

The man said, "You are going to overpower these pirates and get our ship back?"

"Yes," said James, still not moving a limb and even using limited mouth movements.

"You are going to do this alone?"

"Trust me. I will bring others to help. Will you help me do this?"

If you haven't read the first books in the Landlord series, take a few moments to look at these:

Book 1. The Landlord's Inheritance
This was Mickey's first adventure and the one that started it all.

Book 2. The Landlord's Wheelchair Child
Mickey thinks that all is well until he finds a little girl all alone in one of his apartment complexes. He has to help this little girl find her parents.

Book 3. The Landlord's Dead Body
When construction starts at one of his new projects, new CEO Mickey Ray Christianson must find out who killed and buried this young lady in the middle of his project.

Book 4. The Landlord's Ex-Fiancée
When Mickey Ray gets a call from the Oregon police that his Ex-Fiancée was dead, he and James fly out to pick up her body. When they arrive, they determine that Valerie was murdered. The entire Mongoose team assembles to track down her killer. Action escalates in this fast-paced story of love and justice.

The entire Landlord's series is available at amazon.com, barnesandnoble.com and terryjoegunnelsbooks.com.

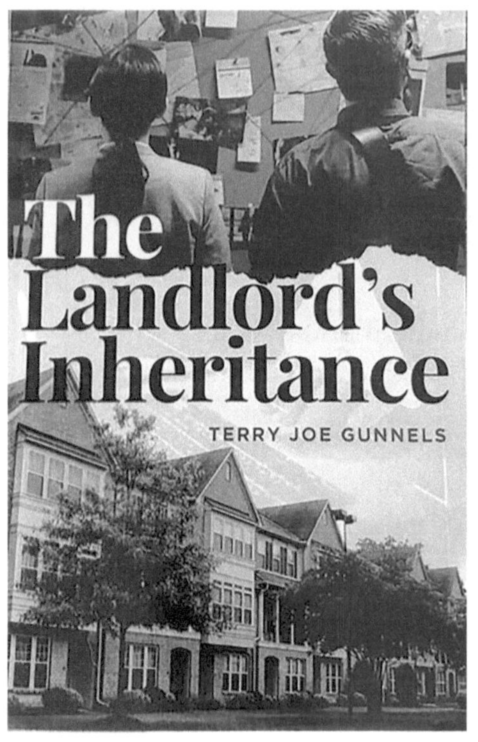

Siblings Mickey Ray and Darcy Jean are informed that the automobile disaster that caused the death of their Mother and their Father's multiple injuries including brain damage was not an accident but an attempted murder. The local police seem ambivalent, and their aunt comes in with a forgotten Power of Attorney signed by their Father, Daniel, and tries to take control of the Real Estate holdings. The brother and sister team begin a power struggle and are physically threatened by unknown thugs which results in Mickey's girlfriend's disappearance which she is presumed dead and Darcy Jean in hiding. James, Mickey's best friend, a disfigured Ex-Military Black Ops operative, assists in the hunt to put a stop to the "takeover."

Simple Detective Work, Internet Research, Adventure, Action and Suspense with a Sprinkle of Romance, and a Fast-Paced, Explosive ending are included in this book of intrigue.

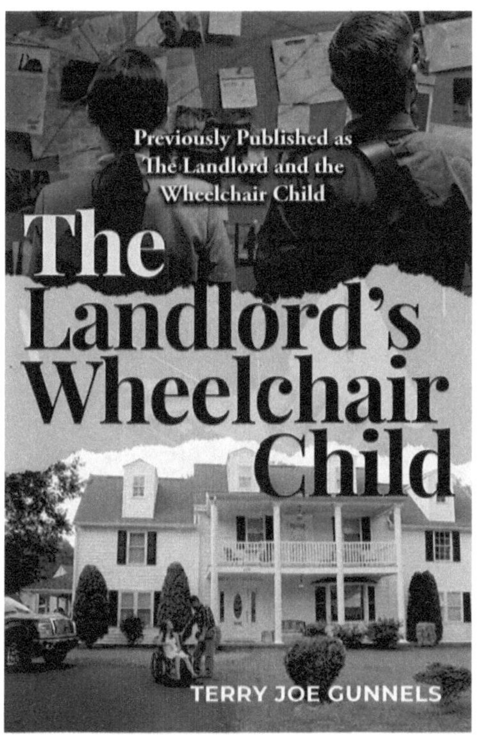

Landlord Mickey Ray Christianson is walking the grounds of his apartment complex late one afternoon, and he sees a little girl in a wheelchair sitting all alone. He sits down beside her and begins talking to her. He then finds out that her mother left her, intending to return. When the child's mother doesn't return, Mickey has the gut feeling that something has gone awry and calls his sister, Darcy, to run a background check on her parents. After Darcy gets permission from the Department of Child's Services to take custody of the child, Carrie, Mickey Ray, and his best friend, James, go hunting for Carrie's parents, assuming they were kidnapped. With help from some of James' past Black Ops teammates, a find-and-rescue operation takes place. After a suspenseful mission and a lot of action, Mickey reunites Carrie with her parents.

I hope you like Mickey and James' newest adventure as they dive headfirst into helping this little child. It is suspenseful to the very end.

After many months of preparation, construction has begun on a new Apartment complex. On the very first day, a worker with a backhoe, digs up a body of a young lady. After the police identify the victim, it turns out that Mickey Ray Christianson and his sister Darcy Jean went to school with her. The victim, Betty Duncan was single, pregnant and lived with her mother in one of their apartments, so Mickey and his best friend and brother-in-law, James Bower set out to find her killer. They start with the obvious suspects, the baby daddy. Along the way, Mickey connects with one of his old schoolmates and thinks he is falling in love with her. After tracking down several leads and dead ends, the case is solved with a huge twist for Mickey and all involved.

I hope this one keeps you on the edge of your seat as it did me as I wrote it. Believe it or not, I didn't know "who dunnit" until the very end!

Mickey and James are back in action with this new action-thriller. The police answer Mickey's call to his ex-fiancée attending culinary school in Oregon. They tell him that Valerie is deceased, so Mickey flies out to pick up the body. The attractive police detective tells Mickey she has a "gut" feeling that it's murder. James, Mickey's best friend, gets a flight to help Mickey find the killer. James brings some others that helped them in earlier cases. Sexy Marie comes to do some undercover work, and little bombshell Alyssa comes to handle technical surveillance. The police detective and Mickey hit it off and she takes vacation time to join in the investigation. James obtains an armored Humvee, munitions, including rocket launchers he got on clearance from an anonymous arms dealer. They have run-ins with thugs, smugglers, and seriously evil men as they go to war to get justice for Mickey's ex-fiancée, Valerie. Ride along with the wild car chases, late-night raids, and the explosive fireball finish of this exciting new Landlord's adventure.

A picture of the Author and one of his collectible autos.

The entire Landlord's series is available at: amazon.com
barnesandnoble.com terryjoegunnelsbooks.com